RETRIBUTION

A Selection of Recent Titles by Adrian Magson

The Harry Tate Thrillers
RED STATION *
TRACERS *
DECEPTION *
RETRIBUTION *

The Riley Gavin and Frank Palmer Series
NO PEACE FOR THE WICKED
NO HELP FOR THE DYING
NO SLEEP FOR THE DEAD
NO TEARS FOR THE LOST
NO KISS FOR THE DEVIL

* *available from Severn House*

RETRIBUTION

A Harry Tate Thriller

Adrian Magson

Severn House Large Print
London & New York

This first large print edition published 2015
in Great Britain and the USA by
SEVERN HOUSE PUBLISHERS LTD of
19 Cedar Road, Sutton, Surrey, England, SM2 5DA.
First world regular print edition published 2012 by
Severn House Publishers Ltd., London and New York.

British Library Cataloguing in Publication Data

Magson, Adrian. author.
 Retribution.
 1. Tate, Harry (Fictitious character)–Fiction.
 2. Intelligence officers–Fiction. 3. Great Britain. MI5–
 Fiction. 4. Kosovo War, 1998-1999–Atrocities–Fiction.
 5. Assassins–Fiction. 6. Suspense fiction. 7. Large type
 books.
 I. Title
 823.9'2-dc23

 ISBN-13: 9780727897923

Severn House Publishers support the Forest Stewardship Council™
[FSC™], the leading international forest certification organisation. All
our titles that are printed on FSC certified paper carry the FSC logo.

Typeset by Palimpsest Book Production Ltd.,
Falkirk, Stirlingshire, Scotland.
Printed and bound in Great Britain by
T J International, Padstow, Cornwall.

As always, this is for Ann, once described as my roadie. Without her help and support, it wouldn't be fun.

Acknowledgements

In this, the fourth book, I would like to thank a few industry people who have helped along the way in bringing Harry Tate out of the shadows:
  Mike Stotter and Ali Karim, of the Shots Collective, for being such stalwart supporters ever since my first book; Matt Hilton, for his help and friendship; Adrian Muller, who always believed in Harry; Myles Allfrey for his knowledge of 'stuff' and things that go bang; Edwin Buckhalter, Kate Lyall Grant and the team at Severn House Publishers, for making it all happen; and finally but not least, David Headley and Roberto Carballeiro of the DHH Literary Agency, for their constant help, input and encouragement.

One

Kosovo, Autumn 1999

The girl slithered over the wire like a silver fish, her thin cotton dress plastered to her body by the driving rain. Globules of water shook loose from the mesh as she climbed, plummeting to the earth around her, a contrasting flicker of tiny jewels against the mud, gravel and coarse grass.

Thirty metres behind her lay a dense treeline of spiky conifers. Beyond that, high in the hills, her brother was in hiding, close to death after a severe beating by a drunken Serb militiaman. She didn't dare approach the hospital for help, didn't trust the international military mission called KFOR that was supposed to be keeping the peace, or any of the local residents.

All she could do was come down here and climb the fence, to see what she could find to help make his last few days bearable.

She crouched, scanning the compound. It was lit by a tall gantry mounted with six floodlights, the glare pushing back the encircling gloom and highlighting the curtain of solid rain that had been falling relentlessly for over an hour. To one side stood a clump of low, interconnected huts, dimly lit. Across the way a clutch of shipping containers formed a tall barrier against the cold, barren hills half a mile away. Mitrovica, the

1

nearest town, was out of sight, a forbidding place of whispers and certain danger.

A flicker of movement made her freeze. A stocky figure stepped out from one of the huts and paced across the yard, footsteps echoing on the puddled tarmac. The girl noted the waterproof cape, camouflage uniform, jump boots and assault rifle. American, she thought automatically.

She knew about soldiers and their weapons; she had seen too many in her young years not to have learned something about them, the main thing being that they represented danger and death, no matter whose side they were on.

As the soldier disappeared among the shadows thrown by the containers, the girl moved quickly towards the huts. This was where the Kosovo Force (KFOR) troopers ate and slept. There was always something lying around.

Food was her priority: powdered milk, sugar, tea, tins of meat, army rations – especially chocolate if she was lucky. It was never going to be enough, but it might keep her and her brother going for another day or two in their hiding place. Anything was better than falling victim to the Serb killer squads roaming the villages.

A brief flare of a match showed from between the containers. It was the chance she had been waiting for. The guard's night-vision would be gone for a few moments. She ran for the nearest hut, light-footed, almost ephemeral in the glitter of rainfall against the lights.

She slipped inside. It smelled of coffee and stale food, making her stomach lurch. She listened. No sounds of snoring here; so this wasn't a sleeping area, which was good. Ghosting along a narrow corridor, she entered a small space on her right. A security lamp threw a dull glow over cupboards, chairs and tables, and sideboards with a kettle and a portable gas stove.

She checked the cupboards, found a tin of coffee and some powdered milk. No sugar but better than nothing. A packet of biscuits lay opened on a bottom shelf, and she took one, the temptation too much. The packet rustled loudly in the silence. She froze. Then she took a bite of the biscuit, followed by another, wolfing down the crumbly sweetness in a moment.

Moments later her stomach rebelled, and she sank to the floor, pain ripping through her. She'd been too long without decent food. She took deep breaths until the pain subsided. She clutched the tins of coffee and powdered milk close to her, trophies too valuable to leave behind, and a panacea. She blinked hard, feeling her eyelids beginning to droop, betraying her. *She had to get out. Selim was waiting.*

But warmed by the residual heat in the hut, it was a losing battle.

It seemed like hours later that she woke with a start. She'd been dreaming, of trucks and men and noise . . . except that it wasn't a dream. She could actually hear them: engines roaring and doors slamming and lots of shouting. She got to her knees and peered out of a window on to the compound.

Trucks. All bearing the white letters KFOR on their sides. Two four-by-four vehicles in their midst, followed by the bull shape of an armoured personnel carrier. Her heart sank. Where there had been quiet and shelter and the soft, measured tread of the guard, there was now a mass of movement. And the inevitable guns.

Some of them were close by, inside the huts. Instinctively, she scuttled inside a cupboard, curling her small body into the tight space and pulling the door to behind her. As a last thought, she reached up and placed the coffee tin on the worktop above her head. If they saw the tin, they might not bother checking the cupboards.

In the dark of her hiding place, she breathed softly, willing herself to relax, waiting for the men to settle down.

Silence fell at last. She slept. But it wasn't for long. Fear of discovery haunted her dreams. She uncurled herself and slowly stood upright, gritting her teeth against the cramp in her legs and stomach.

She turned and picked up the coffee tin. It was open. She glanced at the kettle, saw steam curling from the spout. *Someone had been in here and she hadn't heard a thing.* She replaced the lid on the tin and hugged it to her with the powdered milk. Moving to the door she peered out into the corridor. It was empty. Towards the end away from the entrance was a fire door. It faced out on to the fence.

Her only way out.

She padded softly towards it. It was dark outside, all in shadow, shielded from the compound lights. She could throw the tins over the wire, then follow before anyone saw—

There came a whisper of movement behind her. A powerful hand was clamped over her mouth.

She caught the mixed aromas of man-smell, of damp clothing, and the coarse texture of a camouflage jacket sleeve curling across her throat.

Then nothing.

Two

Afghanistan/Pakistan border, 2012

The man named Kassim came down out of the hills at a steady pace, losing altitude quickly under the growing sun. He had been hustling along for nearly three hours now, raising spurts of dust off the narrow, rocky path. Sixty minutes on the move, ten motionless. For a newcomer to the region, it would have seemed suicidal travelling this way. But nobody strolled in these hills; you moved fast and with the utmost caution. It was a way of life. A way to continue living.

The pace was punishing. He was beginning to tire, his concentration dwindling. He had not eaten properly for two days and water had been scarce. He was beginning to feel the effects of dehydration, and the heat hung heavy like the inside of an oven, rasping his throat.

A buzzard soared overhead and he stopped, moving off the trail. He squatted by a large rock, watching the bird until it became a speck, indistinct against the blue of the sky. He wondered idly if it would encounter one of the many drones sent over by the Coalition forces. Bigger, faster,

5

a bird infinitely more dangerous. Maybe they would soon train buzzards to carry their little cameras for them, filming everything as they floated on the thermals.

The thought drew his eyes back to the valley slopes. He surveyed the trail either side, searching for dust where there should be none, for the darting flight of a hare in panic or the telltale flare of a fox's bushy tail. He was well aware of enemy Special Forces operating in the region, of the heavily whiskered and grubby Taliban hunters, like cave dwellers with sniper scopes and long-range rifles. Up here, this close to the border region, a lone man was viewed with suspicion on all sides, a person to be stopped and examined.

Or killed.

Half a mile away the burned-out, rotting hulk of a Russian helicopter rested on its side where it had crashed years before. Long since stripped of anything useful, it was now a wind-burnished resting place for the birds to perch, a relic of another war in a long list of so many conflicts in the region.

He plucked at his shirt and waistcoat, flapping the warm air around him, and scratched at the beard covering his lower face. He felt a gritty sheen of sweat-soaked dust among the hairs. He needed a bath, and could feel in his mind the embrace of soft, soapy water and the touch of a rough towel.

He shook away the daydream and stood, relieving the tightness in his thighs and calves, then swung his arms wide to loosen his shoulders. He was tall and lean, with no spare meat on his bones after so long in the hills. His hands were powerful, yet with the long fingers of a musician, which his mother had hoped he would one day be. Cruelly, those hopes had died years ago with the death of so many other things, and he had not given the idea another thought since leaving the hills above the shattered village where he had been born. Later, through the madrasas where he had been schooled by those who had taken him in; then in Chechnya and the desert camps where he had been trained and tested; in the many weeks with specialist 'tutors', who had taught him so much, there had been no time for music.

All he had now was the mission.

He dipped a hand into the bag across his shoulder and took out a water bottle. It was nearly empty. He trickled the few tepid drops on to his tongue, rinsing out the dust and spitting it on to a rock nearby. The moisture sizzled for a moment, and was gone.

He chewed slowly on a piece of dried meat, stomach growling for more. He had used a great deal of energy coming down from the hills, and would have to find something soon, before he became too weak. But for now he ignored his body's demands. There would be time for food later.

He stood and set off at the same ground-eating shuffle, the slap of his sandals the only sound to accompany his breathing. He followed a steep path, knees feeling the strain of the descent, and crossed a small wooden bridge over a dried river bed strewn with large boulders the size of cars. There would be water in this area again when the snows melted high in the mountains and

7

gushed down the passes into the valleys below. Until then, it would remain as dry as a biscuit.

He paused briefly on the other side, sniffing the air. He was right on the border with Pakistan, and although patrols were irregular, there were occasional watchers on the high ground, monitoring illegal crossings.

Continuing on down, he passed a herd of scruffy, fat-tailed sheep picking at meagre grazing on the steep slopes. There was no sign of a herder but he wasn't surprised; only the foolhardy trusted strangers on the trails in this area.

An hour later he skirted a tiny collection of dwellings, arousing a frantic barking from a mangy dog. In the distance the cry of a small child was abruptly silenced, testifying that adults here chose to stay out of sight, incurious about the passing stranger and his intentions.

After another hour he reached a track clinging to the side of a hill.

A Mitsubishi truck was waiting, four emaciated-looking goats in the back. The driver was standing by the front, tinkering with the engine. The moment he saw Kassim, he dropped the hood and gestured to him to climb aboard. There was no exchange of words. Kassim got in and dropped his bag between his feet.

After forty minutes they emerged from a narrow valley into Torkham, the official border crossing point. The air was thick with noise and dust and colour, and Kassim felt a spike of anxiety at the crush of people in the streets.

The driver sensed his mood and looked at the bag on the floor. 'You have a weapon?' When

8

Kassim nodded, the driver pulled over and stopped alongside an open drain. 'A pistol?'

'A Makarov.'

'The make is not important. You get caught with it and we might as well cut our own throats. Drop it in the hole.'

Kassim didn't argue. He took out the semi-automatic and dropped it, along with the spare clip, into the mouth of the drain.

The driver laughed as they drove away. 'Don't look so sad, my friend. Someone will take it out later and clean it. It will go to a good home, I promise.'

They passed two American army Humvees at the side of the road, loaded with soldiers. Inscrutable behind their dark glasses and bristling with weaponry, they stood out among the mountain people. His driver waved a vague hand as they drove by, the goats in the back protesting uneasily at the noise, and Kassim felt a burn of irritation at the man's cavalier attitude. Maybe down here things were different; where he had just come from, if you saw American soldiers, you didn't wave – you shot them.

They threaded their way through the crowded back streets, a stop–start journey, finally emerging on the main Torkham to Peshawar road. Here they joined vehicles of every size and description, most carrying bundles of goods of unknown origin, or overloaded with families heading who knew where. Signs of military activity were everywhere, and Kassim felt that he was being assessed and recorded by every pair of eyes he saw. They stopped once at the driver's insistence, at a roadside eating place.

9

Kassim wanted to continue to Peshawar, but the other man insisted it was for the best. He ordered meat and vegetables cooked in red chillies, and sat eating and watching the road, nodding to Kassim to do the same. 'You will see,' he murmured.

Minutes later, a convoy of Pakistani army trucks roared by and set up a road block to the north of their position, stopping every vehicle going south.

It was a signal for the driver to move. 'Come,' he said, wiping his hands and face. 'We go now.'

The traffic thickened and slowed noticeably as they neared Peshawar. Kassim was thinking about the chain of arrangements that had been made for him to come here, starting up in the Hindu Kush and ending wherever his journey might take him. This man, the driver, had not enquired as to his name nor given his own. For whatever reason, he was helping Kassim and that was enough. Kassim felt humbled by the risk the man was taking.

On the outskirts of Peshawar, the man pointed to a bus stop. 'From there a bus will take you to the airport,' he said. 'Your flight leaves in the morning, Insha'Allah, and you should use the time in Lahore to shake off anyone you think is watching you.' He glanced at Kassim's clothing, which was that of the hills, stiffened by dust and sweat, and pointed to the back of the truck. 'There is a bag for you. It contains clothes. Find some-where to change into them before you board the bus. And get your hair cut. The passengers are mostly airport workers and would not let you on the way you are.'

'What is wrong with the way I am?' Kassim had

so far seen more people dressed the same as him on every street corner than in western clothing.

'Because you look like a *Talib*, my brother – or a wild man.' He tapped the side of his head with a stubby finger. 'From now on, you have to think like the unbelievers and be one step ahead. And speak English, the universal language.'

It was an indication that this man was no mere driver, but someone in the chain of command. The risk must have been judged worthwhile for such a person to come down here to see him off. He said nothing, merely nodded in understanding.

Three hours later, Kassim was walking on board a Pakistan International Airlines flight to Lahore, with an onward connection to Paris Charles de Gaulle. He was carrying a sports bag and dressed in dark slacks, leather shoes and a white shirt, and had been shaved clean at a street corner barbershop, his hair washed and cut short with a side parting. He felt restricted in the new clothes, as if his body were encased in a tight sleeve from head to toe, and was convinced he was about to be stopped by security guards at any moment. But nobody paid him the slightest attention.

As he took his seat, he put his hand in his pocket and felt for the piece of soft blue material that accompanied him everywhere he went. As he did so, he muttered a soft prayer and made a firm vow to succeed.

All the talking, the schooling, the training and testing – and the years of fighting – had been aimed at this moment.

He was on his way.

11

Three

Harry Tate stared at the text on his mobile phone. It had bleeped seconds ago. He was trying to ignore it; calls when he was on a job were a distraction. Calls from the person who'd been trying to contact him for two days now, leaving voicemail messages, were even more so than most.

Harry. Plse make Grosvenor Square tomorrow at 18.30? Urgent. Remember Mitrovica. Ken Deane.

For no good reason that he could determine, Harry felt a ripple in his gut. Ken Deane and Mitrovica; the combination wasn't good. Nor was being asked to remember the things he'd seen there. And if Ken Deane was still working for the UN, as he had been when they first met, it was the last thing he wanted. Take on a contract with the UN and you could end up somewhere hot, remote and deeply unfriendly.

He looked up at the door of the house they were watching as a thickset man with ginger hair stepped outside. His name was Terry de Witt. He was supposed to be in hiding.

'He can't be,' Rik Ferris muttered in disbelief, and reached for the door latch of the Audi.

Harry put a hand on his sleeve. 'Forget it. We're too late.' He nodded towards the end of the street.

A black Range Rover had appeared, ghosting along the line of empty cars. To outward appearances just another luxury Chelsea tractor looking for a parking slot, it was nothing of the sort. Three men and the driver, Harry noted.

He knew what would happen next: the car would stop alongside de Witt, and the driver would ask for directions, friendly but puzzled. De Witt would pause and move closer, even though he knew this area of Primrose Hill in north London as well as he knew the far side of the moon. But his naïve side, the side which had got him traced in the first place, would come to the fore in spite of several warnings to stay inside, no matter what.

Sure enough, the two side doors opened and two of the men got out. They were big and moved swiftly, hauling de Witt inside. It took seconds, with no exchange of words. Give it an hour or two, Harry knew, and de Witt, South African numbers man to an Albanian arms dealer, would be overseas and gone for good. Or dead.

'Do we stop them?' Rik asked.

'Only if you want those boys to put some dents in your nice car. Follow at a discreet distance.' Harry dialled the contact number for the security company paying the bill for this job. When the call was picked up, he gave the registration of the Range Rover, descriptions of the occupants and the direction of travel. This was strictly an observe-only assignment and not worth the grief he figured would accompany that particular car with those three men if he and Rik tried to get in their way.

13

'So what was the message?' Rik was trying not to look disappointed at missing the chance of a hot pursuit through the city streets. He started the car and settled in a block behind the Range Rover, allowing a taxi to overtake to act as a screen.

Harry read out the text. 'That's all I know. Something to do with Mitrovica in Kosovo. He's persistent, I'll give him that.' Three voicemail messages and a text so far. It must be important.

'Grosvenor Square?' Rik swerved to avoid a cycle courier. 'That's the US Embassy. What's Kosovo got to do with them? Is Deane CIA?'

'Not unless he had a better offer since I last saw him.'

'When was that?'

'Pristina, Kosovo in 'ninety-nine. He was the UN's local field security rep. So he said, anyway.' He switched off the phone and watched the Range Rover. He had no reason to think Deane had been playing a dual role in Kosovo, but he wasn't going to enter the US Embassy unless he had to. Deane could come and talk to him out in the open.

'Has he seen us, d'you think?' Rik asked. The driver of the Range Rover didn't seem in any great hurry, and was drifting along the street, matching the traffic flow.

'If he has, we'll soon find out.' If they had been spotted and the occupants of the other car wanted to get away, they would wait for their moment, then use the traffic to pull out and be gone. And there wasn't much Harry and Rik could do to stop them. On the other hand, maybe a deal had been worked out with someone that would allow

14

de Witt to be taken out of the country and beyond the reach of the courts.

It wouldn't be the first time.

The Range Rover pulled on to the Marylebone Road and turned west, putting on speed. West was Heathrow. Heathrow was a flight out. Harry dialled the number again and gave them an update.

'Wait one,' came the reply.

Harry wondered how many cases like de Witt ended up dropping quietly between the floorboards, when they had all the attributes of a High Court showpiece. The accountant had conspired to commit fraud on a massive scale, ruining many lives and ending some prematurely. But certain individuals would see his freedom as a relatively cheap price to pay in order to get the men above him – the Albanians and others who were the planners and executioners. The dealers in death.

'Discontinue surveillance.' The instruction was without drama; a female voice, thirty-ish, by the sound of it, confident and precise. Probably government trained and brained. 'They're free to leave. This assignment is over. Thank you for your time.'

Harry acknowledged and switched off. At least she had nice manners, which was better than most. As he'd suspected: somebody had worked out a deal.

'Let's go to your place,' he said. 'I need you to run a check for me.'

'On Deane?'

'Yes. Find out what he does now, where he lives, everything you can.'

Rik glanced across. 'He's not a mate, then?' Harry would know, otherwise. And going into a meet without knowing something about your contact was risky. Standard operating procedure: find out all there was to know first, avoid surprises. 'You don't sound keen.'

'I'm not. He's not enough of a mate to be calling me after all this time.' Their first encounter had been twelve years ago, when Harry had been part of the NATO-led peacekeeping mission in Kosovo. A KFOR unit had been called in when heavily armed Serb militias had tried to commandeer UN trucks to move their troops and armaments into Albanian-held territories. Deane, then the local field security representative for the UN, had been in a tricky situation: risk a fight the lightly armed UN force might not win, or back down and allow the Serbs to take the trucks, thus setting a dangerous precedent.

Harry and his colleagues had been able to defuse the situation, but it had been a close-run thing. Shortly afterwards, he'd been assigned to lead a close protection team in the area. A UN Special Rapporteur on Human Rights had flown in unannounced for a whistle-stop tour, demanding a protection squad to accompany him. Ignoring advice from KFOR personnel on the ground to stay away, the official had dug his heels in. Keen to show openness and transparency, the UN had pressured KFOR to select a multinational squad, and Ken Deane had remembered Harry's name.

Now, it seemed, he'd remembered it again.

Four

Four days after beginning his long journey, Kassim stepped off a Pakistan International Airlines flight at Paris Charles de Gaulle, and took a shuttle bus to the stop at Étoile. It was six o'clock in the evening.

Before leaving him at the bus stop in Peshawar, the driver had handed Kassim an envelope containing a passport, money and tickets, and visa documents to enter the United States. Kassim did not ask how these papers had been produced; he knew only they would be genuine for someone, although not himself. He noted that he was now named Zef Haxhi, a student of dry land agriculture travelling on field studies, jointly funded by the University of Rawalpindi and the American University of Kosovo. The subject was sufficiently boring to keep anyone from questioning him too closely, and with the magic addition of the word American, it should stand up to scrutiny.

The rest, though, would be up to him.

As instructed, on arrival in Lahore, he had used some of the money in the bag to buy western clothes: a cheap suit, shoes, shirts and underwear. He had also purchased a medium-size, dark green rucksack, more befitting a student of agriculture than the bag provided. Being shaved clean had left his skin tender after years of being covered with a light beard; he still wasn't accustomed to

17

the open air on his cheeks. But now he looked no different to a thousand others. Many followers of Islam – notably the Taliban – believed a man should never lose his beard. He thought the view extreme and had shaved so as not to stand out. For what he had to do, blending in was of paramount importance.

Now he was here, he saw that he was, if anything, even lighter skinned than many others, and felt instantly at ease. But he recalled being told in the briefings that in many western cities, making eye contact was to be avoided, and reminded himself not to make simple mistakes.

The air was chilly and the streets of the French capital were busy, but he had no eyes for the architecture and the cold meant nothing. He waited for the bus to move away, then consulted the map he had bought at the airport, before setting off north along Rue Auber. He felt awkward in the new shoes, especially on the unforgiving pavements, but he was grateful to be on his feet again. Although the atmosphere here was loaded with petrol fumes and the smoke of cigarettes, he had room to stretch, feeling the muscles of his calves gradually loosening as he moved.

From Auber he crossed Boulevard Haussmann to the Gare St Lazare. He found the street he was looking for tucked away behind the station. It was a narrow, untidy passage between a jumble of old houses. Litter-filled puddles from earlier rainfall gave the street a forlorn air, and a scavenging dog tugged at a refuse sack outside a butcher's shop, scattering bloody remains across the pavement. Loud Moroccan-style music wailed from a first-floor apartment, and bedding fluttered from ornate balconies, a flash of colour in a drab setting.

He stopped outside a peeling doorway and studied the name written below the doorbell. At his feet a refuse bag gave out an unwholesome smell, and he wondered how people could live in such surroundings. He pressed the bell.

The door opened to reveal an old man in a white *djellaba* and skullcap. He peered at Kassim through thick spectacles, his expression carefully blank.

'I'm Kassim.'

The old man nodded and beckoned him in, checking the street before closing the door again. They exchanged brief courtesies before the old man led Kassim up the stairs to a small room. It contained a rickety card table and two chairs, and on the floor, a cardboard box. On the table stood a coffee pot and two cups.

The old man bade Kassim sit, and poured coffee. It was blue-black and thick, the steam curling upwards and infusing the air with its heady aroma. The two men sipped the treacly brew, eyes on each other. Finally, courtesies over, the old man stood up.

'Your package is here.' He nodded at the cardboard box on the floor. 'I will leave you for a minute.'

'No.' Kassim stopped him. 'Stay. I will soon be gone.'

The old man inclined his head and watched as Kassim pulled the box towards him. Inside was a small pocket-sized binder containing more than a dozen sheets of typed paper. He flipped it open.

Each sheet carried a small photo, and beneath each one was a name and address with some notes for Kassim to study.

Beneath the binder was an envelope containing a thick wad of money. He fanned through it, noting euros and US dollars, all medium denominations. Depending on his travel and accommodation, he had been assured there would be sufficient to last several days. With the money was a single sheet of paper showing the address in New York of a travel agency.

The final item was a heavy bundle wrapped in newspaper. It was a Russian-made Makarov 9mm with a clip of ammunition, a twin of the one he had thrown down the drain in Torkham. He must have looked startled by the similarity, because the old man asked softly, 'There is something wrong?'

He shook his head, wondering if it had been coincidence or a lack of imagination on somebody's part. The gun looked well used but was clean and gleamed with oil.

'Is this all the ammunition you could get?' he asked. He slipped the clip into the gun with a practised movement and hefted it for balance.

The old man seemed unimpressed by his deftness with the weapon. 'Why? Are you going to start a *jihad* – a holy war?' His tone was serious, and Kassim felt instantly chided, like a child that had suggested something outrageous.

'No. Of course not.'

'You must dispose of it carefully afterwards.'

He stared hard at the man, wondering at the departure of his earlier courtesy. Maybe living here in the west eroded the customary traditions of welcome and politeness to guests.

'I know what I must do,' he said gruffly and stood up. Venting his anger on this old fool was pointless. He was merely a contact to be used for limited assistance; he knew nothing of Kassim's mission and probably cared less, and would in all probability be glad to see the back of him, this mountain man from far away.

He placed the gun inside his rucksack, pushing it down between the few clothes where it would not bump against anything. He put the binder inside his jacket, then followed the old man from the room and down the stairs.

At the bottom Kassim took his arm, feeling the thin bones beneath the cloth of the *djellaba*. 'I may need to contact you,' he said, before his host opened the door.

The old man stared at Kassim's hand until the visitor released him. When he looked up, his eyes were cool and unfathomable.

'I will not be here. This is not my home. After you leave I will never come here again.' He spoke with absolute finality, and Kassim wondered at the man's past that he could be so calm, so definite. So controlled.

The old man pulled the door open and stood back. 'Go with God,' he said politely, dipping his head in salute.

Five

Harry stood on the east side of Grosvenor Square and watched Ken Deane walking towards him. The American looked relaxed, in spite of the tone of his text message. Dressed in a neutral suit and sombre tie, the man who was now Deputy Head of UN Field Security could have been any one of dozens of workers from the imposing structure of the US Embassy on the opposite side of the square. He reached the pavement under an angry blast from a cab driver, and grinned in triumph.

'You'd get arrested for that in New York,' Harry told him.

Deane pulled a face. 'Not me, pal – I'm UN, remember? They pull that shit and I'd have a team of Gurkhas come through the windows to haul me out.'

'Actually,' Harry pointed out, 'you wouldn't. They're all in Afghanistan.'

'Damn. Is that right? I can never keep track of where everyone is these days.' Deane pumped his hand, his grip softer than Harry remembered. 'So how are you, bud? How's life in the private sector?' He turned and led Harry around the square, past the heavy anti-bomb barriers and the armed police outside the guardhouse, up towards Park Lane. 'Somehow I never saw you as a PMC.'

'I'm not.' Private military contractors were security personnel working in war zones like Iraq

22

and Afghanistan, often employed by shadowy organizations led by former Special Forces officers. Some regarded them as the blue-chip version of what had once been called mercenaries. 'I'm freelance.'

Deane gave him a quizzical look. 'If you say so. Is it true what I heard – that you nearly got iced in Georgia, courtesy of your own MI5?'

Harry was trying to put that episode out of his mind, but clearly the talk was still rumbling around on the security and intelligence grapevine. After a failed drugs intercept in which two civilians and a police officer had been shot dead, Harry had been sent to a combined MI5/MI6 office in Georgia, code-named Red Station. Ostensibly to get him away from the press furore and the sniping of politicians looking for a scalp, the posting had been a sham; when he'd made noises about coming back, he and his new colleagues, including Rik Ferris, had been made the subjects of a kill order by a man known as The Hit.

'Not all of MI5,' he said. 'Just one.'

'Right. Paulton. He's still out there, isn't he?'

'For now.' Harry didn't doubt that Deane knew all there was to know about his MI5 background and George Henry Paulton, his former boss. He'd clearly made his way up the UN security ladder since Kosovo, which put him in a position where digging around in Intelligence files was relatively simple, and finding people who knew all about men like Harry Tate was no more than a phone call away. It made him impatient to find out what Deane was doing here in London. 'You didn't fly all the way over here just to talk about me, though.'

Deane waited until they had skirted a group of men in white *djellabas* clustered on the pavement by a limousine before answering. It gave Harry a chance to study him. He had the white teeth and smart, brush-cut hair of many Americans, which was little different to how Harry remembered him, but he was beginning to run up some extra weight. Too much time spent driving a desk.

'Yeah, look – I'm sorry about the subterfuge, Harry. It's true I was over here anyway, some business at the embassy. But what I have to talk about has taken precedence over everything. I have orders to keep it away from the embassy and off the wires, and I couldn't think of any building in London where we could meet that wasn't awash with spooks. I've been in this game too long, I guess . . . suspicious of everyone.'

Harry knew how he felt; he'd become far less trusting of people himself of late. Being marked down for elimination does that to a person.

'So why the message?'

'Let's get in the open first,' Deane muttered finally. 'I've been cooped up in planes and cars and offices, and I need some fresh air and the feel of green grass under my feet.' He nodded towards Hyde Park. 'That looks good to me. We could get an ice cream and walk.'

They bought ice creams from a late vendor and walked out across the park, steering clear of being overheard. Deane took the top off his ice cream and said, 'You ever thought of going back in uniform, Harry?'

24

'Why?' Harry studied his cone and dumped it at the foot of a tree where the birds could feed on it. He'd lost his appetite. 'Are you recruiting?' Deane had tried to get him on the UN payroll after Kosovo, but Harry had preferred the army, before transferring to MI5, the Security Services.

Deane shrugged and dumped his ice cream, too. 'In a manner of speaking.'

He seemed tense, and Harry wondered what was coming. He didn't have long to wait. 'You remember your team in Kosovo, when you were dragooned into babysitting Anton Kleeman?'

'Was that his name? It was a long time ago.' Long enough to have shut out some of the memories, anyway.

'You had some close calls out there.'

Harry nodded. 'A couple. Your note mentioned Mitrovica.'

'That's right. You got targeted by a Serb ambush squad and had to duck into a UN container depot for the night, remember?'

Harry remembered, and thought that it was a very specific situation to bring up. His team and their protectee had been travelling in armoured four-by-fours and had joined up with a resupply convoy coming down through the hills. The convoy had run into some mines on the road, losing two men and a couple of trucks. 'We rested up at the depot then got on a flight across the border next morning. Job done.'

'Do you remember any names?' The question was casual. Too casual.

'A couple. Broms, Orti . . . Bikov-something – a US Marine, anyway.' They had only been together a couple of days, not enough to make a lasting impression. 'Why?'

'Because stories are coming out of the region about stuff that happened back in Kosovo in 'ninety-nine. Stories backed up by some accurate details. It's beginning to make serious waves.'

'It was Kosovo. Lots of stuff happened back then. Remember ethnic cleansing?'

'Yeah, of course. But this is closer to home – specifically the UN and KFOR. Actually, it's KFOR, but the UN is the whipping post for all that's bad in international peacekeeping, and it was our mandate that put KFOR in there, so . . .' He paused.

Harry wasn't sure he wanted to hear this, but he was here now. 'Go on.'

'The stories all amount to the same thing.' Deane took a deep breath. 'Sometime in autumn 'ninety-nine, a fourteen-year-old girl was raped and murdered inside one of our compounds, and her body dumped outside the wire.'

Harry had seen too much in Kosovo to be surprised by anything that had happened in that broken region. Even so, this was, as Deane said, closer to home.

'How does that involve me?'

'Because what we're hearing, she was raped and murdered by a UN soldier.' He paused, then added, 'A UN soldier in the container depot on the Mitrovica road. The night you and your team were there.'

Six

Out on the street after leaving the old man, Kassim experienced a faint sense of bewilderment. He'd somehow expected more, as would be the tradition in the mountains. But beyond providing the weapon and the money, this man would help him no further. For now, he truly was on his own.

He strode off along the street, uncomfortably aware of the weight of the Makarov in the rucksack against his hip. His bewilderment was a passing phase, he knew that. After all the lessons and training, where he was watched and coached every day, a sense of isolation was to be expected, his trainers had warned him. Those same men, older and wiser, had seen everything, witnessed many things. But he still wasn't sure if they had done what he was now expected to do. Asking such a question would have met with instant reproof. It was enough that they had heard of his story, blurted out in a moment of anger, and selected him – *him* – to be the agent of destruction.

Barely twenty minutes later he was entering a more prosperous neighbourhood, with a profusion of shops, cafés and businesses. The houses were fresher and well-tended, and both sides of the street were lined nose to tail with shiny cars. He referred briefly to the binder in his pocket, checking one photo in particular.

He turned into a side street. Finding the address he wanted, he passed by without stopping, running a quick eye over the door. He could not tell for certain from such a brief inspection, but it did not look as if there were any special security measures in place. The wood looked normal, without the heavy, studded appearance of reinforcements or extra locks, and a narrow window to one side looked like a single pane of standard glass.

He decided to wait and watch before taking any action.

Nearby was a café with a few chairs and tables outside. He stepped inside, into a wall of choking cigarette smoke and loud talk, and the chink of glasses. He chose a table near the window from where he could watch the street, and ordered a fizzy drink from an aproned waiter.

His timetable was flexible and allowed for problems. If all went well, he would catch a train from the Gare du Nord at 22.01. If not, he would leave tomorrow instead.

All he could do now was wait.

In the building across from the café where Kassim waited, Jean-Michel Orti was going through a series of intensive exercises. His head was pounding with the after-effects of too much *pastis*, and he felt like shit. Much better if he just went to bed and got some sleep. But the routine of his years in the French Foreign Legion was too ingrained to break, so he gritted his teeth and continued, his body breaking out in a sweat in the stuffy room. He reached fifty with a final push and moved into squat-thrusts, his powerful leg muscles – which could normally carry him for miles with a full bergen – cracking from the lack of proper exercise over the past week.

Nearing the end of seven days' special leave before reporting back to the Legion office in Marseilles, Orti was tiring of the city and the faded delights it had to offer. His dutiful visits to his mother and sister, whose apartment this was, had soon become dull for them all, and there were fewer familiar faces around to greet him any more. Those who had not moved away seemed more concerned with family and responsibilities than sinking a few beers with an old friend. He'd been too long in the Legion. He might as well have joined a monastery.

He sighed and stood up. A strong coffee would clear his head and get him in tune for the following morning. If he made the mistake of reporting back to base unfit even for the daily run, the *capitaine* would spot it immediately and have him doing several rounds of the assault course with a bunch of new recruits, to teach him a lesson.

He splashed water on his face and dried off, then ran lightly downstairs and crossed the street.

The Café Sport was bustling with noise from the usual clientele whiling away the evening with pointless chatter about politics and football, the air heavy with cigarette smoke. He ordered coffee and a reheated croissant to soak it up, and sat down at the back of the room, checking the other patrons out of habit. Mostly locals, there were a couple of strangers, clearly business types deep in conversation over a laptop. Near the window a man in a cheap suit was sipping a soft drink and staring out at the street. Strong face, weathered, good shoulders, like an athlete, but lean. Could almost be a Legionnaire. Italian, Orti guessed, or one of the paler North Africans . . . Spanish with a touch of Moor, perhaps. A rucksack sat on the floor between his feet. An immigrant, looking for work.

The coffee was good and strong, and he drank a single cup, washing down the croissant. He made no attempt at conversation with the other customers. Those who knew him were aware of his background and paid him the courtesy of privacy; those who did not saw a fit-looking man in his late thirties paying the price for too many drinks.

Orti paid at the bar and left a tip for the waiter, then walked back across the street, breathing in the night air and looking forward to sleep followed by a morning run. As he put the key in the door and pushed it open he heard a whisper of sound behind him. Instantly he began to turn. But he was too slow, dulled by tiredness and the effects of drink. He felt a savage blow in the lower back and was thrown forward inside and against the wall of the hallway. An arm like a steel bar wrapped itself around his throat and another hand grasped his wrist like a vice and twisted it painfully up behind his back with no more effort than if he had been a child. Before he could make a sound he was dragged along the lower hallway into the kitchen, his feet scrabbling to gain purchase on the floor tiles.

Training as a Legionnaire includes some brutally effective unarmed combat, with moves borrowed from various disciplines such as karate, judo and aikido. Even if unarmed, Legionnaires are expected to meet all attacks with ferocious countermeasures. Yet Orti found himself unable to do anything against this attack. He was slammed face down on the kitchen floor and trussed with a length of clothes line before the full gravity of his circumstances could penetrate his confused mind.

The attacker rolled him over on to his back and placed a foot on his chest, thrusting a tea towel into his mouth with strong fingers. Orti found himself looking into a familiar face: it was the man from the café . . . the immigrant. Dark eyes stared back with little expression, and Orti felt a chill of fear. It was not, he knew, the loud, noisily aggressive men you had to worry about; it was the quiet ones who said little. Like this one.

'You are Orti?' the man said softly.

The Frenchman thought the accent strange; from Spain or Italy, maybe. He shook his head instinctively, his brain fogged but now func-tioning, and fought to draw in air through his nose. He made a grunting noise to show he wanted to talk, but the man ignored him and rolled him over to find the wallet in his back pocket. The details inside clearly confirmed what he wanted to know. He took out all the folded euros inside and tossed the wallet to one side.

But next he did a strange thing. He raised one hand. He was holding a piece of ragged cloth. Light blue with one edge of thin leather, it was worn smooth, as if by constant rubbing.

Then Orti recognized the colour and texture. It was part of a UN beret. He frowned. What the fu—?

31

Whatever the man thought Orti's expression of surprise portrayed, it seemed to disappoint him. His eyes hardened and he took a deep breath. He released the Frenchman for a second, then moved across the room. Seconds later he was back, holding a towel that he wrapped around something in his hand.

Orti caught a glimpse of polished metal and a bone handle, and recognized the object with a feeling of profound sadness. It was his own hunting knife.

Seven

Harry focussed on the basic details, trying to push aside any emotion. 'It could have been anyone. There were guards on duty when we arrived, and the road nearby had passing traffic.'

'Yeah, but the guards all left with the convoy, didn't they – for Pristina?'

Harry was puzzled. If Deane knew that much, he'd evidently done some groundwork. But then he shouldn't have expected anything less. Deane was experienced and had a large security organization at his disposal; checking the facts would have been his first objective. But, as he was admitting, even the UN couldn't know everything.

Harry cast his mind back to that night. After running into the ambush in driving rain, and having a truck with two men blown up and another vehicle crippled, the convoy had barged their way through at speed, following the lead vehicle, an armoured personnel carrier. With the agreement of the convoy commander, a Dutch officer, they had made for a container depot near Mitrovica. It had been the only place Harry had been able to find quickly on the map that offered any kind of safety perimeter. With no evacuation possible before dawn, his first responsibility was the isolation and protection of his UN charge, Anton Kleeman, and his assistant, a woman named Karen Walters.

Within minutes of their arrival, the convoy commander had received orders to leave for Pristina to assist with the protection of a refugee camp under attack from Serb militia. That had left Harry and his team alone in the depot with their two charges. He had given orders to get them out of sight in case the compound was being watched and the team had got them bedded down.

'There was one other man,' he recalled. 'One of the guards. He'd just started his shift and knew the place, and he was a combat veteran, so they left him where he was. I don't recall his name, though.'

'Fine. I can check that out.'

'It still doesn't mean it was anyone in the compound.'

'Actually, that might not be true.' Deane seemed almost embarrassed, and rubbed his face hard.

'What do you mean?'

'There's evidence, apparently.'

'What kind of evidence?'

'A piece of a uniform. We're still trying to sort out what might be genuine information from hype.' He took a deep breath. 'Harry, there's a lot

33

of people out there would like to put us on the rack. It would serve several national interests if we got so tied up with scandal we couldn't operate freely. And there are a few states out there that don't like being landed with peacekeeping forces under a UN mandate, preventing them from sorting out their differences any old way they feel. Add to that the world economy right now, and I can think of a couple of regular members who'd be delighted to have an excuse to drop out of the UN and save some money.' His face twisted. 'United in name only, I'm afraid.'

'So who's generating the propaganda?'

'I wish we knew. A couple of right-wing investigative hacks are jumping all over it, egged on by human rights groups and the usual anti-government, anti-UN, anti-everything nuts. But they're being fed by someone who claims to know enough of the details to make it stick. In fact, right now there's a small bunch of reporters out in Kosovo raking through the ashes and trying to find anyone who was there at the time. A lot of the population haven't returned even now, and that's the only thing slowing down the press investigation. But I don't expect that to last. If there's someone out there they haven't found yet, it's just a matter of time before they do.'

'Do you know who the girl was?'

'Not yet. Local, that's all they're saying. She probably went inside the compound looking for food. One of the reports hinted at a possible name, but they haven't shared it yet.' He shrugged. 'Could be a bluff to stoke the fire and sell a few more copies, but gut feel tells me it's not. There's too much anger being generated. It's as if the detail is there, but they're holding it back for some reason.'

'What do you want from me?'

'Anything you can tell me about that time. Frankly, we're up against it and I don't know what else we can do. It could all blow over tomorrow, but sooner or later the names of the team are going to come out – including yours. You worked with these guys; you might have a gut feel about them. Anything we can do to get ahead of the game is worth a try.'

Harry felt a bristle of anger. 'It sounds as if you've already made up your minds.'

'I haven't. But look at the facts, Harry. A small group of men from various backgrounds cooped up for the night in a remote compound . . . and a girl – a kid. The girl ends up raped and dead. If the evidence these rumours are hinting at is real, one of those men was responsible.'

'Are you sure this isn't an exercise to protect your man's reputation?'

'Kleeman?' Deane shook his head. 'Fuck him. The guy's a politician with his eye on the top job; I could care less about his reputation. He'll move on one day, but in the meantime my responsibility is to the organization.'

'It could be a politically motivated scam.'

'And that's just as bad. This could reflect badly on us for years to come.' He glanced at Harry. 'What do you think? Your gut feel.'

Harry thought about it. Common sense told him this could all disappear with tomorrow's newspapers, overtaken by something bigger and more newsworthy. But it could do the opposite and blow up in their faces. And if anyone wanted to smear the UN, drawing in one of their top officials with a rape scandal involving one of his bodyguards would be a good way to do it.

'I don't know. I don't really remember the others and I doubt they remember me; we were just a bunch of men thrown together for a couple of days. It wasn't an opportunity to make lasting friendships.'

'Jesus, Harry.' Deane looked disappointed, and Harry suddenly realized that there was something else to this visit. To this meeting.

He gave Deane a hard stare. 'I think you should cut to the chase, don't you? What exactly do you want?'

Deane toed the grass underfoot. 'OK. To the chase, then. I need your help in closing this thing down.' He sounded relieved now, as if he'd got something difficult out of the way. 'I asked a few people and spoke to a guy called Ballatyne. He said you were reliable and knew your way around.'

Richard Ballatyne was an operations chief in MI6. Harry and Rik had worked for him on a couple of occasions before, when non-attributables were required for tasks falling outside the scope of any specific government agency. Now, it seemed, Ballatyne was playing at being a part-time job finder, dropping Harry's name in convenient corners.

'You know what he does?'

Deane nodded. 'Sure. MI6. Why – is it a problem?'

'It might be if he ever asks you for a favour

in return. Just don't agree to meet him in an Italian restaurant; the coffee's rubbish.'

Deane suppressed a puzzled smile, no doubt writing it off as British humour. 'OK. Are we on?'

'Why me?'

'Ballatyne said you'd ask that.'

'Good. I'm choosy about the jobs I do. Still asking: why me?'

'What can I say?' Deane shrugged. 'I've got plenty of guys, but not for this. They're too close. I need an outsider. I can arrange for a full UN ID card and whatever facilities you need short of a guided missile, but you'll be outside the dome.'

Harry figured that Deane would have many resourceful and skilled people on his staff, most if not all with military training. But organizations like the UN were rife with gossip, and speculation was a regular party game. Deane also had a secondary reason for calling on Harry: if the rumour about the dead girl was true and names began to come out, then Harry himself was going to be in the firing line. It was a great motivator.

'Let me think it over.'

Deane's face tightened. 'Ballatyne said you'd say that, too. Trouble is, I need your answer now.'

'No.' Harry began to turn away, but Deane put a hand on his arm.

'Wait.' Deane scrubbed at his face, his eyes going walkabout with tension. 'Just hear me out, OK? Two minutes.'

'All right. Two.'

Deane breathed out and said quietly, 'It's not

37

just rumours from the backwoods or some press hack driving this, Harry. We have credible intelligence that there's an organized group behind it, and they intend blowing it wide open in a way that nobody will be able to ignore.'

'How can they guarantee that? The UN has dealt with accusations before and come out smiling.'

'I know. But this is different. Intel suggests they're sending someone. Sounds crazy, huh?' He gave a smile but it didn't reach his eyes.

'To do what?'

'To go after the CP team.'

Harry digested that for a few moments, trying to picture the possibilities. It didn't seem credible. Dramatic as hell, yes. But one man? 'Who is he?'

'We don't know. An Afghan. That's all we have. No name, no description.'

'An Afghan. You're saying this is terrorist-related?'

Deane lifted his shoulders. 'Looks that way to me. Who else would benefit by hitting the UN?'

'And does your intel say what he's going to do?'

'Yes. He's going to find the men who were in the compound that night. And he's going to kill them. All of them.'

In Paris, Kassim made his way to the Gare du Nord. He felt bone-tired, as if he had run into a wall. He'd been stunned by seeing the Frenchman, Orti, enter the café, and for a moment had nearly allowed his caution to overcome him. But then reason took control, and he realized that it was natural for the man to use the café, being in the same street.

In the end, it had worked to his advantage. It demonstrated that the photo in the pocket binder was good, which boded well for the rest. Satisfied that he was looking at the right man, he'd waited for the Frenchman to take his first mouthful of coffee, then got up and left, to find a quiet doorway further along the street.

This one had gone well. Yet he felt a strange sense of disappointment. Something told him that Orti had not understood what was happening, even at the end. The eyes had been too clear to be mistaken. He had not known why Kassim was there.

He bought a ticket for Brussels, the next stage of his journey, and found a seat at the rear of a carriage and sat down, tucking his rucksack under his legs. He did not trust to leaving the bag out of his reach for a second. The Makarov was in the bottom, unused, wrapped in a towel with the hunting knife. There had been no sense in leaving them behind, as it saved him acquiring others later. He checked the right sleeve of his jacket, where he had earlier noticed small spots of blood. He had scrubbed at them with a damp cloth before leaving Orti's apartment, and the brisk walk to the station had helped the material to dry. Now the stains were almost invisible.

He stared through the window at the empty tracks, running over the killing in a series of flickering snapshots: going through the door, pushing Orti in front of him and trussing him like a goat, ready for the kill. The shock of surprise had generated a rush of adrenalin, helping him overcome the soldier in the first few seconds. It was a tactic learned in the training camps, then at first hand in various fields of combat.

Yet he had no sense of pleasure at taking the man's life. It had been a task accomplished, nothing more.

Most of Kassim's killing had been done on the hilly battlefields of Afghanistan, where personal contact was rare and death was meted out at a distance. Occasionally he had used the night to cloak his attacks, overcoming guards with a knife to ensure silence. But always he had managed to move on, brushing aside the dreams that later came to haunt him by telling himself there had been no other way.

This time, though, had been different. He had used Orti's own blade, seen his eyes up close; had felt the other's body warmth, sensed his final breath on his cheek; seen the flicker of something desperate in Orti's face in the moments before he went.

But that wasn't all. There had been a need to mark the killing for those who would understand. His trainers had been emphatic about that. He had closed his mind to what had followed, like a surgeon from his patient, and with a few swift cuts of the knife, his task was complete.

As the train slid almost noiselessly out of the station, Kassim felt relieved. He was not clear yet, but every second took him beyond the reach of any random police activity.

He slept most of the hour and a half it took to reach Brussels, lulled to sleep by the warm air and the hum of the engines. His dreams were vivid and random, a kaleidoscope of scenes from long ago, when life was very different, and those from more recent times. And among them, the image of Orti's face swam up like a fish coming to the surface of a pool, staring up at him. He sat up with a jerk, wondering if he had said anything in the quietness of the carriage. But when he looked round, nobody had noticed.

Eight

'Harry?' It was Deane's voice, dragging him out of a restless sleep permeated with jagged images of narrow mountain roads, snow-covered slopes and war machines. And Paulton's face. That never went away completely.

Harry swung out of bed, the phone clamped to his ear. 'Yes.' He checked his watch. It was just after six. Too early to be anything good. 'You gave me until noon.' Deane had finally relented, seeing that Harry wouldn't be pushed.

'I know. But our situation just got worse. Marble Arch, thirty minutes?'

Harry debated telling Deane to go jump in front of traffic. He had a hospital visit to make. But he knew it would merely be delaying the inevitable. He was going to say yes in the end, and they both knew it. He gave his assent and put down the phone, then got washed and dressed and went out to find a cab.

* * *

41

Deane was standing near the giant Fiddian-Green horse's head sculpture, sipping at a mug of coffee. He handed a second mug to Harry.

'Sorry about this, but I got an alert from my office just over an hour ago.' He led Harry away from a group of early-bird tourists planning their day. 'Yesterday you mentioned one of the CP team. Orti?'

'Yes. French Foreign Legion. What about him?'

'I said this man – the Afghan – was coming.' He stared out over the park. 'Well, I think he's already made his first move. Orti's dead.'

If the coffee didn't blow away the cobwebs, this bit of news certainly did. Harry had seen death enough over the years, as a soldier and an MI5 officer, to have developed a reasonably pragmatic view of it. For men like Orti, it went with the job, especially in an elite Special Forces outfit like the Foreign Legion. Even so . . .

'How?'

'He was tied up and knifed late last night.'

'Where?'

'In his sister's apartment in Paris. She was away and he was using it to bed down while on leave. He'd just got back from a bar in the same street, where he'd been drinking coffee. There were signs he'd been exercising in the apartment – he was due to report back today and was probably sweating off a hangover.'

'Nobody saw anything?'

'No. It was professional and quick – and no signs of robbery. The local cops think Orti must have pissed someone off, maybe an Algerian from way back; someone who recognized what he was and decided to get one back for old times' sake.'

'So what's wrong with that?' There was something in Deane's voice and manner that showed doubt.

'You were in Kosovo . . . you saw what they could do to each other.'

Harry nodded. He knew all right. If every story had been reported in full, they would have had readers throwing up their cornflakes. He had seen the grim results of ethnic cleansing and the terrible revenge attacks by the Kosovars and ethnic Albanians. Gruesome failed to describe the horrors perpetrated on all sides in the name of nationalism and religion. Amid the killings, rapes and beatings that happened daily, there were numerous examples of torture, amputations and live burials.

'There was that thing some of them did,' Deane continued, his voice thick. 'They'd leave a calling card, to show they weren't going away.'

Harry remembered. It hadn't been widespread, but it had occurred often enough to be noticed. One group had cut off the noses of the people they killed; another carved a cross on the forehead. Either way, it was another form of terror, a symbol of the undying hatred on either side and the lengths to which they would go to induce fear in their enemies.

'And this one?'

Deane's eyes looked bleak. 'Orti had the letters "UN" carved into his chest. Throw in the rumours about the kid's murder, it doesn't take much to figure out who the killer had a grudge against – and it wasn't the French Foreign Legion.'

43

Harry felt a tickle on the back of his neck. Deane was right. It was too pointed, too deliberate.

'If Orti wasn't still attached to the UN, how did you hear about the killing so quickly?'

'A fluke of European manners. A customer in the bar told the police that Orti was with the Legion and had once been with the UN in Kosovo. They meant KFOR but my office was copied in on the news as a courtesy. My deputy ran Orti's file to see who he was . . . and up popped Mitrovica.'

'And that rang alarm bells.'

'You bet. It could be a coincidence thing, something in Orti's background with the Legion. But I don't think so.'

Harry didn't, either. He tried to picture the man, but having known him for such a brief time didn't help. Running a short-term CP team wasn't the ideal way to get to know anyone; more time is spent looking outwards than in, watching for threat, not judging the character defects of the man next to you.

'If it was me,' Deane continued, 'and one of my men was hit like that, on the back of the rumours going around, I'd be keeping one eye over my shoulder.' He looked keenly at Harry. 'I looked up your ShootReps and IncReps while you were there. You had a couple of wild incidents.'

'Nothing most other units didn't come across.' He wondered at the change of direction. Shooting Reports and Incident Reports were made by UN or KFOR ground troops. Harry's unit had reported on several 'hot' incidents, some serious, others less so. 'How is that relevant?'

'It's not. I'm just thinking of other angles. Did any of your "hot" contacts involve any collateral damage? Women killed by accident? Kids killed or badly hurt by stray fire? Anything Orti was involved in, maybe on the side?'

Harry considered the question dispassionately. Not all UN or KFOR troops behaved impeccably, although they were generally picked for their attitude and inter-personnel skills. But occasionally the stresses and dangers of a peacekeeping posting could get to an individual and spiral out of control. Boredom was a problem, made worse by being isolated in a compound with not enough to do and men you had already spent too many hours with. That could lead to many things, not least of which was gambling.

By its nature, it inevitably spilled over into the local community, always on the lookout for ways of making money in a desperate situation. Money, or any other form of currency such as pilfered stores and equipment, was always the target. It was part of the desperation economy wherever foreign troops were called in to keep the peace.

'Orti seemed a good soldier, but I can't say I knew him.'

'Pity.' Deane looked glum. 'Looks like we're no further forward, then.' He checked his watch. 'I've got to get to the embassy. There's a press conference in New York today. A couple of reporters have tabled questions about the rumours.' He pulled a face. 'They're not going to let this go. And when they hear about Orti, it's going to gather weight and speed.'

Harry nodded. 'I agree. And the answer's yes.'

'What?'

'I'm in.'

Harry left a relieved Deane to make his way to the US Embassy to do whatever damage limitation he was able to, and walked round to Rik's place in Paddington.

'He doesn't give much away, does he, your mate?' Rik greeted him at the door dressed in a lurid purple T-shirt and jeans, his hair spiky and unruly, as if he'd just rolled out of a hedge.

'He's not supposed to. What have you got?' Harry gestured at a laptop blinking quietly on the table where Rik usually worked, and guessed he'd been up for some time.

Rik spun the laptop round to face him. He'd cut and pasted a variety of documents culled from several sources, but it didn't take long to read. From early enlistment in the US Marine Corps, Ken Deane had applied for a job with the United Nations as a field security officer. He had served in a number of UN operational areas, including Kosovo, rising through the ranks to become a leading figure in the Department of Safety and Security, dealing with everything from security clearance procedures through protection of humanitarian volunteers and UN personnel, and linking to investigations into the behaviour of personnel and claims against the organization. Much of it appeared to be desk driven, but Harry guessed that Deane's major role was as a troubleshooter, ready to up and go at a moment's notice when trouble flared. As it had now.

He pushed the laptop back towards Rik. Deane was looking to nip this thing in the bud before it got out of hand. Speaking to Harry was the logical step in the investigation, trying to ferret out quick answers at first hand and protect the UN's back. He couldn't hold that against the man; he'd have done the same. But the implications for Harry were clear: if the rumours and the intelligence were true and a member of the CP team had been involved in rape and murder, it meant they were all at risk.

He rang Richard Ballatyne on his mobile number. Since the MI6 officer had pointed Deane his way in the first place, he must have a point of view on the matter.

Ballatyne sounded cautious. 'To be honest, Harry, this is not something we want to get involved in.'

'That didn't stop you putting my name forward.'

'Sorry. I should have warned you.' He didn't sound sorry. But then, he never did. 'If you want the general feeling around here,' he continued, 'it would be in all our interests if this thing could be laid to rest. The UN's too vital to all our interests to become embroiled in a long-running scandal with no resolution. And if that means finding and hanging out the guilty party to dry before this escalates, then so be it.'

'Thanks.' Harry felt cornered. He was already mentally committed to helping Deane; Ballatyne had just placed the full stop at the end of the sentence.

'There's just one thing, Harry. If you start on this, there's no dropping the baton halfway. This isn't like our normal work: there are no shadows, no smoke and mirrors. It's in the full glare of the sun and there's already been too much focus on it. If you find anything, it's likely that you'll only be a step ahead of the press and whoever's driving this.'

'So?'

'So make sure you get it right. Close it down.'

Harry put down the phone with an uneasy feeling. He'd just been given official approval, such as it was, to help the UN with their problem. But it was a nod at arm's length and free of any recorded official sanction.

He told Rik everything Deane had said, and gave him the names of the personnel he could remember from the close protection team. 'If the group behind this identified Orti, then they've got all our names and it won't be long before they're in the public domain. See if you can find out what's out there. I'll get full details of the team as soon as I can.'

Rik nodded and made some notes. 'Will do. I'll put out feelers with some people I know.' He looked at Harry. 'Are we getting on board with this?'

'I don't have much choice. If I can identify the guilty party, I might be able to put a stop to it.'

'Not just you.' Rik looked determined. 'So forget the "I" bit.'

Harry smiled gratefully. 'Thanks. I could do with someone watching my back.'

'Are we carrying?'

'We will be.' Harry and Rik were 'carded' – authorized to carry a weapon. It was a rare permission for civilians, and only ever granted to former military or government security personnel. But it came with a proviso: the holder could be called on at a moment's notice to jump into the breach and be ready to use the weapon on government business. Those occasions had been rare, and in Harry's case, often disguised as semi-commercial arrangements. The last one had been through Richard Ballatyne, in the search for a rogue organization using and killing deserters from the military. Since then, Harry and Rik had been working in the private sector, searching for missing persons of dubious repute and providing security-related services to quasi-government individuals.

Now it looked as if they were going to be working for more personal reasons.

He took a cab down to an upmarket flower shop near Fulham, and walked into the usual heady aroma of fresh greenery and blossom and the taste of something metallic. The co-owner, Jean Fleming, was snipping stems and arranging a display for the window. She was tall and slim and smiled when she saw him, and he felt his day brighten as always.

They exchanged kisses and she leaned against him. 'This is a surprise. Do you want me to arrange some flowers for you, sir? We have a special offer on today, for hunky men only.'

'Damn,' he breathed, 'I'm off hunky men this week.'

'That's a relief.' She leaned away from him. 'You're going somewhere, aren't you?' The widow of an army officer, she knew all about sudden absences and goodbyes and not asking where.

'A few days. Week at most. Can you struggle on without me?'

She shrugged. 'If I need company I can always hang around the gate at Wellington Barracks. They keep a spot especially for me whenever you're away.' She pulled him close and said softly, 'Stay safe for me, Harry Tate, or I'll be really cross.'

He nodded. 'Always do.' Their relationship was what she referred to jokingly as 'occasional', but they both knew it was a bit more than that, although neither wanted to say it. It worked fine as it was.

In Brussels, the smell of cooking woke Kassim and set his stomach growling. It was a reminder that he had not eaten for many hours. He knew he could not risk going for much longer without food, since the successful outcome of his mission depended on his strength as well as his skills. To compromise that by not eating would be unforgivable.

He was tucked into a shop doorway not far from the Midi station. The night had been chill and damp, but nothing he couldn't cope with; he'd existed for weeks at a time in far worse conditions in the mountains of Afghanistan and elsewhere. He checked the money he'd taken from Orti's wallet. He already had some, but it had been an opportunity to add to his reserves. He stood up and stretched the kinks out of his limbs, then walked until he found a backstreet café where he ordered a simple meal of lamb, rice and vegetables washed down with plain tea. He was one of several men, each ignoring the others, focussing on their food. Over his meal he checked the pocket binder for his next target. The address was just beyond the city centre and it would probably take no more than half an hour to walk there.

He put the binder away, retaining a mental image of the next man on his list.

Arne Broms. Another soldier.

Nine

High in the United Nations headquarters building overlooking First Avenue in New York, UN Special Envoy Anton Kleeman rocked back on his heels and bit down on a growing feeling of irritation. He was facing a group of select, influential media reporters and beginning to wish he had listened to his advisors. The briefing had been his idea, timed to set the pace for a series of meetings with key people in the permanent member states of the UN Security Council. He had been biding his time for long enough; in this world, if you didn't embrace opportunity when it presented itself, you were fated to be just another name on a wall, soon ignored amid the masses. And if there was something Kleeman found distasteful, it was the idea of being ignored.

It was part of his plan to elevate his own position within the organization at a time when other envoys and special delegates were busy catching the eye of news channels and scoring points in the media

51

and PR battle. His plan had been to brief on reports coming out of Africa about alleged atrocities by UN troops against women, and the older reports about brutalities in Kosovo which were currently making the news and growing day by day. Now he was beginning to wonder if this had been such a good idea. Kosovo's grim past was still too vivid for many, especially with war crimes tribunals involving Serb and other warlords running their course. With any new allegations threatening to send the UN itself into a scandal-ridden spin, the occasion could have been better timed. And he'd forgotten how much of a squalid rabble these media wretches could be. Yet instinct told him there was no other way to hit the headlines.

'Is it true, Mr Kleeman,' opened a man from the *Washington Post*, 'that not all the Kosovar refugees who have returned to their homeland are satisfied with the peacekeeping force out there – with KFOR? Isn't this causing the UN some PR problems?'

Kleeman smiled to disguise his dismay, surprised that it had gone this way so soon. He'd expected to get a few of his own shots in first before things got to this stage. 'I think you'll find it's called UNMIK now – the UN Mission in Kosovo,' he said dismissively. 'As you know, under UN mandate twelve forty-four, NATO-led forces entered Kosovo in June 1999 and—'

'But isn't that the problem?' the man interrupted Kleeman's flow. 'In the minds of the refugees in the region, the two are indivisibly linked. The personnel come from the same countries in most cases.'

'Well, that's a difficult quest—'

'What about the stories we're hearing?' A shrill voice cut across his words, and he felt his blood pressure rising. The voice belonged to Dorrie Henson from *The Times*, a regular pain in the ass of the UN and a confirmed radical. 'Stories about alleged brutalities by UN-attached military personnel in Kosovo, going back several years?'

Kleeman felt a sudden tightness around his eyes as a buzz rose around the room, and glared at the woman. He had not been prepared for this. Henson smiled triumphantly back at him as her words unleashed a volley of questions on the subject, and he wondered if it were possible to get the damned woman banned from the building altogether. See how her editor liked those cookies. With luck she'd be out of a job within days and permanently out of his hair.

He held up an imperious hand and was about to speak when Karen Walters, a long-time aide, standing in his line of vision at the back of the room, shot him a warning look. It said quite clearly, *don't go there!*

He pretended not to have seen her and held up a hand. He'd suddenly seen a way out of this dilemma; a way that would enhance his own reputation and standing and lay the matter to rest – at least, for now. It came from his early days in Wall Street, when he had used his father's fortune to make an even bigger one. Back then, the general motto was, when your back's to the wall, come out fighting.

The hubbub died down, and he addressed the woman from *The Times*. '*Mz* Henson,' he said with deliberate emphasis, his handsome face set in a smile, 'I'm not sure where you get your information from, but there have been no confirmed "brutalities" by any KFOR personnel in Kosovo. The "rumours" as you so correctly call them, are unfounded and unsubstantiated, based on enmity towards the UN and NATO in general. There may have been some incidents by untrained NATO personnel, but—'

'You don't call bar-fights and the shooting dead of an unarmed civilian brutal?' called another voice from the back of the room. 'That was in Gornji Livoc.'

'And the young men beaten up outside a bar in Lausa by so-called NATO Special Forces?'

'What about the shooting of two medical workers by UN peacekeepers in Mitrovica?'

The volley of voices grew as the reporters sensed blood in the air, citing stories of serious behaviour by, among others, Russian, African, Pakistani and Polish troops, and a British soldier sent home in disgrace.

Karen Walters moved swiftly from her position at the back of the room, her arm raised in an attempt to draw attention away from Kleeman, who looked like a rabbit caught in the headlights. Suddenly Dorrie Henson's voice cut through the room with the precision of a surgeon's knife.

'What about the rape and murder of a young Muslim girl by a KFOR soldier at a UN compound in 1999, Mr Special Envoy? That seems pretty darned brutal to me!'

Ten

For several seconds there was stunned silence. Then the room erupted in frantic questioning, some of it directed at Henson by press colleagues desperate to share what she knew.

Kleeman resisted the powerful temptation to rush from the room, and waved his hand until everyone fell silent.

'That is as yet unconfirmed,' he said forcefully. 'We do not have full details of that alleged incident. However, what I—'

'These *alleged* stories are coming out of Kosovo day after day,' Henson said cuttingly, 'and have been for weeks. Some of them through the aid agencies. Surely they're being investigated, Mr Special Envoy?'

'What I *do* know,' Kleeman ploughed on, visibly stung by the heavy irony in Henson's use of his official title, 'is that we are hearing this story – not *stories*, Ms Henson – the same time as you. We have to look into the claims, the same way we look into *all* alleged incidents involving UN personnel. That takes time. I think it does no one any good to jump to conclusions at this early stage.' He looked around for support from the more UN-friendly people present. 'And it does no good for those members of the peace-keeping forces still in Kosovo today to have their role besmirched without – I repeat, Ms Henson

– *without* foundation. They already have a difficult enough job as it is.'

'But it will be investigated?' an elderly, grey-suited Reuters man in the front row prompted with quiet courtesy.

Kleeman fastened gratefully on him and said, 'It will be investigated fully.' He put on his most earnest expression and turned to look Henson straight in the eye. 'And I can promise you this: the trooper responsible *will* be brought to justice, and *will* pay for his crimes.'

'Trooper?' Henson looked startled. 'So you know the rank of this person? What else do you know that you're not telling us, Mr Kleeman?'

It was a mistake and he knew it. But before he could reply, Karen Walters stepped in, planting herself firmly between the press and her boss. If it got up Kleeman's nose, her stance said, she couldn't care less; this farce had gone far enough. She apologized and pleaded an important call from overseas, allowing Kleeman to bustle out. He may have been reckless in giving such a briefing, but it wouldn't do to let the press think he'd been reined in like a runaway horse.

Back in his office, Kleeman wished he dared light a cigarette, but the sensors in the ceiling would have reacted instantly. He gritted his teeth instead and waited for Walters to come in. He had no doubts his aide would be unhappy about the way he had thrust his head out in front of the press pack, but that was too bad. She was there to suit him, not the other way round.

He felt rattled by the ferocity of the questioning.

56

He had faced the media many times, often at moments of acute international tension, but this was the first time he had felt like a rabbit thrown to the hounds . . . even if he had put himself there in the first place. On the other hand, he was pleased with the way it had gone. He was sure he had come across as determined – uncompromising, even. And fair, too. People could relate to fair, no matter what the circumstances.

He opened his diary to check the details of his forthcoming trips. Coming on the heels of this press conference, he would be able to use the meetings to press some flesh with the influential members of the Security Council outside the building rather than under the heavy umbrella and constant gaze of the UN administration.

He had been an also-ran for long enough. The time had come to start the ball rolling and move up a few floors.

'We've got to kill this right now,' Walters muttered, closing the door firmly behind her. She was flushed and angry, eyes glinting like a wild cat at bay. She was tall and slim, and dressed elegantly if clinically in a dark blue suit.

Kleeman glanced at her legs and wondered how in spite of all the trips they'd shared on UN business, he'd never once found himself physically drawn to her. An absence of chemistry, perhaps. He wondered who was benefiting in that direction; it was bound to be someone in authority. Unless she was a dyke.

'What's to kill?' he asked. 'As far as we know, it's true, isn't it?' He waved a hand in the direction of the briefing room. 'They seem to have some evidence – what's the point of trying to deny it?' His eyes glittered, a warning to his aide not to overstep the mark by questioning his decisions. As a Special Envoy, with the ear of people all the way to the top, he was not someone to fall foul of without incurring serious collateral career damage.

Of mixed parentage – grandparents Swedish and Danish, father naturalized American, mother Swiss – he had managed to sweep into the diplomatic arena representing a broad range of flags. To some, this was his main strength. Educated at Harvard and the Goethe-Institut in Germany, and with sizeable investments in the Fortune 500 list of US corporations, he had the credentials and, more importantly, the money to take him wherever he wished to go. With friends in the highest places, cultivated over the years in college and business, he had the political clout to have bypassed a number of other well-placed candidates on the UN career ladder. Watchers in the know were even tipping him for Secretary-General in a few years' time, and in spite of some voices in opposition, no one was betting entirely against him.

'They'll pursue this now,' Walters warned him. 'We must advise everyone on the ground so they can be prepared.'

He nodded. In spite of her subordinate position, experience told him that he would do well to keep this woman onside. Never forget the little people on the way up, his father had often said. Well, he wasn't about to. Not yet, anyway.

'Send a note to Field Security,' he advised. 'I'm sure they're already on to it, but it won't harm to remind them that this could snowball. If the story is true, we have to let it be seen that we're eager to keep our house in order. Ethics are only worth possessing, Miss Walters, if they are seen to be upheld.'

Walters blinked at the absurd pomposity of this statement. 'You realize,' she said, 'this could be close to that base we had to use when we were over there?'

'So?' He seemed indifferent to the connection, and not for the first time, Walters wondered if he was all that bright.

'It would not be good publicity, that's all.'

He almost sneered. 'There's no such thing as bad publicity. If the story's true, there's a soldier out there somewhere who has committed a heinous crime. He must pay for it.' He flicked open a folder on his desk, signalling the end of the discussion. 'Now, let's get on, shall we?'

Karen Walters returned to her own office feeling deeply unsettled. There was, as Kleeman had said, no point in denying the story was out there. But letting the press know the way he had, that a UN soldier *was* involved, even before confirmation of the facts, was like throwing the press a big, juicy bone and telling them to gnaw away. What the hell was he playing at? Was it inexperience that had pushed him to say more than was wise, or was he, as rumours had it in the washrooms of the UN, simply eager to grab the headlines as a means of promoting his own platform?

The briefing had been a mistake. Kleeman was accustomed to the social wolf pack, a cocktail in one hand and a clutch of patron-acquired opera tickets in the other. He had certainly never been exposed before to the kind of bearpit atmosphere he had volunteered himself for today. And she had been powerless to stop him. She should have known better. Putting himself out there had been an act of pure vanity – a way of signalling his career intentions. Unfortunately, the rest of the organization – herself included – was going to have to pick up the pieces.

She shivered, remembering the way he'd sneaked a look at her legs. He'd never tried it on with her, thank God. He was married to a social butterfly with old, New England money, although he had plenty of his own, by all accounts. But that had never stopped men like him in the past. She picked up the phone and put out a call for Ken Deane. He was in the UK on unspecified business. She needed to speak to him directly. There were some things you simply couldn't put in writing.

Eleven

The Major Trauma Centre at King's College Hospital in Camberwell, south London, was unusually quiet when Harry walked through the front entrance and checked in at the front desk. The receptionist smiled in recognition but still checked his details and logged him in before nodding him through.

He knew where to go.

He walked up two flights of stairs and made

his way to a corridor lined with side wards. A security guard sat at the end behind a small desk. He checked Harry's details again and nodded him through. The air was cool and smelled faintly of lemons. There was none of the medical detritus common to many hospitals; the better, he had decided, to hurry patients out of their rooms to emergency theatres without having to run the obstacle course of trolleys, unused wheelchairs and spare equipment.

In this place, speed was essential and taken as read.

His footsteps echoed along the corridor. Each room had specialist monitors bleeping quietly or displaying figures Harry didn't pretend to understand, each linked to a person who had suffered gunshot or similar trauma. Each room was its own small universe, but one where survival was not a given.

He stopped outside the second door from the end just as a nurse came out carrying a tray covered by a cloth. She smiled sympathetically and closed the door behind her. It was a signal to him to wait.

'Any change?' he asked. The last time he'd been here a few days ago, there had been no reaction, just the steady breathing of sedated sleep.

'Some,' she replied. 'She speaks occasionally, when it suits her. Mostly she doesn't. But she's on the mend . . . if she wants to be, anyway.'

Harry knew that this nurse, like her colleagues in the unit, was a specialist in treating the Centre's patients. Part of their remit was to take more than

61

a strictly post-operative and clinical interest in their charges. For most of the inmates, coming round after severe wounds and surgery was to encounter a set of circumstances they could never have envisaged. They were awaking to face a lifestyle that would bear no resemblance to anything they had known so far, a future that was at best uncertain. It required a certain specialized approach by the staff.

'You think she doesn't want to?'

The nurse tilted her head to one side. 'Hard to say. She doesn't give any indication one way or another. She knows she's got a fight on her hands, though. The instinct is there in everyone, so we can only hope.'

'Any other visitors?' He asked the same question each time.

'No. A couple of men dropped by after your last visit, but I wouldn't classify them as sympathy callers.' A lift of an eyebrow showed she knew official visitors when she saw them.

Probably Ballatyne's men, he thought, checking that the patient wasn't stealing the cutlery.

'Can I go in?'

She nodded. 'Of course. Don't stay long, though. She needs lots of rest.'

Harry hesitated, a question forming that he hadn't wanted to ask before. 'Is my coming here helping or hindering?'

The nurse looked at him for a moment, then nodded. 'I know you're not her boyfriend or anything,' she said shrewdly. 'But I'm guessing you have a . . . connection?'

'She saved my life,' he said simply. And got

shot in the process, he wanted to add. Her last words then had been to ask for his help. Would anyone have asked that if they didn't have the instinct to live?

'In that case,' the nurse said, 'I think it helps.'

He nodded his thanks and opened the door. As he stepped inside, the woman on the bed shifted slightly, sensing his presence. Her head swivelled on the pillow.

He still wasn't sure whether Clare Jardine hated him or not. Maybe she just hated everyone. He walked over and stood looking down at her.

'I didn't bring any grapes or stuff,' he said. 'And flowers aren't your thing, are they?'

Clare licked her lips, which were dry, and flicked a glance towards the bedside cabinet holding a jug of water and a pad of cotton wool. It was a mute request for a drink. There was nothing of a personal nature from outside: no flowers, no magazines, no cards. Just the water.

Harry dipped the cotton wool in the jug and touched it to her lips. She nudged forward, trying to get more of the liquid, but he pulled it away. He'd had instructions before about what was permissible, and drinking wasn't.

'Bastard,' she whispered. But there was a flicker of something in her eyes that had not been there for a while.

She was tough, he knew that. And dangerous, with a predilection for cold steel. A former member of MI6, she had shared the Red Station posting with him and Rik Ferris after being embroiled on the wrong side of a honey trap with a foreign agent. Rik had been caught hacking into highly sensitive

63

security and political files. Nobody had thought to mention that they were not meant to come back alive.

He pulled up a chair and sat down, his eyes coming level with the shelf of the cabinet. Inside was a bright pink powder compact. Harry smiled. An ironic gift from Rik Ferris. They weren't friends, but it had been significant because Clare had helped save Rik's life, too.

At least she hadn't had it thrown out yet.

'I called by,' he began casually, as if they were old friends, 'because I might not be in for a bit. It looks as if I'm being drawn into something I can't get out of.'

No reaction. She wasn't even looking at him. Her breathing was low and measured.

'I know how much you value these scintillating chats of ours,' he continued, 'and I wouldn't want you to think I was ignoring you if I don't pop by for a while.'

'Don't let me keep you, then,' she whispered, the sound raw, like sandpaper.

'Great,' he said cheerfully. 'So we are talking. That's nice. Shall I tell you about this new job? Well, it's not really a job yet, but I've got a feeling it's about to be.' No reaction, so he ploughed on. 'You know you get an instinct about some things? Of course you do – you're ex-Six: you get injected with instincts when you join, don't you? Well, I've got a feeling this one's going to be nasty.' He was rambling deliberately, hoping for a response. Anything was better than none, even insults. She didn't disappoint.

She moved her head slowly and looked at him. Her eyes were cold, dark, empty. 'Fuck off, Tate.'

Twelve

The Swedish Embassy was on the Avenue Louise, a main artery into Brussels constantly full of speeding traffic. On either side of the route were exotic and attractively lit shops, nudging shoulders with elegant houses and faceless office blocks, many behind ornate iron gates and security systems.

A notice on the embassy wall said the building was closed. Kassim saw a policeman standing just inside the doors, and a camera peering down at him. He walked another two hundred paces, then turned back, unfolding the street map in the manner of a bemused tourist. The play-acting took him no more than two minutes, by which time he had seen no sign of visitors and absorbed all there was to see of the building.

He turned into a side street and consulted the binder. Arne Broms was a big man, pasty and rounded, eyes dull and uninterested. He would have little problem in recognizing him. Soldiers attached to the embassy, the binder told him, were billeted in a section house nearby. He checked the address. It was no more than three streets away.

He followed the map and found that the section house was just that – a house. He couldn't tell how secure it was, but a camera over the front door made a direct entry too risky. He walked on, stuffing the map in his pocket, formulating a plan. He could not spend too much time here; it was too open. He had to move before he got noticed. As he turned the next corner, which was a deserted building site behind boards of marine ply, he found himself face to face with a man coming the other way. Kassim almost gasped with the shock of recognition.

It was his target: Broms.

The Swede was wearing a nylon windcheater and carrying a plastic shopping bag. He looked bored and unprepared, ripe for what Kassim had to do.

Kassim reached for the knife, every instinct telling him *do it – now!* But then the moment had passed, the opportunity for surprise lost. He continued down the street, the muscles in his back twitching, and a feeling of failure eating at him. If only he had been more alert! He could have been away before the Swede had stopped breathing.

Except that would not have been the right way to do it.

The man had to know.

Later that afternoon, Kassim returned to the street and ducked into the building site. After two hours, he saw the Swede emerge from the section house. He was now in uniform, shoulders back and head up, a man transformed by duty.

Kassim was feeling the strain. It had to be now. There was a flight the following morning, if luck favoured him. But that depended on completing what he had come here for, and in this city environment, opportunities in broad daylight were rare.

Then he saw his chance. Broms was heading towards him. Kassim began to breathe faster, his heart thumping in his chest. He had already worked out what to do, and now the opportunity was here.

He checked the street both ways. It was deserted. Broms was coming down this side, striding confidently, big arms swinging. He wouldn't be an easy man to simply grab hold of as he went past.

Kassim stepped out of the building site and walked diagonally across the street, his back to Broms. As the Swede came abreast of the empty plot, Kassim spun on his heel and slid the rucksack from his shoulder. The knife was resting point down on one side, next to the Makarov wrapped in the towel. But the gun would be too noisy. It had to be the knife.

He ran the last few paces, silent even in the western shoes. At the last second Broms heard him. The man turned, his mouth open, but too late. Kassim hit him full on and plunged the knife with all his strength into the Swede's ribs. There was a popping sound followed by a groan, then the momentum of Kassim's attack carried both men tumbling through the nearest section of boarding on to the building site. The knife was wrenched aside by the Swede's body falling away from him, but Kassim followed him down, landing on top of the other man with a grunt, dropping his rucksack to the ground nearby. He drove his knees either side of Broms' chest, pinning him down, then thrust a hand in his pocket and took out the piece of blue cloth he had shown to Orti.

The Swede was still alive, stunned, a faint spot

of pink froth bubbling at his mouth. His eyes rolling in pain and shock, he focussed on Kassim. 'What—?' he muttered, uncomprehending. He flapped his arms, trying to dislodge his attacker, but his strength was fading quickly. '*What?*'

Suddenly Kassim wanted done with it. He shoved the piece of cloth under Broms' nose, waiting until the man's eyes rolled round to look at it. Just for a second, there was a sign of something, a dim light deep in the pupils. Then nothing.

'I don't . . .' Broms sighed and tried one more time to lift himself off the ground. Then the life force drained out of him in a rush.

Kassim twisted his wrist and pulled the blade from the dead Swede's side. A small gout of blood leaked on to the soil beneath. He slid the knife point under the edge of the windcheater and sliced open the man's clothing, exposing his chest.

When he was finished he jumped up and wiped the blade on the dead man's uniform, before stuffing it into his rucksack. As he turned to leave, he saw an old woman standing across the street. She was staring at him, then at the body of Broms on the ground.

For an old woman she had a scream like a banshee, the noise echoing off the buildings and raising the hairs on the back of Kassim's neck. It was too late to stop her, so he stepped through the broken boarding and walked away quickly down the street.

Two minutes later, he was among shoppers and homeward-bound workers, just one face among many.

Thirteen

'Harry?' It was Ken Deane, later that evening. Harry had his television on with the sound off, thinking about what he had to do. Deane sounded angry. 'I'm on a secure line. Another man's down.'

'Who?'

'Arne Broms. He was stabbed in Brussels this afternoon, near the Swedish Embassy. Word just came through.'

Harry felt a tightening in his stomach. Broms the driver. Big, solid, careful. Not an easy man to take down.

'What are the locals saying?' He was sure Deane's office would already have been in touch with the Belgian police, no doubt pushing as discreetly but as firmly as possible for the basic details.

'They're playing wise monkeys. They think it must have been a political act. Do you believe that? I mean, who the hell gets snitty with the Swedes, for Chrissakes?'

'You think it was the same as Orti?'

A long sigh filtered down the line. 'Yeah, pretty much. There was a witness to the killing: an old lady who freaked out with the shock. Kept shouting about "a man with dark eyes . . . a man with dark eyes". They haven't got a useful word out of her since.' He coughed. 'It chimes with something the Paris police said. A couple of barflies where Orti had his last drink said there was a man with dark eyes in the café.'

'What was Broms doing in Brussels?'

'He was on secondment to the embassy, Two I/C of their security section. The embassy's closed down but they had a skeleton staff packing up and needed a security presence. Broms rotated shifts with two other guards, and lived in a section house nearby. He died of a single stab to the side. The cops say his chest had been mutilated. I asked for pictures, but they haven't sent them through yet.'

Harry thought about what kind of man could kill two experienced soldiers with such apparent ease. First Orti, who would know every possible move of rough-house fighting going, then Broms, big enough to shrug off most men with little effort. Whoever the killer was, he had used the element of surprise backed up with lethal skill.

Deane said, 'You remember Anton Kleeman?'

'How could I forget?' Harry almost had, until now. He vaguely recalled a handsome man in his early forties, smooth and urbane, with the healthy glow of the outdoors common to many Americans; a professional politician but not one you would necessarily like unless he wanted it.

'Well, he's moved up the UN totem pole since Kosovo. He's now a Special Envoy and nobody's taking bets that he doesn't try for one of the top jobs one day. He's got the clout and influence to get his hat in the ring; he just needs something to propel him the last few rungs of the ladder.'

Harry wondered where this was leading. He soon found out.

70

'He called a press conference earlier today in New York. It was supposed to be a follow-up briefing dealing with reports about brutalities committed by UN forces in Africa. Word is, he was using it to beef himself up prior to a number of Security Council meetings. There was certainly no need for any briefing on the subject today. Unfortunately, he got sandbagged about the alleged rape and murder in Kosovo.'

'Which he discounted?'

'Which he did not. He actually said the matter would be fully investigated and the guilty trooper, even if no longer serving, would be charged and punished.'

'But it was twelve years ago.'

'Some other allegations are even older – the accusations against the British in Kenya . . . against the US in Vietnam and Cambodia, the UN in Haiti and Somalia. Memories are long when it comes to injustices.'

It wasn't what Harry had meant; he'd been thinking of the time span compared with more recent allegations. But Deane was right: there was no statute of limitations for accusations against nation states. 'What happened?'

'You can imagine. When he said "trooper", the *Times* reporter nearly had an orgasm.' Deane huffed down the line. 'Man, what an asshole.'

'What do you want me to do?' said Harry, sensing it was his turn.

Deane didn't even express surprise. 'Ideally, find the rest of the team. Go talk to them . . . Koslov, Bikovsky, Pendry . . . see if they've got anything to hide. Oh, and the compound guard,

71

too. See what they say, did they have any scams going on the side involving girls in the compounds – that kind of thing.'

'Why should they tell me anything?'

'You're one of them. They'll talk to you. They won't give me Jack shit.'

'They'll know what I'm doing, though – who I'm reporting to.'

Deane came straight back. 'Listen, we've got two ex-KFOR guys who've been hit and I need to find out why. We wouldn't want this to become a habit.'

'You still think the killings are connected with the rumours about the girl?'

'Maybe. I don't know.' Deane sounded exasperated. 'You know how it works: make enough noise and people start to believe you, no matter how wild or how far back it goes. Piggyback on the shoulders of fresh reports about the same organization doing stuff it shouldn't, and it gets easier to take at face value.'

'Have the two murders been reported?'

'Only locally. But not the full details – and nothing about the links to the UN. So far we're managing to keep a lid on it. Just two soldiers murdered. It happens all the time.'

Harry felt a momentary doubt. He was still adjusting to life after leaving MI5, building up contacts and getting himself known. In a crowded security field, with a lot of Special Forces people also out there looking for work, he couldn't afford to get sidetracked.

Yet a part of him was intrigued by the possibilities Deane had to offer. Working undercover was dangerous, lonely and in the end no guarantee of good health if you stuck at it too long. But this wasn't strictly undercover. And it wasn't for ever.

'What about the other KFOR units over there?' he asked. 'We weren't the only ones.'

'No incident reports have come in – I checked.' Deane had a smile in his voice, like a dog suddenly presented with a juicy bone. 'Not one single death among ex-UN or KFOR personnel that wasn't a certified accident.'

Harry relented, as he'd known he would. This wasn't going away, and he'd rather face up to the situation than let it come and find him. 'All right.'

'Good man. I've booked you a seat on board a US Coast Guard flight out of Northolt tomorrow. It took some doing, but it'll save a lot of hassle.'

'That was a hell of an assumption.'

'Yeah, well, I don't have time to hang around. We need to find the source of this rumour and whether it's connected with Orti or Broms. And to safeguard the other men you need to track them down and talk to them – hard if needs be.'

'Is that what you want me to do – protect them? Or find the guilty man?'

Deane didn't hesitate. 'Do what you have to, Harry. It's all the same in the end.'

Harry wondered how much of his life they had gone through in the last few days; how much detail they had sifted through, how many people they'd talked to. This business was snowballing fast, and some influential strings must have been pulled to get all this organized. If Deane had already spoken to Ballatyne, it was likely that MI6 had provided a full briefing on Harry's background. But to do that and sign it off, they must have had complete confidence in his record in Kosovo. 'Fine. When's the briefing?'

'You just had it. A file with the addresses of each man and their current or last known whereabouts will be delivered with a UN security clearance to your hotel in New York.'

'I haven't told you where I'm staying yet.'

'No need. I arranged that, too. Oh, and I'm arranging for a sidearm and permit to be delivered, too. Just don't go waving the gun around in public. The cops in New York are a little sensitive these days.'

This was outside anything Harry had heard about non-US law enforcement agency or military personnel being allowed to carry weapons in the country. It was a measure of how seriously Deane was taking the issue. 'Is it really necessary?'

'I think so. Whoever this guy is, he's good. He's taken Orti and Broms, so everyone else is at risk including you.'

'In that case, you'd better throw in a spare.'

If Deane wondered why he wanted a second weapon, he saw no reason to argue. 'Will do. You OK with this?'

'I'm fine.' Harry didn't mind being a sacrificial goat – as long as the goat could show some teeth. 'How many people can you throw at this on the research side?'

'As many as I've got. Why?'

'You're going to need them. Get them trawling through airline schedules. Look for single male

74

travellers coming out of Afghanistan, Pakistan and India, and moving on across to Europe.'

'Why not two? It would look more natural. And how do we know it's a man?'

'Two would stand out and increase the likelihood of mistakes. This person took out two experienced soldiers; a woman wouldn't have the strength.' The exception, he thought, was Clare Jardine, who had guile and speed instead. 'A woman would have to get close first, to gain their confidence. He's not doing that – he's going for it.'

'OK, so one man. He could have a change of ID for each flight.'

'He may well have. But changes of documentation take more planning and increase the risk of getting caught. I think he'll keep it to the minimum.'

'Shit. Thanks a bunch, Harry. You've just made this thing ten times – pardon my French – fucking worse.'

'It's a crunching exercise. You might get lucky.'

'Yeah, I can hope. Maybe if he's an Afghan, he'll stand out.'

'I wouldn't bet on that. Look at Hamid Karzai: take away his cloak and hat and he'd pass as French, Italian or Spanish.'

'Ah, shit, Harry, do you give lectures in this kind of stuff?' Deane sounded depressed.

'It's elementary. Hear a man's name and you stop thinking about what he looks like.'

'Thanks, Sherlock. Anything else you want to hit me with?'

'Just one thing. Assuming this business is connected with Kosovo, neither Orti nor Broms was still assigned to the UN.'

'Right. So?'

'So how did the killer know where to find them?'

It was a second or two before Deane grasped the implications. When he spoke, it was softly, a realization that there was a leak in the bucket. 'Oh, shit.'

At Brussels airport, Kassim boarded his flight at the earliest opportunity, to avoid being too long under the scrutiny of the other passengers, and took his seat at a window. He buckled himself in and pulled down the blind, then closed his eyes and settled back. He had no desire to engage in pointless conversation, as his English was sufficient but not fluent. People noticed and remembered accents, his trainers had pointed out. Especially around international flights.

There had been no element of irony in the speaker's voice at this statement.

The rucksack was on the floor behind his legs. He'd regretted having to get rid of the gun and hunting knife, but he could replace both and more on arrival in New York. Until then, he had to remain as unobtrusive as possible. He'd made a point of eating beforehand, so he would not need to be disturbed by the flight attendants.

He thought momentarily about the Swede. Another one who had appeared not to know what was happening. It puzzled him. Unless the man's mind had rejected all memory of the past. In any event, he had died well, if too quickly. Kassim shook off the image and tried to focus on the next task ahead. But he couldn't help the thoughts crowding in, as they always did. He had seen too much over the years.

It was going to be a long flight.

Fourteen

Harry rolled out of bed in response to a repeated knocking, only recognizing where he was by the hotel room décor. His head felt stuffed with cotton wool after the flight from Northolt, and his talk with Deane at Marble Arch seemed a long time ago. The security chief had booked him into a small hotel on East 36th Street, just a few blocks from the UN headquarters.

The visitor was a suited messenger holding up a UN pass for Harry to check, and a black canvas bag with a combination lock. Harry signed an electronic receipt pad and thanked the messenger, then called for an all-day breakfast to be sent up to his room. He functioned better on a full stomach.

After a quick shower he got dressed and opened the bag. It contained several sheets of printed paper and a typed note from Deane, two 9mm Ruger SR9 semi-automatics with four magazines, and two electronic swipe cards.

The note was brief.

Details of the team members. Broms and Orti are included for background. Don't waste time with the Foreign Legion – they'll probably nail you to a door and let the ants eat you. Any problems with US military, let me know. Use the passes with discretion and ring me when you can.

KD

The passes carried a small square on one side. Harry's name and photo was on one, Rik Ferris's photo on the other, but with the name James Morrison. Deane showing his age and a liking for dead rock stars, Harry decided. The shots were official – culled, he guessed, courtesy of someone in Thames House, the headquarters of MI5 in London. The passes described them as representatives of the United Nations Field Security Office, and requested all help be given to the bearer, followed by a 24-hour international telephone number for verification.

Room service interrupted his reading of the biographical sheets and he settled down to eat. Half an hour later, over a second cup of coffee, he had a rough plan of action worked out. He would contact the rest of the CP team – Pendry, Bikovsky and Koslov – in that order. The two Americans because they were closest, the Russian last. With a bit of luck he might not need to go all the way to Moscow, Koslov's last listed posting. All he could remember of the man was a thin figure, pale of face and colouring, almost delicate compared with the other members of the team. But tough, if he was in the Russian army.

According to Deane's notes, Carl Pendry was now a 'black hat' instructor at the Army Airborne School at Fort Benning, Georgia. Don Bikovsky

78

had left the US Marines and gone back to civilian life. His last recorded address was Venice Beach, California.

He tried Bikovsky first, but got no answer. Next he tried Pendry's number. The phone was picked up on the second ring by a man with the threat of a drill-sergeant's eye on his back.

'Sorry, sir,' he replied in rapid-fire speech. 'I'm afraid Sergeant Pendry's on the range, sir. He should be back late this afternoon. I'm Specialist Cantrell, sir. Can I take a message, sir?'

Harry had to remind himself that most American soldiers spoke as if they were permanently on parade and addressing a senior officer. The energized-sounding individual on the other end was therefore behaving normally.

'Just a friend calling, that's all, Cantrell,' he told the soldier in an effort to slow him down. 'My name's Harry Tate. I'm in the Fort Benning area tomorrow and I'd like to call by and stand him a beer. Where does he hang out when he's not shouting at trainees?'

There was an audible sigh of relaxation and Cantrell laughed. 'Well, sir, there's only one place Carl hangs out right now, and that's the Holiday Inn North near Columbus airport. He's there most evenings when he's off free.' Cantrell seemed to find the idea amusing for some reason.

'Is there something I should know about the Holiday Inn, Mr Cantrell?'

'Well, it's no secret, I guess,' Cantrell chuckled again. 'The sergeant's gone and got hisself a lady, sir. She's a vice president there, I think. Shall I tell him you called, sir?'

'Why not?' It sounded as if Pendry was a popular man, which said something about his character. 'Tell him I'll see him at eighteen hundred hours at the Holiday Inn.'

He replaced the phone and tried to picture the huge Ranger alongside any woman and gave up. He just hoped Pendry got the message and didn't decide to make himself scarce. He wanted to keep their meeting as low key as possible.

He tried Bikovsky's number again but still with no answer. It looked as though he was going to have to go out to Venice Beach after he'd seen Pendry. For now, it was time to get moving.

He was about to call the front desk for a cab when the phone rang. It was Ken Deane.

'What you said about how the killer knew where to find Orti and Broms,' he said without preamble. 'It looks like we had a bug in the works. You need to be in on this. A car will be with you any minute.' He rang off without asking if it was convenient.

By the time Harry got downstairs, a suited driver was standing outside with a black Suburban at the kerb. The man ushered him inside and closed the door, then climbed in and took off along the street. They stopped outside a plain, concrete building a stone's throw from UN Plaza, and the driver told Harry he should go to the fifteenth floor, conference room 1217, where Deane was waiting for him.

'Harry. Come in.' Ken Deane greeted him at the door of a small lobby opening into a conference room overlooking the East River. Harry could see two other people already seated at the long table, a large man with receding sandy hair and a woman who looked vaguely familiar.

Before leading Harry through, Deane took his elbow and said softly, 'You got the ID cards and stuff?'

'Yes, thanks. I didn't know you were a fan of The Doors.'

Deane grinned. 'Long time ago. Listen, for reasons that will become clear, I got you on attachment easily enough – we drag in specialists all the time; but Ferris was later than I'd expected and would have been pushing it. I got him a genuine ID card but he's not on the books, although the name Morrison is. Just don't let him get caught in the spotlight. And if he gets shot, you'd better bury him before the press finds out.' He gave a lift of the eyebrows to show that he was aware of Rik's very public gunshot injury in central London a few months ago, and gestured towards the conference room. 'Come on in. Let's get this started.'

'You already met each other some years ago,' Deane said, indicating the woman. 'Karen Walters, Special Assistant to Anton Kleeman.'

Walters was tall and slim, with the power-dressed appearance of the professional senior administrator. She was in her late forties, Harry judged, and if she remembered him, did not show it.

'And Vince McKenna, my deputy.'

McKenna smiled and pumped his hand, but didn't speak.

Deane indicated chairs and said, 'My apologies for the drama, Harry. We're meeting in this annexe because going through the security screens

81

at UN Plaza would take up too much time. Vince?' He waved at McKenna to continue and sat back to listen.

'Right.' McKenna cleared his throat. 'Until yesterday afternoon, a woman named Irina Demescu was employed as an analyst in our IT department. She failed to report in today, which was out of character. Her supervisor tried to contact her at home, but without success. When they checked her workstation, they found her desk had been cleared. That automatically triggered an alert to the departmental security rep, who signalled the central security office.' He blinked as the words tumbled out, as if surprised. 'We, uh . . . ordered an immediate check of any computers she'd been using. That check is still ongoing, but she appears to have downloaded a quantity of personnel data from our archives.'

Harry felt all eyes on him. 'What sort of data?'

'Names, addresses, service history . . . mostly from our DPKO records.' He blinked. 'Sorry – that's our Department of Peacekeeping Operations. It was mostly military personnel, but there were a couple of civilian names, too, because they were all connected by circumstance.' He gave a brief flicker of his eyes at Karen Walters.

Harry did not miss the look. Wariness coupled with antipathy. 'How many people are we talking about?'

McKenna consulted his notes. 'About a dozen. Most were lifted a week, ten days ago, with one copied as late as yesterday afternoon just before she left.' He stopped speaking and glanced at Deane.

Harry wondered if all meetings in the UN were

conducted at this pace, and was glad he hadn't taken up Deane's offer of a job all those years ago. He'd have probably thrown himself in the East River by now.

Deane leaned forward and said, 'It seems Demescu volunteered to work late on several occasions over the last few weeks. That wasn't unusual; she was a conscientious worker, so nobody thought anything of it. It meant she had an office to herself.' He lifted his eyebrows. 'There's a minimum staff ruling in the IT department of no less than two personnel at all times. It's been ramped up since nine-eleven. But there's been a flu virus going round and the department was hit pretty bad. It seems nobody told security and with the shortages there was no regular audit.'

'Did she have the skills to search all the files she wanted to?' asked Karen Walters. She was looking strained.

'Absolutely,' said Deane. 'She came from Microdata after graduating from UCLA in computer sciences. Her supervisor says she was one of the best.'

Harry thought it odd that someone had come from Microdata to the UN; he didn't know the relevant salary levels, but he was willing to bet the UN paid less than a going commercial concern like the electronics giant.

McKenna said helpfully, 'Although she left an audit trail.'

'Audit trail?'

'Right, ma'am – it's an electronic footprint showing who's been in the files. It tells us where she looked, dates, times . . . all that.'

83

'She didn't erase it?' Deane looked surprised.

'Not over the last two days. Early on it probably wouldn't have mattered. She could have come up with half a dozen reasons for being in there. Latterly, well, she probably knew her time was up, so why bother? I think she collated the information as she went, taking it out of the building piecemeal or on a memory stick.' He explained, 'The terminal she was using was blind, with no access to the outside.'

Deane gave McKenna a pointed look as if reminded how susceptible they were to data theft. He said, 'OK, let's move on. Where are we right now?'

McKenna shook his head. 'We don't have a lead on her. We've checked her apartment, but there's no response. We're waiting on a court order to go inside. A neighbour thinks she saw Demescu getting into a cab with a couple of bags late last night. She has family in eastern Europe and spoke in the past of not being able to do enough to help them.'

Walters puffed out her cheeks. 'Well, it looks like she's made up for it now.'

'What exactly did she take?' Harry asked, before the game descended into an interdepartmental wrangle.

'Her supervisor ran a duplicate programme.' McKenna opened a folder on the table before him. He took out a number of sheets of closely printed paper. Each one bore a colour-print photo followed by several lines of information. 'Most of this was downloaded days ago. The supervisor says that anything lifted more recently was just updates of any changes to the files.'

Walters craned her head to see. 'What are they?'

'What he said,' Deane muttered. 'Personnel files on a bunch of people.' He reached across and shuffled the sheets apart, reading out the names. 'Bikovsky, Broms, Orti, Koslov, Pendry, Carvalho . . . and two civilians, Kleeman and you.' He looked at Walters in apology. 'There were a couple of other names, one of them deceased through natural causes.'

Harry recognized the sheets. He'd been given the same information but in a slightly different format. The photos staring up at them were the faces of the CP team, with one exception.

'Who is Carvalho?'

Deane looked at the sheet. 'That's a mistake. He's a US Marine, one of the convoy guards. I don't think he figures in this.'

'Why not?'

'As far as we can figure out, he went to Pristina with the convoy and the other depot guard, a guy named Oakes, from your RAF regiment. The deceased man was a Brit from the Royal Military Police. He stayed on at the compound. With both Orti and Broms murdered, I think we can say that this is categorically part of the threat. A terrorist threat,' he added heavily. 'I don't know Demescu's, uh . . . affiliations, but I gather she's a Muslim with family in Albania.'

'That's outrageous.' Walters looked shocked. Twin red spots had appeared on her cheeks. 'You're saying it's a religious attack because she's a Muslim?'

'You're damn right it's outrageous.' Deane came back at her without heat. 'It's also

85

outrageous that an employee of this organization has conspired to provide a killer with personal data for the purposes of murder. And before you get all feminist on my ass, we still haven't discounted your name being on his list. You were there, too, don't forget.'

Nobody spoke for several seconds, then Harry said to McKenna, 'You said the woman downloaded some information before she left.'

McKenna nodded. 'That's correct. Her supervisor believes she was accessing and updating recent additions to the files.'

'About what?'

'About you. She knew you were coming.' He pursed his lips. 'And now, so does the killer.'

Fifteen

Standing in a rubbish-strewn doorway on the Lower East Side, beneath a latticework of scaffolding up the front of the building, Kassim was watching a first-floor apartment across the street. At ground level was a general store, with the owner, an old Vietnamese man, cleaning the front window. A steady stream of customers had been coming and going, with enough movement to cover Kassim's presence. So far he had seen no sign of occupation, although the page in the binder had given this as his next target's temporary address.

He checked his watch and wished he had

brought something to drink. He was thirsty and tired and beginning to feel the cold. The drop in temperature had been acute after the clammy heat he'd been used to in the mountains, but it was damp here, too, which he was finding debilitating. Maybe he needed to get a coat; one of those padded jackets he had seen people wearing. It might also serve as another layer of camouflage, to help him blend in.

Earlier, Kassim had dug out the address of a contact he had been given on New York's East Side, and found it belonged to a man running a small travel agency. The name he was using was Agim Remzi, allegedly a Kosovar who had been in America for over twenty years.

Kassim was reluctant to put his trust in people he had never met, no matter what their stated origins. But the situation demanded it. Remzi, as part of the extended network he was relying on, had agreed to provide Kassim with money and assistance; he could have little interest in betraying him, since it would lead to his own downfall.

He had walked past the front of the agency twice, noting the layout. It was in a busy district with other businesses nearby. After a truck dropping off banded stacks of catalogues had departed in a cloud of exhaust fumes, Kassim had walked through the front door. A woman was tapping at a computer keyboard beneath garish posters of sun, sand and snow, and the place smelled of cheap perfume and stale cigarette smoke.

The woman had looked at him with dark eyes, her chin raised in mute query.

'Agim Remzi,' Kassim had said simply.

87

The woman disappeared through a door at the back and returned moments later followed by a thin, ascetic individual with startlingly blue eyes and grey hair. Remzi beckoned him through, telling the woman to lock the door. Inside his office he offered tea, clearing his desk by pushing papers into his top drawer.

'It is an awkward time,' breathed Remzi, gesturing at his desk. 'Busy as hell . . .' The Americanism sounded false and Kassim wondered to what extent this man had become part of the culture around him. Enough to betray him if he felt threatened?

'It is the will of God,' he muttered darkly, a terse reminder.

Remzi leaned forward and lifted his chin. 'Of course. What do you need of me?'

Kassim had checked his money reserve, which was dwindling fast. He would need more if he had to travel far over the next few days. But with Remzi running a travel agency, that should be the least of his problems.

'First, money,' he replied. 'Also tickets. You know the places I have to go.'

'Yes. Where to next?' Remzi picked up a pencil and pad.

Kassim reached across and took the pencil from his hand. 'You do not need to know that yet. Only that I will call you when I need them – but they must be ready with any paperwork.'

'As you wish. It has all been arranged.' Remzi opened his desk drawer and took out a bulky envelope. It was creased and banded many times with elastic.

'Used notes, all small, all checked. You should have no problems.' When Kassim looked blank, Remzi explained, 'All notes have numbers. There are many fakes in circulation. Give someone one of those, and you will have Treasury agents sitting behind you closer than a child to its mother.' He grinned humourlessly. 'The best thing about this godless country is that nobody likes being cheated. What else do you need?'

Kassim stuffed the envelope in his jacket and took out the binder. He had already removed the pages bearing the details of Orti and Broms. 'You know about this?'

Remzi nodded cautiously. 'Of course. I know the person who provided the details inside.'

'Good. This information . . . what if it is not correct?'

The man frowned. 'I don't understand.'

'What if I do not find all these people?' Kassim had considered at the start that many of the names in the binder might have moved on; as members of the military, their destiny was not their own.

Remzi scratched a note on a notepad, and passed the slip of paper across the desk. Kassim looked at it. *Irina@hotmail.com.* It meant nothing to him. He shrugged.

'What is this?'

'It's the internet,' Remzi explained, as if to a child. 'Like a telephone . . . but you don't speak, and you can contact someone even when they are not there.' He waved a hand and turned to a computer on the table behind him. 'Watch – I will show you.'

Kassim leaned over the desk and gripped

89

Remzi's shoulder, his strong fingers digging into his flesh. Remzi yelped and sank back, scrabbling to get the hand off him. But it was like being held in a steel vice.

'I know the internet, you fool!' Kassim hissed. 'You think I'm a cave dweller? Huh?' He let the travel agent go. He had used internet cafés in Pakistan many times. It had been part of his training, to communicate with others through anonymous Hotmails that were rarely used more than three or four times before being changed. The Americans, through their National Security Agency and CIA, were constantly monitoring cyberspace for key words or coded numbers, and repetition of certain phrases or names in their hunt for insurgents and members of al-Qaeda.

Remzi apologized and rubbed his shoulder, his face pale. 'Of course. I'm sorry . . . I did not think. Forgive me.' He gestured at the screen. 'There is always someone out there to help you. You just need to reach out.'

Kassim sat down, slightly mollified. 'Who are they?' he asked, 'these people who help me?'

Remzi stared at him, his blue eyes suddenly cool. 'That is something you do not need to know. They do not know you, only that you have come. It is better if it stays that way. Then they cannot compromise you.'

A car pulling to a stop along the street brought Kassim back to the present. It was juggled into position and the engine died. The door opened, followed by a faint double-whoop of the electronic immobilizer.

Kassim shrank back into the shadows as footsteps came down the street and a man approached the door alongside the general store. He had a crew cut and a strong, tanned face, and walked with a firm tread. He was holding one of those large, brown paper bags Kassim had seen people carrying out of supermarkets. He mentally compared the face with the photo in his binder. Carvalho, one of the UN guards, according to the file, and a US Marine.

The door opened and closed, leaving the street empty once more. Kassim began counting and adjusted his breathing, feeling his body settle as he tried not to think of all the things that could go wrong. He'd checked the rear of the building for a fire escape ladder, but there were too many overlooking windows to use that way in.

Five minutes passed before he stepped from the doorway and walked across the street, checking both ways. A woman climbed into a car a hundred yards to his right and pulled away down the street, and a man walked a dog across the intersection to his left. The windows above him were blank. No customers from the general store on the street.

The door the man had gone through was old and warped out of true, and Kassim leaned his shoulder against it, testing its strength. The only point of resistance was level with the lock. He felt in his rucksack and took out a large screwdriver he had bought earlier from a hardware store. He had wanted one of the hunting knives on display in a glass cabinet, but the man looked suspicious, so he'd opted for the screwdriver and a grindstone instead.

He gripped the rubber-sheathed handle and inserted the point between the jamb and the door. It slid with little resistance through the wood until he felt it stop up against the metal latch. With another push the lock gave with a faint creak and the door opened.

The hallway was dark and smelled of mould. A corridor ran away from him towards a flickering flare of light and the sound of a television. He ducked until he could see the length of the floor, looking for obstructions. It would not help if he tripped over something in his path.

Slipping off his shoes, he crept forward until he breasted two open doors, one on each side. One was a bathroom, the other little more than a cupboard filled with junk. He listened, only moving on when he was sure the rooms were empty. A man was humming tunelessly barely six feet away at the end of the hall. Kassim breathed deeply and gripped the screwdriver. In his other hand he clutched the fragment of blue cloth.

Sixteen

There was silence at the table overlooking the East River as everyone digested the information that had gone round the room. Deane stood up and walked over to the window, chewing his lip.

'It seems pretty cut and dried to me,' he murmured. 'Information on former and current personnel is lifted from our files, and within days, two of them are dead.' He turned and faced them. 'In line with what we've heard, someone – an Afghan – is going after the CP team and Orti and Broms were the first. Any guesses as to who's next?'

'If the same person killed both men,' said Harry, 'and he's following a plan, then whoever is nearest. At some point he's going to end up here.'

Deane nodded. 'Makes sense. Let's hope it gives us some time to prepare everyone.'

'What about Special Envoy Kleeman?' Karen Walters asked quietly. 'Is he under threat?'

'Unlikely,' Deane said. 'The stories doing the rounds say it was a soldier, and there's evidence to prove it: part of a uniform.'

'That lets me out, then,' Walters said, with a pointed glance at Deane. 'I hate to be sexist, but last I heard, women aren't equipped for it. Rape, I mean.'

Deane's look was several shades less than friendly for pointing out the obvious. He said curtly, 'And Kleeman's a civilian – we get that. Not that it matters; thanks to his status in the UN, there's a tighter cordon around him than the President's cat.'

'It would help,' Harry put in, 'if we could speak to someone who knew the Demescu woman. Does she have family here? Was she part of this plan or was she pressured to steal the information? Where might she have gone?'

Deane said, 'Her supervisor's outside. His name's Benton Ehrlich. I'll get him in here.' He went to the door and leaned out, spoke to someone. Moments later, a man entered the room. He was slim, bespectacled and nervous, and clearly uncomfortable outside the familiar confines of his department. He blinked rapidly when he saw the printouts on the table.

Harry caught the look. 'You know what these are?'

'Yes, sir,' Ehrlich nodded, his Adam's apple bobbing up and down.

'Did you know Ms Demescu well?'

'Sure, sir. Well, we worked together.' He glanced around at the others, his face flushing under their scrutiny.

'You had no idea she was accessing unauthorized files?'

Ehrlich shook his head. 'No way, sir. Irina – Miss Demescu – always seemed real keen, sir, but she kind of kept to herself.'

'You ever socialize with her, Benton?' Karen Walters put in. 'Did she ever talk about her family?'

Ehrlich shrugged. 'Well, we had drinks a couple of times – I mean with other people, you know. But that was all. She didn't drink alcohol and was kind of private. She didn't say much, although I did hear her mention she had family in the Balkans one time. I figured it was best not to talk about that.'

After a few more questions Deane thanked Ehrlich and told him he could go back to work. The supervisor nodded and left the room as quickly as he could.

Deane thanked McKenna and waited until the door was closed before turning to Karen Walters. 'What's been the fallout from Kleeman's press grilling?'

Walters leaned down and took a copy of the *New York Times* from her briefcase. She dropped it on the table. The front page was framed in red marker ink.

'It's hit the front pages,' she said grimly. 'I didn't bring the *Washington Post* or the foreign nationals – I didn't want to depress you. But it's headline news everywhere. Al Jazeera has been running special broadcasts all over the Middle East, and a number of Islamic countries have come out condemning the news and demanding a response by the UN, saying it points towards an anti-Islamic bias by UN troops and supporting member states.'

Deane pulled the *Times* towards him and stared at the headline.

REFUGEE GIRL RAPED AND MURDERED BY PEACEKEEPER – UN SPECIAL ENVOY PROMISES JUSTICE

UN Special Envoy Anton Kleeman yesterday gave substance to the rumors coming out of the country of Kosovo that a teenage girl was brutally raped and murdered by a UN 'Trooper' attached to the multinational KFOR peacekeeping force during 1999. So far the victim, possibly a homeless refugee, has not been identified, nor has the soldier. Special Envoy Kleeman, hotly tipped for the highest reaches of the peacekeeping and humanitarian organization, yesterday vowed before a press briefing that justice for the brutalized young girl would be swift. Speaking to a select press gathering before leaving on a brief visit to Beijing, Paris, and London for talks with other UN members, he would not be drawn on what this justice might entail, nor how it would be enforced.

Deane shook his head in disgust. '*Brutally* raped and murdered? Is there any other way? Jesus.'

'You can't blame the press,' Walters said with cool indifference. 'They react to what they're told.'

'Right. And he sure told them, didn't he? Who the hell allowed Kleeman to do this?'

Walters bristled defensively. 'I'm his aide, not his nanny. If he wants to set out on a crusade without telling me, there's not much I can do to stop him. You want me to hit him over the head and haul him out of the room any time, give me the paperwork.'

Deane grinned nastily. 'Don't tempt me.' He tapped the newspaper article. 'This trip to Beijing and Europe . . . how come you're not along to hold his hand?'

'He has other people for that: trained diplomat types who know how to behave in front of foreign devils. Don't show the soles of the feet or talk about Chinese human rights abuses, don't insult the euro, ignore the French or mention the war; work the cutlery from the outside in and if someone spits on their plate don't stab 'em in the eye with your fish fork.' She brushed a hair from across her face. 'Frankly, I'm glad to be out of his way for a while.'

96

Harry caught her eye. 'You don't like him much?'

Her look was cool, as if unsure what lay behind the question. She shivered. 'To be honest, he gives me the creeps. He's like one of those Hollywood actor-types, all macho bullshit and Armani, but too good to be true.'

'He's gay?' Deane looked stunned.

'No, not that.' She sighed. 'It's a woman thing: good-looking, rich, sophisticated guys affect us that way if they don't have their hand up our skirts every five minutes.'

Deane said with a wry grin, 'Now who's being outrageous?'

'Are you going to notify everyone in those files?' Walters countered.

'All the CP team, yes. That's what Harry's here for. We've tracked down everyone to a last known address, but we haven't spoken to them directly yet. We figured it would be better done face to face.' He tapped the table top. 'We don't want everyone to hear that there's a killer on the loose looking to waste a whole bunch of UN military personnel.'

Walters looked at Harry as if for the first time, and he knew what she was thinking. 'You were the team leader, I remember.' She gave a faint smile. 'You didn't exactly hit it off with Kleeman, did you?'

Harry said nothing for a moment. He didn't see the point in going over old news. But when Deane and McKenna looked at him, he realized that anything appearing to have been hidden now might look questionable later on.

'He wanted us to mount a hot pursuit following

an ambush by Serb snipers,' he explained. 'We were hit as we drove down a narrow defile in heavy rain at night. Kleeman suggested we hit them back, but that wasn't our mission; we were there to protect him, not engage in a firefight. Going after Serb forces in those conditions was a no-hoper. I told him that. Then, when we reached the compound where we were to rest up for the night before being airlifted out, the convoy commander was ordered to Pristina to help protect refugees under attack. Kleeman wanted to go with them.' He shrugged. 'It wasn't my job to provide him or anyone else with a photo opportunity, so we stayed put. He wasn't impressed.'

Deane pulled a face. 'That might explain why he was so quick to jump on the military. I hope the press doesn't get hold of these names yet.' He flicked idly through the papers. 'When they do, every man on it will be labelled a potential rapist and murderer.'

Walters said, 'Can you keep them secure?'

'I wish I could. But they're already out there. Whoever was using Demescu might not allow it to remain secret.'

'That might work to our advantage,' Harry suggested.

'How do you mean?'

'Having the media looking for the men as well might crowd him and scare him off. And if the guilty trooper is out there, he's bound to be on his guard, too.'

There was a knock at the door.

Deane stood and spoke to a man outside. When he came back, he looked shocked.

'There's been another killing.' He reached out and pulled one of the record sheets towards him, spun it round so they could all see it. 'This time right here in New York.'

Seventeen

Kassim awoke in pain and confusion. Something was crawling over his foot. He jerked his legs up and looked around. He was in the stairwell of an abandoned building, moisture coating the walls and puddled across the floor, the air foetid.

He'd been dreaming, back in the hills, with flashes of blue sky over the mountain peaks and the broad, green-brown sweep of the slopes where villages clung to life like dried plants on rocks. Everything was peaceful: a dog barking, a child laughing, a buzzard riding the thermals. Then a helicopter gunship had streaked over the hill and a munitions truck had exploded. The driver had loomed suddenly in front of him, eyes pleading for help. But it wasn't the driver any more; it was his mother, bony fingers reaching for him as the skin peeled back under the flames.

He shook his head, the dream receding, and remembered the previous evening.

He'd been rooted to the spot when the man he was stalking suddenly appeared before him. Carvalho was holding a vegetable knife, the blade covered with red tomato pulp. Close up, the man looked huge.

99

Kassim launched himself forward. But the Marine's reaction was swift. Pivoting slightly, he launched a high back-kick which connected painfully with Kassim's shoulder. Pain mushroomed down his arm as he went backwards, smashing into a coffee table. Barely managing to retain a grip on the screwdriver, he struggled to his feet. As he did so, Carvalho roared and launched himself at him, casting aside the puny vegetable knife and reaching for Kassim's wrist.

Kassim was surprised the Marine didn't just hit him with a piece of furniture – it would have ended things right there. Fortunately for him, Carvalho's hands were filmed with cooking oil, and his grip on Kassim's arm was momentary. It was the Marine's big mistake.

Kassim lashed out with the screwdriver, laying open the skin of Carvalho's forearm like butter. The Marine ignored it, then wiped his hands on his trousers before coming in low and fast, spinning sideways and connecting with a vicious side-kick.

Kassim gasped as the American's boot sank into his ribs. There was a popping sound as a rib gave way, and the pain tore through him in waves. He sank to one knee, desperately waiting for the follow-up and hoping his adversary would decide to use his hands instead of those lethal feet.

Carvalho obliged and reached for Kassim's arm. He was grinning as if sensing victory, and the intrusion was no longer the issue; now it was pure animal instinct, one man against another. The questions over what Kassim was doing there would come later.

Kassim gagged and sank further, and Carvalho took the arm holding the screwdriver in a vice-like grip. That was when Kassim gathered all his strength and lunged off the floor, snapping his arm free and driving the screwdriver towards the other man with all his weight behind it.

The shank went home, puncturing the Marine's clothing and sinking in up to the handle. Carvalho looked startled, his mouth forming an 'o', before Kassim swept his legs away, dropping him to the floor with a crash.

Kassim bent over and rested his hand on his knees. The pain in his side was intense. He listened for sounds of alarm from the floor above, but if anyone had heard, they made no protest. At his feet Carvalho sighed wetly, his breathing constricted, and one knee came up for a moment before straightening out. Even as Kassim looked at him, the Marine coughed faintly one more time, then was gone.

Kassim cursed. It wasn't how he had wanted it to go. He touched a bruise blossoming beneath his hairline behind his right ear. A small amount of blood was seeping out where he had struck the coffee table, and he felt a dull ache building across the back of his neck.

But he'd survived. Now he had to get away. First, though, he had to clean himself up; walking the streets with an obvious head wound would be a sure way of drawing attention to himself.

He bent and tugged the screwdriver free, then went to the kitchen sink and sluiced his face with water. He dried himself off and checked his appearance in a shaving mirror. Unless anyone noticed the cut on his head, he was merely another tired worker on his way home.

He sank to the floor, listening above the drumming of blood in his head. After a few moments' rest, he stood up and looked around. Carvalho had been preparing a meal. Several tomatoes lay on a chopping board, some already sliced, and he gulped them down to quench his thirst. Nearby was a wallet. He opened it and saw notes, a driver's licence and a cash card. He pocketed the money and licence, and was about to leave the cash card when he noticed that the licence had a four-digit number printed down the side in faint pencil. He added the card to his haul and tossed the wallet to one side.

By the sink was a block of wood carrying several knives of different sizes. He selected a larger version of the vegetable knife and took a deep breath before stepping back across the room and bending over the man's body.

He couldn't speak to the man, but he could leave a message for others.

Twenty minutes later, he was several blocks from Carvalho's apartment, walking at a deceptively fast pace. He felt very thirsty again, and recognized the after-effects of shock. He needed a sweet drink. He saw a coffee shop and ducked inside, where he ordered black tea and a glass of cold water. He took his drinks to the back of the room and poured copious amounts of sugar into the tea. The glucose would help settle his nerves. The shakes would come soon, as they always did. Once it was over, he could be on his way. The pain in his side was subsiding and he forced it to the back of his mind.

Above the counter a television gave out the evening's news. Kassim watched as a familiar face appeared, smiling off-camera. The man turned to climb a set of steps into an aircraft, followed by two security guards. The news anchorman came back to remind viewers that they were witnessing UN Special Envoy Anton Kleeman departing for a series of important meetings in China, France and Great Britain.

Kassim watched with only vague interest. Kleeman's face was in his binder, but the UN man was not important. Not right now.

He pulled his rucksack towards him, checking that the sharpened screwdriver was concealed. Then he took the binder from his pocket and tore out the page relating to Carvalho.

When he left the coffee shop thirty minutes later, the crumpled page went into a trash can at the end of the street. He walked until he saw an ATM, then took out Carvalho's card and licence, and fed the card into the slot. When prompted, he keyed in the four-digit number. He had never owned a credit card, but something he'd learned in training was that people often wrote down the number required to access their account.

Seconds later, he was holding a sheaf of money in his hand.

He sat up. Light was filtering through the wrecked building, and with it the buzz of traffic. It was morning. He'd noticed the place the previous night, seeing a drunk slipping through a gap in some wood fencing around a development site. Beyond the fence the building rose high in the night sky, the window apertures empty of glass, with long, plastic rubbish tubes hanging from the gaps like the intestines of a gutted sheep. Cautiously, he'd eased through the gap in the fence.

The drunk had disappeared, muttering and cursing, unaware of Kassim's presence. A sharp, feral smell of sweat mixed with alcohol drifted back to Kassim's nose, unpleasant and alien.

Kassim had been so intent on not tripping, he'd missed the second man. There was a sudden movement in the dark, and he'd felt an arm wrap itself around his face. The pungent smell made his stomach heave. He was slammed against a wall, his face digging into the plaster and his ribs burning with pain.

'No *pass*!' a voice had grated in his ear, a spray of spit against his skin. 'You ain't got no fucking *pass*, you don't come in without no *fee*!'

Kassim had tried to heave the man around, but it was like trying to move a tree. In the background another voice, distant and higher up, wanted to know what was happening.

'Gotta intruder,' the man breathed, voice barely loud enough to be heard, as though wanting to keep his find to himself. 'Got a silent, tiptoeing intruder wants to take our rights away. Think I'll kill the sumbitch 'n take *his* rights, instead.' There was a snick of metal and the man giggled, high-pitched and unnatural.

Kassim pushed against the wall, the muscles of his back contracting at the thought of the knife and furious at the idea of being stopped in his task, not by the police or the UN, but by one of New York's dispossessed.

'The fuck's goin' on down there?' someone yelled, and a bottle exploded nearby, showering them with splinters. 'Izzat you, Tuck – you fuck?'

The man behind Kassim hesitated. It was enough. Kassim heaved himself backwards, slamming his head into the man's face, feeling bone and cartilage crumble. A grunt of pain and something metallic clinked on the floor in the darkness.

'Tuck? *Fuck* you doin', man?'

Kassim turned. Angry and in pain, he yanked the man towards him, no longer capable of stopping even had he wanted to. The man tried to pull away, sensing Kassim's greater fury and strength. But it was too late. Kassim spun him round and took his head in his hands, feeling long greasy hair and an unshaven jaw. Wrapping his fingers in the man's hair, he gave a ferocious jerk and heard a crunch as his neck snapped.

A scrape on the stairs warned him of more danger. Kassim turned and moved deeper into the building, searching for a hole in which to hide.

He found another stairwell, and a door leading out to a bare patch of ground. It was an escape route. He settled down just inside the doorway, exhausted, pulling sheets of cardboard packaging around him. It was enough to keep him dry. Within seconds he was asleep.

Now it was time to move. With daylight, the area might be flooded with police, searching every available inch of space. He had no idea how the

105

New York police would react to the death of a soldier, but he had to assume the worst.

He had to leave.

He moved out of the building, picking his way carefully through the debris and builders' rubble, not pausing to look back. He walked until he saw a coffee bar with computers on tables around the room. It was an internet café. In the back was a washroom. It wasn't open yet but a couple of skinny youths were slouched outside, waiting for a fix of their favourite narcotic.

Kassim joined them. He needed the tickets and documents for the next two stages of his journey. He knew he could call on Remzi in person or phone him, but it was safer to use email. He would pick them up at a prearranged point away from the agency, since he didn't trust the man to have kept himself secure. Then he would be on his way.

Eighteen

Harry was at Newark, about to board a military flight for Columbus, Georgia, when his phone rang. It was Deane.

'The police have confirmed the identity of the dead man: it's Carvalho, the US Marine who was riding shotgun on convoys.'

'What was he doing in New York?'

'Attending a friend's wedding and staying at an apartment on the Lower East Side. Early estimates say he was stabbed sometime last night. The

106

scene-of-crime officer thinks it was some sort of shank. He'd also got the letters "UN" cut into his chest.'

A shank: a rough stabbing instrument with a sharpened point. The killer seemed to favour cold steel. Was that to ensure a silent kill or did it show a sadistic touch?

'It's the same man.'

'Right. Forensics is still going over the scene and we'll have copies of their report later, but they said the place was bust up, like after a fight. An ex-grunt down at the local precinct had served tours with the UN in Nicaragua. He saw the detail of the mutilation and figured we'd like a heads-up.'

'I thought Carvalho went to Pristina with the convoy? Why would the killer target him?'

'Maybe he switched duties with one of the others. No way of knowing. Whoever is doing this is going through the names he's been fed by Demescu. He's not stopping to ask where they were on the night – he's taking them all out.'

'You'd better warn the other guard in the UK,' suggested Harry. 'Just in case.'

'Don't worry, it's being taken care of.'

'Anything else?'

'A local Vietnamese shopkeeper told them a man had been watching the place earlier. Thin, he said, dark-eyed but not black . . . and foreign.'

'What made him say that?'

'He said he looked too fit, unlike most Americans. One minute he was there, the next he'd disappeared. He thought he heard some noise coming from upstairs, but that's not unusual in the area.'

Harry felt things were getting out of hand. He

wondered how the killer had known of Carvalho's movements. He soon got his answer.

'As soon as you left we re-checked Demescu's audit trail. In the last couple of days she made a point of accessing various military files, checking the whereabouts of the men on the list still serving. She was looking for changes of detail, postings, troop movements – anything that affected their locations. The only one relevant was the US Marine Corps database with details of Carvalho's leave application. She did it minutes before she left, the same time she picked up on your assignment to the UN. I'm sorry, Harry, that was my fault: I've kept this quiet for the most part, but I had to make a record of your involvement with the UN to back up the firearms licence and the ID card. Demescu used a search engine to pull up your name. She'll have seen the notes I made.'

The idea that whoever was behind Demescu and the killer now knew where he was gave Harry an uncomfortable feeling between the shoulder blades. He was accustomed to working in the shadows, not having his location on display like a fridge magnet. 'What about Demescu?' he asked. 'Anything on her yet?'

'We're still looking. I don't think we'll see her again. She's probably out of the country by now.'

'Whoever was using her,' said Harry, 'must have thought burning an asset like that was worth it.'

'Unless she was being coerced. We don't know what her family situation is like back home. I've got people looking into that. If she thought she was going to be dropped once she completed her work, getting out while she still could would have been the better option.'

Harry agreed. 'Any more news on the rape story?'

'Some. A couple of UN interpreters in Mitrovica have picked up stories about a dead girl found years ago outside a KFOR compound. It blew over because of ethnic violence in the area . . . and what was another death among so many? But now it's coming back. There's still no hard information, but it's beginning to take on a reality that's hard to shift.'

'The killings aren't going to help,' Harry said grimly.

'Yeah. Paris, Brussels and now New York . . . maybe this guy's just following his nose.'

'I don't believe that. He got his information on the CP team from Demescu. Find her and we might find out who else is involved. That might lead us to the killer.'

Deane sighed. 'Yeah. I wish I knew where he was right now.'

'On the move,' said Harry. 'I would be if it was me.' He saw a man in crew uniform waving to him. 'I've got to go. I'll be in touch.'

'OK. Listen, if you do go to Moscow to see Koslov, you might swing through Kosovo. Our man on the ground in Pristina is Archie Lubeszki. He can fill you in on any local background. At this stage every little bit helps. And Harry – ring me any time, you hear?'

Harry switched off his phone and followed the crewman on board his flight, a US Army Cessna UC-35. It was classed as a utility flight, and he'd got company in four senior officers, who all stopped talking the moment he walked aboard, their inbuilt antennae warning them of a civilian presence. He ignored them and sat down, closing his eyes. Over the years he'd developed the soldier's facility of snatching sleep whenever the opportunity arose, and right now he needed to pack away as much as he could. He was going to need it.

Harry found the Holiday Inn a short car ride from Columbus airport. A large, 222-room building with conference facilities, fitness room and satellite television, it still managed to look like a hundred other similar hotels.

He parked his rental car near the front entrance and walked into an air-conditioned chill. The lobby was full of men and women dressed in suits or blazers, with sharp creases and little jewellery, badges pinned to their chests.

Harry checked in, then skirted the mêlée and headed for the lobby bar. He needed a cold drink and to check the lay of the land. The bar already held a collection of serious drinkers – presumably colleagues of the group outside – and he found a spot away from the noisiest group. He ordered a beer and nodded towards the lobby. 'Sales conference?'

'Yes, sir.' The bartender placed a beer in front of him. 'You from out of town?'

'New York,' Harry said. 'Down to see a friend.'

'Uh-huh.' The man nodded, as if being from New York explained it all.

'My name's Harry Tate. I'm here to see Carl Pendry.'

The man dunked a glass into a basin of water.

'Carl? Yeah – I know Carl.' He excused himself and moved along the bar to serve another customer, leaving Harry with the uncomfortable feeling that he'd breached some local code of conduct.

Moments later he sensed a movement nearby and detected a trace of perfume. He turned and found a young woman looking up at him.

'Hi,' she said brightly. 'You're Harry, right?' She spoke with an attractive, soft drawl, and was small and slim, dressed in a dark trouser-suit and a frilly blouse. A mass of blonde hair topped a pert face with large, alert eyes.

'Yes,' he said, assuming she was a member of staff. Ten feet away the bartender was watching from the corner of his eye. 'Is there a problem?'

'Not at all,' she replied. 'You've come to see Carl.'

'News travels fast.'

'Only when it has to. I'm Gail Tranter. Carl's a friend.' She signalled to the bartender, miming a drink. 'He asked me to meet you and make sure you were comfortable. He's been delayed at the base, but he won't be long. They have a lot of new arrivals to deal with.'

She collected her drink, which looked to Harry like a straight tonic, and led him to a table away from the other guests.

'Sorry about the crush – when we don't have corporate meetings, we get a lot of military personnel and their families passing through.' She sat neatly and sipped her drink. 'Our policy is to support the military at all times. Carl tells me you were with him in Kosovo?' Her tone ended each sentence on a rising inflection, and Kosovo was pronounced with soft and rounded Os.

111

'That's right.' Harry wondered how much Pendry had told her.

'Close protection?' she said with no trace of irony. 'Does that mean you're like the Secret Service, you have to put yourself in front of the – what is it? – the veepee?'

'Actually, the industry standard is to duck for cover and let the veepee take the bullet.'

'That's what Carl said. I didn't believe him, either.' The look she gave Harry warned him she wasn't a weak, fluffy-headed female who needed protecting from the harsher truths of the world, so he could cut the bullshit. He decided he liked her.

'Have you and Carl been friends for long?'

'Sure. We were at school together. Then he joined the army and moved away. I stayed around here and did college and majored in business studies. We bumped into each other again in Columbus about a month ago.' She grinned at the memory. 'He'd put on about fifty pounds of muscle and grown another ten inches. I hardly recognized him. But we get on pretty good.' She smiled meaningfully.

Then a shadow loomed over their table and a voice growled menacingly through the background hubbub. 'Say, what's a good southern gal doin' with some skinny-assed white dude from England?'

In Columbus airport, Kassim made his way through the arrivals hall and found a cab. He asked to be taken to the city centre.

The driver nodded without a word. He was a skinny Asian with a scrub of jet-black hair over a pale, pockmarked face. He drove single-handed, the other beating time on the centre console to the radio, pausing only to answer incomprehensible bursts of chatter from his dispatcher. Other than an occasional glance in his rear-view mirror, he ignored his passenger completely.

Kassim was happy enough to sink into the rear seat and keep his head down. He was thinking about the Hotmail message he'd picked up in the internet café in New York. He had deleted the words immediately after reading them, but he could still see the text in his mind. It had warned him that the Americans were looking for him, that a pursuer was already out there, waiting for him to make a mistake. The message had also confirmed where he needed to go next.

He stared out at the garish lights of a Holiday Inn as they passed, and toyed with the idea of booking in for the night. At least here there would be no danger; he'd be just another weary traveller looking for a bed. After his night in the deserted building and the fight with the derelict, he needed a shower and some rest. But the faint lure of comfort gave way to the need for action . . . to prepare for what lay ahead.

After a couple of miles the cab stopped behind a line of vehicles edging past an auto wreck. Emergency crews were clearing up the debris, and an ambulance was just leaving. The cab driver applied his brake and sighed resignedly.

'We wait,' he explained shortly.

Kassim leaned forward and said, 'I have to hire a car. You know of a person?'

The driver looked back at him in the mirror. A person, not a place. This passenger hadn't been to the rental agencies at the airport, which had

113

to be for a reason. A bad credit risk, maybe. He nodded. 'Sure. I know. What kind car?'

'Ordinary. Not big.'

'Compact?' The driver slapped the wheel. 'Like this?'

Kassim nodded. 'Ordinary.'

'Sure. You have money?' He rubbed his fingers and thumb together, the international sign for cash. His passenger needed a car without signing any papers, this was the only way.

'I have,' Kassim confirmed, and stared hard at the man in the mirror until he looked away. His message to the driver was brutally clear. *Try to take advantage of me, and you will not live to see the morning.*

He sat back and prepared to wait, thinking about the man who was coming after him. The name had been included in the Hotmail message, and was also in his pocket binder. Maybe this man had a double motive for finding him as quickly as possible: to stop him from carrying out his task and to conceal his own involvement. If so, Kassim reflected, then it would be right that they meet soon.

He pulled out the binder and stared hard at the photo of Harry Tate, committing the face to memory.

Nineteen

Harry looked up to find Carl Pendry grinning down at him, his dark skin gleaming under the

114

soft lights. He was dressed in chinos and a pale shirt, his arm muscles bulging under the thin fabric.

'For a minute there I thought a human being had walked in,' Harry responded drily. 'But it's just a robot grunt in civilian clothes.'

Pendry looked affronted. 'Hey, white boy, don't diss the threads – they cost serious money!' He bent to kiss Gail on the cheek. 'Hi, honey – sorry I'm late. This guy giving you trouble?'

Gail smiled and returned the kiss. 'No, he's been a perfect gentleman. You could learn a thing or two from him.'

Pendry rolled his eyes. 'Why is it all you women think the sun sets on *ginnelmen*?' He threw a mock scowl at Harry. 'See what you done, comin' down here wit yo' fancy English ways? It's gonna take me weeks to get her back to likin' our brutal southern style.'

Gail stood up, her hand on Pendry's arm. 'I've got to go look after these convention folks. See you tomorrow?' Pendry nodded and Gail smiled at Harry. 'It's been nice meeting you. If you need to stay longer, let me know.'

Harry stood up and nodded. 'That's very kind.'

They watched her walk away, then sat down.

'Have you eaten yet?' Pendry asked, his voice becoming serious. 'I guess you want to talk.'

'That would be good.'

They went into the restaurant and ordered, sitting away from the door so they wouldn't be interrupted. Over drinks, they quickly caught up on the years since Kosovo.

For Harry it was out of the army and into the

Security Service, then civilian life; for Pendry it was a standard round of military postings around the world until he became a senior instructor at the Airborne School, Fort Benning. When talk got round to the other members of the CP team, Harry judged the time right to tell him what had happened.

Pendry said nothing until Harry concluded with the murder of a young girl. He left it until last so that he could judge the other man's reaction.

'You serious?' Pendry looked shocked. 'Man, they weren't into any of that shit. Broms – he's what we'd call a good ol' farm boy; the Frenchman was too professional to crap crooked. As for shakin' it with the locals?' He shook his head in bafflement. 'When did we get the time?'

'That's what I thought.' Harry told him about the third killing in New York, of the Marine, Carvalho. 'Did you speak to him?'

'Said hi, probably. He was in the compound after the others left, but he seemed a regular guy – for a Marine, anyway. He get cut the same way?'

'Yes. He fought back, but it didn't do any good.'

Pendry looked keenly at him. 'You figure this killer's working his way through the whole convoy? That's crazy.' He went silent as the waitress came with their food.

Harry shrugged and began to eat. 'Maybe he doesn't know who he's after, so he's hunting down everyone on the list until he finds the guilty man. That's why I'm doing the rounds. Deane's sending out a warning to the rest of the convoy personnel.' He put his fork down. 'I'm going to see Bikovsky next. Do you know why he left the army?'

Pendry shook his head. 'Nothing personal. Had a beef about refugees and asylum seekers, but he's not alone in that. Maybe he was burned out. It happens.' He gave Harry a hard look. 'But you're not here just to give me a warning, are you?'

'You've lost me,' Harry said easily.

'Yeah, right.' Pendry's friendly demeanour was gone. 'You really trailed all the way out here to warn me that I might have a killer freak on my ass? Bikovsky, too? And – what was his name – Koslov? You going all the way to Minsk or Leningrad to warn him? You never heard of the phone?'

A couple of businessmen at a nearby table glanced across as Pendry's words reached them, and the waitress at a dessert trolley paused in the middle of spooning out some gateau.

'Moscow, actually,' Harry replied. 'And if I have to, yes.'

Pendry pushed his plate away. 'I'm done,' he hissed. 'You want to ask me did I run a card game while I was running cover for the UN big cheese? Or in my free time, did I kill and rape a local girl?'

'If I'd thought it was you,' Harry said, quietly dispassionate, 'we wouldn't be sitting here. If the rumours are true, someone did it. It's my job to find out who – and stop the rest of you joining Orti, Broms and Carvalho. One of you might have seen something – something completely innocent-looking but possibly significant. Asking on the phone wouldn't have been enough . . . I have to do it face to face.'

The quiet force of Harry's words drove the anger out of Pendry like air from a tyre. After a second or two he waved a hand and sat back. 'Sorry. I thought you were looking at me for this thing.'

'I'm looking at everyone. And I'm a suspect, too. We all are – those of us who are left.'

'So what now?'

'You watch your back. This killer's taken out three good men so far – all combat trained. If it's revenge for the girl he's after, he's got one hell of an incentive.'

Harry went to his room after saying goodbye to Pendry and lay down to let his mind go blank. Ten minutes later, there was a knock at his door. He opened it and stood back.

'Hello, dear,' said Rik Ferris, walking past him. He looked tired and rumpled from the flight, his hair even more spiky than usual. He was carrying a travel bag and a laptop case. 'Nice hotel, this. Which is my bed?'

'Your room's down the hall. You'll have to check in,' Harry told him. 'Any problems?' He was referring to the flight over.

Rik shook his head. 'No. Normal crap with immigration, but nothing unusual.'

They had discussed Rik's involvement and decided on discretion while on the move. Former MI5 officers were not normally high on anyone's suspect or watch list but Rik had been involved in the same shooting incident in central London as Harry a few months before, and they didn't want to take a chance on his being stopped by an eagle-eyed security officer. And Harry already

118

knew from the Irina Demescu episode how leaky the UN was. Having Rik in the background under an assumed name, rather than some nameless IT geek in the depths of UN Plaza, was a simple precaution.

'This is for emergencies only.' Harry handed him the UN ID card and the Ruger with a spare magazine.

Rik studied the name on the card. 'Wasn't there a Jim Morrison who killed himself?'

'Is that a problem?'

Rik shrugged. 'No, that's cool. Way before my time, anyway.' He checked the Ruger and inserted a magazine, then ejected it again. 'Nice. Who do I get to shoot?'

Harry was watching him carefully. Rik was smiling but it didn't quite look right. He knew why: Rik was thinking about the time he'd used a gun in London. He'd got shot then, but still kept firing. That kind of thing stays with you.

'Nobody, I hope. You're my back-stop. You stay below the parapet at all times. We don't even travel together.'

'Don't you trust your new best friend?'

'It's not Deane who bothers me: the UN's full of holes and I'd rather you didn't figure on anyone's radar. That way we keep an advantage.'

Rik nodded. 'Fine.' He put the gun down and produced two mobile phones. He handed one to Harry. 'We keep in touch with these. I've already fed in my number. Use it and lose it if you have to – we can always get replacements. Deane has your UK mobile number, don't forget; if he wants to find you, he'll put a trace on the signal.'

'You're as paranoid as me.'

Rik gave a crooked smile. 'I learned from the master.'

'Glad to hear it.' Harry pointed at the internet connection on the side table. 'Plug in and boot up. We've got work to do.'

Twenty

Sergeant Carl Pendry had eased his way with care into a clump of juniper, and was waiting for the first of his sniper class to arrive. The morning was fresh with the smell of damp earth, a touch of pine and closer to, the sharp, rich aroma of crushed grass. High in the trees a squirrel scratched away, oblivious to the man below. It was one of the things Pendry loved about this job and always impressed on his trainees: snipers were in a dangerous profession, out on their own or with a spotter for hours, even days at a time. But that didn't mean a man couldn't appreciate his surroundings.

Pendry was dressed in regulation camouflage smock and pants, his head covered by a green woollen net cap dotted with foliage. His face was a blend of wavy green camo paint to break up the darkness of his skin against the background, and in his hand he held an M16 assault rifle. He had been in the same position for forty minutes and was beginning to feel the first pangs of hunger. His mouth was dry from the effects of the drinks with Harry the previous evening, and he wished he'd brought some water. A glance at his watch told him it was just coming up to 6 a.m.

There were five men in the class, all of them better than good. Their task was simple: to approach and 'take out' Pendry without being detected. But it had to be within a thirty-yard kill zone. Anyone spotted before that was in danger of flunking the course or being back-marked. And none of them was keen to go through another six weeks of initiative tests, psychological assessments, assault courses and daily runs considered among the most demanding in the US military.

Their covert skills were still a little rough around the edges, and Pendry had decided to introduce an element of realism to the scenario. Earlier that morning he'd armed himself with a few flash-bangs – giant fireworks which could blow a metal pail several feet. In the words of the quartermaster-armourer, they were harmless to humans unless swallowed or, he'd added drily, if they landed right next to a trainee who was dreaming of his girl back home. The noise alone would blow the shit clean out of his bowels.

A faint scuffle a few yards away and the squirrel ceased its scratching. Pendry half-closed his eyes, concentrating on locating the source of the noise. He was guessing it would be Lloyd; he was the best of the bunch and unbelievably quick. Twenty-one years old and thin as a whippet, the farm boy from the Smokey Mountains could slide through the undergrowth like a snake.

Pendry pulled out one of the flash-bangs. Give it twenty seconds and if Mr Lloyd was sitting in the same spot, his ears would be ringing for a

121

week. If that didn't scare the crap out of him, and some idea of realism *into* him, Pendry had live rounds in his M16 to warm up the atmosphere around the boy's head a little.

A small bird looped urgently out of a bush thirty feet away. It was near the source of the earlier sound, and Pendry heard a faint rasp of clothing. He grinned. Lloyd had snagged himself on a root. Now he was trying to free himself. This was going to be easy.

Then came a muffled drumming, followed by the sound of someone running through the bushes. He frowned. If that was Lloyd, he was going the wrong way!

Pendry exploded out of his hide, his M16 held across his body and the flash-bang spinning away into the grass. Either his star recruit had gone nuts or someone had intruded on the exercise. Damned civilians – they were way out of place this far into the training grounds! Now he had to make sure the stupid fucker didn't get shot by one of the trainees.

He pounded after the intruder, brushing aside the hanging branches and catching a glimpse of a camouflage jacket disappearing into a thicket fifty yards ahead.

'Hey! Hold up there!' he roared, and scrabbled for his cellphone. The man was running like an Olympic sprinter and Pendry knew he'd never catch him. But at least he could keep him in sight and alert security to get the stupid sonofabitch picked up before he got himself killed.

Then he caught a glimpse of a figure lying prone in deep cover, his rifle pointing straight at him. It was Lloyd.

Damn! That clever fuckin' kid had set this up to deceive—

Pendry skidded to a stop. Something wasn't right. He stared down at the trainee, a chill gripping his gut. The farm boy wasn't moving. Lloyd was lying with his face down in the earth, a widening pool of blood spreading beneath him.

His throat had been cut from ear to ear.

An hour later the training area was swarming with security patrols and military police with dogs. Overhead a Bell AH-1Z attack helicopter cross-quartered the sky in a search pattern of the ground below, while a larger version thudded away after dropping off a fully armed search team. All training had been suspended and a military investigation team was on its way in. The whole area was in lockdown.

Harry Tate was studying the layout where the killing had happened, standing within an area marked by white tape. Lloyd's body lay beneath a military groundsheet, the grass around him bright with splashes of blood.

'Go over it again,' Harry told the instructor, who was still stunned by what had happened. Fortunately, after calling security, Pendry had had the presence of mind to ring Harry at the hotel before he left. Harry had phoned Rik on the internal line and advised him to keep his head down and to continue trawling for information on the members of the CP team and any news about murdered girls in Kosovo in 1999.

Getting on to the training area had been surprisingly simple. It was the first time he'd used his

UN pass, and although he'd had to resort to a phone call to New York, it had worked with surprising efficiency. Even so, he had been escorted to the scene of the killing by two armed troopers, who were still posted nearby.

'I heard a noise,' Pendry repeated. 'Like he'd got hisself snagged . . . you know how it is when you're crawling. Then there was this thumpin' noise, like someone was beating the ground. Next thing this guy took off through the trees. I started after him. I mean, I thought it was a civilian . . . we get 'em comin' through here from time to time, even though it's off-limits. They get off on being near the action.'

'Did you see the killer?'

'Tall – about five ten – and wearin' plain camo jacket and pants. Stuff you can buy from any surplus store.'

'Hair? Skin?'

'Dark hair . . . couldn't see any skin. Pale, I think. He could sure run, though – like a jackrabbit.'

A Ranger colonel appeared along the taped trail leading out of the area. A young lieutenant scurried along in his wake like a tug chasing a liner. The senior officer, lean, compact and grey-haired, scanned the area with cool blue eyes, then looked at Harry with flinty hostility. He evidently knew who Harry represented, but all he saw was a stranger – and a foreigner – with no US military credentials. His thoughts were obvious: the UN had no remit on Ranger turf and Harry should be kicked off as soon as he got word from HQ.

'What have we got?' he asked. He clearly knew

124

enough about the workings of officialdom to preserve a sense of courtesy. He also needed to know what Harry had found out while he'd been here, to help his own investigations about this business. Then he could kick the Brit's ass off the area with a clear conscience.

Harry told him in simple and polite terms. 'Your man Lloyd was lying up right here. The killer must have approached from the rear and killed him where he lay.'

The colonel was sceptical. 'You saying he didn't hear the killer coming? I find that hard to believe; he was a highly trained soldier.'

'I'm sure he was,' Harry agreed. 'But he would have been concentrating on his forward area. If he was as good as you and Sergeant Pendry say, he probably knew where Pendry was anyway, so why look anywhere else?'

'Have you ever been in a live situation, mister?' the young lieutenant demanded. He was as rigid as a tent-pole and looked tough and fit. But his eyes flickered too easily towards the colonel. Harry recognized the type: he was aiming at higher things, a future staffer in the making.

'Several times, actually, Lieutenant,' Harry replied. 'Northern Ireland, Bosnia, Colombia, Africa and Kosovo. I've also been on a Special Forces sniper course, so I know what it's like for a young trooper trying to score against the best there is.'

'Thank you, Lieutenant,' the colonel muttered briskly. 'I think we can take it Mr Tate knows what he's at.' He said to Harry, 'If you'll excuse me, I have to get back and meet our public relations boys.'

'The press have heard already?'

The colonel nodded, his expression sour. 'Unfortunately, there are people with nothing better to do than to spend their time monitoring military and police communication channels. Someone on the base mentioned the manner of Lloyd's death and the world at large now knows we've lost a fine young soldier with his throat cut. No way can this be explained as a training accident.' He began to turn away then paused. 'I'll be in my office if you want to share any ideas you might have.'

'Ideas?'

The blue eyes settled on him. 'Yes. How and why can a tough, fit young Ranger in the middle of a US Army training ground get his throat cut without fighting back?'

'He didn't fight because he couldn't.' Harry pointed at twin depressions each side of the body. 'The killer jumped on his back, pinning him face down. Caught in that position, Lloyd didn't stand a chance.'

The colonel flinched at such a stark summary, but didn't argue. 'But why him? And why does your presence here make the back of my neck itch?'

Harry wanted to tell him, but couldn't. He wouldn't understand; the worlds of elite fighting troops like the Rangers and the murkier one in which Harry moved were too far apart. 'All I can say is,' he said finally, 'I believe it was a case of mistaken identity.'

The officer nodded curtly and walked away through the trees, closely followed by the lieutenant and the two escorts.

126

Twenty-One

Harry glanced at Pendry. 'It was meant to be you, Carl,' he told him. It was brutal but necessary, if only to snap Pendry out of his anger and make him aware of his own safety. 'If it was our killer, and not some lunatic with a personal grudge against Lloyd, he'll be back for another try.'

'I know.' Pendry looked across at the body under the groundsheet, his jaw working furiously. 'But why kill the kid? He didn't have no enemies – it was pointless.'

'Not to the killer.'

'What?'

'Lloyd might have got a look at him. He wouldn't have wanted to risk having his description broadcast, especially in an area surrounded by security patrols. Anyway, if it was the same man who killed Carvalho and the others, Lloyd would have been no match.'

'But the way Lloyd's lying,' Pendry argued. 'He was moving forward. He didn't look like he even saw him.'

'He's not facing the right way, though.'

'What?' Pendry checked the body position again, then looked towards the juniper bush. The direction Lloyd was facing was off by a good forty-five degrees. 'I don't get it.'

'My guess is he crossed the killer's trail or saw

him and followed to see what he was up to. Then the killer turned the tables.'

'That means he's combat trained. Christ, who *is* this guy?'

'A professional. One who isn't afraid of penetrating a top military base to get what he's after.'

One of the MPs laying out the white tape called out to them. He was fifty yards away, pointing into some brushwood. They hurried across and looked down. A large knife with a roughened bone handle and a serrated back ridge was lying on the ground.

The blade was red in blood.

'A hunting knife,' Pendry said. 'He must have dropped it when he took off through the bushes.'

Harry looked at the MP. 'I suggest you bag that carefully and get it to the forensics people,' he said. 'This might be the only evidence we get.'

The policeman nodded and began talking urgently into his radio. Pendry squatted and examined the knife where it lay.

'It's just a knife,' he said. 'Around here you'll find a thousand just like it.'

'Maybe,' said Harry. 'But there might be prints.'

Pendry shook his head and stood up. 'What do we do now?'

'We let the investigation team do their thing. He may have left more evidence behind. If so, they'll find it.' He looked up at the helicopter circling overhead a couple of hundred yards away, the down-draught swaying the branches of the trees.

Half a mile away, under cover of a line of scrubby bushes, Kassim watched through binoculars as the activity continued around the site where he had

128

killed the American soldier. He could not see the black Ranger he had come looking for, but he knew he was there somewhere. Unfortunately, he was now untouchable, surrounded by heavily armed military personnel.

He regretted losing the knife, which had been ripped from his hand by a branch whipping back against his thumb. No doubt it would soon be picked up by the investigators and subjected to careful examination. It was inconvenient but hardly a disaster; he had no record in the United States, so any traces on the weapon would lead nowhere.

Now he had to get away from here and get cleaned up. There would be other chances to deal with Pendry, but not right now. Better to move on and come back another time. There was also the presence of the Englishman, Tate. He too would be fully alert, and any chance he had of approaching him was now gone.

He was thinking about money. He was going to have to call on the travel agent, Remzi, again, before he left America. He had enough cash for his immediate needs and his tickets, but the payment for the car had been more than he'd anticipated. After the cab driver had dropped him off the night before near a tired-looking back-street workshop, he had found himself under scrutiny from three large, silent men in grubby overalls. A fourth man was using an oxyacetylene cutter on the wing of a beaten-up Chevrolet.

The haggling had been brief; take it or leave it. He had taken an aged Ford, victim of countless bruises and scrapes, but sound. They had thrown in directions for a cheap hotel and the location of a hunting store with flexible opening hours.

No doubt Remzi wouldn't be pleased to hear from him again, but there was no other way. He slid out from his cover and wormed his way deeper into a belt of trees stretching away into the distance. It meant a long trek back to his car, but he was in no hurry. If they found it in the meantime, it would lead them nowhere.

It was early evening before Harry arrived back at the Holiday Inn. He was tired and tense, anxious to climb into the shower for an hour or so to wash off the dust of the training ground. By the time he and Carl Pendry had been through a lengthy grilling by the US Army investigators and local FBI special agents, called in on the advice of the base commander, the morning had turned into late afternoon. Harry had finally been allowed off the base, and knew it was so that they could shunt him out of the way. He had been helpful but was an outsider. Before leaving, Pendry had given him a direct number in case he needed to call.

He saw Rik in the doorway to the bar. He was holding a beer and fanning himself with a hotel brochure. Harry walked past him and ordered a beer; the shower could wait.

'What's up?' he asked, as Rik sidled up alongside him and put his glass on the bar. The barman was out of earshot.

'I've been monitoring the news channels. The local networks are going nuts. The most accurate is a soldier killed in a training accident, the worst

130

is an entire platoon mown down by a crazed terrorist gunman. How bad was it?'

Harry gave him the basic facts. 'If it wasn't an attempt on Pendry, I'll eat my feet.'

'How did the killer find him? I checked the satellite photos – it's a hell of a big area.'

'Common knowledge. Most of the population here is either military, ex-military or knows someone employed on the base. And I hear there are army freaks who like to sneak in and watch the training. If our man knows what Pendry's job is, it wouldn't be too hard to find someone keen to brag about what was going on where, and pin down the location.'

Rik sipped at his beer. 'He couldn't have driven in; he'd have been spotted. He must have walked.'

'And back out.'

Harry thought about Pendry's comment about the man wearing camouflage jacket and pants. A place like Fort Benning was buzzing with security patrols and troop movements. But that would have worked to the killer's advantage: who would question a man in combat clothing in the middle of a military training area? 'At least we now know something else about him: he's good at infiltration. Did you find anything else?'

'Some basic background on the CP team members, but nothing specific to help us. Bikovsky's the only one who jumps out.'

'Why?'

'I picked up a couple of reports from newspaper archives. He was arrested once for drink driving as a kid, then for assault in San Diego, but released without charge. That's all it said. When I tried to dig deeper, I hit a lot of empty space.'

'What does that mean?'

'It's like the records have been sanitized.'

Harry looked at him. 'That doesn't sound good.'

'Exactly what I thought.' Rik checked his watch. 'I'm meeting a guy later who's got a back door into state court and justice records. He might be able to find out more.'

'You found someone here? How?'

Rik gave a faint smirk. 'I put out a call. There's always someone around if you know who to ask.' Rik had numerous friends and contacts in the shadowy world of computer hackers, most of them embracing anonymity and wary of coming out of their dark corners into the daylight. Harry had met a couple, pale-skinned and unhealthy specimens who would go through fire and water to breach a firewall or step into forbidden cyber territory just to prove that they could. A bit like Rik himself.

But he didn't like the idea of an outsider becoming involved. 'Couldn't you do it?'

'Not like this guy. He's got a rep for digging into Department of Justice files. He knows his way round.' He tried to look modest and failed. 'I could do it, but it would take me longer – and I'd probably trip over something.'

'Can you trust him?'

'Yeah. I've got something he wants.'

'Money?'

'A name. A contact in the community.'

Harry said nothing. If Rik was offering a name, it had to be someone the unknown hacker wanted to get to, someone higher up the ladder of IT geekdom.

'You want me to come?'

Rik rolled his eyes. 'Get off. He'd shit a streak if he saw you.'

'How quaint. What's so scary about me?'

'You look like you represent The Machine, that's what.' Rik did bunny ears with his fingers and drawled, 'Like, Establishment, dude.'

Rik was pulling his chain. He changed the subject. 'What about Koslov – anything new?'

'Other than the details Deane gave you, no. No photos, either. He's either left the army and gone into private work, or he's gone off the grid for other reasons.'

Harry knew what that meant: Koslov was either using his military training and skills working for some rich oligarch, or was now employed by the Russian government in a quasi-military capacity. He'd already fed the number into his mobile along with Pendry's and Bikovsky's. He'd try him when he got a moment.

'And anything out of Kosovo?'

'Bits and pieces. Some repeat chatter about a dead girl from way back, but no specifics. The press are hinting at fresh claims against the UN, but it's all being played down. I get the feeling they're waiting for some hard evidence to come out. When it does, it'll be gloves off.'

'Let's hope they're kept waiting.'

'There's something else.' Rik scratched his head, a sign that he was nervous.

'What is it?'

'Did you know that every time you visit Clare, your name is sent to Six?'

Harry didn't rise to it. He had never told Rik

about his visits to the Trauma Centre because he knew he didn't care for Clare Jardine. But Rik had found out anyway.

'You checking up on me?' he muttered.

'No. No. I just . . . wondered how she was doing.' Rik put his glass down. He looked sheepish.

'You hacked into the records. Are you nuts? Ballatyne will skin you alive if he finds out.'

'He won't. The system's wide open. Anyone could get in there – even you.'

'Thanks. What else did you discover?'

Rik cleared his throat. 'It was scary reading.'

'Gunshot wounds usually are. She was lucky, though; she should pull through.' If she wants to, he thought, echoing the nurse's comment. She'll still be bloody dangerous.

'I guess. There was a record of visitors. Well, one: you.'

Harry wasn't surprised that visits were recorded. Ballatyne would have requested it.

'How come,' Rik asked, 'she's not in a secure ward?'

Harry shook his head. 'Where would she go?' In reality, he knew the answer to that. He'd pressured Ballatyne into dropping any charges against Clare. She'd saved two lives and nearly lost her own in the process, and that, he'd argued, was on the plus side of the balance sheet.

He left Rik in the bar and went to the reception desk for his key. The crowd had gone and the receptionist greeted him cheerfully, handing him his key and a message slip.

'The earlier duty manager said someone was asking for you,' she told him, 'but the caller

134

wouldn't leave a name. With security here, she made a note.'

The call was timed at 2 p.m. It was probably Ken Deane wanting to know how it was going. He'd called him from the base earlier that morning, to add grease to the wheels and update him on events. He went upstairs to put through a call to New York.

Hovering by the hotel entrance under cover of a group of military family members, Kassim watched Tate take his key and a slip of paper from the receptionist and walk away. He noted the Englishman's stocky build and the way he carried himself. Not a man to underestimate, he decided, but given the right circumstances, not a problem. Minutes earlier, he'd observed him enter the hotel bar and order a drink, where he'd been engaged in conversation by another man. This one was younger, with untidy hair and wearing the clothing common to so many Americans: jeans and a T-shirt. There had been no exchange of greetings and Tate had looked almost offhand. Tate had eventually walked back to the reception desk to get his key.

After making his way back off the training area, Kassim had driven into Columbus and found a cyber-café. Remzi had not been pleased to hear from him. His responses were terse and poorly typed, the sign of a man in a hurry . . . or on the edge of his nerves. But he had complied with Kassim's request and told him that a courier would deliver the funds later that day. It had meant telling Remzi where he was staying, but there was no way round it. He would have to trust him.

135

Next Kassim had purchased a change of clothing and returned to his hotel, a cheap commercial place near the station, and taken a shower to wash off the dust and grime of the previous night. Then he'd fallen asleep for a few hours.

It was the middle of the afternoon when he was woken by a call from the front desk. A package to sign for. He drank some water, then went down and signed for a padded envelope. Next he found a local phone book and began dialling hotels near the airport. He was counting on Tate having booked one nearby rather than staying on the base, but it was a long shot. If that failed he would have to think again.

He struck lucky on the seventh try. Tate had a room at the Holiday Inn, but had left before breakfast; on his way, the receptionist thought, to Fort Benning. The irony of how close he might have been to the man yet again didn't escape Kassim. When the receptionist asked who was calling, Kassim had rung off.

Next he'd called the training base and asked for Mr Tate, saying the call was from UN headquarters in New York. As he'd hoped, the Englishman's presence was known and the answer had been immediate. 'I'm sorry, sir – Mr Tate's not available right now. Can I ask him to call you back?'

Kassim had rung off with a satisfied smile. Perfect.

He'd gone out to look for a replacement, no-questions-asked vehicle, and tried three back-street garages before finding a ragged Toyota pickup in a chop shop. The owner had let it go for three hundred dollars. By the time he'd driven

136

back out on to the road running past the training camp and crossed the extensive tract of countryside used by the military, news of the killing had spread to the outside world. It had pulled a gaggle of onlookers, press people and television crews to the area, and he'd found it easy to blend in with the crowd and watch for developments.

When Tate had come out in the back of an army vehicle, Kassim had followed, biding his time.

Now he decided to make his next move.

A new group of arrivals had just entered the lobby and were crowding the desk. Kassim went over to a house phone on one wall and dialled reception. It took a while but a receptionist eventually excused herself to answer the phone.

'Mr Tate, please.'

'One moment, sir.' As he'd hoped, the receptionist sounded rushed. 'You can dial his extension direct.' She gave him the room number with a prefix digit.

Kassim made his way towards the rest rooms, where he found a room number locator. Tate's room was on the ground floor at the rear. His stomach was tight with anticipation, and he felt for the reassuring weight of the hunting knife he'd been forced to buy to replace the lost one. He paused at the end of the corridor to consult the binder one last time, then snapped it shut and slipped it into his pocket.

Soon it would be over.

The air-conditioned quietness of his room did little to lift Harry's sense of frustration, caused by all the pointless questions he'd faced earlier. In typical military fashion, things had gone in circles, accomplishing little and serving only to delay him getting off the base and in pursuit of the killer of Orti, Broms, Carvalho . . . and now Lloyd.

He dialled Deane's number in New York. The phone rang twice before he answered. 'Harry? What's up – can't sleep?'

'Not yet. Sorry I didn't get back to you sooner. Things got a little hectic.'

'I'm not surprised. The brass give you a hard time?'

'Not too bad. Your call this morning helped smooth things over. I'm flying to LA in the morning to see Bikovsky. No point in hanging around here . . . I think our man's backed off for now.'

'Good. How's Pendry?'

'He wants blood for whoever killed the trooper, but he's dealing with it.'

Deane grunted. 'You think he's clean?'

Harry had already dismissed any idea of the Ranger being involved in anything in Kosovo. 'As sure as I can be. He doesn't feel right. I think the guilty man's still out there.'

'How do you know that?'

'Because I know who he isn't.'

'Huh?'

'It wasn't Orti because the killer went after Broms too, then Carvalho. Now he's tried Pendry. Unless he really is planning on wiping out the whole team, he hasn't yet found his target. Do you have any information on the other two?'

'No. Bikovsky's dropped off the radar and Koslov's somewhere in Moscow. Even our reach only extends so far. Keep in touch, Harry.'

'Wait,' Harry stopped him. 'What was it you wanted?'

'Me?'

'You called me earlier.'

'Not me, bud. I've been in back-to-back meetings.'

Harry felt a chill crawl up his back. 'You didn't call at two p.m.?'

'No. Pendry, perhaps?'

'He was on the base with me.'

Deane was silent for a moment, then said, 'Jesus. He knows where you are.'

Harry thought about the photo Deane had got from MI5. It would now be on the UN records. 'And he knows what I look like.'

Deane swore softly. 'Do you need backup?'

'No. I'll be in touch.' He clicked off and reached for the Ruger.

Twenty-Two

'You sure this is the place?' The cab driver eyed Rik in the mirror. They were in Phenix City, Alabama, across the Chattahoochee River from its bigger neighbour, Columbus. 'There are better places to eat, my friend.' His tone suggested that passengers from England didn't usually find their way to this part of town.

'I'm positive, thanks.' Rik peeled off some notes and passed them over. The man took the money with a nod and gave him a card with a cab company logo and a number in big, black not-drunk-enough-to-miss typeface.

'Call that number when you're ready to leave and I'll tell you if I can make it or not. Things get busy later.' He peered over his shoulder and added, 'I'd keep the British accent down a little, you hear? Ain't that they don't like you folks, just some of 'em don't like anyone *different*. You take care, now.'

As soon as Rik's feet touched the grit of the car park, the driver was gone, leaving a trace of exhaust fumes in his wake.

Rik stood and looked around. A hundred yards away the late traffic on Phenix City's 13th Street was a constant buzz, the sound washing over the surrounding buildings, streets and alleys like a gentle flood. This part of town was strictly commercial, with auto repair shops and small engineering units every few yards, and signs offering marine engine servicing, panel work and paint spraying alongside grill restaurants, bars and barbecue joints.

Rik's contact had been wary of meeting anywhere too open, insisting on a place he called Mooney's Bar. 'Any cab will get you there,' he'd said enigmatically. 'Tell him Mooney's off Thirteenth. He'll know. You'll know me, too, when you see me.' He hadn't explained why.

Mooney's was a narrow-fronted, brick-built, single-storey building sandwiched between two auto repair yards. It stretched back a hundred feet with parking spaces along the front and down one side. There were several vehicles around and the sound of country music drifted from the open door. Neon signs advertised nachos, chicken wings and several brand names he'd never heard of. Across the road were more industrial units with floodlit yards and shadow-filled spaces lined with silent vehicles and piles of car parts, and further along, a scattering of trees and bushes with more buildings poking aluminium vents into the night sky, one of them lit by floodlights.

Rik walked up the steps to the door and stepped inside. Mooney's layout was simple; it had a long bar down one side and tables down the other. The music was coming from speakers up on the walls, and he counted twenty customers, mostly couples. A group of four men in plaid shirts and work jeans turned to look but without great interest. A pasty-faced young guy in a black T-shirt and jeans and his hair tied in a ponytail was sitting at one of the tables. He had his nose buried in a computer magazine and was picking at a plate of fries, stabbing them with a fork and feeding them in an abstract manner into his mouth.

Rik wandered over. 'Ripper?' he said.

The ponytail nodded and dropped the magazine, gesturing at the chair opposite with the fork. Seconds later the barman arrived with two beers and stood waiting.

'Give him ten bucks,' said Ripper.

Rik handed over a note and sat down. He studied the man opposite. Some of his fellow hackers wore suits and lived a conventional life, concealing their passion behind an outer veneer of normality. Others did not. Ripper clearly belonged to the darker side. He was as pale as a Goth and the amount of face piercings on view would never have allowed him through an airport scanner on the first try. He probably had more that Rik didn't like to think about, and a flurry of tattoos crawling up his neck and throat. He was trying to look cool but looked nervy and sniffed a lot. Rik wondered if he'd made a mistake coming here.

'So you're Blackjack?' It was one of Rik's tag names. His voice was a surprise; it was soft and melodic, not at all what Rik had expected. 'I heard some good stuff about you.' When Rik didn't respond, he said, 'Not too talkative, huh? Yeah, I'm cool with that. What do you want from me?'

'I was told you can get into court records. That if I give you a name, you can get me the details. Is that right?'

Ripper nodded. 'Damn right. Hazell tell you that?'

'No. Never heard of Hazell.'

'Rodeoboy, then.'

Rik nodded and sipped the beer. It was fizzy and thin. Ripper was testing him. It was common practice, dropping sly verbal traps for anyone asking questions who shouldn't. Rodeoboy was a contact of Rik's from years ago, before he'd joined MI5. He still didn't know where the hacker lived – it could have been on the far side of the moon. But Rodeoboy was reliable and knew a lot of useful people. People like Ripper.

'Rodeo, right.' Ripper smiled and chewed on a fry. 'So what's the name?'

Rik handed him a slip of paper. It carried Don Bikovsky's name and an address in Venice Beach. 'He's not there now, though. It's where the trail ended.'

Ripper touched the paper but didn't pick it up, as if drawing on the details through his fingertips. 'It's kinda sketchy, man, just a name. Not a lot to go on. Could be several Bikovskys in the system.'

'Not unless they're a family of convicted criminals with the same first name. It's all I've got. More importantly,' he pointed out, 'I was told it's all you need.'

'Yeah, that's right.' Ripper sniffed importantly and pushed the plate away, drumming his fingers on the table. It was the first sign of excitement he'd shown. A challenge had been thrown down and he was sniffing at the hook. But there were certain conventions to go through.

'If you can't do it,' Rik said, 'I'll get on the first plane to New York.'

'New York?' Ripper looked confused. 'Is that where you live? You're like, British, though, right?'

'So? We've been known to travel. But the Skeeter, he lives in New York. Manhattan, to be precise.'

Ripper sat up as if he'd been electrocuted. 'You know the Skeeter? I've like, touched base with him, man. He's dynamic. Done some great stuff.' He scowled. 'But he's not right for this job; he's a little—' Ripper flicked a pale hand, the fingers stubby with chewed nails.

'He's what?'

'He's fast, I grant you, and good . . . but heavy-handed. To open the DOJ box of afternoon delights you need the touch of a surgeon.' Ripper smiled arrogantly, a silver nose ring jiggling in the light.

'I'll be sure to tell him you said that.'

Ripper ignored him. 'But you promised me the Stick Man. That's what you said on the line: you could get me a link to the Stick. Him and me,' he rubbed the sides of his two forefingers together, 'we've got similar aims, see – and I know we could make some solid connections. All I need is an in.'

'Really?' Rik began to stand up. 'Who said the Stick Man was a guy?'

'Wait!' Ripper put a hand out. 'I was kidding! Everyone knows Stick's a skirt.' He grinned as Rik sat down again. 'Dude, I was playing with you.' A strange light glittered deep in the hacker's eyes and he threw Rik a sly look. 'Stick's awesome.' He reached for his drink and sucked in a mouthful, his skinny throat working like a pump. 'That's neat tactics, hiding behind a guy tag. Who'd think, huh?' He turned his head away but kept his eyes on Rik. 'You can really give me an intro?' He was almost begging, but trying to hide it.

'I said I would. But I need your expertise to do this for me. Are we on?' He almost gagged at having to lay on the flattery, but it was necessary. Money was one level of motivation with people like Ripper; an introduction to another hacker higher up the ladder was another. Praise by their peers, on the other hand, was what many craved most.

A long, almost painful pause, then a nod. 'We're on. I get you the goods on this –' he glanced at the paper – 'Bikovsky perp, and you drop me the Stick's link and a powerful recommend, right?'

'Absolutely. You've got my contact details. As soon as you can.'

'Ace, man. You're a prince.' Ripper sat back and grinned with a dreamy look in his eye.

'How long?'

'Give me two, maybe three hours. Nobody works nights in Justice except the janitors.'

Rik took a last sip of the beer and eyed the four men at the bar. They were taking more of an interest in him than he liked. The barman was at the other end of the room scooping up empties.

'The guys at the bar, do you know them?'

Ripper shrugged, too sunk into his own private world to look. 'Not really. They come and go, pretty much always together, though. Not real regulars.' He frowned suddenly, as if realizing that their agreement was likely to vanish in a puff of smoke if any trouble broke out. 'You got a car outside? Only, I don't drive.'

'I soon will have.' Rik took out his mobile and the card the cab driver had given him and dialled the number. Getting turned over by a bunch of chancers on their own turf would be no way to get this job done. A familiar voice answered and told him he'd be there in four minutes.

Rik stood up and offered his hand. 'It's done. I'm gone.'

Ripper's grip was flaccid and slightly clammy. 'Be in touch, man.'

Rik walked out of the door and breathed deep, grateful for the cool night air. He'd picked up just a little too much of the smell of French fries and Ripper's body odour. Out here it was cool, with the smell of stale water coming off the river a couple of hundred yards away and a tang of burnt metal on the breeze being carried from a factory venting smoke in the distance.

He stepped down on to the car park tarmac to

145

meet the cab and stretch his legs. The door behind him opened with a squeak of hinges. He turned as the four men from the bar filed out and stood looking down at him. They didn't say a word, just stood looking.

Rik nodded and turned away, his chest pounding. The cab was taking its time.

'Got a light, pal?' It was one of the men, stepping down on to the tarmac and holding up a cigarette. He was tall, with a receding hairline and the sloping shoulders of a weights man. Two of his friends, Rik noted, were smoking, cigarettes curled into their palms. They were all big-boned with manual workers' hands and heavy boots.

'I don't,' he said. 'Sorry.'

'Pity.' A long pause, then a snigger from one of the smokers at the door, who stepped down and moved away to one side.

Rik was certain four minutes had come and gone. This was in danger of getting serious.

'You talking to the geek for?' the first man asked, lighting his cigarette. 'He's some kinda weird, you know? You a weirdo, too? His boyfriend, maybe?'

His friend was shuffling closer. They were bracketing Rik against the vehicles in the parking bays, and he knew they must have done this before. The other two were watching, unmoving, but ready to step down and join in.

Car headlights came off 13th Street and swept across the industrial units, then turned down a gap between the buildings and disappeared. Rik decided these boys weren't going to give him time to wait for his ride. He knew the procedure: he'd

see a close-up of one of the cigarettes being flicked
in his face, then they'd be all over him and gone.
He checked to make sure there were no onlookers
in the cars, then reached under his jacket.

As the first man stepped closer, Rik pulled out
the Ruger. The metal glittered with the reflection
from the neon.

'Whoa, *shit* . . .!' the man muttered, and
dropped his cigarette in surprise. His companion
swung round and walked away fast, losing
himself down the side of the building, and the
two men on the step lifted their hands to show
they weren't involved.

Then another set of lights appeared and the cab
came down the street.

Rik put the Ruger away and walked away across
the car park.

Twenty-Three

At the Holiday Inn, Harry was trying Rik's extension. No answer. He must have gone out to meet
his contact. He dialled the number Pendry had
given him, then switched off the light and stood
in the dark. He was wondering how close the
killer was right now.

He had absolutely no doubts that it had been
the same person calling the hotel earlier. Only
Deane, Pendry and Rik knew where he was, and
there was no way anyone would have got details
from the military base. That meant he'd been

147

tracked from New York to Columbus and pinpointed to this hotel.

But how?

The long, hard way was one explanation: the killer had the same list of names and locations as Harry. If he had the patience to ring round all the likely hotels in the area, it would be just a matter of asking for Harry Tate by name. Eventually someone would have given it up.

'Yeah?' The Ranger's voice was heavy with sleep.

'Our man's here in the hotel.' Harry kept his voice low, one ear cocked towards the door. He explained briefly about the phone call to reception. 'Can you get away?'

'I'm on it,' Pendry replied, instantly alert. The sound of bed springs creaked in the background. 'How do you want to play this?'

'As quiet as possible. If we call the locals, they'll come in with a full SWAT team. There's a convention going on here, so the place is full. I'm going to try to draw him out. I'll wait an hour, to give you time to get here and settle in, then I'll move.'

'Uh-huh. What if he tries before that?'

'I don't think he will. I'm counting on him waiting for the place to go quiet.'

'You want me to stay on the outside?'

'Yes. But watch your back.'

He replaced the phone, then reached across and cut the air conditioning. With the fan going it was almost impossible to hear anything outside the room. He wedged a chair under the door handle and sat for an hour, listening as the hotel noises gradually died down. An occasional voice

148

echoed along the corridor as guests returned to their rooms, and the ice machine clunked noisily every few minutes. Out in the car park vehicles came and went, but at last even that activity ceased, save for an occasional movement.

He was glad of the Ranger's instinctive response. He knew how good the man was and preferred to have him around rather than half a dozen local cops bristling with weaponry and in a mood to shoot anyone who didn't look right.

There was the click of a door. Somebody entered the room next door. Harry tensed, straining to track the other person's movements. A cupboard door banged, two thumps as shoes hit the floor and a grunt as someone lay down on the bed. Then silence.

Out on the expressway the hum of traffic continued into the night.

Harry sighed and tried to relax. Breathed easily and slowly, listening and analysing every sound.

Kassim sat in the dark, immobile. He had learned a long time ago that the hunter who could not remain still rarely caught his prey. He was also listening to the murmur of voices, the ice machine and the traffic on the expressway. For him it was a distraction from the task in hand, to be blanked out and ignored.

The green digital readout of the television clock glowed brightly across the darkened room. It was past midnight. Another new day.

So be it.

He got to his feet, careful to avoid brushing against the furniture. The knife felt good in his hand, balanced and ready. In his other hand was

149

the piece of blue fabric. He was filled with a feeling of quiet fatalism. What would be would be.

One silent step across the carpet took him close to the connecting door. He cocked his head, projecting his senses through the crack around the frame into the next room. He thought he detected someone breathing.

He reached out to touch the door. This had to be hard and fast. There was no time for hesitation. In, do it and out again.

Harry needed a cold drink. Or movement. Either would do. He was tired of waiting in this dark, airless cell, wondering what was going on outside. Waiting had always been a problem for him, but he wasn't usually the target. Far better to be up and moving.

He picked up the Ruger and went to the door. The peephole revealed an empty corridor. Other than the person next door, and some distant voices that could have been a television, there had been few signs of movement for over thirty minutes.

With the lightest of touches he opened the door and stepped out into the corridor. The carpet was springy, silent. The overhead lights were dimmed, and at the far end, a green fire escape sign glowed in the dark. He waited for the ice machine to begin its throaty rattle, then pulled the door closed behind him with a soft click.

First he checked the fire door leading to the car park. It was closed and could only be opened from the inside by depressing the bar. Satisfied his back wasn't exposed, he turned towards reception.

He had barely taken two steps when there was

movement at the end of the corridor leading from reception. A tall figure was moving towards him. Harry waited, trying to get a sense of what the man was like. A suit . . . he was wearing a suit. A flash of white at the chest showed a shirt but no tie. But there was a silvery glimmer of reflected light down by his side.

Harry's throat went dry. He forced himself to continue walking. It might not be the killer. It could be anyone . . . a late-night reveller, perhaps. Harry held the Ruger down behind his leg, ready to bring it up, and wondered if the man had seen it. He'd soon find out; any innocent person would scream the place down.

Harry was halfway along the corridor when the man veered abruptly to one side, and for a second he thought it was to let him pass. Then he moved back, this time with a small shake of his head like a dog emerging from water. His arm moved, again showing a glimmer of light in his hand.

Harry dropped into a crouch, bringing up the gun and focussing on the man's mid-section. His training switched in and coordinated his move-ments. His finger began to take up the slack on the trigger as he watched the man's hand, waiting for the last possible moment before opening fire. In this narrow corridor, the sound of the shot would be like a field-gun.

He stopped, requiring a Herculean effort not to squeeze the trigger, and stood up. Moved to one side as the man lurched by, his room passkey in one hand and a shiny aluminium ice bucket in the other. A wave of alcohol followed him like a flag. He was in his fifties, his skin mottled and flushed, a businessman fixing himself a nightcap.

Harry breathed out, his head pounding with tension. He continued along the corridor to the ice machine, turning once to glance behind him. The drunk had stopped by a door and was attempting to slide his passkey into the lock.

Harry plunged his hand into the chute and wiped two or three ice blocks across his face, grateful for the icy coldness on his skin. From back up the corridor he heard a thump, then silence. The drunk had only just made it home in time.

He glanced round the corner into the reception area. It was empty, the front doors closed. As he paced back along the corridor towards his room, something began tugging at his brain, insistent and disturbing. Something was odd, out of place. The reception area? The front entrance? The corridor?

The drunk. He'd gone into the room next to Harry's.

Harry looked up and saw that the overhead corridor light nearest to his door was dead, leaving that part of the corridor in a pool of shadow.

It had been working earlier.

He felt horribly exposed but continued the last few paces until he reached the room next to his. As he drew level with the door, a groan sounded close by. With the Ruger held high in front of him, he reached out with his free hand to touch the door.

Then the door of his own room opened with a crash and a large, bulky figure stumbled out on unsteady legs.

'What the—!'

Harry tried to make sense of what he was

152

seeing. Then the picture disentangled itself. It was the drunk, head slumped forward over a slash of red on his white shirt front. The man seemed suddenly to have developed two heads . . . and two more legs.

Two heads . . . two people.

The killer had been in the next room.

'Stand still.' Harry centred his gun on the head behind the drunk. But as he did so, the two figures lurched away towards the fire door. Now he could see from the light further along the corridor that the man behind was supporting the drunk with one arm wrapped around his torso, dragging him along as a shield. In his hand he was holding a piece of blue material. His other forearm was curled tight across the drunk's throat, holding a large hunting knife digging into his chest.

'I said, stand still!' he repeated, but the man ignored him, intent only on reaching the outer door.

Then the drunk was standing by himself, half-propped against the wall, and the door had clanked open behind him, letting in a gust of cool night air. In the background the other figure seemed to flit away with barely a sound, and disappeared into the darkness.

Twenty-Four

As the drunk's body finally lost its grip on the wall and toppled forward, Harry heard a shout of surprise from outside. He caught the falling man and lowered him gently to the floor, then ducked low to the ground and slid out of the door into the night.

Immediately to his right was a flower bed with shrubs at shoulder height cutting off his view of the car park. If the killer was anywhere, he could be in the bushes, waiting for Harry to show himself. But what had the shout been? Perhaps he'd run into Pendry.

He slid sideways into a patch of deep shadow created by the security lights spaced around the hotel, and breathed softly, tuning in to the night sounds. The traffic hum from the expressway intruded, and he knew if the killer was anywhere close and saw Harry first, he would get minimal warning before the man was upon him. Better to be out in the open.

The grass was soft and springy, already cool to the touch. He squatted down and edged out to where he could see a line of parked cars. If the killer was among them, the shadows were too dense to reveal him. He stood up and walked along the line, confident that if the man did show himself, he could react in time.

Two minutes later he found a man in a waiter's uniform lying by the open door of a Bronco. There were no keys in the ignition.

He left the man where he was and continued to search the area, heart hammering in his chest. Then a whistle drew his attention and he saw Pendry appear from between two panel vans that bore the logo of a catering company. The Ranger was signalling towards the other side of the hotel complex. In his fist was the sheen of a handgun.

154

'He came out the door and ran into the guy with the Bronco,' said Pendry in a whisper, 'but I guess he couldn't find the keys. Then he went to the front of the building. He'll be looking for a free ride out of here.'

'Not this one,' said Harry. 'He'll have a vehicle. He was trying to distract us by leaving a body lying around. Let's split up. You go to the back – I'll take the front.'

Before they could move, however, the roar of an engine sounded from the other side of the hotel, and headlights flared across the bushes near the entrance. The next moment red tail lights disappeared along the approach road with a squeal of tyres. Damn . . . the man was seconds from the expressway.

Harry ran back to the Bronco and found the waiter sitting up nursing his head. He looked groggy but unhurt. 'Lie still,' Harry told him. 'An ambulance will be here shortly.' He ran back inside the hotel corridor to where the drunk was lying motionless against the wall. His breathing was faint and rapid, and he needed urgent medical attention. Pendry appeared and swore softly.

'I'll call it in,' said Harry, and went into his room to use the phone. As he dialled and spoke to the 911 operator, he saw the connecting door to the next room was open. The wood around the lock was splintered and raw where it had been kicked in.

Pendry joined him after making the wounded man as comfortable as possible. 'Damn,' the Ranger muttered, eyeing the broken door. 'He bust through from the next *room*?'

Harry nodded, remembering the sounds the killer

had made pretending to be another guest. He was clever. Very clever. 'I told you he was good,' he said, and replaced the phone, paraphrasing an old military saying. 'Let's hope he isn't lucky, too.'

Kassim pounded the wheel in frustration as he joined the expressway, earning an angry bray of air horns from a tanker driver as he came close to clipping one of its giant chrome fenders. This wasn't how it was supposed to be, he thought savagely. He had the advantage . . . he should have been able to finish off the Englishman!

He pressed his foot to the floor, aware that he only had minutes to get clear of the area before the police saturated the roads with men and vehicles. Traffic was lighter now, but if he managed to put a few miles between himself and the hotel, he might just get outside any net thrown up to entrap him.

He felt for the rucksack on the back seat of the car. He had to get cleaned up. He might have traces of blood on him from when he'd stabbed the drunk. Another mistake; he should have left him alone. But he'd reacted without thinking, aiming for the throat but hitting the man's chest instead, the knife blade glancing off bone.

After two miles, Kassim's breathing returned to normal and he began to feel calmer. He slowed down. Now would not be a good time to be stopped for speeding. It was time to think. Time to decide on the next move.

Time to do the unexpected.

'What is it with you?' Rik murmured thirty minutes later, after knocking on Harry's door. 'I

156

go out drinking and you're the one who has all the fun.' He had arrived back to find a police cordon around the hotel and the surrounding darkness lit by the lights of emergency vehicles. Harry was being interviewed by a police detective, who seemed satisfied that the attack had been a random room invasion by an opportunist thief. The drunken guest and the waiter had both been taken to the nearest emergency unit for treatment. Pendry had gone to see Gail, who would have heard the news of the fracas and be worried enough to come out. Having her wandering around while the attacker was still out there was not something they wanted to contemplate.

Harry looked at Rik. He had a flush to his face and seemed edgy. Something had happened. 'What is it?'

'Nothing, why?'

Harry waited, eyebrows raised, until Rik relented and told him about the four men. 'It was nothing. Just a bunch of guys trying it on.'

Harry held out his hand. 'You'd better give me the gun. I'm on a military flight to LA, so I can get them checked through. We'll meet up there.'

Rik handed over the Ruger and spare magazine. 'Did you get a look at him?'

Harry shook his head. 'Not really. Taller than average, slim . . . we already know he can move fast. But I didn't see his face; he'd taken out the light in the corridor. When will you get anything on Bikovsky?'

'Ripper said a couple of hours.'

'*Ripper?* What's his real name – Malcolm?'

'Very funny. They use tag names to protect themselves. I'm sure he'll come through.'

'It would be nice if he did before I set off for LA. I don't want to trek all the way over there for nothing.'

'But you'll go, anyway.'

'I have to. Bikovsky's likely to be the next one on the list.'

Twenty-Five

Harry dropped his bag by the reception desk and waited to check out. He was booked on a military flight to the Los Angeles Air Force Base at El Segundo at nine thirty, courtesy of the UN. Deane was pulling strings to move him around with the minimum of fuss and paperwork, and other than having to check in the Rugers to a secure box, he was going to face minimum questioning.

He'd told Rik to make his own arrangements about getting to LA on a commercial flight. The more they were in the same area, the more risk there was of someone making a connection. He didn't think it likely that the killer had someone watching his back, but he didn't want to take the chance.

He was surprised to see Carl Pendry stride through the hotel's main entrance, dwarfing the slim shape of Gail Tranter alongside him. The Ranger was stuffing his military ID into his pocket after being checked through the police cordon outside.

With the coming of daylight, several crime scene investigators and forensics personnel were now quartering the car park for clues, and questioning guests about the previous night, while coloured tape fluttered in the morning breeze, shutting off all non-essential access to the area. So far, though, they had turned up nothing substantial.

Gail was the first to speak, her eyes flashing spiritedly at Harry.

'He won't tell me anything,' she said, nodding at Pendry. 'I know something bad happened out at the training grounds – and here last night with two men being attacked. The whole town's talking about it, what with the helicopters coming and going, and the state and city cops on every route through here. They're saying a trainee got killed . . . is that right?'

Harry studied her for a moment. She was evidently smart and the bond between her and Pendry was close. It would be fair to tell her what was happening, but he wondered if she would react well to hearing that her boyfriend was a target for a killer. He glanced at Pendry, who was impassive and brooding, annoyed by the senseless loss of one of his charges and their failure to catch the man responsible.

'Carl can tell you as much as we know,' he said. 'After that, he should find you somewhere on the base to stay for a few days. Somewhere safe.'

Gail shot a keen look between the two men. 'Why? Is he in danger?'

'Possibly. But if you take precautions you'll be fine. And I can do my job a lot easier. Carl?' He looked meaningfully at the Ranger and stuck out his hand, drawing him to one side. 'I'm off to see if I can find Bikovsky. Get Gail away from here and keep your head down. He failed this time but he might try again. Don't give him Gail as leverage.'

The Ranger nodded. 'Sure thing. But say – any chance I can help? I'd sure like to nail this sonofabitch, and I'm sure I could get a release after what happened to Lloyd.'

'Sorry. He'll spot me eventually; with us together he'd do it even quicker.'

Pendry nodded ruefully, desperate to do something to redress the balance. 'OK. Let me know how it goes, though, huh?' Then he stopped, looking awkward. 'I thought about a couple of things last night. Could be important.'

'Like what?'

'One was the Marine, Carvalho. You thought he was one of the compound guards who went to Pristina, right?'

'So?'

'He wasn't. I remembered he was sick that night and switched with another guy – a Brit. Carvalho knew he'd be no good in a fight, so the Brit agreed to go instead. I don't think they told anyone in the rush to get out, so it wouldn't have been official – at least, not until later when the rosters were checked.'

Harry tried to recall the British soldier, but he'd had his hands full that night and the compound guard had been out on patrol. Then he remembered something from Deane's briefing: the man had been one of two British soldiers, a member of the Royal Military Police. He had since died of natural causes.

Either way, the fact that Carvalho had switched duties at the last minute had eventually found its way into the roster records, and had been picked up by Demescu.

'What was the other thing you remembered?'

'The guy Bikovsky.' He looked awkward, then ploughed on. 'I don't like saying this about another man, but there was some talk around the table the night Kleeman left, before we rotated back to our units.'

'Talk?'

'Bikovsky was being derogatory about the locals, saying they'd steal anything that wasn't nailed down and the women were little more than whores. The guy had a real attitude problem. He was also bragging about not going back to the US at the end of his tour, saying he was going to bug out as soon as he could. I figured it was drunk talk. We'd all had a couple to loosen up, but he'd picked up some extras. Later on he told another guy he'd got into trouble before enlisting and was scared to go back.'

'What sort of trouble?'

'He'd been accused of raping a minor in San Diego.'

Twenty-Six

Harry said his goodbyes to Pendry and Gail, then walked over to the in-house phone and rang Rik's room. There had been no news from Ripper.

'Tell him to look at sex crimes records,' Harry suggested. 'I'm heading for the airport.'

On the way, he rang Deane, but the security

161

officer was out, so he left a carefully worded message. The rumours about Bikovsky's past, if true, wouldn't brighten his day.

He had just checked in for his flight to LA when Rik called. He sounded puzzled.

'Ripper hit a wall. Bikovsky has two arrests for DUI – drink driving – and a couple of misdemeanours as a teenager, but after that, not a thing. Nothing in the sex crimes files, either.'

'So he's clean.' Pendry's man must have got it wrong. Barrack-room chatter building rumours out of speculation.

'That's the thing. He said there are files, but they're marked restricted access. It would take some major work to get inside, and even then there are no guarantees. For some reason Bikovsky's off-limits.'

Harry felt a stirring of interest. He'd heard of records being locked before, but only for security reasons, usually in connection with a government department or the military.

He thanked Rik and rang off, and his mobile buzzed immediately.

It was Deane. 'Harry, I'm getting heat from the US Army Criminal Investigations Command, the Department of Defence and Homeland Security. Your name's bouncing all over the wires.'

'What are they saying?'

'They want to know why you're involved and have asked that you stay put in Columbus until they're satisfied that what happened down there is not terrorist-related. I've hedged as much as I can, but they're feeling antsy and my influence only goes so far.'

'How long will it take? I'm at the airport ready to go.'

'Twenty-four hours, max. I've put word upstairs that they're obstructing our investigations, and I'll let you know as soon as it's good to go.' He paused. 'This thing with Bikovsky: I've been contacting people about this and calling in some favours. Have you spoken to him yet?'

'No. He's not answering his phone. I was planning on going there rather than leaving it to a local cop.'

'Well, when you do, tread carefully. Like your message suggested, Bikovsky's got history. He ran with a couple of small gangs when he was a kid, and got into street trouble. Nothing really serious, though. But about fifteen years ago he was accused of sexual moles-tation of a minor.'

'And they allowed him in the military?'

'The evidence wasn't proven. I spoke to a member of the sex crimes unit in San Diego. None of this is repeatable, by the way. In 'ninety-eight Bikovsky was charged with the rape of a fifteen-year-old girl. His lawyer got him off on a technicality . . . something to do with her testimony being assisted by one of her brothers. Anyway, they couldn't get at the truth and the girl finally withdrew her statement. So, no complaint, no charge. Six months later another girl came forward and said Bikovsky had got her involved in illegal drugs for sex and she'd developed HIV. She was a wild child who dropped out of high school and ran with some undesirables. Her father was a high-powered studio executive with a top lawyer in his pocket. He got him

163

to file for a court order under California's health privacy laws protecting minors. It means her name can't be disclosed . . . and nor can her attacker's. We're locked out.'

'For ever?'

'Probably not, but it'll take a ton of paperwork to gain access on the grounds of national security – and maybe even not then. I've put that in motion with our legal team but it's gonna take time. The studio exec's still around and he's a real hard nose when it comes to privacy. I haven't made this information available to anyone else yet – it's too sensitive.'

'Is there any possibility he's guilty?'

'According to my San Diego PD contact, definitely – and for more than one, in his opinion. But proving it is something else. Fact is, with this rape story coming out of Kosovo, if anyone places Bikovsky there at the time, his history gives validity to the idea. Tread easy with him, Harry. We don't want to spook him and lose him: we want him to answer for his crimes.'

Harry was beginning to have doubts about his involvement in this. 'Shouldn't the police or FBI be doing this? They could have people round there checking on him right now.'

There was a short silence, then Deane said neutrally, 'They will be called at the appropriate time.'

'When will that be?'

'As soon as you find him.' He paused. 'There's more. Pictures of the compound have just arrived. They're hitting the internet as we speak. They were posted by an anonymous contributor on a blog site with anti-American and extremist links. There's even a photo of the spot outside the wire where the girl's body was allegedly found.'

'Have they named the victim?'

'Not yet. As it goes there's very little fact at all, just a brief description with some anti-UN comment. They say more will be revealed shortly. It's like they're taunting us. Most of the press have been sceptical so far, thank God, but this stuff is enough to give a louder voice to those who don't like the UN.'

'Any way of tracking down the origin of the site?'

'Not much. Our guys say it probably passed through several servers before hitting the blog site, and the blogger will certainly have moved on by now. Give it a day or so and it'll come back up from somewhere else. That's not all, though.'

'Tell me.'

'He talks about a "spectacular" being planned.'

It was typical extremist talk, signalling something big in the wind. It could be hot air, to stir up unrest, but Harry didn't think so. This whole thing felt as if it was gathering momentum. It wouldn't take much now for the sparks to be fanned into a roaring inferno.

'Is there a date on the photos?'

'No. But they look recent. Someone's been doing his homework.'

Harry was surprised. Somehow he'd expected the depot and everything in it to have disappeared, along with the changing political landscape in Kosovo. He had only a vague memory of the compound itself, having seen it mostly in the dark and under floodlights.

'Can you email me the photos and send me the link to the blog site?'

'Sure. If I send the link, you'll get the photos anyway.'

'Belt and braces; send both in case the site gets taken down.'

'Good point. Anything else?'

'Get your man in Kosovo to take similar shots of the same locations.'

'How will that help?'

'It might tell us if they're genuine. If your man's shots look different, it's because the ones you just received are a put-up job.'

'And if they match?'

'Then somebody went there to take them. That makes it more real.'

There was a pause. 'No. I think someone's playing us.'

'If you believe that, you're dreaming.' He sensed Deane was still reluctant to believe what was happening. 'This is real – they've gone to too much trouble for a scam or a smear campaign against the UN. With this much organization, someone somewhere has got something that's going to sink you.'

'Christ, you're bad news, you know that?' Deane sounded depressed. 'What's your email address?'

Harry gave him the email he shared with Rik. He wasn't sure how much help the photos would be, but they might refresh his mind about the place where this had all begun.

Deane made a note then said, 'They're on the way. Check back with me when you've had a chance to study them. I need some input, Harry.'

'What are you looking for?'

'Jesus, anything: ideas, thoughts, guesses – anything you've got. This thing's driving me nuts. There's too much that they know and we don't.'

'Such as who "they" are.'

Deane sighed. 'Tell me about it. Take your pick. We've got plenty of anti-UN groups around the world.'

'I've been thinking about that. There's got to be a connection with Kosovo.'

'How d'you mean?'

'They've got a story, a location and a list of UN names, none of it random. Anyone wanting to hurt the UN could have taken any one of several complaints over the years, most of them well documented. But this is too specific to one place and one event.'

'What about the girl's name? Wouldn't they have jumped at making that public by now? It would add credibility to their claims.'

'Maybe it points too directly at the killer or the people behind him. They could be saving that for later once they've got the attention of the press.'

'And here was I thinking it was a single nut job.'

'Get used to it,' Harry said. 'This was never a lone operator. He got the names of personnel from protected UN archives going back a dozen years, with updates on their current locations. So far he's managed to track down and take out three of them in different countries. He's mobile and resourceful enough to adapt to situations as they arise. But he couldn't do it alone. He's got a network, starting with Demescu and whoever used her.'

'Well, maybe it's not all bad news,' Deane said

finally, sounding a little happier. 'We might yet have a face. The crime scene officers at the place Carvalho was killed found his wallet. No driver's licence, no cash and no credit card. What are the odds?'

'The killer took them.'

'Must have. They're trawling through the nearest ATMs that have cameras. If the killer used the card, he'd have done so pretty soon after leaving the body.'

Harry took a cab back to the hotel and booked his room for a further night, then went in search of Rik and got him to check his email. He was impatient to be on his way to LA, and the enforced delay was frustrating. But there was nothing he could do about it. If he left the area before being given clearance by Deane, he might be picked up unceremoniously by military police and shipped straight to Fort Benning and a military lock-up. And the colonel from the training area, accompanied by his junior shadow, wouldn't be far away.

Deane had sent him the link to the blog and some photographs. Rik clicked on the link, opening a vividly colourful site with anti-American and anti-UN propaganda. The sidebars were cluttered with more links to extremist sites and a rolling live feed to Twitter comments demanding an end to the UN and justice for 'Victims of the Satanist United Nations Organization'. Some of the names included 'Islam' or 'Jihad'; many of them Harry had never come across before. There were, however, several familiar groups, including Hezb-e-Islami (HIG) and Army of Islam. The first was a fundamentalist Afghan organization set up over thirty years ago, with a strong political arm and a bloody history of attacks against Coalition forces. The second was a Palestinian group with a list of 'spectaculars' to its name and links to al-Qaeda.

The commentary accompanying the photographs was surprisingly brief.

> *This place marks where a child of God met her end. Inside this compound near Mitrovica, Kosovo, an innocent, loved by God, treasured by family, a child who never hurt anyone, was defiled and murdered by a member of the military United Nations invaders. Her name lives for evermore in the heart, and will soon echo around the world! Allah be praised!*

The first photo showed a concrete base surrounded by a wire mesh fence topped by razor wire, overlooked by security lights on gantries. Inside the fence were several shipping containers and trucks, and further over, a huddle of temporary buildings. Harry couldn't tell if it was the depot at Mitrovica, but instinct told him that it had to be. There had been too much planning involved in this to allow it to fall apart because of a set of bogus photographs.

> *This place of so-called sanctuary offered only death and defilement, within sight of her home!*

The next showed a section of mesh, held by concrete posts and topped with rolls of razor wire.

169

The ground on the outside was covered in long grass and weeds, running away into a stretch of trees in the background. Beyond that, a cluster of old buildings hugged a distant slope, surrounded by a spiky growth of pine trees. It looked bleak and cold, a place lacking in any vestige of comfort or warmth.

Harry wondered which house the girl had come from. It should surely be easy enough to find out. How many young girls could have been living in the area at the time, unless she had been a transient?

> *God take her soul and protect her, and give strength to he who avenges this atrocity! For surely there will be a spectacular which will mark this crime and burn the name of the hated UN forever!*

The fourth was a close-up shot of the grass immediately outside the fence. Someone had planted a short stake in the ground. Tied to it was a small bunch of flowers.

Twenty-Seven

Harry waited while Rik trawled the related links and pages for clues. It was slow going, and Rik complained about the speed of the connections. But he found nothing to indicate the origins of the photographs or the text. Contributions to the site were openly welcomed, and the site's owners, if found, would probably claim that they accepted bloggers' submissions without question, taking advantage of the freedom of the internet, and that this particular submission broke no rules about incitement to violence.

He also drew a blank with the site's location, tracking it through several servers until the trail ran out at a site in Indonesia.

'I could spend a week on this,' he said eventually. 'Whoever runs this has covered his tracks too well.'

Harry was tempted to ask him to get the community of hackers and cyber-geeks to help. But they skated close enough to the wind already, without risking being linked to terrorist or extremist sites.

In the end he called Deane.

'The photos certainly look real enough,' he told him. 'But only an eyes-on comparison will tell.'

'I've asked Archie Lubeszki to take some shots and compare them to those on the site. Beyond that, I'm not sure what else we can do.'

'Get him to check the houses in the area,' Harry suggested. 'See if anyone still there from that time remembers stories of girls going missing.'

'We did that already, but came up blank.'

'Include any who were reported missing due to ethnic cleansing. Concentrate on young girls.'

'OK. I'll get him to try again. It's tough, though, like opening old wounds. The press have been in there, too, stirring up the dust.'

'Well, somebody must know something,' Harry

countered. 'Memories go back a long way in that region.'

'Leave it with me.'

'Something else,' Harry continued, remembering the photos. 'Get him to check the wire, will you? See if there's any way of getting out of the compound near the point where the girl's body was dumped.'

'Like a back gate?'

'Anything. If it really happened, whoever did this had to get the body outside the wire. He wouldn't have been able to risk carrying her out because of the guard patrol.'

'What are you saying?'

'If she didn't go round, she went over the top.'

There was a shocked silence as Deane digested the words. 'He *threw* her over? Christ. Would that have been possible?'

'If he was desperate enough.' And strong enough, he decided.

After the call, Harry prowled the room while Rik continued scouring the net for any mention of Mitrovica, missing girls or references to UN atrocities. But there were too many links, most eventually proving unhelpful and time-consuming. In a region where so much death and violence, so many unexplained disappearances had happened over the years, including whole communities in some cases, it would have taken a vast team of researchers several days to follow up and eliminate each one.

'It's too fragmented,' was Rik's conclusion. He sat back and stared at the screen in frustration. 'If the name hasn't surfaced by now, it probably won't unless the people behind it let it out. That's if they've got one.'

'They've got one,' said Harry with certainty. The closer he got to this, the less he felt it was an elaborate bluff. 'What puzzles me is why now?'

Rik looked at him. 'You think they've been sitting on it?'

'Maybe. Or someone knew but didn't talk about it.'

'How do you keep that sort of thing quiet?'

Harry picked up his key and jacket. He needed a change of scenery. The room was beginning to close in around him. 'Unless the person who knew couldn't talk.'

'What do you mean?'

'I don't know,' he admitted, and shrugged on his jacket. 'But I will, given time.' He picked up Rik's jacket and threw it across to him.

'What's this for?' Rik looked puzzled.

Harry had been thinking that Rik needed reacquainting with some live firing. They hadn't been to a gun range recently, and he was worried that Rik had been too quick to wave his gun at the men who'd approached him outside the bar in Phenix. Rik's memories of being shot would be vivid, still, and Harry didn't want him to rely too much on showing a gun to get out of trouble.

'We're going to get some gun practice.'

He led the way out to the car and drove to an indoor range recommended by Pendry. He could have asked to use the facilities at Fort Benning, but that would have brought Rik under the suspicious eye of the military. And he still wasn't ready to broadcast their connection to anyone he wasn't absolutely sure of.

The range was an anonymous, low building at the back of an industrial estate, with nothing to show what function it performed. The foyer was utilitarian in appearance, save for a wallboard behind the counter holding an impressive collection of guns. The man behind the counter had the lean, fit look of a former soldier. After checking their passports and getting them to sign waivers, he called a colleague, who checked in the Rugers and led them through a rear door to the range, where giant fans clearing the air did not entirely reduce the familiar smell of gunpowder.

At Hartsfield-Jackson airport, Atlanta, Kassim waited patiently while his passport was examined by a female officer. Her plump fingers were cluttered with rings and her fingernails each a different, vivid colour, a stark contrast to her shiny black skin and hair. She looked at him twice while turning the pages, and was fingering the paper of the passport and flexing the covers, looking for signs of tampering. He decided that her carefully contrived outward appearance did not reflect the person within. He kept his face blank; being over-friendly would probably irritate her just as would showing impatience at what was an unavoidable procedure.

She turned away and used a keyboard below the level of the counter, her nails clack-clacking like distant machine-gun fire. Behind the booth an armed security guard watched her working, then glanced at Kassim.

He felt his heart rate increasing and forced himself to breathe easily. He had to remain calm. He was still using the Haxhi documents, but beginning to feel exposed. How long could he continue to rely on them? But to risk using another set of ID presented the same danger: that someone somewhere had made a simple mistake and he would end up being called aside by a vigilant security officer. If that happened, he might never see the light of day again.

'Thank you, Mr Haxhi. Have a good trip.' She pronounced it like 'taxi' with the 'h' in the middle and slapped the passport down on the counter, her attention switching to the next in line.

Kassim walked away, feeling the eyes of the security guard on his back. He didn't look back, concentrating instead on not giving way to a powerful feeling of nausea washing over him. He looked for a sign to the rest rooms. He had a long trip ahead of him, and if he was going to be ill, better to get it over and done here rather than on the plane to Moscow.

Twenty-Eight

The sun was setting low over Venice Beach, Los Angeles, as Harry walked down a paved footpath between two sets of condominiums, leaving behind the busier area of Speedway and the shops and restaurants along Ocean Front Walk. The atmosphere was heavy and still, in spite of the proximity of the ocean, but there were crowds out enjoying the evening air and the sights.

After finally being given permission to leave Columbus yesterday evening, he'd told Rik to meet him in LA, and to make sure he hadn't picked up a tail on the way. There were further delays in the military flight from the airport, with a diversion to collect some senior staff officers, a reminder to Harry that he was being accorded the use of one of the biggest air taxi companies in the world.

After landing at El Segundo air force base, he'd been ferried to a hotel near LA's International Airport. The Rugers he'd checked in at Columbus security had been handed back without comment, and he'd locked them in the room safe. On the way to the hotel, he called Deane to use his influence and get the nearest LAPD precinct house to send an officer to run an eye over Bikovsky's address. The officer's report came straight back; there was no sign of the man and none of his neighbours had been able to venture any comments about his whereabouts.

A meandering cycle path was busy with roller bladers, boarders and cyclists, a moving tide of cut-off jeans, halter tops and open shirts, testimony to the attitude that if you were going to be fit, why not look good, too? A juggler strolled in their midst, keeping five balls in the air and talking on a mobile phone. He looked bored. Harry passed a bronze statue of a cowboy, frozen on a plinth until a girl came too close, then he came to life. The girl shrieked and the cowboy froze again, waiting for the next mark.

176

A young woman carrying a large tabby cat swept smoothly past, her long, blonde hair flowing like a Norse goddess, her sun-bronzed body encased in a minute, sequin-studded bikini. She gave Harry a brief smile and was gone, drawing little more than a passing glance from any of the men nearby.

Harry soon understood why. Another *Baywatch* lookalike cruised by, followed by others, either singly or in small groups. Men too were in the parade, using rollerblades to carry them along at near Olympic speeds, muscular, bronzed bodies swaying elegantly around pedestrians and other bladers. Most seemed intent on their progress, eyes concealed behind sunglasses and ears plugged with stereo earphones.

In lightweight slacks and a cotton shirt, Harry felt distinctly overdressed.

He came to the area known as Muscle Beach, where men with huge chests and hands dusted with chalk powder were pumping iron, like a scene from a prison movie. Seeing them reminded Harry of his comment to Deane: what if the girl's body *had* been tossed over the wire at the compound? It would have taken explosive power to do it, not sculptured muscle. Worryingly, of the men in the CP team, more than one would have had the means.

He veered back on to Ocean Front Walk. More shops, restaurants and small apartment blocks, a wash of varied pastel shades in contrast to the uniformity of the sand. A throbbing salsa beat echoed from one door, an old Beach Boys number from another, and his nose twitched at the smell of pizza, coffee and soul food. He was beginning to see why Bikovsky was living here.

He drew level with a narrow alleyway between a Tex-Mex res-taurant and a souvenir shop, and turned in, stepping carefully past a stack of plastic delivery pallets. The air here was cool after the heat along the front. A black cat watched him, eyes glinting nervously before it swished its tail and slid into an open doorway. Further down a skeletal figure in a cook's apron leaned against a wall, sucking on a cigarette. He returned Harry's nod with a blank look, then snapped the cigarette and walked away.

Harry followed the cat.

He found himself in a corridor smelling of fried food and toffee. Two doors facing each other, and at the end a narrow flight of bare steps disappearing upwards. In here the noise of the beach-front was muffled. The cat had disappeared.

Neither of the doors was numbered. He walked up the steps at the end, shoes crunching softly on sand grains. Three turns to the right took him on to a small landing and a corridor leading off to other doors. The caramel smell of toffee was stronger, clinging to the walls. Two more doors, numbered this time. He found the right one and knocked. Silence. It was fitted with a heavy-duty lock. He pushed it but it remained firm. Bikovsky was still out or had flown.

He left the building and stood in the alleyway, thinking about his next move. It had been a long way to come on a hunch, but he knew that trying to talk to the big Marine on the phone about Kosovo would have got him nowhere. Since learning a little of the man's history, he was even more convinced of that.

He walked out to the beachfront and turned into the Tex-Mex restaurant. A slim young woman nodded a welcome and handed him a plastic menu. She wore a smiley badge on her apron, bearing the name Maria. He sat and ordered coffee and a slice of cake.

When it came he smiled and said neutrally, 'I'm looking for Don Bikovsky. Any idea when he's due back?'

The young woman shook her head, a reflex action. 'Sorry, sir. I don't know him.' Her accent carried a lilt from a long way south of LA.

When she next passed by, Harry scribbled his name on the back of the bill and put down a $20 note. As she picked it up he murmured, 'I'm an ex-army buddy. It'd be good to see him again, that's all.' Then he left. This time the girl said nothing.

He rang Ken Deane, bringing him up to date. 'I'll keep at it until I find him. Any prints on the knife left at the base?'

Deane grunted sourly. 'They're still working on it. They keep telling me any time now. On *CSI* they do it in seconds and in high heels.' Paper rustled in the background. 'Just gotten word from Brussels. The old woman who witnessed Broms' murder? She said the killer waved a blue handkerchief after stabbing him.'

'That's all?'

'That's all. A local shrink's trying to get through to her, but it doesn't look hopeful. Severe mental trauma, they think.'

'A handkerchief? Probably to wipe the blade.'

'Yeah . . . could be. Anyway, keep in touch.'

Harry rang off and got a cab out to the airport. Rik would be here soon and they could try Bikovsky again in the morning. He had an uneasy feeling that he was missing something. He just hoped the ex-Marine didn't get a visit from the killer before they found him.

Over 6,000 miles away, in the Chaoyang district of Beijing, UN Special Envoy Anton Kleeman was sitting in the appropriately named Hall for Negotiations in the People's Republic of China Ministry of Foreign Affairs, smiling across the table at the PRC representatives with a deep sense of satisfaction. The talks had been useful, if protracted and unbearably formal, and he was sure Li Xian, the senior Chinese speaker and a man with a surprisingly commercial outlook, was firmly onside. The subtle promise of extra help in penetrating even further into the valuable US markets had seen to that, as had his decision, he felt sure, to come here rather than simply drive to the offices of the PRC Permanent Mission in Manhattan.

While many American businesses and politicians still viewed China with deep suspicion, especially in these troubled economic times, Kleeman did not. Setting aside his UN hat, which he did with great care so as not to be seen fronting his own business interests and investments, he viewed the commercial potential as bordering on the unimaginable. And if a little two-way talking could help along the way while he was nominally here on UN business, so be it. The main thing was, having the Chinese on his side for his eventual elevation within the UN was well worthwhile. For that, supping their drink and pressing their flesh in endless meetings was a small price to pay. With the Chinese in the bag, so to speak, the Euroblok countries, encompassing the French, German and British, would quickly see the advantages of coming round to his way of thinking.

'Mr Kleeman?' It was one of his aides, whispering in his ear. 'The press conference is arranged. The studio have the footage you asked for – of you in Macedonia – to segue into the release tonight.'

Kleeman wiped his mouth with a silk handkerchief and gave a small sigh of satisfaction. Thank God for the modern media. This kind of exposure on the world stage represented a level of PR that no amount of money could buy, and no kind of energy-sapping, time-wasting lobbying could equal. While of little interest to the majority of public viewers, it would serve to propel him up the UN ladder in the eyes of all but the old turkey necks of that crusty institution. Given time and careful handling, he would soon bypass the slower, more conservative and less forward-thinking candidates.

His time was coming.

Twenty-Nine

The air was sharp and cold in the restricted park when Russian Federal Security Service Captain Alexandr Koslov set out on his morning run. From the clawing warmth of the military apartment block three kilometres into Moscow's southern suburbs, he trotted gingerly down the frosty front steps and headed for the path he always took through the trees. It was a favoured jogging track for any officers who believed in keeping moderately fit, offering a few minutes' brief isolation from the demands of office or, providing one made it obvious enough, the mindless chatter of colleagues.

Not that many of Koslov's colleagues were into running. Even he, at thirty-eight and the youngest in his department, was beginning to feel soft, thanks to the sedentary nature of his largely desk-bound job. But you had to make some effort, he told himself, with an eye to promotional prospects and a coveted foreign posting. Although the FSB was responsible for domestic security, it held a support brief for the conduct of electronic surveillance abroad and watching over nationals on overseas placements suspected of not toeing the line. London might be nice, or Paris.

There were few others out at this early hour. He could hear traffic building up on the ring road towards the city centre, and beyond the trees the sound of a commuter train clacking along the line. Sound carried easily in this thin, cold atmosphere, bringing distant noises much closer.

Ahead of him two senior officers from a mechanized rifle regiment shuffled along like a pair of marshmallows, dressed in black market trainers and enormous American quilted coats. Their brief verbal exchanges fired puffs of vapour into the air, and no doubt much of the talk was seditious, Koslov guessed. Probably complaining about their superiors or why they hadn't received a recent pay increase. Dream on, comrades, he thought cynically. Welcome to the brave new world of economic austerity.

He accelerated past them, his feet flicking lightly on the cold surface, in contrast to their lumbering shuffle. Koslov had always been slim, and in spite of his job, weighed no more now than he had as a teenager. In fact, there were some colleagues who frequently joked that the FSB were now taking boys into their ranks, a jibe at his lack of inches and boyish features. He lifted a hand in greeting as he passed the two men. He didn't expect a response and wasn't disappointed; Russian army officers did not trust members of the FSB. Koslov had long ago given up worrying about it. Their loss, he told himself. One day they might realize the FSB was a replacement for the old KGB, not a carbon copy, and men like him were a reflection of modern times and not out to haunt the daylights out of anyone who coveted a pair of American jeans or the latest iPod.

Koslov had been in the army himself once, on attachment from a rifle regiment with the United Nations forces in Kosovo – a rare show of Moscow's understanding and unity for the common good. Not that anyone had really believed him to be a mere soldier; almost without exception, his multinational colleagues had walked around him as if he were an improvised explosive device waiting to explode, some making silly jests about the KGB in ludicrously bad Russian accents. But he didn't care: it had been a breath of fresh air for him, even if the air in Kosovo had been far from clean or pure.

Finding himself working as part of a close protection team had been an eye-opener for the young sergeant. Although he had undergone special training before going to Kosovo, his experience of bodyguards in the Russian army came from either the GRU – Russian military intelligence – or the various security units attached to each regiment. Not that too many officers needed guarding unless it was from their own men. Any physical threats were largely reserved for the staff officers who spent their time in comfortable postings in Moscow or St Petersburg, cordially loathed for their lack of teeth when supporting their men, and by civilians because it was an ingrained habit to distrust the military anyway.

The Americans he had found surprisingly generous and easy-going, eager to share whatever they had. It seemed they had largely forgotten the Cold War – or were perhaps bored with it – while the British captain treated him no differently to anyone else, an attitude Koslov guessed was entirely normal for the man.

It was his tour in Kosovo which had led to Koslov's early promotion and the desk job which went with it. Boosted by a favourable report from the UN Field Security Division, he had been rewarded with enhanced training courses and the promise of a bright future. Without it, he would have been yet another low-ranking FSB grunt for the rest of his days, serving out his time.

He approached a series of obstacles built into the path. Low wooden hurdles for the most part, placed to interrupt the rhythm and increase the heart rate. But jumping them required care to avoid the inevitable icy patches. There were others too, such as pole hurdles and lines of rubber tyres, but they were best tackled when fully warm or when the ground was softer. A broken ankle while training would not be well-regarded and was a fast track to nowhere.

Behind him, he heard the *slap-slap* of another man coming up on his outside. He moved over, wondering who could possibly be running faster than him.

While waiting for Rik to clear arrivals, Harry checked in with Deane. The UN man would probably be at home by now, but he'd impressed on Harry the urgency of maintaining contact no matter what the time.

He answered immediately. There were still no developments on the knife found at Fort Benning. 'They got some prints,' Deane told him, 'but they haven't yet found a match on any of the obvious databases. They've now switched to broaden the search, but it takes time.'

'He's from outside the US,' Harry said.

'Looks like it – or he's Snow White, which I don't buy.'

Harry didn't, either. The killer was too efficient and skilled. To have overcome three soldiers so easily, he had to have received some intensive military training somewhere. If official, it meant a high probability that his prints were recorded. Unless, like Bikovsky, there was a more sinister reason why no database was coming up with a match.

'What about the ATM machines? Any pictures?'

'I'm waiting on that. Carvalho's card was used

185

five blocks from the apartment where he was killed, and maxed out. They're analysing the film now to match the withdrawals.' He paused. 'You get any sense of our guy being around?'

'Not yet.' Harry had thought about it ever since arriving in LA. He claimed no special talent for locating the enemy, but like most hunters, he had an inbuilt antenna when it came to sensing atmosphere, such as a tickle on the back of his neck when he felt he was being watched. So far that had not happened. He didn't know whether to be pleased or disappointed.

'All right. Give me a call if anything . . . well, you know.'

Harry disconnected. He saw a world datelines panel above the arrivals board. It was early morning in Moscow. He called up Alexandr Koslov's number. He had no idea if Koslov was still active in the military, but he owed him the courtesy of a warning. The number rang six times, and he was about to cut the call when there was a switch in the tone, as if it had been interrupted. Then it continued ringing. He gave it ten more rings.

No answer.

He hung up. It sounded as if the call had been transferred automatically. Was that to a landline or to another mobile? He had no way of telling. He gave it five minutes and dialled the number again and went through the same routine.

This time the call was answered in rapid-fire Russian.

Thirty

As Koslov turned his head he caught a glimpse of a tall, lean figure in a nondescript tracksuit coming very close. At the same time he heard a loud burst of laughter from the two officers he'd passed earlier. The other runner seemed to stutter and swerve at this, as if his concentration had been spoiled. Then he accelerated and sped past, flowing along with the easy loping stride of a born runner. The man didn't look at Koslov, and soon rounded a bend in the path and was gone.

Koslov increased his pace for a while, trying to match the other man. But he'd allowed himself to get too cold and felt the beginnings of a stomach cramp. He eased off to a slower jog.

Five minutes later, within half a kilometre of the apartment block and his mind on the day ahead, he saw a tall figure standing by a tree two hundred metres ahead. The man was leaning against the trunk, rubbing his thigh.

It was the runner who had passed him earlier. Koslov guessed he had overdone it in the cold air and developed a muscle cramp.

As Koslov approached, the man straightened and turned, standing full on in the centre of the path. His face was expressionless and he was no longer rubbing his leg.

Koslov felt a sudden quickening of the pulse. What was this idiot playing at? Why block the

187

path? Surely he didn't expect Koslov to stop for a chat.

Then the man brought up his hand from behind his body. There was a gleam of metal and Koslov's inner alarm bells went off. He didn't question what was happening, nor did he even think of trying to disarm the man. He was in no fit state for a fight, and whatever had brought the man here, it wasn't a random mugging.

He swerved off the track and plunged into the trees, his feet crunching on the thick layer of dead twigs and branches covering the ground. If he followed his present course and did not deviate too much, he would reach the apartment block. He'd have to work harder than he would following the running track, but at least he might get there in one piece.

A flash of movement to his left showed the other man running parallel to him. He was keeping a steady station barely twenty metres away without apparent effort. If Koslov kept going as he was, the man would intercept him easily before he reached the apartment block. If he swerved away to his right, however, it would take him deeper into the trees and the untamed undergrowth. And eventually, unless he managed by an amazing stroke of luck to outrun the other man, he would be caught.

An inner voice told him that outrunning his pursuer wasn't going to happen.

Koslov crashed through a small thicket of thorns, his breathing harsher as his body demanded more oxygen. His trainers were beginning to sink in the softer ground and his calf muscles starting to ache with the extra effort required. The other man, however, was showing no signs of distress.

Koslov crossed a section of pathway connecting with the main circuit. With nobody else in sight he was beginning to feel the first signs of desperation. The feeling was worsened by being isolated among these trees, barely two hundred metres from safety. Damn it, this was crazy! Why didn't he just stop and ask the man what he wanted? Or even stand and fight, if that's what the maniac was after?

Yet everything about the runner's demeanour told him discussion was not part of his agenda, and neither was defeat. Besides, if the man was carrying a knife, Koslov knew his own limitations. A pair of hands softened by desk work were no match for a blade.

He staggered through a hollow, tripping on hidden branches, and felt a pain building in his side and burning up through his chest. His legs, good for two or three circuits on a good day, were now hurting badly with the effort of dragging him over the rough terrain. When he glanced to his left, the other man was jogging, now barely ten metres away and moving closer.

Suddenly Koslov glimpsed space and light ahead, and called on his last reserves of energy. He pushed through some low-hanging branches and out into the open, where he startled the two army officers he'd passed earlier. They were enjoying a breather and a quiet cigarette.

Koslov skidded to a stop, his mouth working frantically, and pointed behind him, his body braced for the inevitable surge of movement and the blow which would surely follow.

But the other runner was nowhere to be seen.

'You on a camouflage and concealment course, Koslov?' asked one of the officers, glancing at the swaying branches where the FSB officer had burst from the trees. 'I think you just failed.' He grinned slyly at his colleague and they both laughed before turning and walking towards the apartments. The army rarely had an opportunity to make fun of the FSB, and took it gleefully whenever it was offered.

Koslov, rarely happier to see anyone else, even if they were enjoying his discomfort, trotted closely in their wake, his back prickling with tension. If he tried to tell these buffoons what he had seen, they'd think he was mad. What he should be doing was getting on to the security office and having the place searched. That would be the sensible thing.

At heart, though, he could already picture the reaction of his colleagues – and worse – his superiors, who had expressed great faith in a man who was going places. *A man with a knife? Chasing you through the woods? Are you sure? What have you been up to, you young dog – playing with another man's property?* He could imagine their coarse laughter and raised eyebrows. Greater careers than his had been ruined on such trivial evidence.

'Captain?' It was one of the support staff from the office, a thin-faced young gofer/driver named Dobrev who spent his days chasing around with messages or ferrying officers about the capital. 'A telephone call came in for you, sir. Urgent priority.'

Koslov threw a final look towards the woods and ducked into the apartment building. 'At the

190

office? Why didn't they put it through to my apartment?' He ran lightly up the stairs to his quarters on the second floor, stripping off his tracksuit top as he went. Calls were routinely fed through to officers' living quarters if they were not in the office, in case of priority requests. Such a call usually meant he was about to travel somewhere on an investigation. He would change quickly and should be in the office within twenty minutes.

'I couldn't, sir.' Dobrev panted up the stairs behind him and followed him into the small apartment. 'Your line is not working. Also, it's against regulations to give staff numbers to foreigners, sir.'

Koslov stopped in the middle of pulling on a clean shirt. A shower would have to wait. 'Foreigners?'

'Yes, sir. The call came from –' Dobrev sneaked a look at a slip of paper in the palm of his hand – 'from a man named Harry Tate, sir.' He pronounced it phonetically, then looked up with a frown. 'At least, that's how it sounded. He was an American, I think – calling from somewhere I cannot spell. It sounded like Veniss Bitch, sir.' He shrugged. 'The line was not good.'

'Venice Beach,' Koslov corrected him. His memory ticked over, matching the name to a face. Several years ago now, the British officer in charge of the protection squad in Kosovo.

'You know him?' Dobrev sounded impressed.

'Yes. His name's Harry Tate, he's British and he was calling from Venice Beach near Los Angeles in the United States. It's like a Black Sea resort only a lot more fun – or so I've heard.' He finished pulling on his shirt and wondered

191

what Tate could possibly want. Odd that the man's name should pop up the same day he had been thinking of him. 'What was the message?'

'None left, sir. He said that he would call again in two hours. He was travelling, I think. I heard a Tannoy in the background . . . like an airport or a train station.'

'Good work, Dobrev. Very perceptive of you.' He picked up an orange from a bowl on the table and tossed it across the room. Dobrev caught it adeptly. 'You should eat more fruit. Is the car outside?'

Dobrev backed towards the door, stuffing the orange in his pocket. He was smiling. He was accustomed to officers in the FSB leaving on the run, but not to any kind of praise.

Koslov followed, pausing only to pick up the landline phone. It was dead. He replaced it, making a mental note to get it checked. After what he'd just experienced, he couldn't help but feel uneasy.

Phone lines to this building were never faulty.

Out of sight among the trees, and beginning to feel the cold, Kassim quickly retraced his steps towards the ring road where he had left his car parked in a service entrance to the woods. He felt oddly elated rather than annoyed at not hitting his prey. The contact would have worried the Russian, so accustomed to being safe here in Moscow, and seriously upset his equilibrium. If it had not been for the two other men, he would have had him.

But that did not matter now. He had seen Koslov up close, had looked into his eyes and sensed his feeling of vulnerability. Yet that had also brought

192

its own revelation: seeing the Russian in the flesh had surprised him. He was smaller than the description in the binder had suggested, with a slim body and the fine, pale features of a girl, almost. Strange how history and rumour somehow made Russians seem so much bigger and more threatening than they really were.

He climbed into the battered Saab he had hired from a black-market rental near the airport and threw the knife he'd bought from a street dealer into the glovebox. He would wait until the afternoon, when Koslov's guard would be down, his attention on other matters.

He sat for a few moments, aware that he should move away from here, but remembering what had been drummed into him. For reasons completely unconnected with his main task, killing a Russian was always something to look forward to.

Thirty-One

By the time Koslov had seen to some urgent paperwork and attended a briefing, the two hours since Tate's message had flown by. In that time he had asked the maintenance manager in the apartment block to check his landline. The man had come back to say that overhead wires into the building had been severed by a falling branch. It was one of those things that happened occasionally, a freak of the weather and nature combined. The manager had assured him that communications would be returned to normal within the hour.

When the second call came in from Tate via the central switchboard, he was ready for it.

'Alexandr,' the Englishman greeted him. His voice sounded subdued, or maybe tired. Not a pleasure call, then.

'What can I do for you, Harry?' Koslov asked politely, responding readily to the use of his first name. Although he had got on well with the English officer in Kosovo, there was still enough caution in his nature to know he shouldn't offer anything unless something came the other way first. Especially since a quick check had revealed that Tate had joined the British Security Service, MI5. Besides, he couldn't be absolutely certain that this call wasn't being recorded by one of his own more zealous colleagues somewhere in the depths of this very building.

He listened with growing unease as Tate described the three killings and the attempt on Pendry's life. He also mentioned the possibility of a connection with a murder in Kosovo, although this was still unproven.

As he heard how Pendry's man had met his death, Koslov felt a spider-crawl of movement up his back. He instantly saw vivid flashbacks of the silent runner among the trees that morning, the sunlight glinting on what must surely have been a knife blade. He knew without a shadow of doubt that he, like Pendry, had come dangerously close to the mysterious killer.

'I believe he is already here,' he said quietly. He described what had happened. Even in the telling it seemed unlikely, yet he knew it must have been the same man.

'Did you get a look at him?' asked Tate.

'Regretfully, no,' Koslov admitted. 'I was not expecting to have to remember a face so early in the morning. He was tall, thin – very fit, of course – and . . .' He paused. There was something else about the man that disturbed him, but remained stubbornly vague. A memory, perhaps – an impression of someone he knew?

'And what?'

Koslov shook his head. The impression was gone. Maybe it would come back when he wasn't thinking about it. 'Sorry. For a moment I thought there was something.'

'Don't worry,' Tate told him. 'In the meantime, you'd better get some cover. This man's good. If he can penetrate a Ranger training base and get within a few feet of you in Moscow, he's capable of popping up anywhere. I don't suppose you have an office inside the Kremlin, do you?'

Koslov grinned at the remark but couldn't help a quick glance at the doorway. He slid open his desk drawer. Inside was a holster and harness containing his service pistol. The SR-1 Vector was an ugly brute of a weapon in his opinion, but it had stopping power. He slid it out and checked the load. He'd better start carrying it from now on.

'Thank you for the warning. I don't understand how he could have found me here, though.'

'He has information on all of us. Someone has hacked into systems in the UN and other databases to track us all down. Yours is no more secure than any others.'

195

Koslov grunted in agreement. For all their secrecy, the FSB and SVR – the intelligence directorate responsible for espionage outside the country – had both found their computer systems under repeated attack over recent years from foreign intelligence agencies, most latterly the Chinese Ministry of State Security or *Guóānbù*. But others were just as skilled, and the information was there if hackers knew where to look. 'You have no clues about the killer from the murder scenes?'

'Only the knife he used on the sniper trainee. It had some prints, but no matches have come up so far. If he's from outside the US, he'll be clean. He's obviously well trained and resourceful.'

Koslov thought for a second. Helping the Americans was not something he would normally have been anxious to do, but after this morning, the situation was too dangerous – and too personal. He took a deep breath; he would soon find out if his calls were being monitored or not. If they were, he'd hear the footsteps of the internal security men charging along the corridor before he even put the phone down.

'Can you send me the prints?' This was dangerous to him personally, opening communications with a member of a foreign security agency.

'I think I can arrange it,' Tate answered cautiously. 'Why?'

'Well, whatever you may have been told about our electronic systems,' Koslov replied drily, 'we have a very good database here in Moscow. It holds many thousands of prints.'

For a moment, Tate said nothing. Then he said,

'Where do I send them – your old apartment on the third floor, or your office?'

'My apartment?' Koslov felt a momentary surprise that Harry knew where he lived when he wasn't in his official quarters.

A laugh echoed down the line. 'Our computer's not bad either. Actually, I'm joking. It'll be quicker to email them. Can you give me an address?'

'Sure. Of course.' Koslov read off the centre's email address. 'Mark it for my attention and I will get them examined immediately. What are you going to do next?'

'I've got a man to find,' replied Harry. 'Take care, Alexandr.'

In the UN building in New York, Karen Walters sat across the desk from Ken Deane. The security man was studying an email he'd just received from their legal team. He looked annoyed and apprehensive.

'I didn't tell you about this before,' he said cautiously, 'but we've learned that one of the CP team in Kosovo, a Marine named Bikovsky, was accused of the rape of a minor in San Diego back in 'ninety-eight. It looks like it wasn't his first and only.'

Walters' mouth dropped open. '*What?*' Her sense of shock was understandable; the implications for the UN were obvious, in light of the rumours coming out of Kosovo.

'Yeah, me too.' He gave her a brief summary of what his contact in the San Diego police had told him. 'Unfortunately, we're being denied access to Bikovsky's records on the grounds that it threatens the privacy of the victim, then a minor. Although she's grown up now, her father's digging his heels in.'

'Bikovsky got away with it? That's appalling!'

He nodded, his expression sympathetically grim. 'I hear you. Bikovsky skipped town before anything could be done and disappeared. Two months later he was in the Marines.'

'Didn't it get on to his military file?'

'No reason why it should. No conviction, no record. And he's not the first man to join the military to escape trouble.' He flipped open the file showing Bikovsky's photo, and stared at it as if it would provide some insight into the man's character. It didn't.

Karen Walters reached across so she could see it, and made a small noise of distaste. 'Oh, him.'

'You remember him?' Deane was surprised; protectees and their CP teams spent periods in close proximity and got to know each other quite well. But he hadn't expected Walters to remember any individuals, since she appeared so aloof much of the time.

'He was difficult to miss,' she replied. 'He was a huge brute. He also had a bad attitude about the locals. As he was escorting us out to the helicopter the morning after the ambush, he made disparaging remarks about them; he said the moment we left they'd steal anything that wasn't nailed down.' She shrugged. 'He was the only one who said anything like that. I was surprised, that's all.'

Deane said nothing. She was naïve if she thought that all attached personnel – even those within the

UN proper, given the events surrounding the theft of the data records – were as pure as driven snow. No matter what checks were made, some bad examples always slipped through. He knew of two middle-ranking staffers attached to the Secretary-General's office who had been discovered engaged in illicit financial activities, and were shortly going to find their contracts swiftly terminated. Karen Walters, versed in the ways and intentions of the people in the building immediately associated with her, clearly had a lot to learn about those outside that close-knit circle.

'Let's keep this quiet for now,' he told her. 'If the press hears there was an accused rapist in KFOR colours serving in Kosovo, they'll have Bikovsky and the entire UN wrapped up, judged and convicted before the day's out.'

'What about Kleeman? Shouldn't we tell him?'

Deane grunted. 'Are you kidding? If he hears about it, he'll want Bikovsky castrated in public. No, Bikovsky may have a dirty history, but we're not throwing him to the wolves just so Kleeman can get some brownie points.'

Deane's phone rang and he excused himself.

It was Harry Tate. He quickly brought Deane up to date on his conversation with Koslov and the Russian's narrow escape among the trees around the apartment block. 'He says if we send him the prints off the knife from Fort Benning, he'll run them through their database.'

'Really?' Deane reacted cautiously. He had his doubts about whether the suits at the FBI or the State Department would be happy to go along with that. They still weren't keen on sharing anything with the Russians without a full sitting of a subcommittee and approval from the Intelligence community. 'I hope he keeps it under his samovar. What's to stop them going public about the killings simply to embarrass us?'

'The Russians won't want to admit that a foreign killer got into the grounds of a residential military complex in Moscow and nearly popped one of their officers. I think this is worth a try.'

'I guess. But I thought their databases were creaking at the seams.'

'Koslov's FSB . . . they've probably got the latest Pentiums or Macs in every office.'

'Courtesy of someone in Silicon Valley, I bet.' Deane sighed in frustration. 'Jesus, this guy gets around, doesn't he? Paris, Brussels, New York, Georgia and now Moscow. We should have him working for the UN!'

'He's mobile and has resources,' Harry agreed. 'He's getting help from somewhere.'

'Did Koslov get a look at him?'

'Not really. He was busy trying to stay alive.'

'Pity. We could use a break.'

Harry rang off and was about to switch off the television in his room when a familiar face and name appeared on the screen. It was UN Special Envoy Anton Kleeman standing alongside a group of smiling Chinese politicians. Then the picture cut to show some older footage of a grinning Kleeman in a camouflage jacket, looking younger and slimmer. Karen Walters stood unsmiling to one side. The backdrop looked familiar, Harry thought, a notion quickly confirmed when the camera swung round and caught a brief glimpse of a Sea King helicopter taking off in the background, a crew member visible in the open doorway. It was the same machine that had airlifted everyone out of the KFOR compound near Mitrovica.

As he packed his things away, Harry listened with half an ear to the reporter giving a bland account of talks between the UN Special Envoy and members of the Ministry of Foreign Affairs in Beijing. The studio was evidently using a collage of the Macedonia footage and other short extracts to show Kleeman's versatile role in the organization over a number of years and his increasing prominence in its affairs, including snaps of his college days when he showed great promise as a collegiate wrestler and rower.

He shook his head at the envoy's posturing and turned off the set, sceptical of the ease with which Kleeman had donned the DPM jacket for the cameras and wondering if it was on his own initiative or that of Walters, his assistant.

At a dismal, rain-soaked truck stop outside Moscow, where the city's vast ring road joined the intersection of the M7 at Reutov, Kassim was eating a cheap meal of stew and potatoes, his eye on a television bolted to the wall in one corner. Around him was a mêlée of drivers and travellers, the air of the cafeteria thick with pungent tobacco smoke and a misting of steam rising from damp clothes.

The sound on the television was drowned out by the volume of talk around him, but the picture was clear enough. What had drawn his attention

201

was the sight of a British military helicopter, and a man talking to a clutch of news reporters. The face looked familiar, and Kassim quickly dug out the small binder from his pocket and rifled through the pages until he found the one he wanted.

Anton Kleeman. UN Special Envoy.

Kassim took his plate and edged nearer the television, peering over the shoulders of lorry drivers at the counter. He still couldn't hear anything, and the language would have made it unlikely he'd have understood in any case, but the same reporter's voice continued talking when the picture changed to a shot of the Eiffel Tower in Paris, followed immediately by Big Ben in London.

At the end of the bulletin Kassim returned to his seat with a thoughtful expression and finished his meal. Even when an enormous trucker, clearly overcome by an excess of cheap vodka, lurched against his table and mumbled an apology, he continued staring into the distance.

He needed to get to a computer.

Thirty-Two

The young woman named Maria was again serving when Harry and Rik entered the Tex-Mex restaurant the following morning. The first crush of customers had gone, leaving a few late risers and one or two even later finishers from the previous night. Most had their hands clasped around mugs of strong coffee as they fought to shake off the effects of insomnia, hangovers or non-prescription drugs.

Outside, the day's parade of the Venice Beach beautiful people had not yet begun in earnest. A few early sun-worshippers eager to stake a place on the sands were there, along with the more serious athletes, joggers and bladers, and on a patch of sandy grass, a clutch of t'ai chi exponents were going through their paces, ages ranging from teens to the elderly. Harry suspected it was the only sane time of the day.

They took a table away from the other diners, and when Maria came over, ordered breakfast. If she recognized Harry from the previous evening, she gave no sign, but nodded once and went away to get their food order.

'You dog,' Rik said neutrally, eyeing Maria's departing back. 'You've been schmoozing with the hired help.'

'Shmoozing isn't in my armoury,' Harry muttered. 'But I'm certain she knows Bikovsky.'

A man in a Fred Perry sports shirt and tan slacks put their breakfasts before them. He was about sixty, with dyed hair, a tanned face and deep lines either side of his mouth. His hands were covered in gold rings. 'I'm Jerry – I own this place. Maria said you was askin' about Bikovsky.'

Harry nodded. 'Yes. You know where he is?'

Jerry gave a minute shake of his head, eyes assessing them both. 'He ain't been around for a few days. He owes rent for his place across the alley, so I'm kinda keen to see the big mutt myself. You're British, right?'

'That's right.'

'Thought I recognized the accent. He owe you money, too?'

'Nothing like that.' Harry decided to stick close to the truth, which would sound more believable than if he told Jerry that Bikovsky's life was in danger. 'I met him some years ago in the army – in Kosovo. I was in the area for a couple of days, so I thought it would be nice to meet up.'

'Yeah, Don was in the Marines out there. He told me about it. Rough place.' Jerry flicked a crumb off the table. 'Sometimes he gets work at the studios and stays on location, you know? Easier than travelling up and down the canyons every day.'

'Acting work?' Harry couldn't imagine Bikovsky as a thespian.

The man's smile became lopsided. 'Hell, no. Not what I'd call acting, anyway. More like stunt work, if you know what I mean.' He laughed coarsely, and when Harry looked blank, rolled his eyes and bent near, his voice dropping. 'Skin flicks. Porno movies. The guy's got the pecs, see . . . he looks good in the flesh. It pays pretty good, too, but personally, I don't think it's all that healthy.'

Harry wondered if things had been tough for Bikovsky after leaving the Marines, and whether his history in San Diego had followed him rather more closely than he'd liked. After what Deane had told him about the rape charge, perhaps it wasn't so surprising that he'd gravitated to the sex industry.

'Do you have an address for this studio?'

Jerry raised his shoulders. 'Who knows? These guys, they move around a lot. Plus Don's been hanging with a strange crowd recently. I think maybe he's in trouble and he's gone to let things cool down.'

'What kind of trouble?'

The man turned away as another customer began to get impatient and a crash came from the kitchen. 'What other kind is there?' he said simply. 'Girls, of course . . . or drugs.' He stopped and put out a finger. 'But if you see him, tell him he's gotta pay me the rent or I let the place to someone else. I gotta make a living, too.' He walked away and disappeared through a door at the back.

They finished their meals, and Harry led Rik out on to Ocean Front Walk. As they drew level with the alleyway alongside the building housing Bikovsky's flat, he glanced around and saw an LAPD patrol car drifting towards the County Lifeguard station a hundred yards away.

'I'll go in,' he said. 'You keep an eye out.'

Rik looked at him. 'You think Jerry was telling whoppers?'

'He probably thought we were. If Bikovsky owes him rent money, he's not likely to let someone else walk in and get first bite.'

'How do you want to do this?'

Harry nodded towards the police car. 'Keep an eye on them, just in case. I'll try Bikovsky's door again.'

Rik nodded and walked away, while Harry climbed the stairs to Bikovsky's apartment. The same sweet smell was in the air, overlaid by a powerful aroma of aftershave. Music came from behind one of the doors downstairs, but there was little sign of life. He knocked at Bikovsky's door and waited.

Nothing. He tried the handle. Locked. He tested the door with his shoulder. It might give but it would make some noise.

A faint scuffling noise sounded from the stairway behind him. When he turned round two men were stepping on to the landing, watching him. One was holding a baseball bat, swinging it loosely between his thumb and forefinger.

Harry stepped away from the door. Years of dealing with threatening situations had given him the ability to read people and their body language. Whoever these two were, they hadn't come here to talk. And he doubted they were looking for a third for a knockabout on the beach. Both were dressed in slacks and sports shirts and baseball caps. The nearest was a hulk, with massive biceps and shoulders straining against the fabric of his shirt. His hands were empty and looked like miniature grabs from a mechanical digger.

The man with the bat was slimmer, although the difference was marginal. He had a spread of designer stubble across his face and his eyes looked oddly slack and dulled. Harry wondered whether he'd overdone the steroids. Both men bore a passing resemblance to Bikovsky, although it could have been the similarity in size and the stance of muscular solidity.

'You got business in there?' the first man asked softly.

Harry flicked a glance along the corridor, where

a glow from the sun was reflecting off the walls from a window at the end. He hadn't checked to see if there was another exit, but he recalled seeing a series of outside fire escape ladders. Getting to one, however, before these two were all over him like a heavy rash, was doubtful.

'I'm looking for the tenant,' he replied, non-committal. 'Would you know where he is?'

'Christ, ain't he polite, Marty?' the batter said to his companion, and sniggered. His voice was reedy and nasal. He smiled and took a deep breath as if he was winding himself up. 'So who are you, pal? What's your business?' He slapped the bat against the wall, dislodging a fragment of plaster. ''Cos we got a prior call on the *tenant's* time, see.'

Marty said nothing, but brought his hands together and cracked a knuckle, shifting his weight forward on his toes. It was a signal that he was about to move. A doer, thought Harry, not a talker.

'That's my business,' Harry replied, and stepped towards them.

They weren't expecting that. They hesitated for a second, but soon recovered. By then he was close enough to have caused confusion. They shuffled their feet, turning to attack, knowing that the advantage was heavily stacked in their favour if they could stay apart and block his way past. But the confines of the corridor worked against them, and the batter in particular was now standing so close to the wall he couldn't bring his weapon into play. It made the other man the more dangerous of the two.

'And mine.'

The sound of another voice echoing along the corridor made them freeze. Harry glanced past the two men and saw a slim figure coming towards them, framed by the sun's reflection.

It was Rik. He must have come up the fire escape. He had his hand out and the Ruger was pointing at the batter's head.

Harry didn't wait for them to recover. They would soon realize that anyone opening fire here would attract instant attention from the police. He stepped in fast, knowing that if they got hold of him, he was in real trouble.

Marty was the first to react. He spun on one foot, drawing up his other foot to launch a side-kick, hands out ready to counter-attack. Harry changed direction at the last second, catching the man with the bat by surprise. Sliding in hard and low, he palmed his right fist in his left hand and rammed his elbow through the batter's guard. He felt a satisfying crunch as something gave which travelled all the way to his fist, and saw the batter stagger backwards. Unfortunately, he was too close to the top step; with a yelp of pain and surprise, he dropped his bat and crashed over backwards down the stairs.

Harry was already turning to face the man named Marty, but found to his surprise that he was frozen, his kicking leg cocked but unmoving. Instead, he was looking at his friend bowling down the stairs, leaving behind a smear of blood from his damaged nose.

Then Harry saw the reason for Marty's lack of movement: Rik had moved in very fast and touched the back of the big man's head with the tip of his gun barrel.

'OK – I'm done,' Marty muttered, and lowered his foot. He was breathing heavily, and clearly knew when a fight was over.

'Eddie? Marty? You OK up there?'

Harry stepped past Marty and walked quickly down the stairs until he reached the man called Eddie. He was staring up, eyes flickering on the edge of consciousness. His bat was lying further down the steps. Harry stepped over him and continued on down.

A third man was standing in the alleyway, peering anxiously through the doorway. He possessed neither the physical size nor the intimidating appearance of the other two, but was trying to look as if he was their equal. A car blocked the far end of the alley, the engine running.

'Who the hell are you?' The man straightened his shoulders and made to step in Harry's way.

'Public Health.' Harry walked directly at him, making him jump aside. 'Your friends said to go on up.'

Across the alleyway at the rear of the Tex-Mex, Jerry was ducking back out of sight and pulling the kitchen door shut behind him.

Harry walked round to the front entrance and stepped inside, banging open the door unceremoniously. He walked straight past Maria, who put out a faint hand to stop him, and pushed open the door to the kitchen. Jerry was standing by a wall phone, muttering something. He took it from him, replacing it in its cradle, and the restaurant owner jumped back as if he'd been stung. A film

209

of perspiration glittered across his face, but it wasn't from the kitchen.

'Where is he?' Harry asked softly. 'And who were those two musclemen? Are they part of the trouble you mentioned or did you call them?'

'I can't tell you that!' Jerry babbled, his voice rising. 'They're trouble. I was looking, that's all. It's my property – I didn't want the place trashed.'

'If you don't tell me where he is,' said Harry evenly, 'I'll have the public health people down here inside the hour. They'll close this place down pending analysis of the junk you call food, and close the apartments across the way because of the rats.'

Jerry's eyes widened. 'Rats? What rats? I ain't got no—'

'The ones on the stairs.' Harry stared at him. 'Who do you think they'll believe – you or a tourist who's threatening to make a big noise to the city management?'

Maria entered the kitchen behind him, her dark eyes full of concern. Harry was guessing she had work permit issues and her words confirmed it. 'Please. Don't do that,' she whispered. 'I need this job. I will tell you where Don Bikovsky is.'

Three minutes later, Harry and Rik were losing themselves among the growing crowds drifting along the beachfront. He didn't expect the men from the apartment building to come after him, but he didn't want to take any chances. At least he now knew where Bikovsky was and could speak to the man rather than waste any more time.

The men, Maria had told him, were local enforcers employed by criminals involved in the porn industry. Their primary function was to close down rival operations and to deter actors and technicians from working for anyone their bosses didn't approve of. With the vast amounts of money to be made from the industry, they made sure their methods were effective. She said the three men Harry had confronted had been sent with orders to deal with Bikovsky.

'He is filming,' she said quickly, as Jerry scuttled away to the sanctuary of his restaurant. 'He tried to get me involved, too. It is good money, but not nice work.' She pulled a face. 'I could never go home again afterwards. I told Don one day he will get something bad . . . a disease . . . but he does not seem to care.'

Harry asked, 'Are you and he close?'

Maria looked shocked at the suggestion. 'No – nothing like that. Don, he's OK, you know. But there are times when he is not such a nice man.' She looked guilty for a second, then explained, 'He saved me once from a guy on the beach. It was just some kid looking for easy money, you know? But Don, he thought he was trying to . . . to hurt me. He beat him very bad. He has demons . . . I think he is a very sad man. Unhappy. In his eyes he is gone away somewhere else. But he never hurt me.'

'Does he use drugs?'

Maria shrugged eloquently. 'I never see him. That is something you will have to ask him.'

Thirty-Three

The traffic on the way up to the canyons above Los Angeles was less frenetic, but still took over an hour, with two accidents and some heavy roadworks to be negotiated on the way. The road began to climb steadily, snaking past large, impressive properties behind high walls and grilled entrances, the grounds planted with arrays of trees, laurel, mimosa and palms. On the way they passed celebrity tour buses full of tourists, and Harry was struck by how the desperate search for privacy by the rich and famous dovetailed so well with the tourist industry.

Rik was navigating, the car's satnav having given up en route, and called out the address Maria had given him. It was beyond the Ventura Freeway past Universal City and Glendale. According to Maria, it was a large house with extensive grounds and heavy security. She hadn't said how she knew that.

Harry turned into the road and drifted along until he saw the house number. Up here the air was warm and less muggy compared with the city or even Venice Beach. With the occasional glimpses he caught on the way up of the ocean and downtown LA stretching away into the distance, he figured he could possibly force himself to spend some time here if the need ever arose.

Maria had been right – it was a large place. Set behind locked iron gates topped with a camera, it owed its style to Spanish and Moorish influences, and Harry wondered how many millions of dollars it would fetch on the open market.

Three cars were parked on the gravel drive, their bodywork gleaming in the sun. A man in jeans and T-shirt was hosing down a green Rolls-Royce, while alongside stood a Lexus and a muscle Jeep bristling with chrome, raised suspension and huge tyres. The porno business evidently paid well.

Harry leaned out and tapped a button on an intercom post at the side of the entrance. Seconds later a voice answered, asking his business. The man with the hose stopped what he was doing and looked in their direction.

'I'd like to speak to Don Bikovsky, please,' Harry told the metal box.

'Sorry – we have no one of that name here.' The response was immediate, automatic and, to Harry, not surprising, given what was allegedly going on here.

He tried again. 'I've been advised differently.'

'Then your information is incorrect, sir. This is a private residence. You can turn round in the entrance.' The box clicked off and Harry heard the buzz of a camera above the gate as it focussed in on his face.

He pressed the button again. 'Perhaps you could you tell Don that I have some urgent information for him. My name's Tate and I believe his life is in danger.'

A short silence, then, 'Wait . . . I'll see what I can find out.'

They sat and waited. Five minutes, then ten. The car washer had disappeared. One or two vehicles passed, glossy and exclusive, followed by the inevitable tour bus, but nobody showed any interest. Other than the faint sound of a water sprinkler and a few birds singing in the trees, the area was very peaceful.

There was a tapping noise on Harry's side window. He turned and saw Bikovsky scowl at him. Harry lowered the window.

'What do you want, man?' The ex-Marine sounded irritated. If he remembered Harry, he was doing a sterling job of hiding it. He was dressed in baggy swim shorts and trainers, his naked torso rippling with bunched muscle. Whatever else Bikovsky had been doing over the years, he hadn't ignored his fitness routine. The effect was spoiled, however, by his eyes, which looked red and slightly out of focus.

'You don't sound surprised to see me,' Harry told him. He climbed out of the car, forcing the big man to step back, and looked at the house. 'Nice place.'

'It's a rental. What do you want?'

'You got my message?'

'Yeah, I got it. So what? I don't have to listen to you.'

'Not even if I can save your life?'

Bikovsky jerked a thumb back at the house. 'Try getting to the point – I'm on someone else's dollar right now.'

In contrast to the muscled torso, Harry noticed

214

his fingernails were grubby and bitten to the quick. There was also a smell of cheap oil in the air and a silvery sheen on Bikovsky's arms and staining the waistband of his shorts.

'Fair enough. I'll be quick.' He spoke without emotion, suddenly wanting to be somewhere else, and trying not to remember what had been said about this man. 'You remember Orti and Broms? And Carvalho?'

Bikovsky's face screwed up in mock concentration. 'Not really. Why – you planning a team reunion? If so, count me out – I don't do that crap.' He began to turn away, but Harry's next words stopped him.

'They're all dead.'

The ex-Marine looked at Harry, then bent to peer at Rik inside the car. A flicker of something crossed his face, then was gone. He shrugged. 'You came all the way out here to tell me that? Why?'

'Because you're next on the list.'

Bikovsky blinked. Hard. Whatever his condition, he wasn't so far gone that he could ignore such a statement. 'Say what? How come? I never saw those guys after we left that shithole. If they were in a jam and got themselves hit, it don't concern me.'

The camera whirred again, and they both looked up. Someone in the house was getting impatient. Bikovsky cursed softly.

Harry said, 'Who says they were in trouble?' There was no answer to that, so he added, 'But I'm not talking about it here.'

'Hey, man – I can't get away just like that.'

215

Bikovsky's voice was urgent, his face turned away from the camera. 'And in case you didn't notice, I left the military and I certainly ain't in KFOR no more. So I don't have to give you squat.'

Harry shrugged and got back in his car. 'Well, if you don't, I'll let Eddie and Marty know where you are. You know Eddie and Marty?' The look on Bikovsky's face confirmed that he did. 'Well, how would your employers like that? It would look bad on film if you picked up a few bruises.' He started the engine. 'By the way, Eddie fell down the stairs outside your apartment. Now they think we're friends . . . and they're not impressed.'

'Shit, man!' Bikovsky protested vehemently. 'What have you done? You can't jam me up like that!'

'Then speak to me. Name a place and make it soon. Then we'll be out of your hair.'

Bikovsky swore again, but finally nodded. 'OK . . . you got it. But this better be worth it. There's a coffee shop on Pacific called the Dolphin. I'll be there about five this evening.' He turned and walked through the gate without looking back.

The camera swivelled to follow him all the way.

'Damn,' Rik said. 'I was hoping for a look inside.'

'Down, boy,' Harry said. 'You're too young for that stuff and your mother would never forgive me.'

The US Army Criminal Investigation Command (CID), assisted by the FBI and prodded by regular

216

calls from Ken Deane, had moved extra quickly on lifting the prints from the knife used to kill Lloyd at Fort Benning. Second only to being sent nationwide to all FBI regions, copies were sent to Koslov at FSB headquarters in Moscow, as Harry Tate had requested.

As soon as he was notified of their arrival, Koslov took the prints along to the forensic laboratory and flagged the job as ultra urgent, to include all databases. Nothing less would get anything moving, and since he had a vested interest in the information, he had no hesitation in pulling rank over several other jobs currently being dealt with. Even so, the civilian supervisor argued as a matter of course, claiming there were already far too many urgent jobs awaiting their turn.

'Do you have proper justification for this taking precedence, Captain?' the man enquired primly. Plainly, to him it meant nothing if the job was done now or next week, but he evidently felt the need to defend his corner, especially with newcomers like Koslov.

'Yes, I do,' Koslov responded firmly, staring the man down. 'If we do not find out who these prints belong to, I will probably die. After that, so will you, for allowing the murder of an officer through dereliction of your duty. Is that justification enough for you?' He nodded at the man's suddenly pale face and walked away.

Fifty minutes later, to Koslov's amazement, the supervisor rang to say they had a match.

'You what?' Holy God, it had been an outside chance, but it had worked. 'Send Dobrev up to me with the details. Immediately.'

Two minutes later Koslov was staring in bafflement at a sheet of printed paper. The details had been copied from Russian Army Intelligence files. After trying all current records, the computer had automatically switched to scanning deeper into the archives and had fastened on a name and prints. From the heading at the top of the sheet, Koslov saw the details had come originally from a specialist Intelligence unit operating in Chechnya. Their unit details had been blanked out, and he knew instantly what that meant: Spetsnaz – Special Forces. The date of 2001 told him more; it was during the period known as the Second Chechen War, which had begun two years before. Islamist separatists fighting for independence from Russia had been spreading their conflict into Dagestan and Ingushetia, drawing in Muslim volunteers from outside the area, some deliberately using the experience gained for training purposes before going to fight in Afghanistan and elsewhere. It had made identifying many of the fighters impossible, but Koslov knew the authorities had made a point of collating and recording thousands of faces, fingerprints and background details of known and suspected terrorists involved in the war. These had been fed into a database which had been kept up to date by security services archivists working for the FSB and SVR.

This man had called himself Kassim. No other name. A notation said the address he'd given was false. His age was given as seventeen years, but that was just as doubtful. Picked up in a sweep of an underground camp outside Grozny, Kassim had been taken to a local militia barracks lock-up for processing along with twenty other suspected fighters. Two days later an explosion had breached the walls and Kassim had vanished, killing one of the guards on the way out. Because of that his file had been kept active for a while, until it was moved into the archives. He was thought to have gone to Afghanistan.

The thumbprint photo told Koslov nothing. Devoid of character or detail like most police mugshots, this one must have been taken and processed by an idiot. It was just a face, nothing more, one he would find replicated outside this building a thousand times, if he cared to go out and look. He stared at the ceiling, seeing once more the face of the man in the trees. *Now* he knew what had been familiar . . . what had been tugging at his memory. It wasn't the man's face, for he didn't know him from a hole in the ground. It was his manner . . . something in the way he moved and the stance of his body as he ran; the purposefulness of his gait. If this information was correct, the American soldier had been killed by an Afghan.

And now Koslov was being stalked by the same man.

He heard a cough and looked up. Dobrev was still standing there.

'Haven't you got things to do?' Koslov asked.

'Sir.' Dobrev nodded. 'Waiting for instructions, sir.'

Koslov smiled. Dobrev was no fool; time spent waiting here was time away from running endless errands for other officers.

'Have you ever seen an Afghan, Dobrev?'

'Umm . . . no, sir. Not up close, anyway.'

219

Koslov spun the sheet of paper round so that Dobrev could see the photo, although he guessed he'd already read the text. 'That man is in Moscow. Right now. He's older now, of course. If you see him, let me know right away. Oh, and start running. Otherwise he'll kill you.'

Thirty-Four

When Harry returned to his hotel, he found an urgent message waiting from Deane. He dialled the number and waited.

The head of security sounded breathless, as if he'd run up a flight of stairs.

'We have an ID on our killer,' he announced. 'Koslov fed in the prints and came up with a name. He's a Muslim fighter named Kassim . . . a *mujahedin*.'

Harry digested the information and felt a tingle of interest in his gut. So, a terrorist connection after all? Time would tell. And while they didn't yet know why this Kassim was intent on wiping out members of the UN, at least they could now begin working on possible motives.

'Did he explain how he got it?'

'He was happy to,' said Deane. 'Russian Military Intelligence kept close tabs on the various *mujahedin* factions during the Second Chechen War, especially when they noticed how many foreigners were turning up in the region. They recorded thousands of fingerprints, names, some photos – and ethnic groupings. They finger-printed every male they came across, active or not. Even if there was no evidence of them being in one of the rebel factions they sent the details back to Moscow. Kassim was kept in a lock-up for a couple of days, then the local rebels staged a breakout. He killed a militiaman and his prints later came up on a captured RPG-7 which brought down a Russian helicopter. According to Koslov this would have put him on a search-and-kill list, but they never found him. He was probably a volunteer and left the country for Afghanistan or Pakistan when things got hot. Kassim's probably an Uzbek . . . they're mostly nomadic types, according to my researchers, so moving around the hills wouldn't have been a problem. And they get used to staying out of the way from the moment they're born. That might explain how he was able to sneak up on the Marine sniper so easily.'

'Is there a photo?'

'Yeah. It's lousy quality, according to Koslov, taken under what he calls battlefield conditions. He's getting it scanned and sent over. I'll email it you and send copies to the FBI office in LA. They might be able to match it with the cameras at the airport.'

'But why an Afghan if the rumours are about Kosovo? And how can a hill tribesman be moving around like he is?'

'I don't know. Maybe he's not just a tribesman. Some *mujahedin* are incomers educated in the west. They only went over to fight against the common enemy, like in Chechnya and Iraq. I'll start making enquiries through the FBI about Aeroflot flights to Moscow. Most of them go out of New York, so he'd have had to come through here from Columbus to make a connection. If he's travelling on a non-Russian passport, there can't be too many names to look through.'

'Why Aeroflot? Aren't there US flights to Moscow?'

'Sure there are, but I figured getting on an Aeroflot flight would be easier – and cheaper.'

'If you say so. What about tickets and visas? You can't pick those up on a whim.'

'Must have been pre-arranged. I'll get on to that, too. I'll leave you to speak to Koslov – see if you can get him to dig around at his end on the immigration and arrivals register. They might be able to come up with something. Have you tracked down Bikovsky yet?'

'I have, but he's reluctant to speak. I'm meeting him tonight.'

'Uh-huh. What's he doing?'

Harry explained what the waitress Maria had told him about Bikovsky's work.

Deane was silent for a moment. 'Any young girls involved?'

'No idea. That's something the FBI will have to address.'

He hung up and dialled Koslov's number, but was told the Russian FSB officer had gone home and would be back later. He told the operator he needed some urgent information and would call back. The man recognized Harry's name and said he would get the captain to ring when he came in.

While he waited he went over what he knew, trying to make a connection which would make sense. If the rape and murder in Kosovo was the linking factor, it still didn't tell him why an Afghan would be tracking down members of the UN. More importantly, how was the man getting the resources to accomplish what he was doing? Flights didn't come cheap and neither did local transport. And if he was using cars supplied by helpers, it would still cost money. Stealing vehicles was a possibility, but risky. On the other hand, renting a car from an official agency was impossible without a driver's licence. Which meant, unless he had forged documents, which was possible, he would be using backstreet dealers. As far as tracing cars would go, that was a dead end.

The phone rang, startling him, and he realized with surprise he'd been sitting there for nearly forty minutes, turning things over in his mind.

'Harry Tate?' It was Koslov. 'You have the information – the Afghan?'

'That's good work, Alexandr,' Harry congratulated him. 'Now all we've got to do is find him. Ken Deane's got the FBI trawling through flight records to Moscow; could you ask your immigration people to do the same? Our guess is he's travelling on a non-Russian passport. But that's all it is – a guess.'

'I've asked them already. They will let me know as soon as they have something.' Koslov sounded excited, the reaction of an investigator close to the conclusion of a hunt, when he could smell the quarry. 'There was something about this man that was familiar – I told you, huh? I have seen the type before. There was something about the way he moved. And the face: he is pale, like many Afghans, and could pass easily for a European. But there was a power in his face . . . you will know what I mean when you see him.'

'I understand. If he's a *mujahedin*, he's superb at adapting to his surroundings and blending in.'

Koslov was silent for a moment, then, 'You have taught young soldiers how to fight – how to defend, yes?'

'Of course.'

'Also you have put yourself against them . . . like in competition. They try to be better than you, but they never do. You know why?'

'I'm more experienced.'

'Is true,' Koslov agreed. 'But more than that, is because you do not think – ever – that you will be beaten by trainee. Is not possible. You are senior . . . so does not enter your thinking. *Mujahedin* are the same, Harry. Not better, but never think of failing. To fail is to die. To die is to lose.'

'You sound as if you admire them.'

'Admire, no. Respect, why not? This Kassim has decided he will win. To win, he does not see obstacles. They do not exist.'

'It's all in the mind.'

'Damn right, my friend. All in the mind.'

Harry thanked the Russian for his help and disconnected. He felt suddenly infected as much by Koslov's enthusiasm for the hunt as daunted by his reading of the *mujahedin* mind. He

224

wondered what the Afghan's next move would be.

Private Anton Dobrev pulled up outside the apartment block to pick up Captain Koslov, and switched off the engine. He had a few minutes yet, and decided he'd enjoy the time while he could, in the warmth of the car. He'd been on his feet since clocking on this morning, and was feeling tired. He yawned, and watched as a man with a broom and cleaner's cart entered the courtyard and began sweeping the ground around the edge of the main building. He decided there were definitely worse jobs than his own. Doing anything outside in this crappy weather was no joke. Probably another conscript on punishment duties.

He tilted his head back, then thought better of it. Wouldn't do for Captain Koslov to come down and find him asleep on the job. Especially with a killer around.

He sat up, wondering if the good captain had been pulling his leg. Why would an Afghan come to Moscow, anyway? He'd be crazy. Although, maybe they were a crazy people and did stuff like that – like the Chechens and some of those other people further east.

He gave a start, realizing that the cleaner had moved closer, and was digging his broom into a corner, teasing at a grating in the ground but not really accomplishing anything. The man was gaunt and wearing a rough padded coat, but surprisingly, ordinary walking shoes. And civilian pants, rather than work trousers.

Dobrev sat up. The man had looked across at

him, then ducked his head quickly. What the hell was he—?

Suddenly he felt a shock like a physical blow. *It was him. The Afghan!* He looked to his front, chest pounding. No. It couldn't be. He was mistaken, daydreaming. Koslov would have his balls if he sounded the alarm and the cleaner was innocent.

He looked again. The man was older than in the photo – but Koslov had said it was taken twelve years ago, according to the document . . . which he wasn't supposed to have read, but what else do you do to brighten your day?

He clicked open the door and stepped out of the car. The cleaner looked up. Face blank, hands gripping the broom. Just a cleaner, surely.

'How's it going?' Dobrev meant to sound friendly, casual, but his nerves made his voice come out as a bark.

The effect was instantaneous, and frightening. The cleaner dropped his broom and crossed the space between them in three quick strides. Before Dobrev could move, the man was on him, a knife blade gleaming in his hand. His eyes looked mad and his teeth were bared, like a dog. Dobrev scrabbled with his hand and managed to hit the car's horn. The blare sounded uncommonly loud in the enclosed courtyard, startling them both. At the same time, he waited for the first stab of pain that was surely going to follow.

But it didn't happen.

Suddenly the man backed off, looking around. The mad look in his eye seemed to fade, and he shook his head with apparent annoyance.

Then he turned and ran.

Dobrev hit the horn again, and felt horribly sick.

Koslov put down the phone with a feeling of satisfaction. It felt good to be working like this, instead of pursuing endless petty roads which led nowhere, or hunting down harmless dissidents who couldn't get together the means to set fire to a bottle of paraffin without burning themselves. The Americans – and Harry, too – were professionals. They had the means, of course, to buy the best facilities to help them with their work. Which was why he felt proud at having come up with the Afghan's identity so quickly. Just think what he could do with their massive computer resources . . . he'd be able to discard all the antiquated card-file systems still being used in so many corners of the Russian security apparatus.

He heard the blast of a car horn. Dobrev, waiting to take him to the office. Cheeky young bugger was getting above himself. Drivers were supposed to come up and knock, not sound the horn like a damned cab driver. He gathered his things together and thought he'd go out to Sheremetyevo instead and take a look at the immigration records and the camera hard drives. He might tread on some toes in the process, but since it had become an international manhunt, and the request from the UN and the FBI had been about as high-powered as it could get, he would have the backing of his superiors.

As he shrugged on his coat, there was another loud blast of the horn, this time longer.

'Dobrev, you insubordinate little shit!' he shouted. 'I'm coming!' He took a last look around, flicked a used shirt into a drawer, then picked up his pistol and went downstairs.

He walked across to the car, and saw Dobrev standing with one foot inside the vehicle. The young man looked terrified and was pointing at a cleaner's cart and broom lying on the ground.

'The Afghan,' Dobrev stuttered. 'He was here!' Then he turned and threw up.

By the time Koslov was being grilled by military security investigators, Kassim was on his way to Moscow's Domodedovo airport. He flung the knife he'd almost used on the Russian driver through the car window at the first opportunity, and straightened his clothing. He was breathing fast, as if he'd run a race, and he felt light-headed. Tiredness, undoubtedly, catching up on him. Yet he'd been awake for much longer in the past, and under far more stressful circumstances. Perhaps it was a sign that he wasn't eating properly. He drank water from a plastic bottle and spat some out of the window. Water was purity; purity was strength. It would have to do for now.

His instructors had warned him that operating at peak effort, whether in a war zone or not, could very quickly drain his mental and physical resources. The only way to sustain himself, they had told him, was by eating at every opportunity, and by observing his daily devotions. He wondered if these men with their wise words had ever done what he was doing, or carried the burden he was carrying. In any case, serving his devotions had never been high on his list of priorities, although he had not dared let them know that. Some things were best left unsaid, when surrounded by zealots; even those who had helped him and brought him to this point.

He couldn't tell what had stopped him killing the driver. The stupid man's challenge had unnerved him. A couple more minutes and he could have been inside the building and looking for Koslov. But the driver had spotted him and was surely about to raise the alarm.

His response had been automatic, the ingrained need to protect himself. But he'd stopped and turned away. Why? He shook his head, seeing the young Russian's face, an unshaven fuzz on his lip and the look of abject fear in his eyes.

Perhaps it had just been his lucky day.

He stayed alert for signs of police activity, and eventually joined a stream of traffic heading into the airport perimeter road. He left the car unlocked in a long-term car park next to the Airhotel. From what he had been told about this place, it would be gone before the day was out. Then he made straight for the check-in desk for flights to London, and to meet the man who would provide him with what he needed for the next stage of his journey. He wouldn't mention that he hadn't killed the Russian, though.

By midday UK time, he would be landing in Heathrow.

Thirty-Five

The Dolphin coffee shop and restaurant on Pacific Avenue was a single-storey building with its own car park, set between an apartment block on one side and a golfing store on the other. There were few cars in evidence, and only a handful of heads visible inside when Harry arrived just before five. He parked across the other side of the road with a clear view of the entrance, and wondered if Bikovsky would turn up. The ex-Marine's attitude at the house in the hills hadn't been exactly helpful, and Harry was half expecting to have been sent on a wild-goose chase just to get him out of the way.

Beside him on the seat was an envelope he'd collected earlier from the local FBI office on Wilshire. It contained copies of the Russian Intelligence file on Kassim and mug shots of the *mujahedin* fighter from Chechnya, taken when he was scooped up in a random raid on a warehouse in Grozny.

The photo was a face-on shot taken against a rough brick backdrop, the overhead lighting casting shadows beneath Kassim's eyes and across his gaunt cheeks. He looked too young to be any kind of fighter, his beard wispy and thin, the early attempts of a teenager trying to look tough and grown-up. But the colour of the hair matched the darkness in his eyes, which were staring into the camera in sullen defiance. Harry could only speculate about how much he had changed since then.

'We've put this out to all our field agents,' Bob Dosario, one of the Bureau's special agents, had told Harry when he was admitted to the LA office. 'And I'm arranging for copies to go out on the streets and to our office at the airport. I can't promise anything, but if he comes here we stand a chance of eyeballing him. Pity is, we don't know what he looks like now, but we might be able to get our guys to build up a facial projection from this photo.'

With Kassim's record so far, Harry had serious doubts about the FBI's chances of catching him unless he made a mistake. And apart from killing Lloyd, which he would have seen as unavoidable, he hadn't shown any signs yet of doing that. He left Dosario and drove down to Pacific Avenue to meet Bikovsky.

A faded, open-topped Suzuki four-by-four turned off Pacific Avenue and bumped the gulley into the Dolphin's car park, narrowly missing a tourist fighting with a folding map. A large figure in jeans and T-shirt climbed out. It was Bikovsky. He stomped across the car park and disappeared through the doors of the Dolphin.

Harry drove into the car park and followed him inside.

Bikovsky was seated at a back table, sipping at a glass of iced water and looking sour. He said nothing when Harry greeted him, but signalled for the waitress to bring a coffee and Danish.

Harry ordered the same and sat down.

'I just got word from a friend about Eddie and Marty,' Bikovsky said briefly. 'Those two guys you met at my place?'

Harry nodded. It was time for the other to lead the way. He might learn far more by letting the man talk.

'You really riled them,' Bikovsky continued, rubbing his knuckles together. 'Eddie, especially – the one you threw down the stairs. Now they're really pissed and looking for payback. The people I'm with, they don't need this kind of shit. They're trying to run a smooth operation, and this kinda noise pulls in too much static from the cops. The people Eddie and Marty work for don't play nice, neither.' He sneered. 'I could have made some decent side money selling this meeting to them, let me tell you.'

'Why didn't you?' Harry resisted taking a look out the window. It wouldn't do any good now, anyway, and he was relying on Rik playing the tourist outside to watch his back for such eventualities.

'I don't trust them even more than I don't trust you.'

Harry ignored the insult. 'Rival operators?'

'Yeah, kinda.' A nervous tone had crept into Bikovsky's voice, and Harry guessed he'd been sent down by his bosses with orders to sort things out.

'In that case,' he said, 'you help me and I'll be out of your hair.'

Bikovsky nodded and took another sip of water. 'Sounds good.'

In a few terse sentences Harry told him everything he knew so far, other than the rumours about
the rape and murder at the compound. He doubted
Bikovsky would have seen anything on the news
reports, and if he was the man responsible, he
didn't want to tip the ex-Marine's hand and risk
him clamming up or disappearing altogether.

'If this Kassim is tracking members of the
team,' he said, 'he's not doing it because someone's feelings got bruised. Something serious
must have happened at the compound. I'm trying
to find out what that might be.'

Bikovsky looked defensive, his eyes flicking
towards the door as if seeking an avenue of
escape. 'What – and you think it may have been
something *I* did? Like what? Man – I was wasted
that night, same as everybody else.' He sat back,
making the seat creak, and swept a large hand
through the air. 'You know what it was like; it
was in, bed down and out again. Anyway, the
compound guards could've been doing stuff
before we even got there. With nothing to do all
day except pound the wire and keep out the camp
rats, who could blame them? Maybe they got
some of the local girls in there for a party and
the locals got pissed.'

'You might be right, except that Carvalho was
rotated out of the convoy to stay with us. He arrived
and left when we did, and the other compound
guards went on to Pristina. So far they've been left
alone.'

'So what are you saying?'

'If something happened, it was the night we
were there. Nothing else makes sense.'

233

The waitress arrived with their orders and Bikovsky shrugged, then took a large bite of his Danish. 'Well, I can't help you. Wish I could, you know?' He finished off the pastry in a few swallows and gulped down his coffee. 'So where to next, huh?' His tone was suddenly relaxed, seeing the meeting as done.

Harry sipped his coffee and pulled a face. 'Moscow, probably. How about you – are you managing to make a living from the films?' He kept his voice casual.

Bikovsky smirked, his manner easier now the talk was no longer of any possible misdemeanours. 'Pretty good. It ain't what my mother wanted me to do, but doin' what comes natural and being paid for it . . . well, it's OK until something better comes along, right?'

Harry glanced around, then edged forward, his manner conspiratorial. 'So what kind of girls do you work with, then?' he asked, in what he hoped was a guy-to-guy manner.

Bikovsky laughed. 'The people I work with, they're at the top end. They distribute right across the States – even Europe. And the chicks, well, they have to be a certain standard.' He smirked, eyes hooded. 'I tell you, some of them, they ain't gonna make it in Hollywood, but, man, they're still classy. If I wasn't in the business, there's no way I'd ever get to party with them. As it is, though . . . well, I get to play with some of the finest ass you'll ever see, let me tell you.'

Harry pushed his coffee away. He badly wanted to knock Bikovsky out of his seat. He had no real recollection of how good the man had been as a soldier, but guessed that underneath the uniform he had never been any different from when he was out of it.

'Are they young?' he asked.

Bikovsky frowned. 'Man, I don't know. Long as they've got the right equipment in the right condition, who cares? If it ain't willing, ready and able, it don't get the job, that's the only rule.'

Harry suppressed his distaste. 'Teenagers? Kids?'

'Sure – I guess. Eighteen, maybe seventeen.' He looked suddenly wary. 'I ain't never heard no one ask for their birth certificates, if that's what you mean. As far as I'm concerned, they're the same as me: do the job and take the money. We done?'

Harry nodded. He'd had enough. If Bikovsky was into young girls, he wasn't about to admit it. He took a copy of Kassim's photo from the envelope and slid it across the table so Bikovsky could see it. 'This is Kassim – or was about ten years ago.'

Bikovsky frowned at the poor reprint. 'He's just a kid!'

'He was. He's grown up a lot since then.'

Bikovsky feigned indifference, but Harry guessed it was an act; his service in the Balkans would have given him a clear idea of what revenge attacks could be like. And age was no guarantee of inability to kill a man.

'Looks a mean little asshole,' was his only comment.

'He's worse. As well as killing the others, he got within thirty feet of Carl Pendry on a sniper

235

training range – and Carl was expecting company. He makes Eddie and Marty seem like pussycats in comparison.'

'So how come he didn't try nailing Pendry again? And if he's so freakin' awesome, how is it he hasn't come after me?'

Harry stood up. 'He missed his chance with Pendry, so he moved on to take a shot at Koslov instead. He's keeping us guessing. It doesn't mean he's given up.'

Bikovsky looked sour. 'What are you saying – that I should leave? Run away? I can't do that.'

'Fine. It's your life.' Harry glanced at Bikovsky's mobile on the table. 'Give me your number. I'll try to warn you if he comes back.'

The Marine shrugged. 'Suit yourself.' He read out the number and Harry keyed it into his own phone. 'The sooner I can forget this shit, the better.'

'Do that. But remember one thing: Kassim won't forget you.'

Thirty-Six

Deep in the picturesque Cotswold hills of southern England, at a small helicopter flight base off the old Roman road, the Fosse Way, Corporal Malcolm Oakes of No. 51 Squadron RAF Regiment was watching the coming of dusk. The silhouette of one of the hangars was turning black against the sky, the vast roof curving down at the sides. As the light faded, the adjacent maintenance work-shops would be swallowed too, followed by the admin block nearby and the perimeter fence three hundred yards away, leaving only the outer and inner security lights to push back the night.

Oakes shivered. It was only his third day here and it was a sight he hadn't tired of, this coming of the evening. Yet he couldn't explain even to himself why he found the sight so compelling. Maybe it was something deep in his psyche he'd never fully grasped, this small, low-key ending to the day.

He'd seen more dramatic moments over the years, in different places, especially on a posting to the Falklands, when the sun came up over the South Atlantic like a shock to the system. Then, he'd witnessed colours more intense than he'd ever seen before, an event he felt should have been accompanied by a swelling chorus of music to do it justice. Even on his last tour in Iraq, the sunset over the desert possessed a cold, ethereal beauty that touched the land as if trying to compensate for the ugliness and killing that had gone on over the generations.

He continued his patrol between the hangars, which housed a collection of training helicopters and fixed-wing aircraft, and spotted his colleague, Andy Killick, disappearing behind a vehicle garage near the admin block. Killick was slipping off for a quick smoke. One day he'd get caught and then wonder why the might of the RAF rulebook was descending on him like a ton of bricks.

Oakes checked his watch. Another thirty

minutes, then he'd be off duty. A few hours' sleep and he'd be heading for a day's hiking along the Windrush. He hadn't done the walk through the Cotswolds yet and it was time to get his boots out and exercise his leg muscles before he was posted somewhere else less inspiring.

He stretched and heard the crackle of the envelope in his top pocket. He'd picked it up earlier when he'd clocked on. He hadn't opened it yet because he was sure he knew what it was; a bollocking for getting heavy-handed with a couple of local men who'd strayed on to the base two days ago in search of whatever wasn't tied down. His method of dealing with trouble had cost him dear in promotion over the years, and his current tenure of the rank of corporal looked like being shorter than ever. One of the men had thrown a punch and made a run for it, but Oakes had brought him down within thirty paces, managing to roll on the intruder's throat in the process. The youth had ended up in hospital, bitching about being beaten up.

He stood for a moment, breathing in the clean air. It made a change from some bases, where the taste of aircraft fuel lay on your tongue all day long.

A brief flare of light came from No. 2 hangar, which housed three Lynx helicopters undergoing maintenance. Oakes froze, looking off to one side of the hangar. It came again . . . definitely a light.

He edged closer, his approach silent on the thick grass, glancing towards the garage in case Killick was watching. He reached for his radio, then decided to leave it; he was already too close and the noise would carry.

He wanted this one to be a real surprise.

A small side door was open. As Oakes stepped inside he heard a scrape of noise echo through the hangar. He hefted his heavy rubber flashlight and moved towards the bank of switches that would illuminate the overhead lights.

He felt rather than heard the door swing to behind him, and a swish of disturbed air ran across the back of his neck.

'Hey – come out—!'

His words were choked off as he was slammed back against the wall. His head connected sickeningly with a heating pipe, and a spray of lights burst in front of his eyes.

Oakes possessed some expertise in martial arts, and had represented his squadron in inter-service bouts, holding his own against younger men. Dazed as he was, he instinctively moved sideways and lashed out with a boot, a move designed to drop his attacker where he stood. But the man was no longer there.

He flicked on his torch, and instantly felt a sharp pain in his hand, as if he'd been electrocuted. The torch fell from nerveless fingers and hit the floor of the hangar, the bulb popping with the impact. He heard a sharp intake of breath barely four feet away, then a vice-like hand gripped his throat.

In the darkness, Oakes realized with awful certainty that whoever this man was, he was no local thief looking for what he could steal. Even as he thought it, he experienced a sharp pain in his gut, like the very worst kind of belly cramp, and his bladder gave way, flooding his pants with a hot gush of urine. Through the pain, he wondered how he was going to explain this to Killick and the others, being taken down like a novice.

Then he was sliding down the wall, the hand gone from his throat and his legs no longer holding him upright. He hit the floor in a sitting position, head lolling, his breath sliding out of him in a rush. God, he felt tired.

A beam of light stabbed through the darkness, and he saw a vague face in the background staring down at him.

'What the fu—?' he tried to ask, then gave up, the effort too much.

The last thing he felt as he rolled on his side was his head hitting the oil-scented concrete floor of the hangar. The last image he saw, looming overhead in the reflected torchlight, was the familiar blade of a Lynx helicopter.

Kassim slipped out of the giant hangar through a rear door and walked towards the fence where he had prepared an escape route. He slid through the gap and jogged across the fields, sticking close to a stone wall until he reached a narrow lane. He thought he heard a faint shout behind him, but it might have been his imagination.

Dealing with Oakes had been easy. But it had brought no satisfaction. The man was just a name, a person on the list. He hadn't even been at the compound. But his instructors had been adamant: not every death would have a connection, but each was about laying a confusing trail.

He was feeling nauseous again, with frequent

attacks of bile rising in his throat. He had put it down to the rigours of his travels and the intense stress he was under, but a small part of him was beginning to wonder.

Parked up against the wall near a clutch of trees was a battered Ford Fiesta collected from a dealer at a used car lot in an area called West Drayton near Heathrow airport. The man had barely spoken, merely handing him the keys and wishing him God's protection. The car was old and tired, but it had served well enough to get him here, allowing him to stay off public transport and dictate his own pace. He jumped over the wall and climbed into the car, and drove away back towards the M4 motorway.

Thirty-Seven

'Jesus, this guy's a fucking killing machine,' Ken Deane muttered helplessly on the other end of the telephone. 'Who the hell's next?'

Harry stared out at a bus full of airport workers going off duty, and wished he had an answer. He was back at El Segundo military base for a flight to Pristina in Kosovo. He knew that the only way to move this business along was to go to the source of the problem: the compound near Mitrovica. Deane had nobody on the ground sufficiently skilled in investigative work, and Harry was the only person he could call on. It meant a long flight with no guaranteed outcome, but they had no choice. Harry wasn't prepared to sit around waiting for the next grisly development.

'I've got you on a military jet to the Slatina air base complex at Pristina International,' Deane had explained, after Harry told him what he wanted to do. 'It should take about ten hours.'

'Make it two seats,' said Harry. 'I'm taking backup.'

'Ferris?'

'Yes. Is that a problem?'

'No. I figured you had him around somewhere. Just keep him out of the limelight.'

After finishing with Bikovsky, he and Rik had been forced to spend the night in a hotel. While waiting for the flight, Harry had called Deane to see if there were any updates. It couldn't have been much worse: the reports of yet another KFOR-associated murder, this time in England.

With regular flights between Moscow and London Heathrow, Kassim had probably walked on to a plane after his attempt on Koslov and straight off the other end, with no reason for anyone in UK immigration to detain him. The following evening a security alert at a small helicopter base in Gloucestershire had revealed a dead RAF corporal, Malcolm Oakes, also with the UN sign carved into his chest.

'Oakes was due for a tour of the Falklands,' said Deane. 'He'd just finished a training course in the north of England and was on a temporary posting at the base in Gloucestershire to beef up security while they had people coming back from overseas.'

'Didn't he get the warning?' Harry asked.

'He did. Your Ministry of Defence sent out a written letter telling him to remain on the base pending developments.' He sighed. 'They found the envelope in his pocket. He hadn't opened it.'

So Oakes had received the same treatment as the others. But with no close witnesses, there was little to go on and nothing significant from anywhere else, either. A woman cleaner at Moscow's Domodedovo airport had seen a thin-faced man 'vigorously' washing his hands and forearms, then being sick in the toilets. It had been odd behaviour but hardly pointed towards a serial killer; go almost anywhere in Moscow and you could see people being ill following a heavy session on bootleg vodka.

The man's description could have fitted any number of people in transit through the airport, and so far there was no camera footage available to back up the cleaner's claims. At the helicopter base where Oakes had been murdered, a fellow guard named Killick had seen a figure hurrying from the hangar towards the perimeter fence, but had been too far away to make pursuit possible. He'd taken it to be another opportunist intruder . . . until he'd discovered his colleague's body.

'You realize there are only four of you left, don't you?' Deane asked. 'Bikovsky, Koslov, Pendry and you.'

There was silence as they contemplated what had happened, and what would happen again if Kassim wasn't stopped. If the newspapers got a sniff, they would have a field day about the UN's inability to protect its own against a knife-wielding maniac bent on revenge.

'Have the Aeroflot passenger lists thrown up anything?'

'We're narrowing it down – or at least the FBI is. There are three possibles at the moment, all unaccompanied male passengers who flew from the US to Moscow on Middle East or European passports. They're running a check of late flights from Moscow to London as we speak. Once they've got the right one, they'll have a name and passport details, and where he got his tickets. I'm willing to bet it'll be right here in New York.'

'Nothing on the woman, Demescu?'

'Not a whisper. She's either gone to ground in the local community or she's back in central Europe.' Deane sighed, his frustration at being so in the dark and helpless clearly showing. 'I just wish we knew where this Kassim was going to pop up next. It's like he's got a fucking crystal ball.'

Harry rang off and looked for Rik, who was chatting to a young woman in a USAF uniform. They had another hour before boarding their flight. He couldn't help wondering if they were wasting their time going to Kosovo when Kassim might even now be heading back to the States, and any information he picked up in the Balkans could prove futile. On the other hand, if he kept on the move, at least Kassim wouldn't know where he was, which was good.

He stopped in mid-stride, his brain spinning. Something Deane had said . . .

He rang Deane again, who said, 'What's up – miss your flight?'

'You said Oakes was on a temporary posting to the base in Gloucestershire.'

'That's right. He'd been there three days.'

'With Demescu in the wind, how would Kassim have known that?'

The silence on the other end was palpable, then Deane said, 'I'll call you back. When's your flight?'

'Just under an hour.'

Thirty minutes later, Deane called.

'Remember Demescu's supervisor – a techy nerd named Ehrlich?'

'Yes. A nervous type.'

'And with good reason. They shared drinkies, he admitted that at the outset. It looks like she's been playing him. Security checked his work-station and found a memory stick concealed in the handle of his rucksack. It was full of data from the personnel records. Ehrlich's been carrying information out of the building to Demescu, and from her to Kassim. The last data he downloaded was about Oakes, lifted from British MoD personnel movement records.'

'So he took over from her.'

'Yeah. He had a programme running that updated any new information on each of the names. We should have spotted it.'

'Does Ehrlich know you're on to him?'

'Not yet.'

'Good. Let him run. Demescu must still be out there somewhere. She probably knows who some of Kassim's other helpers are – like the source of the tickets he's using.'

'Hell of a way to operate; they must have known we'd make the connection sooner or later.'

'Maybe. But it was never meant to be a long-term arrangement. They probably figured on being long gone before then. And Kassim wouldn't care.'

'What do you mean?'

'Everything he's done indicates he's on a one-way trip. He's not using multiple documents to travel and he's taking bigger risks. It's as if he knows when this is over, he'll be burned, and the others will fade into the background. Let Ehrlich run but monitor his movements.'

'You got it. This guy's gonna be more carefully watched from now on than the Secretary-General himself. What are you going to do?'

'I'm staying put in LA. Kosovo can wait. You'll have to pass my apologies to the military. I want to draw Kassim in.'

'How?'

'By laying some bait.'

'What are you suggesting?'

Harry had already had an idea which might draw Kassim out of the woodwork. 'We can start by updating the UN computer records on Bikovsky. Put him back in his apartment in Venice Beach, say, nursing a broken leg.'

Deane gave a grim laugh. 'Christ, a British hunting trick from the days of the Raj. Put out a wounded goat and wait for the tiger.'

'More or less,' Harry agreed. He didn't care for Bikovsky, but he drew the line at coldly using the man as such obvious bait. But he could use the address and Kassim's knowledge of its location at no risk to anyone else. 'You'll have to spice it up a bit,' he added. 'Make it really worth his while coming.'

'How do we do that?'

'Put in something that Ehrlich will be bound to pass on.'

'Like what?'

'Let him know I'll be there as well.'

Thirty-Eight

In the cramped toilets of the flight from Heathrow to Los Angeles, Kassim's urine looked luridly purple under the bulkhead light. He stared at his reflection in the mirror with dismay; the last few days had done more to wear him down physically and mentally than the years in the inhospitable hills of Afghanistan. Then, he'd been in constant danger of being caught by the Americans or the Afghan army, or being vaporized by one of their drones. Yet nothing had wreaked more visible damage on him than the days since leaving the hills on this mission.

He'd developed dark shadows beneath his eyes, making his cheekbones more prominent, and his shaven jaw was like that of a man only days away from death, with a sallow greyness to his skin. Assaulted by rushed convenience meals snatched between flights, and rare stretches of sleep which were becoming increasingly restless and disturbed, his body was beginning to rebel. His digestive system, schooled after years of deprivation in the hills to exist on a meagre diet of dried meat, coarse bread and little water, was now collapsing, causing him acute stomach pains and loose bowels.

He filled a plastic beaker with water and swallowed three of the pills he'd got from the man who had supplied the car in West Drayton. He had explained that he needed something to help him make the long drive without stopping, and to overcome a pain in his gut. The man had told Kassim that his sister was a pharmacist and knew about such things. He'd made a brief phone call and within minutes a small bottle with a dozen pills was Kassim's, in exchange for fifty English pounds.

As he emptied the cup he recognized that it wasn't merely his physical self he needed to preserve; his mental shell, armoured over the years to shut out the disabling emotions of fear and doubt, was showing signs of severe strain. He wondered what kind of pills he could take to rectify that particular problem.

Someone rattled the folding door and a warning tone sounded, followed by an announcement that they were shortly coming in to land. Kassim put the remaining pills in his pocket. He would keep them for later, for as much as he had so far accomplished, there was still a lot to do. And though the binder in his jacket was now thinner than it had been, his task was still far from over. Apart from the Americans, Bikovsky and Pendry, who still lived, there was their leader whom he had come so tantalizingly close to.

He took out the binder. He now knew a little more about the Englishman, Tate, than he had before. He was a member of the British Security

Service known as MI5. Kassim knew about such operatives; they were trained in covert work and were skilled investigators as well as experts in counter-offensive methods. It could not be long before their paths crossed and, God willing, if he was strong enough and watchful, Kassim was sure he could take this man, too.

He returned to his seat and fastened his seatbelt. The overhead television screen was showing CNN highlights. He slipped on his earphones and watched a smiling group of politicians, hair gently ruffled by a breeze gusting off a river behind them. Kassim recognized the building the English called Big Ben, on the River Thames.

In the foreground, his arm around the shoulders of another man, stood the figure of Anton Kleeman.

Evening was approaching in Venice Beach, as a young woman skater glided gracefully along the bike path, virtually silent on rubber wheels. A group of three old women, skin etched deeply by years in the sun, talked and watched their dogs perform. Elsewhere the sound of homeward-bound traffic drifted across the rooftops, signalling the close of another Californian day.

Harry adjusted his position and sipped from a bottle of spring water. From his position on the sand by a trailer used for carrying jet skis, he was able to see the spread of the sidewalk, giving him ample time to study the faces going by. Behind him the Pacific was whispering on the shore two hundred yards out, and a few lone walkers stood outlined against the gleam of the water.

He'd spotted the position earlier, while he and Rik were trawling for observation points. The pool of shadow thrown by the trailer was ideal, and as a vantage point it was as good as he was going to get. Satisfied that it covered all angles, he had made his way back between the bungalows and low-rise apartment blocks, to a narrow back street of art galleries, cafés and souvenir shops. At the end was an army-surplus store selling bleached chinos, jeans and swimwear. Rik was already dressed to blend in, in T-shirt and jeans, but Harry needed something similar. He selected bleached khaki shorts, a baseball cap and a dark, baggy sweatshirt. After changing in the store's fitting room, he went to another store and bought some deck shoes, then left his normal clothes in the rental car and made his way back down to the beach.

Like any other solitary stroller looking for peace and quiet, he'd wandered down to the shoreline and paddled in the water, allowing it to pool around his legs and splash up his pants. By the time he'd wandered back up the beach, his gait a little unsteady, Harry had become a rumpled beach bum, hazy-eyed after too much booze and sun, one of the invisible injured spirits with nowhere special to go.

He squatted down in the shadow of the trailer, pulling an old tyre beneath his head and adjusting the baseball cap over his eyes. The position gave him a good view of the alleyway between the Tex-Mex restaurant and Bikovsky's apartment block. If he lifted himself carefully, he could see down the alley to the road at the far end. With the exception of one or two food stalls and the weightlifting area, which was now deserted save for a solitary figure doing stretching exercises, he had an uninterrupted field of vision for a hundred yards each way.

He took out a small radio handset borrowed from the security office at El Segundo and inserted the earpiece, then keyed the button.

'Very fetching look, dude.' It was Rik Ferris in the weightlifting pen. 'Wait 'til I tell Jean you've gone native.'

Harry smiled. 'Watch and learn, junior. Don't go pulling a muscle.'

'It's about the only thing I will pull down here. If the local talent isn't doing a ton on blades, they've got a dog in tow. How's a guy supposed to strike up a conversation like that?'

'You're not. You're here to work. You set?'

'I'm set. You think he'll come?'

'Depends when he flies in. But he'll come. Don't count on spotting him too easily, though.' The photo of a young Kassim received from Koslov had been almost useless, and no amount of enhancing by Rik or the FBI's own attempts had made the face any more recognizable than a hundred others in the area.

'No problem, boss. Hey, does the budget allow me to buy some of those fancy leather weight-lifting gloves? These bars are really rough on the hands.'

'Dream on, sunshine – and keep your eyes open.' Harry cut the connection and used his mobile to check in with Deane. Earlier, he'd had to fight off the security man's suggestions to flood

251

the beach with LAPD SWAT teams and FBI special agents. At any other time it would have made sense; right now they would have stood out like a marching band. Kassim would smell armed men as soon as he came anywhere near.

Deane had given in reluctantly, conceding that an open firefight within sight of the beach would be a public relations disaster. He had settled instead with getting them the use of radios to keep in touch.

'How's it looking down there?' he asked.

'Clear,' Harry told him. The nearest person was a tiny old woman in a long, shapeless shift and worn tennis shoes, shuffling along the sand twenty yards away.

'Good. The LAPD have got Bikovsky under guard in a safe place. And we think we've got the name Kassim's been using. It's Zef Haxhi. The FBI used one of their fancy algorithms to pull up name repeats related to all the airports and places where the kills have been made.'

'Good work,' said Harry.

'Well, he's not trying too hard to hide, as you said. He's used the same passport all the way, into the US from Brussels, down to Columbus, then to Moscow and London, now back to LA. His entry form describes him as a student of agriculture from Rawalpindi University. The trip was arranged under their student overseas study programme, and we're re-checking the details down to the last dot and comma. But it could take time.'

'Who arranged the visas?'

Deane gave a humourless chuckle. 'There's the

252

irony: the field study programme he's travelling on is funded jointly with the American University of Kosovo. Can you believe that? I suspect that's where the paper trail began.'

Harry sympathized with his mood. They had been clever. Any student travelling from Pakistan would have many hoops to jump through; one linked to an American university based in Europe, however, might have an easier ride. 'The name's not Pakistani, though, is it?'

'No. It's Albanian. Another neat trick: there are a few eastern Europeans and Pakistani nationals on exchange programmes with both campuses, and I'm betting we'll find a Zef Haxhi on the roll somewhere. They'd have needed something that stood up to a cursory check, at the very least.'

Another indicator, thought Harry, of the planning behind this. He sat up, trying to read what was going on here. 'This isn't a terrorist exercise.'

'What?' Deane sounded surprised.

'Kassim hasn't just come down from the hills to knock off a few UN soldiers. This is something bigger. What did that blogger call it?'

'A spectacular. But there was no connection that we could find. It could have meant anything or nothing. You know how these nut jobs build up the chatter to get air time and headlines.'

Nut jobs. Harry's experience of nut jobs was that they were never dangerous, but neither were they this organized or focussed.

'There's something else,' Deane added. 'Ehrlich, the IT nerd who was helping Demescu? He's dropped out of sight. Ditched the watchers we put

253

on him and vanished. We've changed all the access security codes, so Kassim or Haxhi or whatever the hell he calls himself is now running blind.'

Harry didn't think that would slow Kassim down. He'd proved himself to be a careful operator so far, creating mayhem at will. If he found he couldn't raise a response from Demescu or Ehrlich, he would almost certainly drop right off the grid and abandon any other contacts as no longer safe.

Then something Deane had said earlier hit him. 'Wait . . . You said *back* to LA? Was that supposition or is Kassim back already?'

'You mean the FBI didn't tell you?' Deane swore softly. 'An unaccompanied male named Zef Haxhi travelling on a European passport flew in from London Heathrow two hours ago. He's probably already somewhere in the greater Los Angeles area.'

Thirty-Nine

Harry's neck stirred uneasily at the knowledge that Kassim was already here. With the airport just a few miles away, and even allowing for lengthy delays at immigration, it meant he could now be sitting somewhere very close, watching. With his kill record so far, it was an uncomfortable sensation.

'I'll get back to you,' he told Deane, and cut him off in mid-sentence. He looked across to where Rik was doing some lazy stretches, and hit the transmit button on the radio. 'Our man's already here. He landed two hours ago.'

'What? You kidding me?' Rik muttered something obscene and stopped what he was doing. 'Do they know who he is?'

'He's down as a student, using the name Zef Haxhi. Eyes wide open, you hear?'

'Yes, Dad.'

Harry cut the connection and went back to studying the area in front of the shops and apartment blocks. The evening visitors were already beginning to show themselves along the sidewalk, a colourful mix of after-work strollers, ancient hippies, pairs and singles, moving aimlessly in their own world, content to be in the cool anonymity of the evening shadows. Among them was a new breed of bladers and riders, their outfits even more garish than their daytime counterparts as they swooped and glided along the pathway.

There was an increase in traffic, along with one or two police patrols and the occasional delivery van. A sanitation truck rumbled along the edge of the sand, emptying garbage cans, while a sweeper buzzed along the cycle path, damping down the day's dust with a fine spray of water.

A yellow pizza van nosed into the alleyway from the far end and stopped outside Bikovsky's apartment block. A young man in whites leapt from the cab and disappeared inside bearing a flat box, and reappeared moments later folding something into his trouser pocket. He reversed the van with smooth skill and disappeared out the far side.

Harry relaxed; even if it had been Kassim, he

wouldn't have had time to get to the first floor and back down.

'Boss.' It was Rik, sounding puzzled. 'Two hundred yards at nine o'clock . . . guy in a yellow shirt, jacket and jeans. Isn't he supposed to be somewhere else?'

Harry shifted his weight and focussed on a knot of strollers in front of a café and an ethnic jeweller's. At first he saw nobody he recognized. Then he felt a jolt of surprise. A large, muscular figure was ambling along the path, hands in his pockets. He appeared unhurried and relaxed, nothing like a man whose life might be hanging in the balance.

Harry rang Deane. It was quicker than fighting his way through the LAPD network. 'I thought you said Bikovsky was in a safe place under guard?'

'He is.'

'Not from where I'm sitting. Right now he's walking towards his apartment.'

'Christ . . . can you stop him?'

Bikovsky was just passing the Tex-Mex. As he did so, Maria appeared in the restaurant doorway. She glanced at him without reacting, then turned and walked back inside.

'No to that,' said Harry. 'Not without breaking cover.' He cut the connection and rang Bikovsky's mobile, hoping he had the sense to pick up. It rang a dozen times. No answer. He keyed the radio and said to Rik, 'There's nothing we can do. Hold your position. He'll have to take his chances.'

'Amen to that,' said Rik.

Back in the alleyway, a small panel truck stopped alongside a pile of cardboard produce boxes

256

stacked against the wall of the Tex-Mex restaurant. The driver climbed out and began throwing the boxes into the van. Behind him, a trail bike pulled up and the rider leaned it against a wall. He was wearing a white apron and took a pizza box from the pannier on the back.

Everything about the place was telling Kassim that this was wrong. His antennae were buzzing, a sure sign of trouble that had helped him avoid Russian forces in Chechnya and American Taliban hunters in Afghanistan. Yet there was nothing obvious to cause him concern. People were coming out for the evening, minds on their excesses, and everything about the decadent beach community seemed as normal as it ever could. Yet he felt an underlying movement in the air, like the buzz of night flies around his head.

He had retrieved the pizza box from a nearby garbage can, and a white towel tucked into his trousers gave the appearance of an apron. Pizza delivery boys in America were numerous and practically invisible. It made perfect cover.

Yet the memory of his trip through immigration at Los Angeles was making his head hurt. Three times he had been sick on the way here. He'd cursed himself for not thinking sooner of a change of passport. It was an unforgivable lapse. All it needed was for the Americans to have picked up on the frequent use of the Haxhi passport in the last few days, and they would have him.

In the immigration queue his heart had been thumping wildly, and the pulse in his temples seemed set to explode. When the uniformed immigration officer had queried his reasons for visiting, Kassim had not heard him. The officer, a muscular young man in crisp white shirt and dark pants, had peered hard at Kassim through steel spectacles.

'Tough flight, huh?' he'd said sympathetically. Then he'd repeated his question.

It had been too close for Kassim's increasingly fragile peace of mind. Once he was clear he'd gone straight to the washroom and thrown up. He'd emerged feeling dizzy and nauseous, and realized he needed something to regenerate his energy. He'd found a cheap restaurant and forced down some food, fighting against his lack of appetite and an over-abundance of grease.

After eating, he'd located a phone box and called Remzi in New York.

The travel agent had not been pleased to hear from him. 'You should not be calling me,' he'd hissed. 'What do you want?'

'I need new papers,' Kassim had said, brushing aside Remzi's arguments. 'Also a passport. Send them to the Marriott Hotel on West Century Boulevard near Los Angeles airport. I will collect them.'

'I cannot—' Remzi began, but Kassim interrupted him.

'You can – you *must*!' he snapped. 'The Americans know I am here.'

'*What? But you must flee! What if you are caught?*' Remzi's voice rose to a screech, and it was clear that he feared for his own freedom. If Kassim were picked up, his own situation was compromised.

'That's why I need new papers and tickets, you

idiot! If I use the Haxhi papers again, they will take me.' He overrode the agent's protests by telling him where he was going next, and that it had to be soon.

It was enough to get Remzi to agree. 'I will use a person in Los Angeles,' he said, as if talking to himself. 'Yes, that is what I will do. He is very good but very expensive . . . but the situation demands it. Absolutely, we will do that, I—'

'When?' Kassim finally cut him short. This cowardly idiot might go on for hours.

'What?'

'When will I have them?'

'Oh. Yes. I should be able to get a passport to you by this evening. It will be enough to get you out of the country, but that is all. Wait one minute.' The phone went down with a thump.

Kassim waited, knowing that Remzi was only doing it as a means for his own safety; the sooner he got Kassim out of his hair, the sooner he would be able to go back to his normal life.

Remzi came back moments later to explain that Kassim's new name would be Roberto Lucchini, a third-generation Italian from New York. The paperwork would be good, Remzi warned, but might not stand close scrutiny.

'It does not matter,' Kassim told him. Just one more journey, he thought, and it would all be over.

'I will also enclose travel vouchers for your next trip,' Remzi added. 'You must pick up the tickets at the airport using your new passport.'

Kassim thanked him and cut the connection. Then he made a phone reservation at the Marriott, explaining that a package would be arriving and to hold it for his arrival later that evening. He had no intention of using the room, and he doubted the authorities would ever think of looking for him in such a prestigious establishment. As his trainers had explained, a hotel was an ideal post box.

Next he needed transportation. Walking out of the terminal, he had narrowly missed stepping in front of a courier on a weather-beaten trail bike with a noisy engine. Unbelievably, the young rider had left the bike at the kerb without taking the key. Like all *mujahedin*, Kassim had ridden mopeds and Japanese motorbikes extensively in the mountains, often loaded with weapons; LA traffic was easy by comparison.

Now, walking down the alleyway, Kassim noted the garbage collector out of the corner of his eye. He ignored the rumble of nerves in his stomach and kept walking. The man might be genuine or he could be a policeman waiting for Kassim to make an appearance. A young woman peering out of a side door across the alleyway shooed off a scavenging dog, then went back inside. Another police officer?

Then he was in the doorway on his left and walking down a gloomy corridor. A sweet smell hung in the air, and the faint sound of music came from behind one of the two doors on the ground floor. He walked up a flight of bare concrete stairs. He hesitated on the landing, sniffing at the air. A large window at the end of the corridor let in the dying light. No signs of anyone lying in wait.

He had already torn away the edge of the pizza box nearest to him, and slipped his hand inside, grasping the rubberized handle of the shark knife he'd bought earlier from a local dive shop. He muttered a faint prayer and glanced at the fragment of blue cloth in his other hand.

He knocked on Bikovsky's door.

'*Pizza*,' he chanted, the way he'd heard the delivery boys do it. Here, his accent didn't matter; most delivery boys were of foreign extraction.

There was a shuffling sound inside, and a grunt as Bikovsky approached the door. Kassim felt his stomach tighten and a buzzing began in his ears as the adrenalin kicked in. A glimmer of movement showed in the peep hole, then the door clicked and swung open.

Kassim had a momentary flash of recognition as the man in the doorway emerged from the gloom within the apartment, followed by a fleeting second of doubt. Then the hunting mechanism took over. He flung the pizza box to one side and lunged forward with the knife, his arm as rigid as an iron bar. The blade bit deep, ripping through flesh and vital organs, and Kassim used his free hand to palm-heel the stricken man in the chest, causing him to stagger backwards until his foot caught on a rug and pitched him over with a crash. He lay still, making a hollow keening sound, his eyes wide with shock.

Kassim followed him down, pinning his shoulders. The man's heels drummed on the floor as shock crashed through his system, and his breathing became ragged.

Then Kassim stared at him with a sense of

puzzlement and disbelief. *Something was not right.* He stood up and rolled the dying man on to his front. With the bloodied point of the knife he ripped open his rear pocket and took out his wallet, flipped it open to reveal a driver's licence.

It wasn't Bikovsky.

Then his nerves got the better of him and he was up and running, out of the room where death was hovering and along the corridor. He'd walked into a trap. Instead of Bikovsky, he had killed a police officer – maybe a member of the American FBI. It had been a close resemblance, but in the poor light of the apartment building, an understandable error.

As he ran past an open doorway, a woman stepping out saw the bloodied knife and screamed, a nerve-jangling wail which ran through the whole building.

Forty

Harry and Rik heard the blood-curdling scream and were up and running together, scrabbling for purchase on the soft sand. Harry switched channels on his radio and called for backup from the LAPD, then concentrated on getting towards the alleyway through the groups of evening strollers.

As they entered the building, there was a crash of breaking glass from upstairs and the woman screamed again.

'He's outside,' said Harry, and turned back

towards the alleyway while Rik continued up the stairs. 'Check Bikovsky – but be careful!'

Outside a cluster of curious onlookers had gathered, forming a barrier across the alley. Over their heads Harry saw Maria, backlit in the kitchen door of the Tex-Mex. She was gesturing towards the far end, where the alley opened into the back streets of Venice Beach. He drew his gun and forced his way through the crowd, instantly making progress once people caught sight of the Ruger.

As he burst out of the alley, he nearly collided with a trail bike wheeling away with its engine screaming, the rider casting a glance over his shoulder. His face was thin and his eyes burning, and Harry knew without a doubt that this was the man they were looking for.

Kassim was heading across a patch of open ground towards Pacific Avenue, where Harry guessed there would be a hundred and one ways for him to disappear. For a brief second he considered trying for a shot at the killer, but two kids on bikes appeared in the background and he lowered his gun.

In the distance he heard the wail of police sirens, and thumbed the safety catch, slipping the Ruger under his shirt. This was no time to be caught waving a handgun in the middle of Los Angeles by a nervous and trigger-happy cop who might shoot first and ask questions later.

'It wasn't Bikovsky,' he told Deane twenty minutes later. He was watching a paramedic drape a green sheet over the body in Bikovsky's

263

apartment. The dead man was Eddie, the batter. It explained why Maria had shown no signs of recognition when the man had walked by.

Further along the corridor other officers were questioning the woman whose screams had alerted them to Kassim's presence. She had been fortunate to survive with nothing more damaging than a jolt to her system and a small cut from flying glass when Kassim had made his exit through the window.

Harry handed his mobile to a crime scene officer so that Deane could vouch for his and Rik's presence. The detective listened and handed it back with a nod, and Harry promised to call Deane later when they were cleared to leave.

It took only a few minutes, with the arrival of an LAPD crime squad lieutenant named McKenzie, to add a surname and occupation to the dead man.

'It's Eddie Cruz, professional scumbag,' the cop muttered coldly. 'He finally got his true and just deserts.' He bent and peered with professional interest at the knife wound, then into Eddie's sightless eyes. 'I guess it's true: there is a God up there.'

'You know him, then?' said Harry. The cop probably knew all the local names on his territory, right down to their shoe sizes.

McKenzie looked sour. 'Yeah, more's the pity. He was a strong-arm guy for a local organization and reputedly moonlighting for one or two others. He breaks things for people . . . arms and legs, mostly. We figured him for a recent murder up in Bel Air. Some kid making porno movies was getting too big a share of the market. The established guys didn't like it and they warned him off. He kept working. Next thing was we found him in a dumpster with his head caved in. We couldn't prove it was Cruz who did it, but the signs looked right.'

'Do you know his friend Marty?'

The cop looked surprised. 'For someone who's only visiting, you get around the nicest people. Yeah, we know Bell. Him and Cruz are two of a kind, like evil twins. How come you know them?'

Harry explained briefly about his encounter with the men, drawing a fresh look of appraisal from McKenzie, who looked as if he would like to have seen it.

'When that news gets round,' he said shortly, 'you'll make a lot of new friends – mostly in the porno business.'

A few minutes later, Harry and Rik were walking down the stairs.

'Where are we going?' Rik asked.

Harry had got away from McKenzie by using the excuse that he needed to confer with Deane in New York. What he really wanted was to talk to Bikovsky before the LAPD and the FBI put the ex-Marine off-limits.

'I've got a feeling Bikovsky knows more than he thinks . . . or more than he's letting on.'

They were met outside by a crowd of onlookers being pushed back behind a police cordon. Among them were Jerry, concerned about the apartment he let to Bikovsky, and Maria. She was hugging her arms around her, face creased with concern.

'It's not Bikovsky,' Harry explained to Maria. 'Just a man who was unlucky enough to look like him.'

Maria nodded, relief flickering briefly across her face. 'Thank you,' she said, and turned away, disappearing into the crowd, anxious to distance herself from the presence of so many police officers.

'Hey – what about my apartment?' Jerry demanded, pushing forward. 'Did they tear the place up? Am I gonna have to get the place cleaned or what, huh? That no-hoper, Bikovsky . . . he's nothing but trouble!'

A few miles away, on the outskirts of Los Angeles International, Kassim pulled out of the heavy evening traffic and turned in to a block of cargo warehouses. Satisfied he was unobserved, he killed the engine and dumped the trail bike behind a garbage skip, retrieving his rucksack and throwing it over his shoulder. He could see the airport buildings in the distance, and quickly made his way on foot towards them. He was beginning to shake from the kill and the subsequent chase, and was experiencing dizziness again and loss of vision. He badly needed to get cleaned up and to rest, to let the reaction pass before showing up at the Marriott to collect his new passport and travel vouchers.

He arrived at a perimeter road, on the other side of which were the terminal buildings and public car parks. He remembered belatedly that Americans never walked if they could ride, and that he could have used the bike without standing out. He'd been careless, but he put it down to not feeling well. Even so, it was a lesson for the next few hours.

He arrived at the nearest terminal building and found a deserted washroom where he was able to clean himself up and change his shirt. He was covered in a film of perspiration and dust from his ride across the patch of rough ground, and had some minor cuts on his hands where he had burst through the window of the apartment block into the alleyway.

He glanced down and saw a patch of blood on the thigh of his pants from where he had shoved the knife before jumping from the building. He pulled the blade out and rinsed it under the tap, then wrapped it in some paper towels and put it in his rucksack. He would have to dispose of it later. For now, though, he felt safer having it within reach.

As he was holding his leg under a hot-air dryer, he felt a shock penetrate his gut. Something was missing.

The fragment of blue cloth. He'd dropped it!

He searched everywhere, but knew it was no good. He felt as if a piece of him had been ripped away. This was bad. Very bad. He walked up and down, shaking his head, trying to figure out what to do. It was pointless going back; he'd be seen and locked up – or worse, shot dead. Yet it represented a major part of why he was here . . . why he was doing this. How could he have been so careless? It must have happened after he'd killed the American, on his way out of the building.

He forced himself to remain calm and took a deep breath, then drank some cold water. It was time to let go. He could still complete his task. But first he needed to change his profile.

The men chasing him back at the apartment buildings would have got a partial look at him at least. One in particular, who had emerged from the alleyway just as he was leaving on the motorcycle: the Englishman, Tate. It had been close – too close – and he was amazed Tate had not used a weapon. Had it been him, Kassim would not have hesitated.

The outer door rattled and Kassim ducked his face into a basin. A man came in and used one of the cubicles, then stepped across to the basins to wash his hands. He was carrying a sports bag in one hand and in the other a lightweight tan windcheater with a dark blue lining. Kassim went into a cubicle, noisily locking the door, then counted to five before silently slipping the catch and stepping out again.

The man had his head down, soaping his face. His windcheater lay on top of the sports bag at his feet. As Kassim stepped past him, he reached down and scooped up the garment, and was out the door before the man even knew it had gone.

Ten minutes later, having reversed the windcheater and flung it across his shoulders, Kassim found a cafeteria and took a spare seat at a table of Spanish tourists, nodding gratefully as they made room for him.

As he drank a glass of iced coke, allowing his nerves to settle, he noticed a *Herald Tribune* lying on a chair. On the front was a picture of a wartorn building, scarred by fire and pockmarked by shell holes. The photo looked dated, with a woman standing in the centre of the shot, staring in shock at a body lying twisted and burned among the bricks and dust. Kassim was about to look away when he noticed a familiar name in a side column. He picked up the paper and followed the page reference.

UN SPECIAL ENVOY KLEEMAN RETURNING TO KOSOVO.

Inside was a large photo of Anton Kleeman.

Forty-One

Harry also noticed the headline as Rik was scrolling for news on his laptop. They were in an airport hotel, waiting for Deane to call back. Harry had asked him to use his influence to gain access to Bikovsky. He would have to go through the FBI and the LAPD, both of whom were probably claiming primary control over him; the police for questioning about events at his apartment and the FBI for the wider investigation into the UN team murders.

'This can't be good,' Rik commented. He clicked on a link and brought up the picture of Kleeman in a camouflage jacket, smiling into the cameras. It was not a current picture and Kleeman had put on a little weight since 1999.

'It's not.' Harry immediately saw the significance and rang Deane. This couldn't wait.

'When was Kleeman's Kosovo trip planned?' he asked.

'I don't know,' Deane admitted. 'I'd have to check. Karen Walters is right here.'

'Ask her. It's important.'

Deane turned away and there was a rumbling of voices before he came back on. 'It's been on his itinerary for a while, arranged over four months ago. I think it's part of his schedule for worldwide domination.'

'Then that's when the planning began.'

'What planning?'

'The plan to kill him.'

'*What?*' Deane yelped.

'You've got to call it off.'

'Can't be done. What are you talking about, kill him?'

Harry took a deep breath. He didn't know if Deane was being deliberately obtuse or simply in denial. 'Don't you see this is a set-up? The whole thing: the killings, the timing of the rumours, the drip-feed of details to the media, the talk of a "spectacular" – and now Kleeman going to visit Kosovo. It's all linked.'

'Harry, you're— Are you serious?'

'Think about it. Kleeman's on the kill list with everyone else. He might not be the guilty party, but that hasn't mattered to Kassim. What better way to give the UN a bloody nose than by knocking off personnel who were in Kosovo at the time *and* gaining major headlines by rounding it off with the assassination of the Special Envoy they were guarding at the time?'

'But . . . why would they?'

'Because it's not the team they're after – it's Kleeman. *He's* the "spectacular". Kassim's going to be waiting for him.'

There was a stunned silence on the line, then

270

Deane said, 'I still don't see it.' But now he didn't sound quite so sure. 'I mean, this guy's proved he can go anywhere he likes – even Moscow – so why not make the hit in New York? Jesus, Kleeman's an assassin's wet dream: he even strolls down the street to get a lunchtime hot dog. Why wait until he's in Kosovo?'

'Because in New York his death would be meaningless; just another random murder eclipsed by the latest economic recovery forecasts. In Kosovo it would have resonance. This has been their plan all along; and since hearing he's going to Kosovo, it's fallen right into their lap.'

'I hear you.' Deane sounded conflicted. 'OK, say you're right, how do we keep him safe?'

'There's only one way: by stopping Kassim. Have you got approval for me to speak to Bikovsky?'

'I'll call you back. Give me five minutes.'

While Harry was talking to Deane, Rik Ferris contacted Ripper, using the Hotmail account he had used to set up their meeting in Phenix. He kept it short and sharp.

Another job – urgent. Airline flight details. Can do? Blackjack.

He waited three minutes before a reply came.

Airlines easy. Name me the names and dates. Rate? Ripper.

Rik typed, *Passenger: Haxhi, Zef. M. 28 yrs. Euro p'port. Travelled orig Pakistan – Paris – Brussels – NY – Columbus – Moscow – UK, poss now LAX + others + future bookings. Need name of ticket source. $2000 to any account U name. Has to be quick.*

271

He waited only a minute this time. *Consider it max priority. Account will follow. Thnx for contact w Stick. Major grats.*

Rik made sure his mobile was fully charged, then sat back. Ripper was a happy bunny. That would help. He could have done the airlines search himself, but it would have taken time and patience. And something told him they would be on the move shortly. Ripper was better placed to do the job, and fast in his field. Anyone who could get inside the Department of Justice servers and ferret around undetected would find the airlines easy meat. The UN and FBI were probably working on digging out the same information, too, but he knew how they worked. Rulebooks and precious lines of delineation aside, they would give out only what information they thought necessary, and at a speed far below that of pro hackers like Ripper.

Forty-Two

Thirty minutes later, in the foyer of the Comfort Inn on West Century Boulevard in Inglewood, Harry and Rik showed their details to two LAPD officers. They were escorted to a room on the first floor with two uniformed guards stationed outside.

Bikovsky was watching television and sucking on a beer. The bedside table held the mangled remains of a meal, and judging by the number of crushed cans in the waste bin, he'd been drinking most of the day. He was unshaven and looked a mess, and Harry wondered what else he had taken to keep himself going.

The ex-Marine showed no surprise at seeing them. When Harry picked up the remote and muted the television, he started to protest, but thought better of it. Instead he pointed at the screen.

'We just been on the TV with that prick Kleeman. He looked a jerk, but we looked cool as hell.' He sank another mouthful of beer. 'You can put a prick in a uniform, but no way can you put the uniform in a prick.'

The flickering image on the television was the tail end of an evening news item about ongoing international development plans in Kosovo and Bosnia. Old footage of shell-torn houses swam into view, overlaid with white block titles of the location and a scrolling text beneath.

'You and Eddie Cruz,' said Harry, dragging Bikovsky's attention back into the room. 'You look pretty similar, did you ever notice?' A close-up of Anton Kleeman sprang into view, a politician's smile on his smooth face, against the backdrop of the UN building in New York. It looked recent.

'Can't say I did,' said Bikovsky. 'Why?'

'Because he was waiting for you at your apartment.' The news report changed to commercials, and Harry switched off the television. 'Then along came Kassim.'

Bikovsky showed no emotion, and Harry guessed the man was too far gone for the information to penetrate.

273

Rik shook his head and went over to the window, checking the car park.

'Eddie's now got his own drawer at the city morgue. He took the knife that was intended for you. He was standing in the doorway to your apartment at the time.'

Something finally seemed to reach Bikovsky's beer-soaked brain, and he rubbed his face. He started to get up to move towards the light.

'I'd stay away from the windows,' Rik told him. 'If Kassim doesn't have another try, Marty Bell might.'

'Wha—?' Bikovsky blinked and sat down again. 'What're you sayin'? I didn't kill Eddie Cruz.'

'You know that and so do we. But his friends don't. Look at it from their point of view; Eddie sits in your apartment waiting for you to turn up. He opens the door to a knock and ends up sliced and diced. Pretty easy to jump to conclusions about who might have done it, don't you think? Especially since Eddie's friends don't even know Kassim exists.' Rik smiled coldly. 'But they know you do.'

Bikovsky looked alarmed as the information sank in. 'Hey – that ain't right!'

'Scary, isn't it?' Harry said coldly. 'Let's talk about the compound at Mitrovica, shall we?'

'Aw, man,' Bikovsky protested, waving his hand. 'How many times I gotta tell you . . . I don't know shit about that place. I told you, the compound guards musta had somethin' going – or maybe this Kassim's just a twisted fuck who likes cuttin' people. I wasn't into nothin', I didn't do nothin', 'cos I didn't have time!'

274

A knock at the door had Harry and Rik reaching for their weapons. It was one of the officers from outside.

'It's Lieutenant McKenzie at Venice Beach,' he announced. 'Says there's something you have to see.'

Telling Bikovsky they'd be back, they left the hotel and drove back to the apartment building. When they arrived at the alleyway the crowd had gone, with only a few curious latecomers craning their necks to see what was happening.

They found Lieutenant McKenzie standing at the end of the corridor where Kassim had made his exit through the window into the alley. Portable lights had been erected, highlighting the area round the smashed glass, which was dusted in forensic powder. McKenzie was holding a plastic evidence bag.

'We found this snagged on the brickwork outside the window,' he said, holding up the bag for them to see. 'It didn't get there by accident.' He studied both men with serious eyes. 'You two are with the UN, right? This should interest you.'

Harry didn't explain their precise relationship with the organization, but took the bag. Inside was a piece of blue fabric, stained with dirt or rust. One edge was trimmed with leather.

Rik said, 'It's part of a beret.'

'Bingo,' McKenzie muttered, eyes glittering. 'So he does speak.'

Harry recalled what Deane had told him about the old woman's words after seeing Broms killed in Brussels. She said the killer had waved a blue handkerchief. Was this what she had seen? If so,

275

why was Kassim carrying it? And did he wave it at his victims – always assuming he'd done the same to the others – as a kind of talisman or trophy? Or was it a symbol of whatever was driving him on?

'See this?' McKenzie asked, pointing at the rust stain. 'It'll be analysed, but I don't need no lab to tell me what it is. It's dried blood.'

Harry nodded in agreement and thanked him, then signalled for Rik to follow him outside. He needed to think. Everything had happened so quickly it was beginning to feel like a film on fast-forward, and he was in danger of missing something.

They were halfway down the beach when he had a thought. Every man in the CP team had been issued with a UN beret. It was something Kleeman had requested, to show a united front. Most chose not to wear it, preferring their own regimental headgear. Some occasions, however, demanded it, especially when the UN had to be seen and identified quickly. He dialled Carl Pendry's number. The Ranger answered immediately.

'What did you do with your UN beret after your tour?'

Pendry was silent for a moment, then said, 'Handed it in, I guess, along with everything else that wasn't my own kit.' He paused. 'Why you asking?'

'Just checking something.' He gave Pendry a brief run-down of what had happened in LA and Moscow, and with a cautionary note to keep his eyes open, cut the connection. Then he rang

Deane and told him about the fragment of UN beret.

Deane recognized it as the final piece of the jigsaw – the proof the rumours had been hinting at. 'Jesus, that's all we need. OK, I'll check to see if we still have the inventories for that time. But people lose equipment. It doesn't prove this fragment came from a beret in Kosovo. It could have been picked up anywhere.'

'I know. But what are the odds?' The only way to prove it would be by forensic examination of the cloth . . . and the stains.

Deane agreed to call back as soon as he had something, then disconnected. When Harry looked up, Rik was frowning.

'What?' Harry had learned to recognize the look.

'Back at that hotel: Bikovsky was watching a news report from Kosovo.'

'I know. What about it?'

'It was old footage from when you were over there. He saw himself and Kleeman . . . and the rest of the team. Wasn't that across the border?'

'Yes. We'd crossed into Macedonia after leaving the compound. The cameras were waiting for Kleeman to do his piece.'

'What headgear were you wearing?'

Harry thought back. Rik was right: they should all have been wearing blue UN berets. Karen Walters had been there to manage the press briefing, to reinforce the UN's image. He called Bob Dosario at the FBI office on Wilshire Boulevard and explained what he wanted. The special agent was immediately helpful.

'Come on round and I'll have it sent in. I think I know which station it was.'

They drove over to Wilshire and were shown into a conference room with a large flatscreen display. A young female technician in a crisp white shirt was running through a section of film on a DVD player. Dosario welcomed the two men and gestured them to seats.

'Should be there any second. I heard about the killing down at Venice Beach. How's this going to help with your investigation?'

Harry started to explain, then was interrupted by a scene of Anton Kleeman walking away from a Sea King helicopter, his shoulders hunched under the down-draught. He was wearing a DPM smock and flanked by the security team, with Karen Walters fussing in close attendance like a mother hen.

Pendry was big and hard to miss. Behind him was Broms, scoping the crowd of press representatives with a brooding stare. Both wore blue berets. He saw himself stride into picture, signalling to someone to move position, also wearing his beret. Then Orti, the Frenchman moving in a sideways stance just behind him, and further back was Koslov's slim figure turning like a dancer, checking his back. Blue beret.

'Bikovsky,' Rik murmured. 'I don't see him.'

The picture changed, showing a smiling Anton Kleeman in front of the press corps. He was playing them like the experienced politician, lifting the collar of the camouflage smock and pulling a wry face, evidently in response to a comment by one of the reporters. The security team had moved out of the frame, forming a cordon around him but leaving him room to manoeuvre.

When the report ended, Harry turned to the young technician. 'Can you wind it right back to where we exit the helicopter?'

She did and Harry waited while the film ran again. After a few seconds he told her to stop and freeze-frame. On the very edge of the screen a familiar figure was staring off to one side, eyes in shadow.

Bikovsky.

He was wearing his Marine-issue green beret.

Harry turned to Dosario, and moments later the special agent was through to the agent-in-charge at the Comfort Inn. Bikovsky came on, his speech even more slurred.

'C'mon, Tate,' he protested. 'Leave me alone or get me outta here, will you? This place is driving me nuts. They won't even let me use my phone.'

'You'll get out when we're ready,' Harry told him. 'What did you do with your UN beret after your tour in Kosovo?'

'What?' Silence filled the line as Bikovsky tried to work out if it was a trick question. 'Shit, man . . . my *beret*? What you gonna do – bill me for some cruddy piece of military *equipment*? Is that what they pay you guys to do? I thought you was chasin' some freakin' killer.'

'Answer the question,' Harry said harshly, 'or I'll turn you out on the street and let Marty and his friends know where you are.'

'Hey, man . . . c'mon,' Bikovsky said quickly. 'Lemme think . . . it was a long time ago.' The

279

line hummed for a moment. 'Hey – I remember: the beret, yeah. I handed it over, but I never got it back. They gave me a hard time about that. But you tell me who hands in everything? It was a war zone, for Chrissake!'

'What do you mean you handed it over?'

'Like I was told to. When the convoy left, Pendry said to find spare jackets and stuff for the two civilians, 'cos they stood out like tits on a bull. I found two DPM jackets but only one helmet, so I handed over my blue beret. No way was I going to wear that pussy's colour. I was a Marine.' He laughed and gave the US Marine battle cry: *'Hoo-agh!'*

'Who did you give it to?' Harry was holding his breath, although he already knew the answer.

'Who'd ya think?' Bikovsky's voice contained outrage. 'To UN-Special-fuckin'-Rapporteur Kleeman.'

Forty-Three

Kassim stood in front of the Marriott Hotel on West Century Boulevard and checked the area for signs of police activity. It was nearly nine thirty and the eighteen-floor building was a blaze of lights. So far he had seen nothing to alarm him, save for a couple of hotel security guards checking cars in the main car park.

In spite of the late hour, the traffic entering and leaving was considerable: cars, shuttle buses and cabs streaming in and out in a constant flow, passengers mixing with aircrew. The sheer bustle of activity made Kassim feel momentarily secure, but he didn't relax his guard. If there were any police about, they were showing unusual patience; but if they were good, that was what police did the world over.

He finally stepped through the glass entrance, latching on to a group of European travellers from an airport shuttle. He felt nervous at the sheer size of the place and the surroundings, but he'd been trained for this; all he had to do was look bored – or tired. Either would do. And not catch anyone's eye. He felt uneasy about approaching the desk to check in. He didn't want to stay here, so what was the point? Then he spotted an internal phone and veered towards it.

'Concierge.'

Kassim asked if a package had arrived for him. A knot built in his gut while the man went to check. He came back and confirmed that it had.

A few minutes later, among another influx of arrivals, he approached the desk and asked for the package in the name of Roberto Lucchini. The concierge, too busy to care, barely looked at him before handing it over. Two minutes later Kassim was out of the hotel and climbing into a cab. He needed to be on the move again.

'Take me to another hotel,' he told the cabbie. 'Somewhere smaller.'

Further along West Century Boulevard, in the Comfort Inn where Bikovsky had been under guard, Harry and Rik were staring at an empty

281

room. After briefing Bob Dosario at FBI head-quarters and tossing around ideas, they had gone over the tape again frame by frame. It had been a tiring process, confirming only that Kleeman did not appear to have a UN beret, either on his head or tucked under his epaulette.

'I remember thinking we had to get them some kit,' Pendry had confirmed on the phone. 'They were both wearing DPM jackets, but I don't remember what they had on their heads.'

'Bikovsky could be lying,' Dosario had suggested reasonably.

Harry didn't think so. The Marine's response had sounded too genuine. 'He'd be taking a risk. Who would you believe – him or Kleeman?'

Dosario grinned. 'Good point. An all-state college sports champ turned international diplomat versus a sleaze with prior for rape who's now working in porno movies. Mmm . . . wonder how a jury would vote on that one?'

Harry stood up. 'Only one way to find out. Let's go see him.'

They had driven over to the Comfort Inn to talk with Bikovsky, but the ex-Marine was no longer there. An embarrassed officer who had been on guard outside the door was trying to explain how his charge had disappeared while his colleague had taken a comfort break.

'Bikovsky said he needed some ice and to stretch his legs,' muttered the officer, a fifteen-year veteran. He pointed to a machine down the corridor. 'I watch him try it, and he calls back that it's broken. He says he'll go down to the next floor, and I start to follow. Just as I do, the room phone rings and I go get it, thinking maybe it's important.' He pulled a sour face. 'When I get downstairs, he's gone. My lieutenant's gonna have my ass for this.'

Harry didn't bother trying to make him feel better; the officer had been unbelievably negligent. They left him to his fate, while his colleagues began organizing a search and Bob Dosario put out a city-wide alert to his FBI agents in the area.

On the way back to their hotel, Rik checked his email. There was a brief note from Ripper.

> *Zip file on way. See cloud. Should I be worried about Homeland Security dogging my ass? Ripper.*

There was a hypertext link to a secure cloud box where the full file could be seen, with no connections back to Ripper or the source material.

Rik waited until they were back in their hotel before responding. He wanted to see what quality of information Ripper had come up with.

He opened his laptop and clicked on the link to the secure site. There were several pages collated by Ripper taken from airline databases of passenger manifests, each with a separate link for Rik to follow if he wished. There was also a link to a travel agency in New York. He clicked on it. It belonged to a small company called Life Style Travel in Allen Street on the Lower East Side. Run by a man named Agim Remzi and offering cheap deals to resorts worldwide, it was a bucket shop offering cheap, no-frills airline travel for passengers who didn't mind going the long way round and maybe finding their own way back.

'Neat way to avoid obvious checkpoints,' Harry commented, when he saw the website. 'I wonder how many operators he's moved around the world?' He waited for Rik to pull up the pages of airline data that Ripper had uploaded. They ran to several sheets of plain text and figures showing flight numbers, airport acronyms, passenger names, seat numbers and departure and arrival times.

The name Zef Haxhi had been highlighted on each one, and the pages arranged in line with dates and times, showing Haxhi's movements beginning with Peshawar and rolling through Paris, Brussels and New York, then to Columbus and on to Moscow and London.

'He gets around, this boy,' said Rik, clicking on the link to Life Style Travel. 'Bingo.'

The details were a summary from Remzi's PC matching those of the bookings made in the name of Haxhi. The in-bound trip from Peshawar to New York via Paris had been arranged some weeks beforehand, no doubt to prepare the necessary immigration paperwork. But it was clear that Remzi had organized a series of open tickets more recently. Wherever Haxhi had wanted to go, Remzi had smoothed the way like a magic carpet.

'This was no impulse job,' Harry commented. 'There's been too much advance planning.'

'How do we get this to Deane?' Rik queried. 'I don't want to compromise Ripper.'

'You don't need to. Send Deane the link to Life

284

Style with a copy of one of the flight schedule pages, and he can do his own hacking. He doesn't need to know how we got it.'

Rik did so, and hit the button to send the message on its way. 'What do we do now?'

Harry shook his head. 'Nothing we can do. Bikovsky's gone, and this is his turf; he could be anywhere by now. Best leave it to the FBI and LAPD to deal with him. We've got more important things to do.'

'Such as?'

'Kassim or Haxhi, whatever his name is, won't be waiting around. He'll know by now that he's come out too far and we've got a line on him. He'll give up on Bikovsky and go on to bigger things.'

'But isn't that breaking with his plan to go after every member of the team?'

'Perhaps. But I think he's a realist. He knows by now who he *isn't* after, so he's not wasting time or running unnecessary risks by chasing them all down. He left Pendry alive and he didn't wait to take another shot at Koslov. That must mean something.'

'Like what?'

'Once he'd seen them up close, he knew they weren't his targets.'

Rik looked up from the laptop screen. 'How could he know that?'

'I'm not sure.' Harry had been thinking about what made Pendry and Koslov different from the other men; something that allowed them to live. The most obvious point with Pendry was that he was black. Koslov, on the other hand, was white, like the other men. The only thing that set him apart was his size. Yet the girl's murder at the compound had supposedly happened in the dead of night, save for security lights. And the murderer would have avoided them. So any sighting would have been vague at best.

Then he had it. Witness details always differ slightly from one telling to the next – a change of hair colour or body size here, a few inches in height there. Every pair of eyes sees things differently. It made a second-hand description of the killer too vague, too unreliable, especially after all this time.

But if Kassim could tell the difference between one man and another with any degree of certainty, it could only mean one thing.

He had been right there at the time.

Forty-Four

In the UN headquarters in New York, Ken Deane rubbed his eyes and stared down at the busy streets below. On his desk lay a scattering of information. It was both good and bad.

The good was a collection of stills from an ATM machine not far from the scene of the Carvalho killing. They were grainy, with some interference from dust particles on the lens cover of the camera, but good enough to show a white male, thin-faced, possibly of Latino or Mediterranean stock. He was using Carvalho's cash card.

The man hadn't been too concerned with hiding his features, intent on using the keypad and taking the money. Deane had compared it with the photo of the man named Kassim sent over by Koslov, but he couldn't see much of a resemblance. The Chechnya photo was of a kid in his teens, skinny as a stick and looking scared. The still showed an older man, taller, harder and with not a trace of fear about him.

Alongside this were the not-so-good and the plain bad. The first was a rash of printouts from various international intelligence organizations warning of chatter claiming to be from a group promising 'a strike' against the UN. The exact nature of the group wasn't clear, but it seemed to consist of a loose conglomeration of extremist names sworn to overthrow western influence and domination in Afghanistan and the wider region by striking at what they called the 'soft underbelly' of US aggression – the United Nations. Intelligence and security analysts from the US, France and the UK, aware of the rumours surrounding the Mitrovica compound, had added notes about the dominant group behind the chatter. Most were pointing the finger at Hezb-e-Islami as the most likely instigators, having the money, contacts and network capable of mounting such an exercise. The fact that it was a strike not planned to take place in Afghanistan, said the analysts, was a clever distraction: any blow was worthwhile if successful, and the effects would ripple out across the region.

Top of the pile was the bad news; a report from Archie Lubeszki, Deane's field security officer in Pristina. It confirmed that the rumours about a young girl murdered in 1999 were gathering pace, and with enough detail to make them worrying. She was found, it was being claimed, lying in long grass immediately adjacent to a UN container compound near Mitrovica. She had gone missing one night, according to her young brother, while looking for food inside the compound. He had been found wandering, traumatized and sick, along a nearby mountain track the following day. Some hours later, a local woman helping with the search had stumbled across the girl's body right outside the perimeter fence. According to locals, a doctor from Médecins Sans Frontières had made an examination, and claimed she had been raped then suffocated, her breathing cut off by the pressure of a thumb or forefinger pinching her windpipe.

She was just fourteen.

The news had been slow in emerging at the time due to a spate of ethnic killings, and the absence of any clear infrastructure to investigate the reports. Nobody had been able to trace the doctor who had made the initial examination, and Médecins Sans Frontières had no records of a medic operating in that immediate area, although they couldn't discount the possibility.

The story had gradually faded and died, due possibly to the lack of anyone able to keep it alive. Rape, in any case, for them was the final insult in a land which had seen too many horrors inflicted in the name of religious cleansing. Why defile her further by broadcasting to the world the details of her ignominious end?

Eventually, however, on the heels of UN Special

Envoy Anton Kleeman's announcement that the man responsible would be punished, the story had finally been teased out by the relentless probing of reporters desperate for some kind of truth. What they had not included, however, was a verbal addendum by Lubeszki over a scrambled telephone line ten minutes ago.

'I've talked to a woman who knew the girl,' Lubeszki had said, during a follow-up phone call. He sounded tired and angry, the distortion on the line unable to conceal the emotion he was feeling. 'When they found her, she'd been gagged to stop her crying out.'

'Gagged how?'

'The woman who found her says she'd had some cloth jammed into her mouth. Part of a UN beret.'

'Give me strength.' Deane felt a wave of despair. So it was true – they had something.

'The killer must have tried to remove it,' Lubeszki continued, 'but the girl's teeth had clamped around it and it tore off in her mouth. From the position of the body, it looks like she was dumped over from the inside.'

'He *threw* her over?' It was just as Harry Tate had suggested. He kicked a drawer shut in frustration. The last thing the UN needed was confirmation of this kind of news. Overstretched already, the agency was struggling to retain credibility in its day-to-day operations. It didn't need the world to know that one of its number, chosen to give help to the needy, had sunk to the lowest of atrocities.

He thought about the discovery of a fragment of

a beret at the scene of the killing in Venice Beach. It tied in with what Lubeszki was saying. But was it the same fragment? If so, who had it belonged to?

'Do they still have the cloth?' He almost didn't want to ask the question.

'No. It disappeared. When the translator pressed the woman, the shutters came down.'

'Why didn't the locals complain to the authorities when they found the girl?'

'Maybe they did. It's not easy getting anything out of these people. The translator asked about the brother of the dead girl, but he disappeared shortly afterwards. He was most likely taken by the Serbs.'

'I hear you. Christ, what a mess.' He sighed. 'Are you ready for Kleeman's visit?'

Lubeszki gave a disgruntled snort. 'About the same as if my mother-in-law was coming to stay. Hasn't someone told him this might not be a good idea right now?'

Deane didn't want to get into that. Lubeszki was right, though; Special Envoy or not, Kleeman was poking his toe into a tender spot by returning to Kosovo. What they didn't need was another high-profile desk-jockey turning up on a white charger promising the world just so he could score some media points – especially if it became known that he had been in the compound the night of the murder.

After telling Lubeszki he'd be in touch again, he called Bob Dosario of the FBI.

The special agent confirmed that the fragment of cloth found at the crime scene was on its way to be analysed at the LAPD forensics laboratory. 'What are you looking for, exactly?'

'Blood,' said Deane. 'Blood and saliva . . .'

Forty-Five

On second shift the following morning, in a ground-floor washroom of Terminal 1 at Los Angeles International Airport, Norm Perrell, the deputy shift superintendent, was cursing roundly and emptying overflowing trash cans. Two members of the cleaning staff had failed to turn up for work and he was having to fill in while a replacement was found. By Christ, he'd have something to say to them if they ever bothered to haul their asses in, the lazy sonzabitches!

He upended the last can and shook his head at the things people threw out when they visited the washrooms in LA International. A pair of boxers? And what looked like a bedroom slipper? Jesus . . . why come to an airport to dump their crap?

He frowned as the last few items floated down into the reinforced garbage bag. Looked like a passport photo. He bent and retrieved it and saw it was indeed attached to a page from a torn passport. Further down was another page and the pasteboard cover. Hey – what kind of idiot throws away a passport?

Seconds later Norm was scuttling along the corridor towards the airport security office, his chest buzzing with excitement. He'd found a driver's licence as well, and knew some of the security guys might be interested in this stuff. Could be from a mugging, of course, but who knew? The owner's name was weird, though. Haxhi. Zef Haxhi. What kinda name was that? Sounded like a Klingon. Sure as hell wasn't American, he'd bet his last paycheck on *that* . . .

Harry was collecting his stuff together from the bathroom when the phone rang. He went through to the bedroom and picked it up.

It was Bob Dosario calling from FBI headquarters on Wilshire.

'Don't you ever sleep?' Harry asked politely.

'No. They hang me in a closet each night,' Dosario muttered. 'Looks like your man Kassim-stroke-Haxhi got out through LAX this morning.'

Harry swore silently. Still one step ahead of them. 'Do we know the flight?'

'Not yet, but we're on it. A cleaning supervisor found a torn passport in a trash can this morning, in the name of Haxhi. A driver's licence went with it, complete with photos. Both were good but false. It'll take time to check all the passenger lists, but I'm putting extra people on it. Since we don't know what name he's using, we can't tell which flight he took. I've got some of my team checking security cameras in case they can spot him.'

'He might have stayed somewhere local last night. Could you get the photos shown around the hotels? I doubt he'd have wanted to risk hanging round the airport all night.'

'We're on to that too, but with the shift

changeovers, it's going to take time. It's an odd thing, trashing the photos. He must know they could've been found. You think he's had a change of face?'

Harry felt a flutter of certainty growing in him. What had been an unthinkable possibility the previous evening was now solidifying. It was as if the game was being played out to its end, and was about to spin off into another dimension. Now, with the discarding of Kassim's Haxhi documents, there seemed no other reasonable option to consider. 'I don't think it's that complicated. Kassim knows it doesn't matter any more.'

'Huh?'

'He's leaving the country for good.'

'But what about Pendry and Bikovsky? I thought he was after them, too.'

'He was – at first. As far as he knew – as far as we all knew – that piece of cloth came from a UN beret used by one of several men. He's been working on the basis all along of one down, all down, just to be sure.'

'And now?'

'I think he's given up on that. Pendry and Koslov are obvious outsiders.' He explained about the variance in size and colour which were the only things that set them apart from the others as the possible murderer of the girl, and how he suspected Kassim had seen him, albeit not clearly.

'So where does he go now?' Dosario asked. Harry noted that he had made no reference to the fact that Harry was one of the targets, too.

'He's adapting and going after bigger game. I

think you should check all international flights going to Europe.'

'Why?'

'Our focus in this has been on the CP team members – me included. But we were missing someone obvious. Someone we probably didn't want to consider. That person's now on his way to Kosovo. I think that's where Kassim's going.'

'Jesus,' Dosario's voice was flat. 'You mean . . .?'

'Kleeman.'

Harry put the phone down and walked along to Rik's room. He got him to do a search into Kleeman's background. He was remembering what Dosario had said about Kleeman being an all-state college sports champ. But a champ at what? He'd forgotten.

He soon had his answer.

'Interesting.' Rik found a page from a résumé about the Special Envoy. Anton Kleeman had shown a particular talent for contact sports, rising swiftly through the ranks in judo and collegiate wrestling, then switching to Greco-Roman style. One photo showed him hoisting an opponent off the floor, and in another he was slamming a fighter down on to his back. In both pictures he was grinning triumphantly, showing little apparent effort. Harry read further and saw that following a leg injury, Kleeman had switched to rowing, where he had quickly won a place in the college first team, helping them to two successive state championships.

'Strong,' Rik commented. He knew what

Harry was thinking and added, 'Stronger than he looks.'

Harry nodded. 'It's him.'

Two hours later, as he was studying the photo of the man at the ATM machine near Carvalho's place, Dosario called again.

'Bingo.' The FBI man sounded purposeful. 'It looks like Kassim took a direct shuttle to Chicago. One of the airport security officers spotted his face on a tape, filmed on the boarding ramp. A bit grainy, but it matches the photo found in the trash can. I've alerted Chicago to check the security footage for everyone coming off that shuttle.'

Harry glanced at his watch. By then it would be too late. He'd searched security tapes himself and knew how long it took. Kassim was still ahead of them. 'He'll be long gone by now.'

'True. But we can still check the cameras. If he's heading outside the US, he has to present his passport. If any names match up on two flights, we're a step closer. We'll follow this guy all the way across the world if we have to.'

'I believe you.' Harry heard the frustration in his own voice. They were all playing catch-up. 'How about lab analysis of the beret fragment?'

'Blood and saliva . . . some grease, too . . . probably sweat and hair gel. If we get matching substances, we can nail down the provenance. If we can get to the girl's remains we might be able to run a DNA test and compare them. Same with Bikovsky. If either of them came near that piece of cloth, we'll prove it. But it'll take time.'

'Good luck with that,' Harry said drily. 'Find

Bikovsky before Eddie Cruz's friends do, or you'll be testing body parts.'

'What about Kleeman? This could be FBI jurisdiction, you realize?'

'I know. But I'd rather we argued over that later. Right now it's a UN matter, especially as he's in Europe. I've got to make sure Kassim doesn't get near him.'

He called Deane, filling him in on Bikovsky's statement and the news of Kassim's latest movements. As they were speaking on an open line, he avoided using Kleeman's name directly.

Deane's voice came back dull with shock. 'You think Bikovsky was telling the truth?'

'I do, yes. But there's no way of knowing until we have the DNA tests.'

The line ticked as Deane digested the information, and Harry guessed he was picturing the compound, swept by wind and rain and threatened by the possibility of gunfire from the surrounding hills; of a young girl hiding inside the cabins. On one hand she'd have been terrified of discovery, on the other she would have surely felt she was safe among the friendly faces and uniforms of the peacekeepers . . . but finding that her situation was nothing of the sort. He was also likely to be picturing the girl in some dark and dirty corner of the Portakabins, a hand clamped over her mouth to prevent her calling out.

'How was it *possible*?' Deane asked finally. 'I mean, you know the layout of the buildings there. Could he – *anyone* – have actually done this thing with all those people around?'

'Apart from the guard detail,' Harry replied calmly, 'everyone was asleep. It had been a tough couple of days; nobody was volunteering to stay awake when they could get some shut-eye. There were a couple of rooms which weren't used, so it's possible the girl was hiding in one of them. But the rain was hard and making a lot of noise. Whoever did it would have been aware of the guard patrol and could have slipped out the back door without being seen.'

'Lubeszki confirmed your thoughts: that she was probably thrown over the fence from the inside. That would have taken some strength.'

'She weighed next to nothing,' Harry replied. The thought made him feel sad, picturing the lifeless body being punted into the air like a sack of potatoes, to land with a sickening thud on the far side of the wire. He took a deep breath. This was where things could get difficult, but he had to say it. 'But for a collegiate and Greco-Roman state wrestling champion, used to throwing men his own size around, how hard would an under-nourished child have been?'

'*What?*' Deane sounded strangled. '*Kleeman?*'

'Look at his background,' said Harry, and cut the connection. It was brutal but he knew Deane would have no option but to run a check.

He sat and waited.

Forty-Six

'You were right.' The wait had been less than twenty minutes. 'I should have noticed. I've seen Kleeman in the gym; he's not big, but he's strong.

I hear he joined the in-house judo club until he found there was no one could match him on the mat. He was into wrestling and rowing in a big way at college, so, yeah . . . I guess.'

Harry didn't say anything. It must have been a shock for Deane to find out that Kleeman, a rising star of the UN, had feet of clay. But it had been necessary for him to discover it himself. Anything less would have been dismissed as speculation. Even so, he was surprised that he hadn't had a fight on his hands.

'Jesus, Harry, are we both saying we believe this? Have I got to ask a UN Special Envoy for a *blood* test?' He sounded appalled at the notion, using Kleeman's name and title openly now. 'Have you any idea what that would do to us if it got out? That's even assuming I'd be allowed to ask him.'

Harry wondered if Deane was after some kind of approval to look the other way and pretend it was all beyond the realms of reason. Keep the name of the UN spotlessly clean no matter what. Then he realized he was being unfair; Ken Deane would no more sanction that than fly to the moon.

'Someone has to.'

'I guess. But that someone ain't gonna be me. This is where my esteemed superior gets to earn his paycheck. However, before I go speak to *him*, I need your report – Dosario's and Pendry's, too – and the statement from Bikovsky. If the shit's gonna hit the fan, I need as many people backing me up as I can find, otherwise I could find myself counting ice-floes in the Arctic Circle.' What he meant was, the more people involved, the more difficult it would be for anyone to arrange a cover-up. 'What are you doing now?'

'We're getting that flight to Pristina.' It seemed many days since Deane had first arranged a military jet to the Slatina air base in Kosovo, so much had happened.

'That reminds me, not so interesting but important. The FBI has been looking at the travel agency name you sent me.'

'Anything interesting?'

'If it wasn't before, it is now. Remzi's been in the US for about twenty years. He came originally from – surprise, surprise – near Pristina in Kosovo.'

'Anything known?'

'Not a thing. He's the original faceless man. No criminal record, clean bill with the IRS and he pays all his parking tickets on the nail. Model freaking citizen, in fact. If he gives up anything about Kassim, I'll let you know.'

Harry was surprised to hear Deane swear, and guessed the frustration of not being able to get ahead of Kassim was getting to him.

'How real is the connection to HIG – Hezb-e-Islami?' He'd been sceptical at first when Deane had sent him the breakdown of the inter-intelligence agency analyses. But the more he thought about it, the more it seemed to make a weird kind of sense. Presented with someone like Kassim and his thirst for revenge, any organization looking to make a tactical strike against the UN using the power of the press and the internet, both of which they could harness simply by releasing the news, could hardly fail to make an impact.

'It's real enough. The bigwigs' thinking is that

299

HIG is acting as a facilitator for a bunch of different groups – but mostly themselves. Anything that puts a dent in the UN right now is fine by them. And if they can put an end to the career of a hotshot like Kleeman at the same time, all to the good.'

'One hand washes the other.'

'Exactly. And the ripples move outwards, causing a lot of turbulence. It's win-win for them: they get to dictate what happens *and* gain the kudos, but at no great risk.'

It was a different kind of war, thought Harry, but a war all the same.

'It'll soon be old hat,' Deane continued. 'You and I know that. But it's already achieved what they wanted, which is to undermine us.'

'And Kleeman.'

'Yeah, Kleeman. Even if we find by some miracle that it's all an elaborate put-up job and Kassim's a fake, I think that asshole's finished.'

'That sounds definite.'

'Well, this is for your consumption only. Five years ago, Kleeman's wife, Rose, was admitted to a private clinic in Hyannis Port, Cape Cod. She and Kleeman had been staying on Nantucket Island. She claimed she'd choked on a piece of fish at a beach barbecue one evening, and had stopped breathing for a while. Kleeman used his UN muscle to get the US Coast Guard to fly her to the mainland.' There was a soft rustle of paper. 'The clinic recorded the treatment and passed a report to the local police department. During the examination they found severe bruising at the base of the throat, consistent, the ME said, with someone pressing the windpipe with both thumbs. She had related bruising to the back of the neck consistent with finger pressure, and a nurse noticed older bruising to her lower back, buttocks and legs.'

'What did Kleeman say?'

'Nothing. His wife said the neck thing had happened when her husband tried to dislodge the piece of fish, and the leg and back bruising was after a fall while out hiking.'

'Could both be true?'

'Yeah. But the clinic's director does consultancy work with specialist medical teams. He's seen similar lower-body injuries in rough-sex or rape victims.'

'Did it go any further?'

'No. With no complaint from the wife, the police could take no action.'

'Why has it come up now?'

'Records. When someone gets a high profile in the UN like Kleeman, we trawl through their lives to see what's waiting to come out and bite us. If we don't, the press will. Although if your suspicions are correct, it's all a bit late. Anyway, six months ago Kleeman made one of several visits to London, part UN business, part private. One evening he cried off a semi-official dinner and ate in his room. Said he felt tired.'

'It happens.'

'Not that tired. A girl was seen leaving his room just after three a.m.'

'Ah.'

'When I say girl, I mean thirteen years old. A Thai girl in the employ of an escort bureau. Apparently Kleeman's used them before. The

British CID traced her and got a statement from her and her employers. They said Kleeman likes it rough and the same girls never go back.'

Harry saw where this was going. It was tenuous but showed past behaviour consistent with a man with a taste for violence. But did it make him a rapist and killer?

'What's the risk to the UN?'

'Kleeman desperately wants to get to the top of the UN ladder,' Deane said. 'That's why he scheduled his recent round of visits to Beijing, Paris and London . . . to gather support among other members. Kleeman's a planner . . . he takes the long-term view, like the Chinese. He's looking five years ahead, but on current performance and with no hard proof of bad news, he could make it in three. He's already got a number of foreign government representatives on his side, promising commercial ties and trading agreements if they play ball and their UN representatives give him favourable backing.'

'Isn't that against the spirit of the UN?' Harry asked.

Deane grunted. 'I don't think anyone's been so overt about it before now. Usually people like Kleeman go for a seat in government, where they can exercise control in their own country. But things are changing; power in the UN is sexier – and global.'

'What do you want me to do?'

'Keep Kassim off his back and make sure Kleeman comes back here to stand trial. In a perfect world it would be better if we let Kassim do his job and sink the twisted fucker. But this is a Special Envoy of the United Nations we're talking about. I'll tell our mission HQ in Pristina that you're coming.'

'Fine,' Harry said. 'But let's keep contact to the minimum. There's still a danger Kassim might pick up information about us coming.'

'No problem. Lubeszki's the only contact you need.'

As Harry and Rik made their way to El Segundo for the military flight, a cutting wind was battering the doors of the main terminal building at Pristina airport, showering the glass with a volley of collected litter and sleet. Kassim shook off the thin layer of icy water dusting his shoulders and shivered in the sudden down-blast of warm air from a heater above his head. Out on the far side of the car park sat a Toyota pickup he'd bought an hour ago from a street dealer working the airport terminal. The man had been desperate for a sale but Kassim had driven a hard bargain. The vehicle was battered but serviceable, and would blend in perfectly. Not that he planned on keeping it for long, but it was safer than having taxi drivers asking too many questions.

It had been strange using his native language once more, although he no longer felt any affinity with the country; he'd been out of it too long now, and it was a different world in every sense. He'd brushed off the dealer's queries about his accent with vague half-truths about working abroad. Fortunately the man's desire for money had quickly overtaken his curiosity.

Kassim eased through the crowds of travellers,

greeters, traders, military and other security people milling around the main concourse, and found a snack stall where three UN policemen were taking a break. Tall and blond, in crisp blue shirts and trousers, they exuded a foreign healthiness alien to Kosovo. Scandinavians, Kassim guessed, and felt a stab of anxiety as they all turned and looked at him. When he held out a pack of cigarettes and an open palm with a questioning look, they seemed to relax before moving aside with sympathetic smiles. Another soul trying to make a buck, their attitude seemed to say; why hassle the poor bastard?

He nodded his thanks, reflecting that it was unlikely anyone else would trouble him while they were here. Hiding in plain sight, he'd learned a long time ago, was very effective if applied properly.

He bought a plastic mug of thin tea and took the opportunity to study the terminal building. A much-promised rebuilding project he had read about on the flight in seemed to have made little headway, and like the potholed road outside, the terminal held little welcome for first-time visitors. The main danger for Kassim was that it was small enough for him to stand out more than he liked; the plus side was that if danger presented itself, he would see it coming.

The UN policemen finished their drinks and moved away, and Kassim realized they had been watching the arrivals board. Simultaneously, there was a growing commotion among a small group of press cameramen gathered near the arrivals door, hoisting their equipment ready to capture footage of whoever was about to emerge.

Two of the policemen went to stand in front of them, while the third joined a couple of troopers from an American infantry regiment standing by the main exits. Outside, two more troopers in full battledress stood watching the approach road and car park, their Hummer vehicle standing a few yards away.

Kassim sipped his tea and yawned deliberately, turning to check the arrivals board. As he'd expected, the UN envoy was going to be heavily guarded while he was here, with a very visible security presence.

And it wasn't going to do him a single bit of good.

Forty-Seven

The compound near Mitrovica hadn't improved at all over the years since Harry had last seen it; it seemed smaller than he remembered, with fewer containers and the concrete base pitted and cracked, weeds sprouting towards the grey daylight. The floodlights high on the gantry looked battered and weather-beaten, and the gantry itself had a line of rust running its length like dried blood. Most of the Portakabins had been burned, and one only had to turn and look at the surrounding mesh fence with a roll of razor wire along its top, to gain the feeling that this was a ghost camp long overshadowed by the spectre of what had happened here.

Archie Lubeszki, the UNMIK security man, unlocked the gate and led the way inside. They had left his white UN vehicle on the road with a driver standing guard. The atmosphere was damp and sour, like an old garage long unused, and a lingering whiff of burnt wood hung in the air. In the remaining Portakabins, the electrical fittings had been torn from the walls, the wires left hanging bare, and whatever else had been salvageable had gone.

'Locals,' Lubeszki explained. He was a stocky Canadian in his fifties with a beard and thick glasses. 'They broke in a week ago without warning and trashed the place.'

'If it had been me,' said Rik with feeling, 'I'd have done the same.'

Lubeszki nodded. 'I guess. But it's been here a while, so why now?' The last part was rhetorical.

Harry walked across to the huts and along what had been a linking corridor, his footsteps drumming on the warped and rain-soaked floor. A soulful hum sounded as the wind passed through broken windows, and a length of wallboard flapped like a funereal drumbeat. He shivered and tried to get some feeling from the place . . . some sense of memory. But it was too cold, too insulated now by time and events. Whatever badness had happened here had leached out of the place long ago, leaving nothing but a sense of failure.

Lubeszki led them round to the rear of the buildings. The perimeter fence stood less than thirty feet away. Beyond the mesh a stretch of rough grass and weeds ran into a thick belt of trees. The interior looked dark and forbidding, a shifting mass of shadows, and a dread hush hung over the place as if all life had been stilled along with the girl who had died here.

High on the fence was a scrap of pink ribbon. It was knotted in a bow and secured by a piece of wire.

'They say that's where her dress caught on the wire,' Lubeszki explained. 'As she went over.' His voice was neutral, neither confirming nor denying that he believed it. He pointed through the mesh to a spot on the ground beneath the piece of material, and the small wooden stake Harry had seen in the photograph. It had been replanted with a bunch of flowers; fresh and colourful, they looked recent. 'And that's where she was found, right there.'

Rik stared up at the top of the wire and blew out some air. 'Strong,' he murmured, 'to do that.'

There was no arguing with that. The fence here was at least ten feet high. Harry couldn't recall if the roll of razor wire had been in place back then, but it would still have taken muscle to throw the girl over. Bikovsky could have done it; Pendry, Broms and Carvalho, too. Orti would have lacked inches, but he'd been a tough character. But not Koslov.

Lubeszki seemed to be reading his mind. He said, 'She wouldn't have weighed more than a scrap. Folks here lived on what they could find and everyone was undernourished. Come on – I'll take you to see the woman who knew her.' He turned and led them out of the sad compound, locking the gate behind him. 'Don't know why I bother doing this,' he grunted, snapping the lock into place. 'Nobody's coming back here, not since the news broke and they trashed the place.'

That will change, Harry wanted to tell him. If Kleeman is the man, all hell will break loose and this place will become the most photographed symbol of failure on the planet.

The woman Lubeszki had found lived in a decaying ruin of a cottage halfway up a steep mountain track. Scattered piles of bricks showed that there had once been a huddle of houses here; too big for a hamlet, too small for a real village. But a community nonetheless. Hers was the only one still in use. Harry wondered aloud how she survived. And why.

'She's still here because she refuses to move,' Lubeszki replied softly. 'Beats me why, after everything that happened here. But I guess it's all she's got.'

He knocked respectfully on the warped wooden door. It opened to reveal an old woman in a black headscarf and a grey dress. She had a face lined by the elements and too much sorrow, her eyes dull and devoid of expression. Her cheeks were contoured by a lack of teeth, and she eyed the three men one by one, studying their eyes.

Lubeszki spoke gently, indicating Harry and Rik. The woman nodded and invited them in.

It was a tiny room piled with ancient, tired furniture that had long lost its bloom, a storeroom of effects that Harry thought probably reflected the old lady's life. She indicated a bench for the three to use and sat down on a hard-backed chair, and waited.

When they were seated, Lubeszki spoke again at length. The old woman turned her head and stared at Harry for a few moments, her eyes suddenly alive, but dark. Then she began speaking, and Lubeszki translated.

'The girl's family lived up among the trees, over there.' Lubeszki pointed towards an area described by the woman, who did not turn to look, but merely gestured over her shoulder as if it would be bad luck to face the spot. 'They arrived two years before, she does not know from where, and kept to themselves. The man was a mechanic. He worked wherever he could. There were two children and the mother. The family name might have been Tahim but she cannot be certain; they had an accent and besides, she did not care because they were nice enough, so what does a name matter?' He waited as the woman talked on. 'One day Serbs came in trucks. They were heavily armed and drunk, looking for men and boys to kill. The father was taken away and shot. The mother was violated then hung from a tree. The house was burned down. She thinks the children were in the forest at the time, collecting wood, and stayed hidden. She herself was too old so the Serbs ignored her. The children learned to fend for themselves, coming down only to get food. They were small for their age . . . under-nourished. But tough. They hid out for weeks.' The old lady talked on, gradually finding a rhythm with Lubeszki and filling the gaps.

Her face softened at one point in the narrative.

'The girl would come down in the night and I would give her what I could. It was not much. She was so pretty . . . an angel among the ugliness of this place. Then she was taken.'

'Taken.' Harry leaned forward. 'You mean killed?'

Lubeszki nodded. 'Back then, it meant the same thing.' He listened again as the woman spoke. 'Her body was found near the wire, like a piece of discarded rubbish.'

Harry said softly, 'Does she know the girl's name?'

Lubeszki asked her. 'It was Aisha. A beautiful name for a beautiful child, she says. But nobody was surprised that she got caught; she took too many chances, trying to look after her brother, who was sick.' He asked the woman something and she explained briefly. 'The boy was badly beaten one evening by a Serb militiaman. He was kicked unconscious, but he was lucky: the militiaman was alone and too drunk to finish him off, and fell over. The girl, Aisha, helped her brother get away, but he was never very strong after that.'

'What happened to him?' Harry asked. The odds sounded less than slim. Already sick and weakened through malnutrition as he was, the weather out in the woods would have been fatal to him.

'She never saw him again. Probably in a hole in the trees, like so many others.'

Harry began to turn away. Then, for no reason he could think of, he said, 'What was the boy's name?'

Lubeszki asked the question and the woman replied.

'Selim, she says. It means "Peaceful".' The woman chattered on and Lubeszki added, 'But the boy didn't like the name. He chose another one instead – one he said meant "Protector". It wasn't a meaning she had ever heard, but he was just a boy.' He echoed her shrug. 'He was small for his age and weak, but at sixteen, every boy thinks he can take on the world.'

Sixteen in 1999, seventeen if the Russian file was correct. Either way, it would make him twenty-eight years old now. If he'd survived.

'What name did he choose?'

'Kassim. He took the name Kassim.'

Forty-Eight

They thanked the woman for her help and walked back down the slope in silence. Harry's mind was in a whirl. Kassim. The same name cropping up twice in connection with the same time and place; what were the odds?

It had to be the same person. The youth picked up by Russian forces and recorded in Chechnya ten years ago . . . formerly Selim, the brother of the dead girl, Aisha . . . now a killer on the rampage. It all made sense. For whatever reason, the boy had stayed silent over the years, maybe traumatized by what he had seen. Leaving his homeland and drifting, then surfacing in Chechnya

311

and briefly held before disappearing into God alone knew where.

Had Chechnya been the youth's training ground, learning the art of guerrilla war and taking it elsewhere? A legacy born of a senseless and brutal act hundreds of miles and many years away? They would probably never know, no more than they would ever know who was behind him.

Harry wondered at the people who had somehow fastened on and used Kassim's past. It must have been like a gift from heaven, plucking a damaged young man out of whatever hole he was in and training him, grooming him to become a fixated, relentless killer. Because one thing had been clear from the start: Kassim was no amateur revenger on the loose; he was as skilled as any soldier and had clearly received top-level schooling to get him this far. His controllers must have worked hard on him, preparing him for travel across the west, teaching him to blend into the background and move around undetected, feeding him with the motivation to keep himself going against all odds. And those odds must have been formidable. Yet a young man with little formal education, a wealth of hate and trauma and nothing to look forward to, had overcome them.

In the end it would have been too tantalizing to miss: the opportunity to kill a high-level UN envoy with history to justify their actions. They couldn't possibly know whether he was guilty or not, any more than Harry did; but they would have seen the opportunity it presented. He would be guilty by association and judged accordingly in the public eye. The publicity from the girl's murder was already gaining ground, and once confirmed, would explode on to the world scene as effectively as any bomb, nullifying the reputation of the UN in one hit. The fallout would echo around the globe, dragging down tainted member nations by implication, especially America.

And Kleeman's death would be the crowning triumph, seen by many as a just result.

Harry almost admired the men who had brought Kassim this far. They had done well, gaining his trust, drawing his story out of him and using it to give him a focus after so many years of – what? He didn't like to think. Whoever Kassim had been and now was, he was a tough individual mentally and physically. His trainers would have spotted that early on. It was the kind of thing that set men apart. He wondered what had come first – the individual or the plan?

Lubeszki dropped them at a city centre hotel where they could freshen up, with a promise to come back later and take them to the National Library. There was a heavy security presence, with military and police vehicles everywhere, and Harry asked him if this was for Kleeman's visit.

'Not really. There have been flare-ups of violence between various factions, mostly because of lack of jobs and infrastructure, as well as ethnic tensions. The government decided to bring in heavy reinforcements to put a dampener on it. Some of the trouble is purely crime-related, some religious. Kleeman's holding talks with government officials and business leaders here in the city, and he's scheduled to perform an official opening of a new room at the library tomorrow. It's a

313

glad-handing exercise and photo opp, but shouldn't take more than an hour. He'll come in by car from the residence where he's staying, then straight out again, on to a helicopter and away.' He grunted non-committally. 'We got him to keep it short because of the trouble, but his office insisted that the talks with government officials were pre-arranged and non-negotiable.'

'What are the security arrangements?'

'He has three security men, plus half a dozen locals, and Deane's arranged for a team of UNMIK personnel in uniform,' he told them. 'We've circulated pictures of Kassim, but Kleeman will have wall-to-wall visible cover. It'd take a mouse to get through.' He nodded and left the two men to it.

'A mouse would be easy,' Harry murmured drily. He looked at Rik. 'Can you call up some details of the library? I don't really want to wait to see what we're dealing with.'

They went to the room Lubeszki had booked and Rik opened his laptop. First he trawled for details of Kleeman's travel plans to Kosovo to see what was already public knowledge. So far there was very little save for an announcement about the inauguration of an International Studies room at the National Library, but with no time-table announced.

Harry gave it a brief look and shook his head. 'It's already public. Kassim won't have missed that.' He wondered where Kassim was right now. Something told him he couldn't be very far away. He'd always stayed on the move so far, never allowing himself to get boxed in, and there was no reason to suspect that was going to change.

Rik pulled up maps of the library and the surrounding area. He whistled softly. 'I don't fancy Kleeman's chances much if Kassim goes for a long shot.'

Harry looked at the map filling the screen. It showed an irregular mass that was the National Library, sitting on a patch of land open on all sides, in the middle of a box formed by roads. Two of the roads ran north–south on either side, one of them linking up with the main M9 leading south-west to the airport eighteen kilometres away. The other two roads ran east–west either side of the library site, completing the box.

'Show me some photos,' Harry said.

Rik hit the keys and a photo of the library sprang into view. It was a startling sight, resembling a space-age version of a beehive on heavy concrete blocks, a knobbly structure covered in a metal latticework, more a citadel than a place of information and learning. Paved footpaths approached from all sides, leading over open grass and sandy ground, with no obvious cover.

Any target being dropped off would have to be driven right up to the building, but would have to stop short because of the structure of the plinth-like base. From there a walk in the open was unavoidable. A helicopter would have to stand further out, presenting an even greater danger.

Either way, a sniper would have a clear shot.

Kassim had finally found what he was looking for. After leaving the airport, he'd cruised the city's back streets until he found a group of young

Albanians, aimless and angry through lack of jobs and direction. Here was where information could be bought for a packet of cigarettes. Carefully phrasing his questions, he was finally directed to a shell-torn bar where he sat over an apple drink for twenty minutes, watching the street. Eventually a nervous youth slipped through the door and beckoned him outside.

'You want guns,' the youth said. It wasn't a question; people came here for two things: weapons and drugs.

Kassim nodded and showed the youth a ten-dollar bill, as a sign of good intent. He told him what he wanted. The youth nodded and used a cellphone to make a call. He spoke briefly, then beckoned Kassim to follow.

Two minutes later the youth stopped outside the ruins of a house in the Old Town and pointed to a sagging doorway leading to a cellar. When he held out his hand, Kassim gave him the ten dollars and watched him scuttle away down the street.

Before entering, Kassim picked up a short length of lead pipe. He knew better than to walk unprepared into a meeting place like this. He also had a wheel wrench tucked inside his coat, just in case. Stepping over a pile of rubble, he descended the stone steps, feet crunching on a scattering of gravel. At the bottom he passed through a door and found two men standing behind a heavy table in what had once been a kitchen, with a recess for a fire and a broken stone sink. The atmosphere was cold and damp and smelled like a pig farm.

One of the men had his hands behind his back. Kassim ignored him and dropped some money on the table. It was his opening bid or a deposit, depending on how they wished to play it. Their eyes told him nothing, not even bothering to check the money, and he guessed they were wondering if he had more money on him and whether they could take it. He was under no illusions about the danger of the situation, and guessed they were also dealers in drugs, petrol and whatever else they could trade. Killing him if they chose to was probably a matter of whim.

The men listened to his request without expression. In Afghanistan, Kassim reflected sadly, there would have been an offer of refreshment and talk before getting down to business. But not here. Maybe it was better this way. One of the men turned and disappeared through a brick archway at the rear of the room, and returned moments later lugging a heavy wooden box, which he placed on the table.

They could not have been prepared for his visit and he guessed their cache of supplies was not far away. They were stupid, he decided. And therefore dangerous.

The first price was exorbitantly high – enough to buy a car. Ridiculous, Kassim told them bluntly, in a country where you could get an AK47 for a few dollars. But he didn't want an AK47. He added more notes to show willing, then clasped his hands in front of him, signifying his final offer. He had no time for playing games and did not trust these two for a moment.

As the two men consulted each other, he heard the scrape of footsteps on the stone stairs behind him.

317

It was a set-up.

He remained calm and nodded towards the box. One of the men flipped the lid open. Inside were three handguns: a .38 Browning, a Spanish Star and a Makarov with a damaged butt. Also a selection of loaded magazines. It was little better than scrap, but good enough. He indicated the Browning. The man took out the clip and showed it to have a full load, and without thinking, handed both items separately across the table for Kassim to inspect. He probably thought the gun being unloaded would be no threat.

It was a mistake.

Before the man could rectify his move, Kassim took the gun, slipped the clip in place and pointed it at the head of the second man in the space of a split second.

The second man still had his hands behind his back. He went very pale and stared down the barrel.

The atmosphere in the cellar suddenly became very still, and all Kassim could hear was the men's breathing. He nodded at the table, and the man took his hands from behind his back and very carefully placed a semi-automatic pistol on the table. It was another Browning and looked in much better condition than the one Kassim was holding. It was fitted with a suppressor.

They had come prepared for this, he realized. Silenced pistols are not for show. He therefore felt no regrets about what he was about to do.

Smiling coldly, he picked up the gun and calmly shot both men. The noise was little more than a double snap of a twig in the closeness of the room.

Then he stepped back across the cellar floor and fired once more, and watched as the youth who had brought him here dropped a revolver and tumbled down the steps in front of him.

Forty-Nine

'Kassim was seen at the airport.' It was Archie Lubeszki on the phone. 'Three UN cops think they saw him but they only realized it was him after they saw the pictures we circulated. I told them to scour the airport buildings and surrounding area, but I think he'll be long gone by now.'

Harry felt a tightening in his stomach. With it came a reluctant admiration for the man's ability and commitment. Coming out of the mountains of Afghanistan, if that was where he'd been, he'd trailed across Europe and the US, picking off his targets along the way, and was now on his home turf and frighteningly close to his goal.

He switched the phone to loudspeaker so Rik could hear. 'What was he doing?'

'Drinking tea and panhandling. They said he looked rough, like he'd been sick. Unless he was faking it.'

'Could be genuine. He must be living on adrenalin by now.' He wondered what Kassim had been up to. If he was sticking to form, he would have arrived in Kosovo some time before being spotted, so he must have been hanging around the airport for a good reason.

319

Lubeszki unwittingly supplied the answer. 'He was probably watching the press frenzy about Kleeman's arrival. But he wouldn't have found out much about his itinerary. Nothing's been issued yet and won't be. He might know he's going to appear at the National Library, but he'll be behind a wall of protection there. It'd be suicide for him to try anything.'

Harry said nothing. Seemingly suicidal moves were something of a speciality with Kassim, given his attempts on Pendry and Koslov.

'How about tonight?' Rik queried. 'Where's Kleeman staying?'

'The Grand. It's where all the VIPs stay. The place is wall-to-wall with security screenings, armed guards and even a few off-duty Special Forces heavies littering the place. Kleeman's not the only big hoo-hah in town tonight. There's someone from the German government, two representatives of the Dutch government and a few European Central Bank suits. The hotel staff are hand-picked and never replaced without a thorough vetting, so he won't be able to suddenly turn up as a cleaner or a room service waiter.'

'You've been watching too many films,' said Harry. 'If Kassim does anything, it will be what nobody expects.'

Anton Kleeman yawned with relief as the armoured limousine that had carried him from the airport on a tour of the city, followed by a second vehicle carrying his staff and extra protection team, finally entered the high-security cordon around Pristina's Grand Hotel. Military and UN police officers were everywhere, and even before the car stopped, the three members of the protection team riding with him were outside and clearing a path towards the entrance. Overhead a US Army helicopter clattered in a tight circle, a watchful figure leaning out of the fuselage with one booted foot swinging over the skid.

After a day of meetings with various government members, Kleeman was tired and snappy. He had been herded about like a child, pushed, pulled and virtually bullied from one point to another by officials and his close protection team, sparing little or no thought for his status. The bodyguards, increased on the recommendation of New York after some ludicrously over-egged threats against UN personnel, were sticking closer to him than yesterday's sweat and filling the car with their silent presence. He wouldn't have minded but there wasn't a single spark of conversation among them, and they were as jumpy as two-day-old chicks.

The team leader beckoned him forward with what Kleeman considered a less than respectful gesture. He climbed from the car and allowed himself to be swept into the foyer of the hotel, where at least there was some semblance of warmth and comfort. The general décor was worn and in need of revitalization, but staying here had been a political move. At least the staff knew how to treat someone in his position.

As he walked across the well-trodden carpet through the bustle of VIPs, military and UN officials, he saw two men standing to one side, oblivious of the hubbub around them. Dressed in casual civilian clothes, they seemed out of place in this predominantly military setting. Yet there was about them something indefinably regimented and watchful.

He glanced at the leader of the protection team, but the man seemed unconcerned and continued past them towards the stairs.

Kleeman stopped, recognition slowly filtering into his mind. He remembered. *That damned compound.* He swallowed, feeling a vague twinge of unease that had begun at the airport that morning. It had started while he was preparing to address the press. Glancing over their heads for a moment, he had locked eyes with a tall, thin man staring at him from the back. He was poorly dressed and showed signs of malnourishment – not an unusual sight here. Kleeman was sure he had never set eyes on the man before, but the intensity of his gaze had crossed the room with an almost tangible power. It had left him momentarily shaken, until a question from the press had drawn him back. Next time he'd looked, the man was gone.

Now these two. One young, with a colourful shirt under a sports jacket and fashionably dishevelled hair. A stranger. The older man next to him, though, he recognized immediately. Kleeman had a memory for faces. This man had been the leader of the protection team last time he was here. What was his name? Stait? No, *Tate*. British, he recalled, and insubordinate. But efficient. Odd that he should be here. The thought added to his sense of unease, but he fought to suppress it.

He approached the men, causing the two bodyguards to swerve sharply.

'Tate,' Kleeman said warmly. It was a trick that served as well in politics as it did in commerce, especially with his recent visits to China and France. It was something the inhabitants of those two countries had in common; they liked to think they were important enough to be remembered after a single meeting.

Tate nodded without making a big deal of it and lifted a thumb at the bodyguard who had nearly fluffed his manoeuvre. 'You should signal before you turn,' he said. 'It throws them off when you do something unexpected.'

Kleeman was piqued by Tate's tone. Was the man laughing at him? 'I'll try to remember that,' he said coolly. 'Are you still in this business?'

'I wasn't. But the UN asked me back. Rik Ferris, my associate.' Tate nodded towards the younger man beside him. 'He's helping out.'

Kleeman felt another twinge of unease. The two men were study-ing him as if they shared something, some secret. Suddenly he regretted having stopped. 'Helping out with what?'

'The business at the compound.' It was Ferris this time, his voice as flat as gravel pouring into a bucket. 'At Mitrovica. You know – the rumour you said was going to be investigated?' Ferris's eyes were cold and unfriendly.

'Compound?' Suddenly Kleeman felt a burst of panic. 'I don't think—'

'You know. Where that little girl was raped and murdered back in 'ninety-nine. Then thrown over the wire like a sack of garbage. We're here to pick up the man who did it.'

Kleeman felt as if Ferris had reached into his

323

throat and pulled out his lungs. He stepped back momentarily, winded, looking at Tate. But the older man's face was just as cold. Alongside him, Kleeman's bodyguards shifted, puzzled by the change in tone.

Kleeman cleared his throat and wondered, if he were just to walk away, whether Tate would follow him. 'Are you? That's good . . . very good. I expect to hear details as soon as you can release them. Do you have the man in custody? I seem to remember hearing it was a soldier.'

'Not yet,' Tate replied. 'We're looking at some new evidence. Then we'll nail him.'

'Evidence?' The air around Kleeman's head seemed suddenly very warm, and he had a desperate urge to run for the stairs and lock himself away somewhere dark and safe, away from these men of violence and their aggressive manners.

'Blood samples. DNA. That sort of thing.' Tate gave a half smile. 'Amazing how long that stuff hangs around. Like a signature. Excuse us, won't you?'

Kleeman watched the two men walk away, then allowed himself to be propelled up to his room, where he went straight to the bathroom and was violently sick.

'You think we rattled his cage enough?' Rik asked, as they left the Grand Hotel. They had talked it over on the way there, deciding to unsettle Kleeman and see how he reacted.

'If we didn't,' Harry murmured, 'nothing will. You're getting good at the scary stuff.'

324

'Well, I try my best. I hope we're right about him.'

'We're right. I can feel it. Saw it in his eyes.'

'And if we're wrong?'

'You'd better take my gun away, otherwise I might just go and shoot him for the hell of it.'

Fifty

From a part-renovated building three hundred yards away, Kassim watched the front of the ten-storey Grand Hotel. He had seen Kleeman's arrival, counting at least twenty armed security men around the UN envoy and on permanent station as part of the standard security cordon. He sat back, chewing his lip to fight the now permanent nausea he was feeling. He brushed it aside; he was sick, he knew that. But he couldn't let it derail his plan.

Getting in the hotel would be impossible; it would be like throwing himself at the front door with the word 'bomb' strapped across his chest. So he had to think of somewhere else.

He thought back to a phone conversation he had overheard outside the airport terminal building earlier. A British journalist had been phoning in his report, listing to his editor a last-minute, press-eyes-only itinerary for Kleeman. It included a tour of Pristina University followed by a meeting at the National Library building at noon the following day.

325

So. Two possibilities: the university or the library. Kassim slid backwards from his observation point and made his way down the stairs, spilled plaster and brick-dust crunching under his feet. As he walked away, he made his choice. The chase was closing in, and time was fast running out. He had to do it.

The library.

Three in the morning on a building site in Pristina and heavy rain was gusting on a cold wind coming down from the surrounding hills. Sheets of board across half-completed windows snapped like gunshots, and fires in open braziers made of oil drums hissed and spat as the rain hit the red embers, dusting the figures huddled around them in a swirl of vapour and damp ashes.

For Kassim the weather was a blessing. He eased himself from inside a sheet of corrugated cardboard and stretched his arms above his head, feeling the stiffness in muscle and sinew incurred by spending the night on a bare concrete floor. He performed a dozen squats, his thigh muscles protesting until they began to feel the warmth of blood circulating, followed by thirty quick press-ups. The exercise brought a renewed bite of hunger to his belly, but he dismissed it. It would not be the first day to have dawned without him eating, and given a safe outcome of his day here, would not be the last.

He peered through a crack in the front of the building, watching and listening for signs of movement. He had counted five security patrols during the few hours he had been here, checking papers and people, but they had no regularity

326

or set pattern. The last one had passed by just five minutes ago, and he had lain still, waiting for it to pass. So far there had been no attempt to check the building. That might happen at daylight.

Now he had to move.

The rain was like a cold slap in the face, making his skin itch. He pulled his coat around him and slid along the street. His desti-nation was the National Library. He had scouted it out late last night, studying the building and the ground around it.

It was here that Kleeman was due to come in just a few hours.

Kassim slid across the street known as Agim Ramadani and worked his way around the edge of the open area encompassing the library complex to the rear of the building, watching for patrols. The security here seemed lax, but he guessed the bulk of the effort would be reserved for later, in the two hours before Kleeman's visit. By then it would be as tight as a drum.

By then he would be inside.

He sat for a few minutes, tuning in to the dark and allowing his breathing to settle. When he'd got his bearings he reached down and felt for a large section of prefabricated aluminium casing, part of an abandoned central heating system which had never been cleared away. By chance, his earlier foray had shown a maintenance plate on the wall revealing what lay underneath. He eased the aluminium carefully to one side to reveal a square inspection panel set in the ground. It had a lifting ring in one side. A faint grinding noise and the panel came up, bringing with it a gust of foul air. Kassim ignored it; he'd been in worse and could live with whatever was down there. He felt for the rungs of a ladder and stepped down carefully until his shoulders were level with the ground. Then he pulled a paper package from his coat pocket. As he unwrapped it, the pungent smell of human excrement rose to his nose. He dropped part of it on the ground at the lip of the hatch, and some on the lid itself. The paper he discarded on the ground nearby. It would be enough to confuse any patrol dogs.

His final move was to tug the aluminium casing over the panel, then lower both to the ground, concealing his point of entry.

At the base of the ladder he squatted in a pool of water and took a slim torch from his pocket. He flicked it on, illuminating a small tunnel, the light reflecting off curved walls glistening with damp and hung with wet, viscous strands of cobwebs. The atmosphere here was musty and heavy. Halfway along the tunnel walls were two openings, each the size of a man's head. They were the out pipes from the library sewage system. Beneath them was an area of crusted sludge. He knew enough about buildings to realize that there would soon be another panel above his head, this one set in the boiler-room or maintenance-room floor of the library. From there he would have access to all areas of the building.

Kassim gritted his teeth as his stomach threatened to empty itself, ignoring the slime beneath his feet and the skittering sound of small creatures just beyond the glow of his flashlight. He began to make his way forward along the tunnel.

Fifty-One

'I think Kassim's made a move.' Lubeszki on the phone, sounding tense.

It was nine o'clock the following morning and Harry and Rik were sitting in a borrowed Mitsubishi four-by-four watching the close protection team assigned to Anton Kleeman comb the area around the National Library. Sniffer dogs ran excitedly around the structure seeking traces of explosives, while technicians with electronic equipment scanned for radio emissions that might betray a remote detonator. Elsewhere members of the UN police supported by military patrols made a floor-by-floor check of all the surrounding buildings to a distance of 500 yards where a sniper might gain a line-of-sight advantage. This included the art gallery, the radio station and several university buildings, all of which had virtual open access.

'Three local arms and drug dealers were found shot dead yesterday evening,' Lubeszki continued. 'They were in a cellar in the Old Town. The police had been keeping them under surveillance, but lost contact late yesterday.'

'Could it have been a turf war?' Harry didn't want to start chasing the shadows of a local gang feud gone bad.

'Unlikely. Rivals would have made it messy – as a message to others. These guys were taken out professionally, one shot each. A kid who worked as a gofer said they had a visit from a guy wanting to buy a gun. Tall, thin, looked sick, like he was burning up. Spoke the language fluently but with an accent. A second kid took the guy in, then left them to haggle. When he went back to check but didn't show up again, the gofer went in and found the bodies.'

Kassim. It had to be. 'Any idea what he got?'

'Difficult to say. There was a rifle box containing a couple of used handguns and some ammo, but no rifle. Is he the sort to go for a long shot?'

'Not from what we've seen. He likes to work up close. But I wouldn't put it past him.'

'Do you want to see the bodies?'

'No. We'll stay loose.' It wouldn't help, Harry decided. They were better off staying out here and trying to figure out what Kassim would do next. Much of that would depend on Kleeman's movements, which they wouldn't see for a while yet.

He shifted the Heckler & Koch MP5 submachine gun across his body. It felt awkward carrying the weapon after so long, as did the bulk of the armoured vest he, like Rik, was wearing. They had been issued with sets of borrowed combat gear so as to blend in; it seemed a contradiction, but among the many security personnel present, two civilians would stand out immediately.

Already a substantial number of journalists had gathered, with camera crews and commentators and their portable units and satellite dishes which would transmit Kleeman's words on to television screens around the world. They were currently being kept behind a safety cordon while a security sweep was made of the building, before being admitted into the main hall of the library.

The Dutch UNMIK officer responsible for Kleeman's protection team approached the car. Captain Rekker was tall and slim, his cheeks pinched white with cold. He carried a submachine gun and wore a camouflage smock over a bullet-proof vest.

'This is our second sweep,' he told Harry. 'Nothing found so far. We've checked the surrounding buildings out to three hundred metres, but it's a spoiling exercise. All a gunman has to do is wait for our men to leave, then slip back in behind them. We plan to go into the library one more time, then we seal it until Kleeman arrives. Everyone here has been briefed about this Kassim and told to expect something.'

Harry nodded, relieved the Dutchman didn't feel his toes were being trodden on and clearly knew his job. They had made contact through Lubeszki the previous evening, and had agreed to stay clear of the building while the security checks were in progress.

'What's his likely exposure time?' Because Kleeman's vehicle would not be able to get right up to the building, there would be a dash of some six or seven yards to reach the door, surrounded by members of the CP team.

'Ten seconds – fifteen at most. We asked him to practise, but . . .' Rekker shrugged, his face blank but the meaning clear; Kleeman was being difficult. It was the biggest problem facing protection teams;

331

some VIPs are oblivious to danger, others prefer to face it with equanimity in the pursuit of their jobs. Harry wasn't sure what drove Kleeman, but suspected it had more to do with ego than courage. Whatever, it spelled danger for everyone around him if he so much as slowed down a fraction on his way from the car to the library entrance. If Kassim was out there with a rifle and had a clear field of fire, he would nail the UN envoy the moment an opportunity presented itself.

He looked at Rekker. 'If you want my advice, grab him by both arms and lift him inside if you have to. Deal with the hassle later. At least there's a good chance you'll be alive to do it.'

'You think this Kassim is really here?' The Dutchman looked concerned, not fearful. He was experienced and had been in similar circumstances before.

'It's what he's been working towards. He wouldn't miss it.'

'I've seen the reports.' The captain stood away from the car as his second-in-command, a French lieutenant, signalled the all-clear. 'OK. We are going inside. You wish to join us?'

They walked up the mound and stepped past the clutch of security men through the entrance. The air smelled damp and musty, overlaid with a hint of coffee and spicy cooking. They could see through some swing doors into a large hall, where chairs were being laid out in rows against tables. At the far end was a small dais where technicians were setting up a batch of microphones.

Ahead of them two sniffer dogs darted in and

out of every corner and crevice, urged on by their handlers. Behind each handler stood an armed man. They were taking no chances.

'They have brought in lunch,' Rekker told them, nodding towards two women carrying plates. 'Everything has been checked and sealed. The dogs will make a sweep, then my men will go through one more time.'

They walked through the building, the captain pointing out obvious concealment areas such as wall cavities, cupboards, false ceilings and storerooms. Piles of books stood on vast tables, some damaged and torn, most covered in dust.

'It got left when all the power went out,' Rekker explained. 'They're trying to get it catalogued all over again but they can't get the staff.'

As they walked along a corridor between administration offices, Harry looked up at the ceiling. It was a latticework of struts supporting polystyrene tiles interspersed with neon lights.

'Anything up there?' he asked.

The captain shook his head. 'First place we checked. The struts won't support a man's weight. The whole thing is held by thin wires, so if anyone gets up there, the structure begins to move.' He smiled grimly. 'But we'll check it again anyway.'

They continued their inspection, more evidence plainly visible in the surrounding rooms of the previous searches made by the protection team. Cupboards had been left open, doors left at angles to prevent their use as blinds, inspection panels in the floor taped over with vivid yellow-and-black zebra markings, ceiling tiles removed and stacked on the floor. The skin of the building was too thin to provide concealment, and the windows were sealed shut and staked out by armed troops.

Along the corridor from the main hall, a tiled washroom echoed with their footsteps, the air sharp with the tang of cleaning fluid and the softer scent of detergent. The cubicle doors hung open, and an inspection panel for the master cistern lay against the wall, revealing the crawl-space behind.

Towards the rear of the building they arrived at an open door.

'This leads to the basement,' the captain explained. 'Boiler room, storerooms – fuel storage area. There's a single delivery chute from the outside which we've sealed shut.' He led them down a flight of stairs to a series of chambers lit by single bulbs. The air smelled strongly of fuel oil and damp, and was gritty with the taste of disturbed dust.

They passed a desk spread with yellowed papers and old, curled binders, and on the wall a line of hooks hung with grey uniform coats. Everywhere lay typical institutional evidence of a place used as a dumping ground: packing crates, scarred tables and damaged chairs, broken neon strip-lights, two ancient typewriters, old bookshelves, the detritus of used items set aside and forgotten.

Harry walked through the rooms, passing first a huge boiler and in another a smaller one. Oil-fired, he assumed. This was confirmed by a fuel line running along the wall and disappearing through the brickwork towards the outside. The tank, he guessed – if it was still intact – was somewhere out there. He walked back to the first boiler, which was coal-fired. Sacks of solid fuel were stacked against one wall at the far end.

Some had fallen over, scattering their contents across the concrete floor. Harry kicked one of the lumps, sending it skittering away into a puddle where weeks, maybe months of damp had gathered together in a scummy pool. A thin wisp of black dust rose around his ankles before settling down again in the still air. Two empty coal sacks lay crumpled nearby.

Nothing big enough to hide a man, though.

Back upstairs the security sweep was coming to an end and the building emptying ready for the event to begin.

'How is he leaving afterwards?' Harry asked the captain as they reached the front entrance. Something was tugging at his brain, demanding to be heard.

The Dutchman pointed to an open stretch of ground next to the library, where a large 'H' had been marked off in thick white tape. 'By air. From here he goes to the airport, gets on a flight to Frankfurt, then New York.' He grinned. 'I wish it was as easy for me.' He excused himself and went to gather his team to return to the Grand Hotel to collect Kleeman, leaving Harry and Rik standing at the front entrance.

'You feel anything?' Harry asked. He was talking about that inner sense common to most security teams. He'd felt it in houses, offices – even out in the country. Sometimes he'd been proven right, others not. But he never ignored the feelings.

And right now they were screaming out loud.

Rik shook his head. 'I thought I did – back there. Just for a moment. You?'

Harry nodded. 'He's here. I can feel him. Something's off but I can't put my finger on it.'

'What – inside? There's no room for a cat to hide in there. Anyway, if he's got a rifle . . .'

Harry felt a shiver run down his spine. Something was definitely wrong.

They walked around the outside of the building, fetching up at the rear where maintenance men and builders had turned it into a minor wasteland of aluminium ducting, assorted wood and building materials. None of it looked as if it had been disturbed recently, and it had about it the desolate air of things man-made rendered useless. Like an old quarry long fallen into disuse.

An UNMIK dog handler conducting a final sweep among the refuse with a sniffer dog cursed and stepped back with an expression of distaste. A piece of soiled paper was attached to his boot and he scraped it off on the ground. The dog seemed uninterested and tugged at its lead.

The dog handler's radio crackled into life. He looked at Harry and Rik.

'Kleeman's on his way. ETA five minutes.'

Fifty-Two

Beneath the boiler-room floor, Kassim suppressed a cough as coal dust tickled his nose. He'd listened with nerves jangling as the security sweeps had come and gone. At one point a dog had whined just inches from his head, the thickness of the inspection hatch and some coal between them. He'd pulled back in alarm before telling himself the animal wouldn't be able to sense his presence through the dust and oil from the boiler.

Minutes later came footsteps and the sound of something skittering across the floor. Someone had kicked a loose piece of coal. He'd closed his eyes, imagination threatening to take over as he pictured the man above kicking the layer of coal aside and spotting the outline of the inspection hatch Kassim had covered during the night. He'd balanced bags of coal against the hatch, then let it drop after descending, and listened as the rumble of coal had covered it over. But the footsteps moved away and there was the thump of a door closing.

Kassim flicked on his torch and checked the time. Thirty minutes to go. He doubted there would be another security sweep now. It would soon be time to move.

Before doing so, he took a last look at some maintenance drawings he'd discovered in the boiler room. They showed a tracery of access ways and utility spaces in the building, and he memorized them carefully. His life might depend on it. Then he folded them away and braced his shoulders, pushing upwards. For a second there was solid resistance, and Kassim felt a momentary panic at the thought that he'd miscalculated. Then he heard a rumbling sound across the metal hatch and saw light through a shower of coal dust pouring around him.

He pushed all the way up and stepped into the basement, tensed for the shout that would indicate he had been seen. All his experience told him that if he was spotted, there would be no second chance.

He tore off his clothes and stood naked on two empty coal sacks, rubbed the black powder from his hair, ears and eyes. A bucket of water stood nearby where he had placed it hours before, ready for this. He doused his head and face, careful not to splash the surrounding concrete floor.

This was as close as he was going to get to the ritual cleansing his trainers had insisted on in their naïveté and lack of combat experience, but he had never held himself to be that committed to the ritual, anyway. He dried himself on an old blanket, then put his shoes, trousers and shirt back on, adding one of the grey uniform coats from the wall rack. A quick check of his hair and face in a piece of broken mirror, and he was ready. He stepped towards the stairs. In the coat pocket was the solid weight of the .38 Browning with the silencer.

Harry glanced at his watch. The press lunch was in full swing and he could see Kleeman working the crowd of journalists and officials, patting shoulders as he moved among them. His speech had been measured and controlled, skipping delicately over the more sensitive points of UN involvement in the area, and settling on matters which, while at times controversial, were calculated to set him in a good light. Firm on the continuing bouts of violence in Kosovo, he had shown a reassuring mix of anger and regret at the delays in getting aid to the more remote areas of the country.

Surprisingly, nobody had raised the thorny issue of the murder at Mitrovica. Agreeing on the need for sensitivity due to ongoing investigations, and the desire not to inflame local feelings, it was left to their colleagues at home to do that.

'Let's take a walk,' said Harry. They set off round the building, passing other men patrolling in pairs. Once away from the hubbub of the meeting, the library had a ghostly feel about it, like a school at half-term.

In a large anteroom, two UN policemen were examining a pile of books and laughing. Behind them a figure in a grey cloth coat shuffled slowly along a line of shelves with a pile of heavy tomes, placing them one by one in empty slots. He moved with the slowness of age or infirmity, and the methodical care of the worker who has a lifetime to complete his tasks.

They moved on and checked the washroom, where they found an armed MP on guard, and alongside him, a supply of fresh towels and soap. 'For the big man,' he explained in a thick Glasgow accent, a faint hint of disgust at being given such a menial task. 'The rest of the minnows have to cross their legs.'

They left him to it. As they drew level with the basement door, guarded by a solitary soldier, Harry stopped. Something about their last visit down there still bothered him. But what was it?

'Anyone been in or out?' he asked the soldier.

'No, sir.' The man had a French accent. 'No one is permitted.'

Harry nodded. Must be his imagination, looking to find clues where none existed. Even so, as he turned away a series of images flickered through his mind: the stairs down to the basement, the coats on the wall, the coal across the floor; the puddle of damp. And the skittering lump of coal he'd kicked accidentally, and the ensuing swirl of dust around his feet.

The coal . . .!

'He's inside!' Harry swore and stepped back to the basement door, surprising the soldier. 'Call Captain Rekker,' he told the man. 'Tell him Kassim's *inside* the building. But don't let the press get wind of it, or there'll be a stampede. That's just what Kassim wants.'

As the soldier keyed his radio, Harry pushed the basement door open and stepped cautiously down the stairs into the boiler room, Rik behind, covering his back. The air rose to meet them, damp and pungent. They scanned the area around the base of the stairs, then in a series of overlapping moves covered the entire basement, checking every corner.

Harry toed the coal. Nothing moved in the air.

'When I kicked it earlier,' he said softly, 'the dust rose in the air. Damp coal doesn't do that – I know from when I was a kid; I had to fetch coal in from the shed every day.'

Rik nodded. 'Could be a maintenance worker or a security guy knocked a bag over. The bagged coal would have been drier.'

'Just what I was thinking,' Harry agreed.

'What about a local, got down here for a look-see while the place was open?'

'No. It's been locked tight. If anyone else had got down here and found there was fuel to burn, do you think they'd have left it here?'

'I guess not.' Rik bent to peer into a bucket of water standing against the wall. He prodded the surface with a tentative finger. 'You're right – someone's been here. There's dust everywhere else but on this.' A clatter of footsteps came down the stairs and both men turned as one, the barrels of their MP5s swivelling to cover the entrance. It was Captain Rekker and two of his men. He looked grim.

'I've persuaded them to cut things short. They agreed. Lift-off in five minutes. What have you found?'

Harry explained, indicating the coal. He moved some of the lumps aside with his foot. The outline of an inspection hatch appeared. 'This is where he came in.' He indicated the bucket of clear water and the wet coal sack. 'He used the water to wash off the dust.'

Rekker frowned. 'But I thought he stole a rifle from some black-market dealers. Why would he bother if he planned on getting inside all along?'

'He didn't. There was a rifle box; we just jumped to the wrong conclusion.'

The three members of the CP team moved back to give covering fire while Harry and Rik cleared away the rest of the coal. The captain took out his radio and issued instructions to his men to check for an exit point outside the building.

Rik slung his weapon to the rear and grasped the lift-ring, then counted to three and threw open the hatch.

'You could get a small army in there,' Rekker muttered. His expression was one of disgust at the failure to spot the obvious. 'This does not

341

appear on the plans we were given – but I should have thought of it.'

'Forget it,' Harry told him. 'It's too late – he's already here.' He looked across to where the line of grey coats hung on the wall, another image coming to his mind. There had been an unbroken line of them.

Now one was missing.

'The side room,' he said to Rik. 'The old man putting books on shelves.'

'Old man?' Rekker queried.

'He looked like a member of staff.'

Rekker shook his head with a growing look of concern. 'But we gave specific instructions. There are no staff working today.'

Fifty-Three

Kassim sensed his time was nearly up.

He was stuck in a side room of the library, away from where the meeting was being held. He now realized that he had an impossible task. He'd been waiting for an opportunity to move along the corridor towards the main hall, but there were too many guards around. All he needed was access to the entrance and a clear field of fire, and his job would be complete. Not as telling or shocking as he had managed with the others, but that was a matter of fate. The one thing he'd been counting on was that none of the guards would dare open fire among such a crowd; the carnage among the press and government officials would never be lived down.

But instinct told him his presence had been discovered.

He moved towards the door and heard the clatter of footsteps in the distance, and closer to, the cold *click-clack* of weapons being cocked. The sound bounced along the walls of the corridor, making his already stretched nerves jump alarmingly. There was no shouting, no sound of panic. But they knew he was here.

Word had gone out.

Kassim slipped out of the room with an armful of books. This could work to his advantage. He ventured along the corridor and peered round the corner just as two armed guards stationed themselves at the doorway to the basement. He ducked back and hurried to the washroom, where he stopped and listened outside the door. He could just pick out the echo of heavy footsteps pacing up and down inside.

Taking a deep breath, Kassim opened the door – and found himself face to face with a uniformed military policeman.

'Who're you?' the MP asked, just as Kassim dropped the books he was carrying and thrust the Browning into the man's stomach below his body armour. He pulled the trigger and felt the gun jump in his hand, the suppressed shot muffled further against the other's body.

The MP staggered backwards and fell, blood spreading across his stomach. Kassim stuffed the gun in his pocket, locked the door, then bent and dragged the body across to the furthermost cubicle, where he heaved it on to the seat. Then he knelt between the dead man's legs and ripped away the zebra-tape on the floor sealing the rim of an inspection hatch. He could already hear shouts coming from out in the corridor, and commands for the building to be evacuated and sealed off.

The hatch cover came away, revealing a narrow concrete shaft carrying waste and oil pipes for the heating system, with just enough space for a man to crawl along. It ran off in two directions, one to the rest of the building, the other towards the basement.

Someone banged on the washroom door and called out a name. Kassim cursed and dropped into the hole head first. He'd been intending to take the guard's clothes, but it was too late. He began to pull himself along the shaft, scraping the skin of his elbows and knees as he brushed over the coarse cement bottom. He muttered a prayer, scrabbling desperately to propel himself to safety and ignoring the confines of the shaft, reliving nightmares of childhood in a small cave, hiding from his friends in a boyish game gone wrong.

But this was no game.

He heard a crash follow him down the shaft as the washroom door was kicked in, and redoubled his efforts. Already he could imagine a gun being poked down the shaft, a hail of bullets burning towards him.

He felt the shaft tilt downwards, and let gravity help his progress until he reached a dead end and the touch of soft, damp fabric on the floor of the shaft. It was the blanket he'd dried himself with earlier. He stopped and took a deep breath, then reached backwards and took the Browning from his pocket. One opportunity was all he had. If they were ready for him, he would die right here, in this suffocating little hole with barely room to curl up and meet his maker.

In the basement, the soldier who had earlier been guarding the door stood over the open hatch leading to the outside, where the man named Kassim had come in. He heard a faint sound behind him, and walked back through the connecting chambers. Probably one of the others, come to relieve him—

The grey uniform coats on the wall seemed to explode outwards, and a small metal door appeared, revealing a black hole where there should have been none. A figure tumbled into the basement, the dull glint of metal in his hand, and the guard felt a sick helplessness as he realized his own weapon was pointing away and it was too late to do anything but watch.

Kassim smashed the guard across the side of the face with the Browning. The man fell in a heap and Kassim leapt on him and dragged him out of sight of the stairs towards the open hatch in the floor. He quickly stripped him of his clothes and armoured vest, then took off his own clothes and dressed in the guard's uniform. It wasn't a perfect fit, but good enough. He dumped the unconscious guard down the hatch and threw the cover in on top of him.

345

At the top of the stairs he checked the mechanism of the guard's submachine gun. It was loaded and ready. He placed his ear to the door. Heard shouted orders echoing along the corridor, and beyond that, the noise of a helicopter's engines gathering power.

Kleeman was leaving!

'He's gone down the shaft!' The MP who had broken down the washroom door levered himself up from the hatch in the toilet cubicle. Two of his colleagues had pulled the other soldier out and were checking for signs of life, but to no avail.

Harry walked in and looked at the hole. 'Where does it lead?'

The MP pointed off towards the rear of the building. 'Back that way. But it may change direction . . . it's too dark to see.'

Harry nodded. 'Dump something heavy in there to seal it off.' He beckoned to Rik. 'Come on – I want to stick close to Kleeman.'

They could already hear a helicopter's engines winding up to maximum pitch, and shouts as the CP team began to hustle Kleeman through the mass of journalists towards the main entrance.

Suddenly more cries echoed along the corridor, followed by the sound of a shot.

'He's down in the basement . . . heading for the outside!'

Harry ran along the passageway and saw two soldiers disappearing down the stairs. Another was running towards the front, presumably to cut round the outside to where the tunnel came out.

'Kleeman's on board.' Captain Rekker appeared, signalling to Harry. 'We're lifting off any – who the hell was *that*?' He was staring at the soldier disappearing through the entrance. 'Hey!' he shouted. 'He's not one of ours!'

A volley of shots rang out, flat and puny against the thudding noise of the helicopter's engines. Harry ran towards the main doors and barged aside a group of journalists, his MP5 held aloft. A sick feeling was already building in the pit of his stomach.

Kassim had outwitted them after all.

A windstorm of noise and movement hit them in the face as the rotors of a French military Super Cougar 725 blasted them with dust and debris. A UN policeman lay sprawled a few yards from the front entrance, and three of the CP team were bunched in a heap close by the helicopter's main door, their weapons scattered. Elsewhere other soldiers and police had all dived for cover.

'Where's Kleeman?' Harry asked a stunned guard.

The man pointed towards the helicopter. 'In there. A guy started firing as he came out the door. They didn't stand a chance!'

As if to confirm the guard's words, two men appeared in the opening to the helicopter's fuselage. One was Kleeman, looking stunned; the other, standing behind him, wore combat gear and an armoured vest. It was Kassim, calmly staring out at the dramatic scene.

Kassim ducked back and pointed his submachine gun at the loadmaster. He was holding Anton

Kleeman by the throat and felt unnerved by what he'd just seen. Two more men in combat uniform had emerged from the library entrance, and he recognized Tate and, alongside him, the younger man he'd seen with him in the airport hotel near Fort Benning.

They'd been following him all along!

He felt a ripple of anger and was tempted to open fire. But he decided against it; he might need to conserve ammunition. Instead, he tapped the loadmaster on the head with the tip of the gun barrel and pointed upwards. The man swallowed hard, then flicked his intercom mouthpiece into place and gave instructions to the pilot.

The lumbering craft, capable of carrying up to thirty people, seemed to sink on its haunches for a moment, before gathering itself and lifting off the ground with a renewed down-blast of air, leaving the security guards on the ground staring helplessly into the sky.

Fifty-Four

Harry turned to Captain Rekker, who was busy on his radio, his face taut with frustration at the disaster which had overtaken his team.

'We need another helo,' Harry shouted above the noise. 'We have to follow him.'

Rekker nodded and held up two fingers. 'Coming in now . . . a Black Hawk. The Super Cougar's being tracked by ground navigation.'

The Dutchman walked away, his jaw clenched, and Harry let him go. There was little he could say to assuage his feelings, and he guessed the captain was now facing the prospect of a fore-shortened military career.

The Super Cougar was already a dot on the grey afternoon horizon by the time another engine noise heralded the approach of a second heli-copter. They turned to see a Sikorsky Black Hawk thudding down towards them, a crew member leaning out of the door to assist the pursuers' entry.

The Black Hawk was slower than the Super Cougar, but not by much. They were already far behind and the weather was closing in. Harry knew there was every possibility Kassim might complete his murderous mission by simply throwing Kleeman out of the door, then forcing the pilot to ditch somewhere in the hills where he would be impossible to find.

But why hadn't he already done that?

They leapt aboard and fastened themselves in. Apart from Harry, Rik and Captain Rekker, there were two other members of the CP team and an army paramedic. Two journalists trying to get on the flight were dumped unceremoniously out of the door.

The Black Hawk rose in the air like an express lift and heeled over to follow the distant Super Cougar, throwing the passengers about in their seats. The pilot had been briefed on what was expected of him and was responding with relish.

The centre of Pristina rushed by through the open door. Within minutes they were out over open countryside, dotted with houses and farm buildings and lots of empty space in between.

'He's heading north towards the hills.' It was Rekker, holding an intercom earpiece, from which he could hear the exchange of conversation between the pilot and the ground-control operator following the flight of the other craft. 'Where the hell's he going? There's nothing up there but open country.'

Harry shook his head. He doubted Kassim himself knew which way to go, only that he had a mission to complete. Even sitting on his tail rotor, there would be precious little they could do to stop him without putting the lives of Kleeman and the crew at risk.

North? Harry pulled a map out of a bracket by the door and found Pristina. He stabbed his finger on it so Rekker and the others could see. North of here was Mitrovica.

Kassim was taking Kleeman back to the compound.

It meant he had no walk-out plan; this was the end of the line for both of them.

The Black Hawk began to buck around as it hit wind turbulence coming off the hills and funnelling down the jagged valleys. The CP team members looked unconcerned, accustomed to such uncomfortable transport and bleak conditions, intent only, as Harry knew they would be, on retrieving their man.

'We're catching up!' Rekker shouted, and pointed through the open door as the Black Hawk swung round a tree-covered hill. Ahead of them, about two miles away, the Super Cougar was dropping down into a valley with a river running along the bottom, a sliver of white against the grey-green landscape. Slopes rose sharply on either side, seeming to close in deliberately on the two aircraft, the engine noise hammering back at them.

'He's losing speed deliberately,' Rekker commented. 'Bleeding off gradually so Kassim doesn't notice.'

Harry was impressed by the pilot's courage. If he did it carefully enough, there should be insufficient change in engine noise to alert their captor. As long as Kassim didn't think to take a look at the air speed indicator.

They followed the craft down, skimming in low over the river. Below them, white water foamed over gleaming rocks and coursed swiftly down a series of rugged falls, fed by incessant rain high in the hills. It was a cold and brutal scene, but possessed a coarse, natural beauty at odds with the wretched villages and towns nearby.

'He's going in!' the crew chief shouted. The Super Cougar had dropped abruptly as if a string holding it aloft had been cut. It seemed about to hit the trees. Something must have happened on board. The machine's rear rotor seemed to brush over the top of a giant pine tree as it crested a ridge, and there was a collective intake of breath. Then, at the last moment it dipped, and the rotor exploded with a flash and a puff of smoke.

Inside the lead helicopter, Kleeman and the load-master were huddled together under Kassim's gun, desperately hanging on as the pilot tried to regain control of his craft. A trickle of blood was running down from inside his flying helmet, after Kassim had noticed the decrease in speed and fired a shot close to his head. He'd intended it as a warning, but the movement in the heli-copter's flight had thrown his aim off, the bullet ripping through his helmet and grazing his skull.

Kassim locked his arm through a section of cargo webbing and stared through the open door at the wildly undulating picture below. In the distance he caught fleeting glimpses of the following Black Hawk, which had gradually drawn closer.

The floor dipped as they rounded a tree-lined slope, and Kassim felt his stomach heave. Abused by bad food, irregular sleep and severe stress, he was now in a death-ride across the Kosovan coun-tryside. Yet he felt almost serene.

He had done what he set out to do, and reached the man who was responsible for the murder and violation of Aisha, his beloved sister. Now that man would pay for his crime. He spat out a mouthful of acid burning his throat and stared at Kleeman, who had not taken his eyes off him since leaving Pristina. The Special Envoy was looking deathly pale, but beyond an initial protest, had said nothing. Kassim had seen in his silence a confirmation that the man knew who he was. And why he was here.

He stared out at the blurred scenery below, the hills and valleys, the houses and farms and rolling woodlands, and considered the wider reasons he had been chosen to do this: to bring shame and disgrace on the organization that employed this man, which would be a giant fist against the Americans and their Coalition partners. He had been eager to be useful in the struggle, even if not in his own country, which was spinning by below. Now he was home, he realized that all of that seemed to matter very little. All the teaching, the training, the mantras about killing Americans, the special lessons in the way of the west, the constant drip-feed of hate, which he knew had been carefully tailored to influence him in his moments of doubt; just as the teachings of the Koran were used to wipe away doubts in those chosen to give their lives along the back streets and patrol routes used by the hated invaders. That all now seemed unreal – a vague and misty dream. In the minds of the ones who had schooled him and brought him this far, it had been their plan, their dream.

Now it was all his.

'Brace!' the pilot screamed as the machine's tail dipped. There was a loud bang and the helicopter was wrenched violently to one side, as if swiped by a giant hand. Electronic alert signals began sounding and lights flashing, and he heard someone scream. He hoped it wasn't him.

So be it, thought Kassim, and raised his gun. And as the great machine tilted sideways and hung for a moment above the trees, defying gravity, he looked across at Kleeman and murmured a brief prayer for Aisha recalled from his childhood in the valleys below.

He pulled the trigger.

Fifty-Five

The Black Hawk pilot was already dropping his machine towards the ground as the stricken Super Cougar plunged out of the sky, the fuselage turning lazily as the pilot fought vainly to keep it level. A heavy worm of black smoke from the remains of the tail rotor trailed the helicopter's descent.

'Brace for landing!' A crew member shouted a warning through the intercom as the ground came up to meet them with dizzying speed. Three hundred yards away the Super Cougar rolled lazily on its side and hit some trees with a crash, debris arcing into the air and one of the five rotor blades spinning away like a giant boomerang. Then the fuselage sank out of sight into a large gully.

Harry and Rik were out of the Black Hawk before it touched down and running towards where a plume of black smoke was rising into the air. The tops of the trees where the helicopter had impacted were burning, emitting a crackling sound as oil-fed flames ate into the wet branches.

Behind them, Rekker and his men broke wide to approach the crash site from the side and give covering fire, while the crew member and medic brought fire extinguishers in the hope that they might be of some use.

Harry arrived at the lip of the gully and stared

down at a spot a hundred feet below, where the wreckage of the helicopter had finally come to rest. Held in place by two enormous pine trees above a series of waterfalls and a deep gully, it was lying on its side, the fuselage bent and torn with great gashes along the side.

For a moment nothing moved, save a piece of damaged rotor swinging in the wind and a renewed surge of dark, oily smoke from the remains of the rear assembly. Then the remains of a side window in the forward section popped out, and a figure in a flying suit emerged and rolled down the damaged fuselage. Another man followed and they both took off flying helmets. It was the pilot and co-pilot. Both appeared injured but mobile.

A third figure appeared in the main doorway of the machine, his face covered in blood. He wore combat gear and was holding a submachine gun.

Kassim.

There was too much vegetation in the way for a clear shot, and Harry began a cautious descent of the steep slope between the trees, aware that if he slipped, he wouldn't be able to stop until he landed right in front of the helicopter. He kept his eyes on Kassim, who seemed unaware of how close the pursuers were, and was struggling to get clear of the wreckage.

Then Kassim looked up and saw Harry and Rik, and to one side, Rekker and one of his men.

He tumbled from his perch on the fuselage, his weapon sweeping towards them.

His first burst sprayed through the trees,

355

clipping off branches and chunks of wood. The second burst caught one of the men as he moved down, throwing him on to his back.

It was Rekker.

Kassim switched his attention to Harry, sending a burst of fire past him, one round tugging at his sleeve. It was enough to spin him off balance, and he slammed against a tree, feeling the rough scrape of bark against his face.

'*Down!*' Rik shouted, and Harry dropped to the ground just as Kassim took aim again.

Rik fired two three-shot bursts. The second caught Kassim in the chest. The impact flipped him over and out of sight down the slope, his submachine gun falling to the ground.

Harry skidded the last few feet down to the Super Cougar and looked beyond it, to see Kassim's body floating in a pool of water fifty feet below. He reached up and hauled himself over the lip of the helicopter's main door, and stared down at two figures lying against the other side of the fuselage. Both were covered in blood. He recognized Anton Kleeman. The other was a crew member.

Rik joined him, coughing through the smoke. 'They dead?'

'Can't tell,' replied Harry. The air inside the cabin was thick with the powerful stench of aviation fuel and the sickly smell of burning rubber. He handed his MP5 to Rik and slid inside the helicopter, the movement producing a rasping groan of metal as the machine slipped against the trees.

He bent to check the crewman. He was barely

356

conscious, with a serious gash across his chest and a bullet wound in one shoulder. A steady flow of blood was pumping from the chest wound, and Harry knew they hadn't long to get him some help.

'Get the medic,' he told Rik, then turned to Kleeman.

To his surprise the envoy was conscious, his eyes watching Harry but dulled by shock. Harry checked him over carefully and found a bullet wound in the man's side. Kassim must have shot them both, the intended *coup de grâce*.

'Get me . . . out . . .' Kleeman breathed hoarsely, his skin white and greasy. He tried to pull himself up by using the injured crewman as leverage, but his leg was caught under the bench seat that had collapsed under the craft's impact. 'Damn you . . . get me out! You can see to him later.'

Harry felt a cold anger clutch him at the man's selfishness, and wondered if Kleeman had ever shown true compassion about anyone. Somehow he doubted it.

He bent and grasped the bench seat and braced himself, then heaved upwards, feeling the metal beginning to straighten. It moved sufficiently for Kleeman to pull his foot clear, and the envoy scrabbled away, gasping and coughing.

'Who . . . who was that man?' he asked, touching his side and inspecting his bloodied fingers. He seemed surprised to see the splash of red, as if he'd never considered that he might bleed like anyone else. He slumped against the crewman, eyes rolling, and waved away a spiral of smoke drifting across the cabin.

357

Harry stared at him. 'You don't know?'

'No – should I?' Kleeman coughed again, and a small spot of blood appeared on his lip. If he noticed, he made no sign.

'But you remember the compound at Mitrovica,' said Harry.

Kleeman's gaze faltered, eyes moving away. It was as if the envoy had decided that, for once, silence might be safer than words. It might have worked had he not said, 'You knew that crazy bastard was coming after me! I saw him at the airport, yet you did nothing to stop him – any of you!'

It was enough. Suddenly Harry knew – *knew* without a flicker of doubt that Kleeman was responsible. It was in the air around them, in the sickly pallor of the man's face, in the expression of his eyes, the set of his mouth.

'You raped her,' Harry muttered softly, his words dropping dully into the cold air of the fuselage, loaded with contempt. 'A child. You stuffed a beret in her mouth and raped her. Then you carried her outside and tossed her over the perimeter fence like a bag of dirty laundry.'

Kleeman's eyes flared in defiance. He gasped and clutched his side as a sharp pain coursed through him, and tried to struggle upright, away from Harry's accusing words.

'You're mad, Tate.' Kleeman's smooth veneer had gone, replaced by the ferocity of a snarling animal at bay. 'You fucking *moron*. You don't know what you're saying – I'll have you put away for this!' As he moved again, the fuselage shuddered and tilted with a sickening lurch, emitting a loud groan of tortured metal as it shifted against the trees holding it up.

'You OK?' It was Rik in the open doorway. Behind him was the other member of the CP team. Rik's gaze rested coolly on the injured Kleeman, but he was talking to Harry with steady urgency. 'The paramedic's coming down and I sent the crew guy back for an anchor line. Harry, this thing's either going to blow or go south. You need to get out. Now.'

Harry felt the fuselage shudder. Rik was right; there was no time to wait – for the paramedic or the anchor line. He could also feel the heat as fire began working its way along from the tail section, and smoke began boiling up into the tree canopy above their heads. If the flames didn't take them, they'd all end up at the bottom of the gully a long way below.

Ignoring Kleeman, he grabbed the injured crewman by his harness and dragged him as carefully as he could to the lip of the doorway.

'Take him. Get him out of here.'

Rik and the CP team member reached down and lifted the wounded man clear of the fuselage and began dragging him up the slope.

'Hey!' Kleeman protested. 'What are you doing? What about me?'

'I'll get you out,' said Harry coldly, 'once you tell me what happened at the compound.'

'What? *Are you insane?*' Kleeman's mouth showed a trace of pink froth, and his eyes flashed wildly at the thought of being left a moment longer in the wreckage. He snatched his hand away from the skin of the cabin, where it was growing hot, and tears sprang in his eyes. Then there was another jerk of movement beneath them. He nodded wildly, his expression desperate. 'OK . . . *OK* – I'll tell you. Get me out of here first!'

Harry shook his head. He was beginning to feel dizzy from the acrid smoke swirling around in the cabin. 'We've got time. Go ahead.'

Kleeman looked as if he couldn't believe what was happening to him. But he clearly saw the resolve in Harry's face, and finally buckled.

'*All right* . . . it was me! Is that what you want to hear? I found her . . . she was in the canteen.' His voice dropped to a wheedling tone. 'I went to get a drink, that's all. I couldn't sleep. She was probably there to steal food. What one of your men called a camp rat. She was *nothing*!'

'A victim, actually,' said Harry. 'She was a victim.' He felt a huge sense of anticlimax at hearing the final confirmation from Kleeman's own lips, and fought to resist the urge to stamp on the man's face, to thrust the contemptible words back down his throat. 'We were supposed to be protecting kids like her, remember?'

'For Chrissakes, why should *you* care?' Kleeman gave a shrill scream as something cracked like a gunshot and sparks began joining the smoke pouring into the cabin. His face was blood red and he began to sob in fury and desperation, like a child denied a treat. He stared up at Harry, his eyes no longer possessing any sign of sanity, and little vestige of anything human. 'You've killed people, haven't you, so why the moral fucking judgement?'

Harry heard a shout from up the slope. He glanced back. Rik and the CP man were clear with the injured crewman, and waving frantically at him to get out. Whatever they saw from up there must have been bad.

Then Kleeman grabbed his ankle. The envoy was struggling to get out, clutching desperately at Harry's clothing and trying to push him to one side, babbling incoherently. For just a second, Harry was tempted to respond and pull him clear, to take him back to face justice for what he'd done. Then he realized that there would be nothing adequate to deal with this man. Whatever the fallout against the UN was going to be, it would be dealt with, no matter how brutal. But individuals like Kleeman always knew too many people, carried too much influence. A word here, a touch of political pressure there; they had built their lives on contacts and used them whenever trouble threatened. And if Kleeman left this place, it wouldn't be to stand trial, of that Harry was certain.

Ballatyne was going to be pissed off, he figured. No happy endings. But that was too bad. He'd get over it.

As he swung his feet out of the cabin, he felt a sickening lurch as the helicopter dropped further, and heard the tearing sound of the trees giving way underneath.

'Harry – she's going!' Rik shouted.

'Wait!' Kleeman cried. 'Tate, you can't leave me. Come back here! *You can't do this!*'

Harry didn't answer. He slipped over the rim of the doorway. When he looked back, Kleeman

361

was staring at him like a man looking up from the bottom of his own grave.

He turned and made his way up the slope to where Rik was waiting.

As he reached the top, the flames billowed around the side of the fuselage and began licking through the open door. Then the broken machine finally slipped out of the clutches of the trees and plunged into the gorge below, a long metallic-human squeal following it all the way down.